Caught in passion's raging storm,
they surrendered their hearts
to the tempest's fury

TEMPEST

"I'm hurting you!" she protested, trying to pull away.

"No. Yes. I ache with wantin' you darlin', that's all."

Along with everything else, this was a new and startling revelation to her. Beneath that rough, tough exterior lay a tender, vulnerable man.

"I think I want you, too."

Her words were little more than a whisper, but he heard them as clearly as if she'd shouted them in his ear. They vibrated through him like a quivering arrow, darting straight for his heart.

"Then take me, sweetheart. I'm at your tender mercy."

"How?"

"Kiss me, Charity. Steal my breath away, and give it back again."

CATHERINE HART

TEMPEST

AVON BOOKS ◆ NEW YORK

AVON BOOKS
A division of
The Hearst Corporation
105 Madison Avenue
New York, New York 10016

Copyright © 1991 by Diane Tidd
Inside cover author photograph by Olan Mills Studios
Published by arrangement with the author
Library of Congress Catalog Card Number: 90-93601
ISBN: 0-380-76005-3

First Avon Books Printing: May 1991

AVON TRADEMARK REG. U.S. PAT. OFF. AND IN OTHER COUNTRIES, MARCA REGISTRADA, HECHO EN U.S.A.

Printed in the U.S.A.

RA 10 9 8 7 6 5 4 3 2 1

I dedicate this book
To Maria Carvainis, agent extraordinaire—
For guiding me through the trenches!
And
To Ellen Edwards
For her editorial finesse.
All of which led me to stretch my creative wings just
a little wider.
Thank you both very much.

CHARITY Prindle rode next to her husband on the hard buckboard seat, oblivious to any and all discomforts of the bone-jarring ride. It seemed absolutely ages since they had last been to town, and Dodge City was teeming with activity on this sunny Saturday morning. While John handled the horses, deftly maneuvering the wagon along the busy streets, Charity's sparkling blue eyes hungrily took in the sights, her bonnet bobbing swiftly to and fro. A brilliant smile danced on her lips, a becoming flush of excitement staining her cheeks.

"Hello, Mr. Mullenhour! Good morning, Mrs. Williams!" she called out with a merry wave of her gloved hand. At the musical sound of her voice, heads came about; and even those who didn't know her could not help but return her friendly greeting with an answering smile.

Beside her, John chuckled softly and warned, "Charity, if you don't stop twisting your head about like that, it's gonna come right off. At the least, you're gonna fall off the seat and land in the street."

Far from taking offense, Charity merely turned the full force of her smile on her young husband, and he, too, was lost in her radiant charm. "I'm happy,

1

Johnny," she said on a bubbly sigh. "I'm just so happy I could burst with it! The crops are in, the sun is shining, I'm married to the most wonderful man on earth, and the world is a fine and glorious place!"

John's grin widened, his coffee-brown eyes laughing even as he shook his head at his bride of just more than a year. At eighteen, Charity was still a child in so many ways, still the young girl he'd known and loved since they were both no more than babies. "Some folks are just easy to please, I guess," he teased in his quiet way. "Still, I know how you feel. God sure has been good to us this last year. He gave us rain when we needed it most, and fine, dry days while the wheat was ripening for harvest, and a good yield on our first crop. A farmer can't ask for more than that."

It was typical of John to neglect to add that he had single-handedly done the work of ten men in the past several months. Rising before the sun, he had put in long, backbreaking days plowing and planting and reaping; not to mention worrying over the fledgling plants, fretting over the weather and crop disease and a multitude of other disasters that might threaten to destroy an entire season's labor. Now, with most of their major worries behind them, at least until next spring, the resulting relief made him nearly as giddy as Charity was.

With a skill that belied his own scant twenty-two years of age, John pulled the wagon neatly behind another at the side of the street. "Looks like this is as close as we can come to the mercantile for now," he said lightly, leaping from his seat and coming around to lift Charity from hers. As his large, work-calloused hands spanned her trim waist, he felt a familiar burst of pride that he had won the heart of the prettiest, sweetest girl he ever hoped to know, especially since she'd had several other suitors from which to choose.

"We're closer to the post office here, though," Charity pointed out in her cheerful manner, "and I'm fairly itching to see if there is any news from back home." No matter what, John could always count on Charity to look on the bright side of things—that was just the way she was, always a ray of sunshine, even on the darkest days.

"You, my girl, just want to catch up on all the local gossip, and you know Dinah Mae is sure to know and tell all!" He couldn't resist teasing her, and he adored the telltale blush that crept up her face. "I always have to wonder if our postmistress gathers her news by steaming open the mail before she hands it out," he went on, taking his wife's elbow and steering her along the wooden sidewalk toward the combination drugstore–post office several doors down.

"Shame on you, Johnny!" she said with a giggle. Her chortle became a startled shriek as the window nearest her suddenly shattered, spitting shards of glass and two burly bodies into her path.

The young couple didn't have time to jump out of the way before the two men hurtled into them, knocking both John and Charity into the dusty street. As Charity rolled applecart over appetite, all was a wild kaleidoscope of blurred colors and amplified sounds. A horse whinnied shrilly and stomped its hoofs dreadfully close to her head; nearby, fists pounded flesh with dull thuds, the combatants grunting like pigs at a trough and cursing colorfully; people shouted; a shot rang out; someone screamed.

When the world stopped spinning, and the dust settled once more, Charity found herself lying on her back in the dust, John half over her. Her skirts and petticoats were twisted about, and one leg was bared almost to her thigh. Her bonnet was askew, and a long strand of golden blonde hair dangled over one eye, tickling her nose.

"Johnny!" she wheezed, pushing at him in an attempt to dislodge him from her chest.

Immediately his weight lifted from her. Propped on his elbows, he scanned her face with anxious brown eyes. "Charity! Are you all right?"

"I think so, but I did get the breath knocked out of me for a minute or so. You're not hurt, are you?" A quick glance about them revealed a crowd gathering, and Charity was torn between embarrassment, concern, and an absurd sense of how ridiculous they must look.

"Just a couple of bruises," John assured her. He levered himself to his knees. His arm came about her shoulders to help her up, but before he could stand, several bystanders were there to assist them to their feet. Friends and strangers alike exclaimed over them. Helping hands brushed the dust from their clothes; someone—she didn't know who—cocked Charity's bonnet back into place.

"My stars!" a woman exclaimed. "I thought for sure you were both going to get trampled to death!" Charity recognized the speaker as Mrs. Trumble, the hardware store owner's wife. "I swear!" the lady continued stridently. "This town is nothing but a lawless den of iniquity! Another Sodom and Gomorrah! Why, it's a wonder we don't all wake up murdered in our beds!"

This comment brought more than a few chuckles, especially when Sheriff Masterson and Deputy Marshal Earp stepped forward to counter the woman's claims. "Now, Edith," Bat Masterson refuted gently, "if you were murdered in your sleep, I somehow doubt you'd wake to tell about it. And Dodge City might be either a Sodom or a Gommorah, but surely it's not evil enough to be both rolled into one!"

Shaking her finger under the sheriff's nose, Edith stood by her statement. "Just how do you think Dodge came to be known as the 'wickedest little city in America' then, Sheriff? Why, every newspaper in the country has noted the lawlessness of this town."

Here, Wyatt Earp spoke up. "Why, ma'am, how can you say such a thing, when Bat and I have hardly taken time to sleep, trying to protect the citizens of this fair town."

"Hmph! When the two of you, and your underlings, aren't gambling in the saloons, you're taking up with some floozy! If you're lacking sleep, that's more than likely the real reason! And where were you when poor Charity and John were thrown into the street and nearly killed by these drunken cowboys, might I ask?"

"Please, Mrs. Trumble, it's quite all right," Charity said softly, trying to soothe things over before tempers flared out of control. "John and I are fine, as you can see, though I do wish someone could explain what happened. Why, one minute we were walking peacefully along, and the next I found myself lying in the dirt!" Her voice quavered slightly, revealing her shaken state.

"These two yahoos," the owner of the Longhorn Saloon bellowed, "decided to see who could throw the other through my new front window the fastest." His beefy fists were firmly planted on his ample hips as he stood over the two inebriated culprits, giving them a fiery stare. "Now, either I see five dollars out of each of you boys for damages, or I take it out of your worthless hides right here!"

Deciding the saloon keeper could handle his unruly patrons well enough himself, Sheriff Masterson turned to the Prindles. "Are you folks sure you're okay?" he inquired. "Edith was right about one thing. That was a nasty spill you took, and you might have been trampled by the horses, not to mention hurt from all this glass flying about.''

No sooner were the words out of his mouth than Edith cried out, ''Good gracious, Charity! Your arm is bleeding!''

Indeed, the left sleeve of Charity's dress was turning a bright red. Even as Charity watched, the stain grew. ''Oh, dear!'' she gasped. ''How did that happen?'' Then the little farm wife, who had wrung many a chicken's neck and helped butcher many a hog, felt herself begin to sway. Looking up, Charity beheld a bevy of multicolored spots, all converging into one huge blob. Suddenly, John's voice sounded very far away—then it faded to nothing.

When Charity awakened, she was lying on a couch in Doc Nelson's examining room. ''Good heavens!'' she exclaimed weakly. ''I do believe I must have swooned!''

''That you did, little lady,'' the doctor confirmed, coming to stand next to her. ''Nearly scared ten years out of that poor husband of yours, too. How do you feel now?''

Her lips trembled slightly. ''A little wobbly, and my arm throbs a bit.'' Casting an uneasy glance at her shoulder, she noted the pristine bandage beneath the gaping sleeve. A frown creased her brow.

''I pulled a sliver of glass from your arm, though it was just a small cut,'' he assured her. ''I had to cut your sleeve to bandage it, but Sue will be happy to help you mend it and sponge out the blood before you leave. I know how you ladies are about fashion, and that's too pretty a dress to ruin—and a very pretty young lady wearing it, too, I might add.''

He watched with amusement as she blushed at his compliment, then smiled as she thanked him sweetly for tending to her so well.

"Where is Johnny?" she asked, scanning the room in search of her husband.

"Don't fret, Charity Prindle. He's right in the next room. You can see him as soon as Sue finishes wrapping his hand." The doctor's sister often acted as his nurse, which worked out well for both of them. Since neither of them was married as yet, they lived and worked together. Sue Nelson was also one of Charity's dearest friends.

"His hand? What's wrong with his hand?" Charity tried to sit up too quickly, and those lovely spots began to dance before her eyes once more.

"Whoa, there! Just lie quietly for a few more minutes," Dr. Nelson advised. "John is fine. His hand is bruised, though not broken, I'm glad to say. From the looks of it, I'd guess a horse stomped on it. In the excitement of the moment, it seems neither of you realized your injuries right away."

Shaking her head ever so slightly, Charity wondered more to herself than the doctor, "I can't believe I fainted at seeing a little blood. Why, I've never done such a silly thing in all my born days!"

Andy Nelson nodded, one eyebrow arching upward. "I was wanting to ask you more about that, young woman," he confessed, his eyes twinkling. "Not to be poking my nose in where it doesn't belong, but could you be in a family way, Charity?"

"Oh, my!" she breathed in hopeful awe. "We've been so busy trying to get the crops in, I guess it just didn't cross my mind at all!"

"Then it is a possibility? Have you had any other symptoms? Tender breasts? Nausea? Fatigue? Dizziness?"

"Yes, yes!" Charity's eyes were glittering with joyous tears, her face wreathed in happiness. "A baby! Imagine that! Won't Johnny be surprised!"

Doc Nelson's answer was a low chuckle. "I can't imagine why he should be. Unless they've been teaching us wrong in medical school, the father usually has quite an active part in conception. It would appear that your husband has been planting more than wheat seeds, my dear Mrs. Prindle. My hearty congratulations to the both of you!"

It was a deliriously happy couple that left Doctor Nelson's office a short time later. John had been stunned at Charity's news, then as excited as Christmas. Sue was thrilled to share their glad tidings, promising to help Charity sew a layette for the baby. She also agreed to deliver the pies Charity had baked for several fellow church members who were ill and elderly, thus affording Charity more time to shop and celebrate with John.

"You're too kind, Charity," Sue told her with a smile and a shake of her head. "Don't you know that folks take advantage of people like you? Besides, you make the rest of us look mean by comparison. It really isn't fair, you know."

Now, as they walked along, Charity's face was glowing, and John nearly strutted at her side, both of them ready to burst with pride and joy. They had come to town to stock up on supplies, to pay the final assessments necessary to make their small farm solely their own, to place the remainder of their money in the bank until it was time to order more seed for replanting, and to celebrate the success of their first year's labors, as well as their first year of married life. Now they had even more to celebrate!

"I'm going to buy my wonderful wife the best dinner this town has to offer," John told her, his eyes gleaming down into hers. "You've made me the happiest man on earth, Charity. There is no way I can even begin to thank you, or to tell you how much I truly love you." If they hadn't been standing on Front Street, in broad daylight, he would have pulled her into his arms and kissed her soundly.

"Oh, Johnny, I love you, too, with all my heart."
The tenderness glowing in her face would have
melted the hardest heart. "Do you suppose we can
come back into town tomorrow, to attend Sunday
church services? It's a lot to ask, I know, two trips
to town in two days, but we really should thank
God for all His wondrous bounty. He's given us so
much, Johnny."

"Dear one, if you asked me for the moon right
now, I'd try to get it for you. Yes, we'll come back
in tomorrow, and maybe we'll even take time to visit
with some of our friends, but for now we have some
business to take care of while the stores are open."

"We can spare a little extra to buy cloth and yarn
for baby clothes, can't we? Oh, I simply can't wait
to start knitting booties and caps for our own little
darling! And I must write Mama a letter right away!
Oh, Johnny, can you believe it? A baby! Our own
baby!"

The Dodge City gossip mill was alive and humming. They had walked the short distance from the
doctor's office to the post office, and no sooner had
they entered the small establishment than Dinah
Mae gushed, "Charity! John! Congratulations! I just
heard about the baby!"

John and Charity gaped at Dinah Mae, exchanged
disbelieving looks, and burst out laughing. "It's a
good thing you told me in Doc Nelson's office," John
whispered into Charity's ear, "or they'd be picking
me up off the floor about now. Talk about a grape-
vine! This one could beat the telegraph any day!"

There were three letters awaiting them, all from
"back home" in Pennsylvania farm country. One
was from John's older brother, relating all the news
of their own harvest season and sending hearty
greetings from all of John's family. Another was
from Charity's mother, also relaying love and greet-

ings. The last was a cheerful note from one of Charity's dearest friends. Also, to Charity's delight, there was the new Sears catalog, displaying the absolute latest in ladies' fashions and household items, as well as farm implements.

As they quickly scanned their mail, Charity shook off a wave of homesickness. It had been a year since she'd seen her family or John's, a year since they had boarded the train and set out to claim their farm in Kansas and start married life on their own. Though they had made many new friends among the landowners and shopkeepers in and around Dodge City, Charity often wished they could have settled closer to home, but John had insisted that an opportunity such as this did not come along every day. If they didn't buy the farm in Kansas, it might be another year before they could save enough to afford a place of their own in Pennsylvania—and until then, they couldn't marry.

Given the choice of waiting to wed, or moving west with John, Charity had chosen Kansas, and she had not regretted it—though she had wanted to turn around and run the other way when she'd first seen the old ranch house that came with their acreage. It resembled a large, weathered shed more than a house. Moreover, it seemed to list to one side, and looked as if a strong wind would blow each and every warped board from its weak-kneed beams. If possible, the barn was in even more disrepair.

In the following weeks and months, John had seen to the structural repairs. He'd patched leaks in roofs, braced and replaced main supports, reframed windows, and put new hinges on doors, straightened the front porch to the house, and replaced most of the steps. He'd even built a small mud room onto the back of the house.

Meanwhile, Charity had tackled the inside with broom, bucket, and vigor. No mouse, bat, bird, or spider stood long in the path of her mop! Crisp gingham curtains soon covered glistening windows. Colorful scatter rugs brightened the floors. Jars of dried potpourri lent their scent to that of freshly baked gingerbread and cinnamon-apple cake. Together the young lovers turned the old house into a charming, cozy haven that shone with love and care. It was old, and often drafty, and it still needed another coat of paint, but it was their first home, and they filled it with their love. Now, in just a few short months, the house would know the sounds of a baby's cry.

"Who is *that*?" Ella nudged the woman standing next to her on the landing and pointed over the stair railing at the tall, handsome man leaning with his back to the bar. Her eyes widened appreciatively as she took in the stranger's long, lean build, the broad shoulders, the cool glint of emerald eyes in a hard, tanned face.

Marie shook her head and offered a rare bit of advice to the younger barmaid-cum-whore. "You'd best get a few more men under you before you tackle the likes of Luke Sterling. He's more man than you can appreciate right now, sweetie, and he's never struck me as the type to have much patience with a novice."

"Meanin'?"

"Meanin', he wants it clean, fast, good, and with as little talkin' as possible. He ain't one to chitchat. With him, it's slam, bam, thank you ma'am, and your time or his ain't wasted. He pays top dollar for a job well-done, and he expects to get his money's worth."

"You're sayin' he's only interested in his own pleasure then?" Ella asked with a disappointed sigh.

Marie laughed and shook her head. "No, honey. That one's good—real good. But he's a gunslinger from the top of that dark head to the tips of his boots, and definitely not a man to cross. He's real private, quiet and sort of moody, and I get the feelin' maybe some woman hurt him real bad sometime and he's keepin' his distance now. But I tell you, I've never had it so damned hot in bed with someone so cold!''

Had he heard, Luke would have been surprised to know how accurately Marie had assessed him. He was, indeed, someone to be wary of, a man with a chip on his shoulder and the means to keep anyone else from knocking it off. He was a lone wolf, forging his own way through life, and had been from the time he was young. Even at the orphanage, where Luke had spent ten of his most formative and miserable years on this earth, he'd stood apart from the others.

Undoubtedly, part of the reason he hadn't fit in well with the other children was that he'd been deliberately and eagerly abandoned, not at birth or under dire circumstances, but at the impressionable age of four. Being an especially perceptive youngster, it had been readily apparent to Luke even then that his mother was a self-centered bitch bent soley upon her own pleasures. And it was no longer convenient to have a child tied like a millstone about her neck. Lila Sterling had places to go and men to deceive, and no snot-nosed runt was going to slow her down. With nary a tear in her eye, or a word of regret, she'd dumped him at the orphanage and hightailed it out of there.

Luke was forced to live with the knowledge that his mother was a heartless whore and his father was unknown. He doubted even Lila was sure who had sired him—which meant he couldn't even pretend someone might have once cared, as some of the other children were fond of fantasizing.

It was that simple, and that complicated. With no

one to claim him, Luke was consigned to what amounted to hell on earth for a small, confused boy. The word "bastard" became synonymous, and regularly interchangeable, with his own name. In fact, for a short while he actually believed it *was* part of his name, until a couple of the older boys took it upon themselves to enlighten Luke to a few of the facts of life. It was a bitter lesson he'd never forgotten.

He'd come a long, hard road since then, and woe be to the son of a bitch who dared call him a bastard these days. And if he viewed women warily, with a lack of tender feeling and sweet words, who could blame him, really? What he'd learned as a child, he now carried forth as a man.

His cool green eyes swept the crowded, smoke-filled barroom, ever wary, intimately assessing; his every instinct attuned to possible danger. On the second pass, his glance paused to linger on the two women still poised on the staircase. One, the older of the two, was familiar to him. Luke had bedded her once or twice on previous trips through San Antonio. *What was her name? Marlie? Mary? No, Marie.* That was it; Marie. She was good—and quiet, as he recalled. Not the type to expect a lot of talk or sweet words, or to get her feelings hurt if she didn't receive them.

She caught his look, her brow raised in question, and Luke nodded once, brusquely. Yes, he could use a woman tonight, to ease the tension that even a hot bath hadn't taken from his travel-weary muscles. Marie would do nicely indeed.

His mind made up, Luke downed his shot of whiskey with a flick of his wrist and shoved away from the bar, moving to the stairs with the supple grace of a prowling panther. He was within arm's reach of Marie, her smile beckoning him, when a reckless young ranch hand barged between them, grabbing Marie's arm.

"C'mon, honey. Let's have us some fun!" The cowboy laughed drunkenly.

Marie's smile froze on her face as she tugged her arm from the luckless man's clasp, wordlessly refusing to follow him up the stairs. Her eyes darted anxiously between the foolhardy cowboy and the dangerous man standing just two steps down.

Luke's words emerged in a low growl, his emerald eyes narrowed into smoldering slits. "It's a little hard to have fun in hell, boy, if you take my meanin'. Now, if you don't mind waitin' your turn, Marie and I were about to retire to her room for a spell."

"And if I do mind?" the man dared to ask, drawing a gasp from Marie.

"Then they'll be cartin' your carcass out o' here feet first, and the lady and I will still be goin' to her room."

The cowboy seemed to sober up enough to realize that this wasn't just some trail bum he was facing. The man before him was too relaxed, too sure of himself, and his hand was hovering mere inches from the gun strapped securely to his thigh in the distinct manner of a gunfighter. That green gaze was as steady and lethal as a snake's, silently awaiting the next foolish victim.

"You'd kill a man over a whore?" he queried hesitantly.

"No, but I will kill you for your lack of respect, your bad manners, and your incredible stupidity. It's your choice."

"Hey!" the cowboy said with a nervous laugh, his hands coming up in a sign of surrender. "I can wait! I'll just have me another beer, maybe play a couple hands of poker. Why, I got the whole night ahead o' me."

"Now see?" Luke taunted with a twisted smile. "Already you're smarter than you were two minutes ago. Here." He reached into the vest pocket of his shirt and tossed a quarter-dollar toward the other man. "Have a drink on me while you wait."

With that, Luke claimed Marie's arm and escorted the woman to her room, noting wryly that she repeatedly cast worried glances behind them, as if she was afraid the cowboy would renege on his decision and begin shooting them in the back at any moment.

A short time later, as he lay alone in bed in his hotel room, Luke sighed contentedly and blew smoke toward the ceiling, glad he'd decided to employ Marie's talents this evening. She was worth much more than he'd paid, but he wasn't about to tell her that. Neither would he ever reveal that he'd first been attracted to her because she reminded him of a girl he'd known at the orphanage.

Rosie—Rosie O'Day, he reflected. Yes, at the ripe young age of thirteen, Luke had fallen prey to temptation in the blossoming form of that "older woman" of fifteen. It had been Rosie's chosen task, and a delightful one for both of them, to strip Luke of what little remained of his innocence and to initiate him into the joys of the flesh. It was an education to which Luke took a definite and immediate liking.

Mistaking gratitude on his part, and lust on hers, Luke had incautiously tumbled headlong into his first case of calf love. Three weeks later, after having mooned himself half-sick over her, Luke caught the fickle Rose in the broom closet with another young lad, and abruptly the blinders fell away. Rosie's disloyalty only served to reinforce Luke's deepest feelings about women, to remind him once more how selfish and callous they were. Then and there, he had resolved to enjoy them, to take what they so freely offered, but never, ever to allow himself to care for one of them again.

Since then, Luke had traveled a lot of territory in his thirty years, met and bedded many women, and learned many more of life's numerous lessons. But he had yet to meet a female who could change his opinion about women. Not that he hated them; no, indeed. They were soft and warm and came in right handy when a fellow had the urge. They were what they were, and Luke supposed they just couldn't help it, that deceit was just part of their nature. Luke was not going to hold a grudge against the entire sisterhood for what a few had done wrong, but it would take a rare and special woman to make him risk his heart again, or to gain his trust.

As he crushed out his cigarette and settled down to sleep, his gun close at hand even now, Luke wondered if he would ever meet such a woman.

2

$\mathbf{B}$Y the time John and Charity started back for the farm, it was much later than they had anticipated. The sun had set while they were enjoying their celebration dinner, and it was now full dark.

"If I'd known we'd be so late, and coming back to town tomorrow, I would have made arrangements for Stan Myers to feed the animals, and we'd have stayed in town for the night," John told her, pulling Charity tight against his side. Stan was their nearest neighbor to the west, another Kansas farmer.

Giving a contented yawn, Charity nodded. "That might have been nice, but I'd have worried all night if we had. As dry as it has been, I went off and left the bedroom windows wide open, and as sure as we'd have stayed in town, we'd have had a storm the likes of which we've never seen." Another yawn caught her unawares. At least now she knew why she had been so tired these last days. It was her pregnancy.

With a dreamy smile, Charity leaned her head against John's shoulder. "You know, Johnny, earlier today it struck me that we should be very careful about naming this child."

17

"Oh?" John glanced down at Charity's moonlit features, thinking how delicate and ethereal she seemed in the dim white light.

"I've rarely complained, but I've often wished my parents had named me something else."

"I had no idea you were discontent with your name. Charity is a lovely name, and it fits you remarkably well. Sweetheart, you are the most loving, giving woman I have ever known."

"You, dear husband, are extremely prejudiced." She tapped him lightly on the arm in mock reproval.

"Why don't you like your name?" he persisted quietly.

Charity sighed. "I suppose I've always wondered what would have happened if I'd turned out to be a little hellion, instead of the little darling my parents envisioned. Johnny, could it be that I've always known, deep in my heart, that my parents would be devastated if I didn't live up to the name they had given me? Is that why I've always tried so desperately to be good, to do what is right, to be kind and sweet, even when I felt like screaming or throwing myself on the floor in a rage?"

Just the image of Charity behaving in such a manner made him laugh. "Somehow, I can't see you doing such a thing, Charity. It would go completely against your character."

An exasperated sigh escaped her lips. "See, Johnny? Even you do it."

"Do what?"

"Expect me to be continually perfect! Do you, with your nice, ordinary name, know what a burden that is?"

"Until now, no," he conceded. Then he added softly, "To me you *are* perfect, Charity. Now, tell me, what name would you rather have had?"

"Mary, Jane, Emma?" Charity listed the most common names she could think of. Laughter bubbled into her throat as she added, "Bob, George, Sam! Anything but Charity!"

John's teasing laughter joined hers. "What about Faith, or Hope?" he suggested, his eyes twinkling in the moonlight. "Ah, but I forgot! The greatest of these is Charity—and she's all mine!"

They rode in silence for a while, Charity's head bobbing lightly against John's shoulder as she half-dozed. The shouts, when she first heard them, made her heart race in her chest. Beside her, she felt John's muscles tense as he, too, jerked to alertness.

"War whoops, Johnny?" she whispered, her eyes wide with fright. Everyone for miles around had been in an uproar since hearing about the escape of Dull Knife's band of Cheyenne from their Fort Reno reservation. Accounts of Indian attacks, pillaging, and killings had run rampant as the Northern Cheyenne fled north across western Kansas to their former lands.

John pulled the team to a halt, the better to hear the ruckus ahead of them. The voices came clearer now in the still night air. A shot rang out. More yelling ensued. Horses' hooves beat against the earth, coming closer with each passing moment.

"Johnny?" Charity's voice shook, and she clutched her husband's arm, seeking reassurance in the hard muscle beneath her fingers.

He shook his head. "I don't know, Charity. We'd best get off the road." He spoke softly, his eyes straining to see in the darkness ahead of them. With a light crack of the reins, he urged the horses off to the side of the worn path, into the taller prairie grass. There, the animals labored harder to pull the laden wagon, but John knew that without trees or brush to shelter them from view, their only chance of remaining hidden lay in getting far enough away from the road to blend into the blackness of the night.

The friendly half moon, which had lit their path with its pale light, was now their enemy.

Over the creak of the wagon wheels and the clank of harness, they could not know that their own noise had now attracted the attention of those they wished to avoid. It was several minutes before John realized that they were being pursued by men on horseback.

"Hang on, Charity!" he warned, lashing the team to greater speed, knowing even then that it was too late. Despite the warning, Charity nearly flew from her seat as the wagon lurched forward. Too frightened to cry out, she braced herself as best she could and prayed.

Beside her, John spared a glance behind them, his mouth a grim line as he saw the riders gaining on them. "Damn!" he muttered. That alone told Charity how worried John was, for they both came from good Christian families, and John never cursed.

Charity saw John jerk before she heard the shot. Still, it did not register on her befuddled brain that he had been hit, until he groaned and slumped against her. The reins dropped from his limp fingers.

Then she saw the blood. Not red, but black as sin in the night. It was blossoming over the back of his jacket, high on his right shoulder, wetting her dress, dripping over her fingers as she caught his limp body in her arms. It was warm and sticky, with a sickly-sweet smell, and it kept streaming over her fingers. She screamed, terror hitting her like a thunderbolt. Clutching him to her, sheltering him with her own body, Charity huddled in the wagon seat and screamed—and screamed—and screamed.

Spooked by the woman's shrill cries, and with no one manning the reins, the horses ran wild, the wagon careening behind them. In her panic, Charity scarcely realized the new peril. Nor did she take much notice when two of their pursuers caught up with the runaway team. Riding up on either side, they grabbed the harness, gradually and steadily pulling the horses to a standstill. Vaguely, she registered the thought that these men were not Indians. But with John lying across her lap, that fact brought no comfort. Whoever they were, they had shot John, and he was dying in her arms!

Stunned and terrified, Charity bent protectively over John's body, her howls having diminished to a pitiful moaning. Hot tears streamed down her cheeks, dripping onto her husband's head as she cradled him to her. "Johnny!" she wailed softly. "Oh, Johnny! Don't die, Johnny! Please, don't die!"

Had not one of the men grabbed her arm and tried to pull her from the wagon, Charity might have continued that way all night. But, this new assault served to awaken her from her stupor. Suddenly, she was a screeching tigress fighting for her mate; scratching and clawing and clinging to John's unconscious body until her attacker managed to yank her from the wagon. She fell at his feet, sobbing and shrieking, until he seized a handful of her hair and dragged her upright.

"My, my!" she heard him croon to his cohorts. "Lookee what we've got here!"

To her left, another man laughed. "Whatever it is, Jeb, it looks like it ain't full-growed yet! Throw it back till it's ripe!"

"Oh, it's ripe enough," Jeb answered, a sneer in his voice. "Get an eyeful of these and tell me these ain't sweet pickin's!" With one hand still tangled tightly in her hair, his other hooked inside the bodice of her dress and tore downward. The sickening sound of rending cloth filled Charity's ears, her heart nearly pounding out of her chest as she struggled to free herself from her captor. Her own screams rang in her head and echoed through the night.

Her hands clawed at his as he reached up to rip

her petticoat to her waist, now tearing at the delicate laces of her chemise. Her shoulders burned where the straps seared the skin before giving way under the man's rough assault, but Charity had no time to bother with such insignificant pain. Wild with terror, she watched helplessly as six pair of lusting male eyes eagerly devoured her bare breasts.

"You're right, Jeb. For such a tiny little thing, she sure has nice tits! Let's see the rest of her!"

Raw fear lent her strength, that or Jeb was so busy ogling her breasts that his hold had loosened. With a violent twist that left Jeb holding a handful of hair and little else, Charity broke free. Stumbling, sobbing, she ran on wobbly legs.

Her freedom was short-lived. Three short strides, and she was caught by her bonnet and jerked backward with such force that her hat strings nearly snapped her neck before she came up hard against a man's chest. Gasping and choking, she shivered with dread as he drawled in her ear, "Now, honey, you don't want to leave yet. The fun's just startin'!"

With a demonic chuckle, he grabbed one bare breast and squeezed until Charity squealed in pain. Then he shoved her roughly into the center of his circle of friends.

There were six of them, each more frightening than the other. It was like being set upon by a pack of ravening wolves. Clutching the tatters of her dress to her, Charity swallowed hard, literally tasting her own fear. Slowly, dizzily, she turned, seeking a way out of the ever-tightening circle, searching in vain for just one kind face, just a glimmer of humanity in any of them.

"Please!" The appeal came in a hoarse whisper. "Please don't hurt me!"

Coarse laughter and a chorus of crude suggestions met her plea. Hands reached out to tear at her clothes, to grasp at her flesh. When she backed fearfully from one tormentor, another's hand clawed at her. For long minutes, they toyed with her as a cat would a cornered mouse. It was all just a game to them, but for Charity it was a deadly game she could not win.

"Take your hands off my wife!" At the sound of John's voice, Charity gasped and reeled about. Her captors turned more slowly, a few faces registering surprise while others were carefully blank. John was braced half-in, half-out of the wagon, his features a pale grimace. He balanced a shotgun on the edge of the seat, its barrel aimed toward the outlaws.

For a moment everyone stood as if frozen. If there was a signal, Charity failed to see it; perhaps it was when she took her first step toward John. Almost immediately, guns were fired. Amid the chaos, she found her arms bound tightly to her sides and the sharp blade of a hunting knife pressed to her throat. Held from behind, she could not see her captor; she could not fail to see John clutch his side and tumble from the wagon.

"Johnny!" As his name tore from the depths of her soul, the knife bit into the tender flesh of her neck. From the shallow gash, Charity could feel her own warm blood wetting her neck. Nausea rose up, and for an awful moment she feared she might vomit. If she did, she would either choke to death or succeed in cutting her throat on her assailant's knife! Her knees threatened to buckle beneath her, but the arm under her breasts held her upright.

"Weasel! Bronc! See to the farmer! If he's still alive, get him conscious!" The man holding her was issuing the orders. While they waited for his fellow outlaws to see if John was still alive, the man hugged her tightly to him, the knife blade still pressed firmly against her neck. Through her skirts, Charity felt him rubbing himself lewdly against her buttocks.

Eyes closed, Charity bit back a protest. Salty tears

streamed silently down her colorless face and ran
into the open gash in her neck, while she tried not
to flinch at the stinging pain. She wanted to pray,
but she wasn't sure if she should pray to live, or to
die quickly. Her heart cried out to John, hoping
against hope that he was still alive. Then she wondered if it wouldn't be better, for his sake, if he were
already gone. At least he would be spared more pain
at the hands of these madmen.

The man behind her gave an evil laugh and deliberately rubbed against her again. Dread settled like
a ton of ice in Charity's stomach. There was no doubt
in her mind that this man intended to rape her. Most
likely, his friends would also. Only a miracle would
save her from the fate awaiting her, and miracles
seemed in short supply tonight. Fresh tears wet her
cheeks as she thought of the tiny life now nestled in
her womb.

"Oh, God, please save my baby!" she prayed silently. "Please save my baby!"

"Hey, Cutter! He's still alive! Whatta ya want us
to do with him now?" Blinking back her tears, Charity stared at the men slapping John and pouring water over his face in an effort to revive him.

Cutter, the man holding her to him, answered
with a gruff laugh. "Tie him to the wagon wheel,
and make sure you do it so his head is up, so he can
see everything that's goin' on. We don't want him
to miss any of the fun, do we?"

Whenever Charity recalled the hours that followed, what she remembered most was the pain.
Though she lost consciousness once or twice, for the
most part she was awake. Shock cushioned none of
the terror, lessened little of the agony, as each of the
six men took turns at her.

Once, just once, at the start of it, Charity turned
her head and caught John's tormented eyes. They
were overflowing with unbearable anguish, and she

knew they mirrored the look in her own. Twisting her head away, she did not look at him again; she could not bear to witness his pain. Instead, she concentrated all her energies toward surviving the horror of this night.

Instinct made her fight them at first. To have them take her body and abuse it so violently without trying to stop them, without fighting to save her newly conceived child, was unthinkable! The one called Cutter was first, while another held her down by pinning her arms over her head. It was strange, but even as Cutter's fingers gouged into her thighs, spreading them roughly, even as he plunged into her, tearing her tender flesh and making her scream with the pain, Charity's mind was memorizing everything about him and the others, mentally detailing all that was happening.

It was as if she had become two persons. One Charity was standing outside the other, watching this vile animal rape her, taking note of every movement, every smell and sound, no matter how small. Even as she prayed for numb mindlessness, her senses seemed to sharpen and everything came much more clearly to her in her pain. How clearly she heard John's agonized howl as Cutter claimed her with his first rending thrust. It was the sound of hell's gates opening, of a man's soul being torn from his body.

Against her own wishes, her eyes remained open, watching in tear-glazed horror as Cutter relinquished his position over her to a man he called Whitey. When Whitey's tongue violated her mouth, raping it even as he was raping her body, Charity gagged. Then, without thought to the consequences, she bit him. She tasted his blood in her mouth. Then his ham-sized fist came into view just before he hammered it into her jaw. Pain exploded in her face, bright colors spinning in her head, then blessed oblivion.

A new, sharper pain jerked her to awareness. Her ragged cry brought another kick to her searing side, her ribs on fire and feeling as if they'd been caved in. Incongruously, an absurdly handsome face loomed over her. "Now don't you go faintin' like that again, missy," the man hissed, his white teeth flashing below a meticulously groomed, flowing mustache. "When Dandy makes love to a woman, he wants her awake to enjoy it!"

During this, the third unholy ravagement, Charity felt something break way inside her, as if something had torn loose. By now her voice had given out, and her pleas were but hoarse moans, hardly audible. Inside her head, she shrieked as loudly as ever for the loss of that innocent life her body had harbored for so short a time, that precious life that would never be.

After that she ceased to fight them. Though aware of Jeb climbing atop her and biting viciously at her breasts, she lay quiescent. As she prayed for death that did not come, she heard the one called Weasel curse and say, "Hey, dammit! Don't kill her before I get a turn at her! Christ! She's bleedin' like a stuck sow!"

Nearby, John groaned out sorrowfully, helplessly, "No; no; no!" Her own weak voice repeated her husband's name over and over again, like a prayer.

Though acutely conscious of the continuing attack and excruciating pain, Charity finally found a small, protected niche inside her mind and forced her broken soul to crawl into it. What seemed an eternity later, she knew she must be hysterical, for when the ferret-faced Weasel mounted her, his thin face looking down into hers, she felt an insane urge to laugh. Either she was becoming numb to the pain, or Weasel was skinny all over, for she felt no increase in pain when he penetrated her, as she had with the others. This small, insignificant victory brought giggles bubbling up her throat. Perhaps she was finally getting her wish for death. Maybe that was why it didn't hurt so badly.

Her laughter dissolved unvoiced as the last man, Bronc, climbed onto her battered body. Not one to be satisfied with a half-dead woman beneath him, he instructed Whitney to release her wrists. "Let her scratch and claw if she wants," he said with a laugh. "If there's one thing I love to do, it's break a wild mare! Watch careful now, fellas, and I'll show you how it's done."

Seated astride her, as if on a horse, he pawed at her breasts, tormenting her torn, swollen nipples until she whimpered helplessly. As he rammed himself into her with abusive force, he taunted, "Come on, little filly. Try to buck me off!" With that, he brought his boot heels alongside her bruised thighs. "Move, damn you! Move!" he ordered gruffly. Then, doing what no one anticipated, he raked his spurs down the length of her upper legs. From hip to knee, the skin tore open.

Pain lanced through her like white-hot lightning. Her thighs were on fire, as if branded with hot pokers. Through no volition of her own, Charity lurched upward, giving Bronc the satisfaction he sought, but bringing her bruised insides even more excruciating pain. One final, soul-searing scream tore from her raw throat, rippling on the midnight breeze. Before the sound of it had faded, Charity gave herself gladly into the dark, beckoning arms of unconsciousness.

3

So this was hell! Despite the damp, bitter cold that invaded bone-deep, Charity knew this had to be hell. Crazed laughter rose into her chest. Oh, wouldn't everyone be surprised when they discovered that the devil's realm wasn't a blazing inferno after all, but a cold so chilling that it seared your soul and set your teeth chattering in your head like an angry squirrel.

Hell was darkness so complete it was smothering, like being wrapped in a black shroud and buried alive. It drenched you in your own foul-smelling fear, a fear that defiled the nostrils and coated the tongue. It was pain, mind-numbing pain that pushed so hard into your brain that thinking of anything else was nearly impossible.

Piteous moaning reached through the enveloping black fog, telling Charity she was not alone in her suffering. Only then did she realize that she, too, was making those same horrible sounds. Funny, but knowing that her misery was shared did not ease it. Rather, it compounded her own agony, sending salty tears trickling helplessly from her eyes.

"Charity . . . dear God . . . Charity . . ." The voice came out of the darkness, weak and thready.

28

"Johnny?" she thought confusedly, despair weighing heavy in her heart. Was Johnny here in hell, too? But he'd been so good! And so had she, at least she'd tried to be. The thought crossed Charity's mind that a fair number of decent folk were in for a shock when they discovered for themselves how hard it was to get into heaven. Hell must be populated with disappointed Christians!

"Char . . . ity."

"I'm here, Johnny," she called out, straining to see him in the inky night. The effort of speaking made her wince. A wretched whine rose up, increasing her anguish. Inside and out, her throat felt lacerated, her words emerging as a raspy whisper.

"S . . . Sorry. So sor . . . ry."

Confusion and pain clouded Charity's mind. Sorry? What about? What was Johnny saying? Carefully, intuitively knowing that the slightest movement would bring more excruciating pain, Charity tried to shift her body in the direction of Johnny's voice. Spears of white-hot pain lanced through her. A scream shredded her throat, and the surrounding darkness became an even heavier black, blocking out the sound of Johnny's voice, blocking out the tastes and smells of hell.

How she wished the prairie wind would cease its eternal wailing! It was such a mournful sound, so sad and filled with suffering. No! No, that wasn't the wind at all. It was the sound of her own agony blending in the night with Johnny's. Slowly she opened her eyes and breathed a sigh of relief. At least it wasn't completely dark now. She could see clumps of grass beside her head and other shadows nearby.

For a moment fright froze her heartbeat, as Charity thought the still shadows were those of her attackers. Then she recognized the shapes as those of the buckboard and horses, and went weak with relief. The outlaws were gone! Thank God, those awful, murdering beasts were gone! The slight, shuddering sigh made her chest feel as if it were caving in; it hurt merely to breathe. Weakness and pain brought the ever-ready tears once again.

"Johnny?" Gathering what little courage she still possessed, Charity stared at the night sky and whispered her greatest fear. "We're going to die out here, aren't we, Johnny? Right here . . . tonight . . ." Sobs threatened to choke her, but she forced the words past her trembling lips. "Here in the dirt . . . and our own blood."

Somewhere nearby, to Charity's left, John groaned in answer. "Charity . . . Oh, God! Char . . . Sorry. Should have pro . . . tected you," he gasped.

"I'm scared!" Her frail, frightened cry seemed loud in the still night, and startled them both. "I'm scared to die, Johnny. As a Christian . . . I know I'm . . . not supposed to be . . . but I am." Her words came out in jerks and starts, pain pounding her like an anvil, but the need to speak, to be close to him, gave her the strength to endure.

"Please . . . don't!" She could hear the tears in John's voice as he begged her not to cry, not to think about it, not to be afraid. "Wish I . . . could hold you."

"Me, too." By straining her eyes, Charity thought she could see him a few feet away, near the wagon. She supposed he was still tied to the wagon wheel, but she couldn't tell for sure. That, or like her, he was simply too weak and in too much pain to crawl nearer to her. With each passing moment, Charity could feel the life seeping out of her. Fuzziness was creeping into the edges of her vision, and odd waves seemed to be sweeping through her, making her dizzy. And she was cold, so very, very cold!

Minutes, or maybe hours passed. Finally John

spoke again, his voice no more than a hoarse sigh. "Forgive me. Love you."

A horrible dread sent fresh chills through her as Charity realized how weak John sounded. Terror brought a sharp edge to her words. "Johnny? Don't die, Johnny! Don't die and leave me alone here! Please! Please don't do that!"

His labored breathing was music to her ears. At least it was proof that he was still alive, that he hadn't left her to face her own death all by herself. "Hold on, Johnny. Just a while longer. Please? Maybe . . . someone will find us."

"Pray," he croaked.

That one word helped force back the panic nipping at her heels. "Yes . . . yes . . . Lord's Prayer." Strange how much lighter she felt all of a sudden, how her mind wanted to float away from the pain. The comforting words of the familiar prayer wouldn't come to her until John began to recite them—softly, earnestly. Together, their waning voices linking them in the lonely night, they prayed, "Our Father . . ."

John never finished that prayer. Neither did Charity. When she heard his voice drifting away, her own dwindled to nothing. "Johnny?" she whispered. Holding her breath, she strained to hear the sound of his. An eerie silence was the sole reply; then a sound, like a slight breeze, like the brush of angels' wings on the air. As fright danced over her flesh, making gooseflesh rise in its wake, she screamed his name past her tortured throat. "Johnny! Johnny! Johnny!"

One pale, trembling hand reached out for him, seeking reassurance that never came. Tears blurred her vision, and for one blessed moment he seemed to stir, but it was only her tears making his shadowed image waver before her eyes.

Gathering every ounce of strength she had left,

determined to ignore the pain she knew would come, Charity lurched toward him. Bolts of brilliantly colored lightning jolted through her, so agonizing that her breath left her lungs in a rush. She couldn't see; she couldn't hear; she couldn't even scream, it hurt so terribly. Warm, wet blood gushed from between her legs. As she clawed to within inches of her husband's body, Charity could feel the blood pumping from her body, bathing her thighs a sticky bright red—her blood—her child's blood.

From somewhere over her, a cloud threatened to smother her in its dark folds. She no longer had the strength or the will to fight it. As it swept her away, she tried once more to pray, but without Johnny, all she could manage was a feeble "Our Father . . . Our Father . . ." To save her own life, she could not recall the remainder of the prayer. No matter—Johnny would help her to remember it soon enough.

When Mano first stumbled across the wagon, the dead white man, and the naked, half-dead woman, his first inclination was to keep right on riding—just as fast and as far as his horse would carry him. The scene reeked of blood and death and violence, and Mano needed trouble like he needed three armpits.

For days now, he had tried to stay as inconspicuous as possible, ever since Dull Knife and his band of Northern Cheyenne had broken off of the reservation and headed north. Being a half-breed, and looking more Arapaho than white, was not a healthy thing these days. White men were not real smart about telling one tribe from another, and most of the time they couldn't care less anyway. Usually, they shot first and asked questions last, and Mano had learned caution as a basic rule of survival.

He'd already skirted around and gone several paces beyond the wagon when he heard the woman moan. He reined in, turned to look in her direction, then shook his head and forced himself to turn away. Though he hadn't gone close, he could tell she had been raped. Anyone with a brain could deduct that, since she'd been stripped of her clothing and there was blood all down her legs. From the looks of it, she would join her man in death before the sun rose much higher. Better to stay clear of this trouble, since the woman was going to die anyway, he told himself.

The woman groaned again. Mano closed his eyes and the sound echoed in his head. Damn! Why couldn't she already be dead! Once more, he reined in his horse, this time turning his mount back toward the wagon. He could only hope that this foolish impulse would not lead to his own destruction. Perhaps with a sip of water and a pat on the hand, and the comfort of knowing that she would not die alone, the woman would oblige him by passing on as quickly and quietly as possible. Then, if he were extremely lucky, he could go his way once more, with little delay and none the wiser.

Trouble was Dodge City's middle name. Fistfights, gunfights, prizefights, bullfights—you name it, and Dodge had seen it. Calm was a rare phenomenon, even in the dead of winter when the cattle drives were just a summer's memory. With sixteen saloons and almost as many bawdy houses in a town with a population of less than a thousand full-time residents, there was always some sort of trouble brewing.

So far, this year alone, there had been an attempted train robbery; the brutal killings of two law officers, one of whom was Bat Masterson's older brother, Ed; numerous shootings and assorted confrontations with thieves, rustlers, murderers, outlaws, and unruly cowboys who couldn't hold their liquor. Now the Cheyenne, with their trek through western Kansas, had everyone in an uproar, seeing Indians behind every rock and bush and shooting at anything that moved. And it was only September!

It took a lot to shock people who lived with so much violence on a regular basis, but the sight of the half-breed riding slowly down the street, an unconscious Charity Prindle clasped in his arms, brought a collective gasp from all along the route. Behind Charity and the bronze stranger, a second horse carried the body of John Prindle tied across its back.

Since it was Sunday morning, usually the quietest time of the week in a cow town like Dodge, Mano had hoped to accomplish his mission of mercy without causing a stir. As luck would have it, however, their arrival created an avalanche of commotion. It started with a young boy returning from a trip to the outhouse. The lad stopped short, his mouth and his britches hanging open as he stared. Then the boy was off and gone, buttoning his pants on the run, screaming for the marshal, the sheriff, the army, anyone and everyone he thought should know that Indians were attacking the city and had already killed the Prindles!

When they heard the ruckus, people began pouring out of homes and churches, hanging out of bedroom windows, rubbing the sleep from whiskey-red eyes. They gaped wide-eyed, exchanging stunned looks and worried whispers. The farther Mano traveled, the more people crowded into the street, until finally he halted his horse and just waited.

The first to approach him, hesitantly, were a man in a dark suit and a lady with curly brown hair and the beautiful golden eyes of a cat. The gentleman reached up for the woman in Mano's arms. "I'm a doctor," he said simply. "I know this woman."

Carefully, as if she were made of the most delicate crystal, Mano leaned down and transfered Charity into the doctor's arms. "Take care," he warned as a low moan tore from Charity's swollen lips. "Her ribs are broken, and she's been bleeding badly most of the way here."

Doc Nelson nodded grimly and exchanged a look with the Indian that said neither of them thought she would live much longer. Once more, for a mere heartbeat, Mano's silver gaze caught that of purest gold, worried and wary and warm as a winter's fire, and his heart lurched in his chest. Before she turned her eyes from his, he thought he glimpsed his soul in their glowing depths, and then the moment was past.

Even through the thin blanket Mano had wrapped around Charity, the doctor could feel the fever raging through her. "God, it's as if she's on fire! Has she regained consciousness at all?"

A wry smile twisted Mano's lips. "Only long enough to see me, scream, and faint again. She's muttered a time or two, but I think she's out of her head."

Nelson wasted no more time. "Sue! Let's get her home and see what we can do." Several concerned friends followed behind the doctor and his sister as they headed for his home and office on the next street. Mano watched them go, and wondered briefly what this woman called Sue, with the strange golden eyes, was to the doctor. Was she his woman?

"What about John?" someone asked.

Others gathered about the body of their friend and neighbor, shaking their heads in dismay. "He's dead," another man confirmed sadly. "Best get him over to the undertaker's." It seemed the only thing left to do for him.

Women were weeping. Men were trying to comfort them. Voices rose, sharing grief, and anger, and disbelief over this tragedy which had befallen their friends. A couple of men were already leading John's horse away.

Amid the confusion of the moment, Mano turned his horse around and started out of town the way he had come. Right now, everyone was still stunned; but given a few minutes, their anger would build and they'd be looking for someone to hang by the heels. Mano wanted to be miles from here when this bewildered crowd became a mad, mindless mob.

Suddenly a man stepped into the street in front of him, a Colt .45 leveled squarely at Mano's chest. Mano took one look at the man's smart suit, the pearl-gray bowler perched jauntily atop the dark head, and froze. There was no need for an introduction. Though he'd never met Sheriff Masterson in person, the lawman's formidable reputation was enough to make Mano certain that despite the sheriff's dandified appearance, this was not a man to be taken lightly.

"That's far enough, Indian," Masterson growled. "Dismount slowly, and keep your hands in plain sight. You're about to be a guest of the Ford County jail. How long and how healthy you stay will depend on how well I like your answers to my questions."

Masterson's silver-tipped cane prodded Mano in the ribs. "Let's go, breed."

"Hell fire, Virgil! What you doin' throwin' that ace away?"

Virgil grabbed his head and groaned at his own stupid play. The first decent hand he'd had all night, and he'd literally given it away. His resentful gaze searched the smoky saloon and found the man dressed all in black who was drifting from table to table like a devil's wraith. "Well, dammit," he complained, "how's a body supposed to concentrate on his game with that gunslinger breathin' down his neck? And if you try an' tell me he don't make you as jittery as a bug in a hot skillet, you're lyin'!"

"Wonder what he wants?"

"Trouble most likely," another player mumbled.

"I heard he's been goin' all over Austin askin' about some fella called Dandy."

"What's he want him for?"

"You wanta know, you go ask him. I'm not fool enough to. I figure that's his business."

Luke thought so, too, but he wished someone could tell him positively where to find Dandy now. So far he'd ridden over half the state of Texas trying to find his quarry, with little luck. In El Paso, he'd been told that Dandy had last been seen in San Antonio. There, he'd heard that Dandy had headed north, toward Austin. If he'd been here, he was long gone now, and Luke had no idea where to look next. Texas was a big state by itself, with many a rat hole for scum like Dandy to crawl into and hide, not to mention Mexico and half a dozen neighboring states he might slither through. It was now mid-September, and if he didn't find him soon, winter would slow his search, or delay it entirely until spring.

Deciding he'd wasted enough time here, Luke left the saloon and started down a dark alley, a shortcut to the rear of his hotel the next block over. He'd gone perhaps a third of the way when his razor-honed senses alerted him to the presence of something or someone close by, lurking in the shadows. He stopped, stood stock-still, and waited. At the first slight sound, though his eyes could still discern no movement, Luke's hand flew to his holster, drawing his gun and aiming with lightning speed.

"Don't shoot!" came the frantic cry. "I just want to talk to ya!"

"Step out here then, where I can see you," Luke ordered gruffly, weapon cocked.

A shadow moved and became a thin, bearded man who reeked of whiskey. "Please, mister! I don't mean no harm. I just heard you was lookin' for Dandy, and I thought you might be willin' to pay a little for some information."

Still wary of a trap, Luke asked. "Why didn't you approach me in the saloon? Why wait in a dark alley?"

"Mister, I might be a drunk, but I ain't that addled yet! You think I want Dandy to find out who told you about him, so he can come after me if you don't find him first? Especially with the company he's keepin' lately."

Luke's interest perked suddenly. "Oh? What company?"

"You'll pay?" the drunkard asked querulously.

"First you tell me what you know, then I'll pay you what I think it's worth," Luke countered. "Now, who has Dandy been keepin' company with, old man?"

"Well, rumor has it he's joined up with a gang of worthless yahoos who're no better'n bushwhackers. Supposed to be followin' the cattle trails, headin' north through Texas, the better to ambush a trail boss or two carryin' big cash back home, I reckon."

That made sense to Luke, and it sounded like something Dandy might do. The most money for the least effort. Luke hadn't expected him to team up with anyone else, though. Dandy usually played a lone hand.

"Are you sure we're talkin' about the same man?" he asked. Some might scoff at information gained from a drunkard, but Luke had gained good leads that way before and didn't discount it out of hand. A town drunk was always hanging around the saloons on the fringes of important conversations and schemes, ignored for the most part as being too inebriated to make sense of anything he might chance to overhear. Meanwhile, he was privy to more gossip than a hen party, and more confessions than a priest. The trick was to filter the worthwhile information from the trash, and that was what Luke was trying to do now.

"Dresses like some high-falutin' gambler," the old man said, scratching his scraggly, bug-infested beard. "Has a slicked-down mustache and thinks he's a real ladies' man."

The description fit. "Is he supposed to be heading up this gang of no-goods?"

"Naw. The leader's somebody called Cutter. Supposed to be danged good with a knife. Likes to cut people. A real sweetheart."

Holstering his gun, Luke flipped a coin at the drunk, and grinned when the old man caught it with a deft swipe of his gnarled hand. "Buy yourself a bottle."

The ten-dollar gold piece would buy several bottles, and they both knew it. "Since you're bein' so generous, I'll tell you somethin' else that might come in handy. The day he left Austin, Dandy's horse came up lame, and he traded him to some Indian for an Appaloosa."

Luke's grin widened. Even though the trail drives were almost finished for the fall, if Dandy kept the Appaloosa, he should be easier to track from here on out. Tapping a finger to the brim of his Stetson in mock salute, Luke thanked the old drunk. "Much obliged, mister. Much obliged."

4

$\mathcal{A}$NDY Nelson dragged a weary hand over his eyes, resisting an urge to rub his knuckles into his eyeballs. It was now Monday, mid-morning, twenty-four hours since he'd first begun trying to save Charity Prindle's life, and he and his sister had managed precious little sleep in that time. Sue had taken the last bedside watch while he had grabbed a quick catnap.

"How is she?" he asked.

Sue shook her head. "No change. Her fever is still raging, no matter how often I sponge her down. She keeps calling for John, and when she isn't doing that, she mumbles something that sounds like 'more father' or some such thing. She just keeps muttering that one phrase over and over again." Sue's brow wrinkled as she caught her brother's eye. "What do you suppose it means?"

"I have no idea." Dr. Nelson released his sister's hand and bent to check Charity's pulse. "It's a little stronger now that we've stemmed the bleeding. We have that in our favor, at least."

"Andy? There was never any hope of saving her baby, was there?"

"No, Sue." He shook his head as he shared his

40

sister's dismay. "She probably lost the child sometime last night."

"Do you suppose she knows that? Do you suppose she even knows that John is dead? My God, Andy! How awful! Her husband is being buried today, and she might not even know he died!"

As if disturbed by Sue's words, Charity groaned, her hands flailing weakly at her sides. At once, Doc Nelson attempted to soothe her. "There, there, Charity. Don't you fret now. Everything is going to be just fine. Sue and I are here to help you." His big hand brushed the damp hair from her forehead.

Sue sighed. "Ah, well, perhaps she'll remarry one day and have more children, though I know she would have wanted John's child, as a reminder of him and their love."

With a sad shake of his head, Andy said, "No, Sue. I truly doubt there will be any other children for Charity, at least none of her own body. She's just so torn up inside, and there will be a lot of scarring. If she ever conceives again, it will be a miracle."

Charity was swimming up through a swirling mist, trying to find her way past the pain. It was like being thrown into the center of a big vat of freshly picked cotton. She could see vague, shifting images, but couldn't focus on anything. She could hear voices, but dimly, as if they came to her from a great distance. Try as she might, she could not work up the energy to respond; she was just too sick, too weak, too tired—tired of fighting and tired of living.

It was strange, then, that she should regain her wits so well, just in time to hear Dr. Nelson tell his sister that she would likely never have children of her own. No children. Not now; not ever. Of course, she had guessed that her baby had not survived the repeated rapes. Now, weak and feverish and grieving for both John and their unborn child, Charity wished she had not survived either.

Scalding tears trickled from the corners of her eyes, trailing down her temples into her hair. Gentle fingers—Sue's or the doctor's, Charity supposed—wiped them away. She tried to wet her lips with her tongue, but her whole mouth seemed dry. Her entire face hurt as she forced her lips to move. "Let me die."

"Charity?" Dr. Nelson called her name, his fingers prying at her eyelid. The light made her eyes hurt, and she tried to pull her face away. "Charity? Did you say something? I've given you something for the pain, dear. It should be better now."

Once more, though it cost her tremendous effort to create just a gruff whisper, Charity forced words past her swollen lips. "Let me die."

Sue's gasp was loud in the still room. For a moment Andy said nothing, as if he, too, were stunned. Then his gentle bedside manner, his doctor's training, took over. "Now, Charity, I know you don't mean that. We're going to make you well again, and you are going to help us. Your life is precious, Charity. You must try."

Charity didn't answer. She merely rolled her head to the side and let the mists envelop her again.

As if they had taken Charity's agreement for granted, Sue and Doc Nelson worked tirelessly to keep her from succumbing to death's beckoning embrace. For more than a week they battled the fever that ravaged her body, weakening it and dangerously depleting her bodily fluids. Most of the time Charity was not lucid. Had she been capable, she might have thanked the doctor for the repeated doses of laudanum that eased her pain and kept her in that dream-place where nothing was quite real enough to touch her.

Then the dreams became too real, with ogres leaping upon her at every turn, beating her with clubs and stabbing her with hot pokers, chasing her and taunting her endlessly. Too often, the faces leering down at her were those of her attackers, those real-life demons who had destroyed her happiness and made her world a living hell.

Time after time, Charity would jerk awake, her heart pounding in her chest, her breath rasping in her throat. Fear was a living thing, drenching her in perspiration and setting her entire body to shaking. Asleep or awake, her life had become a nightmare.

As she began to improve, some of Charity and John's friends stopped by to check on her recovery. With awkward sympathy, they came to her bedside with bright, false smiles and too cheerful words of encouragement, even as pity glazed their eyes and dark curiosity laced their voices. Most seemed uncomfortable or embarrassed, not really knowing what to say to her; a few could not quite meet her eye, as if Charity's attack had shamed them all, somehow.

This, at least, was honest, and more aligned with Charity's own feelings of shame and guilt. Rationally, she knew she had nothing to feel guilty about; certainly she'd done nothing to warrant being viciously attacked and raped. Yet the very fact that she had lived, while John and their baby had not, was enough to swamp her with remorse and guilt, as if her immense grief over their deaths was not penance enough for her.

And the disgrace of having been used so carnally by six strangers! Oh, dear God, the shame of it all! She felt so eternally soiled, as if their filth and evilness had invaded her body and now lurked inside of her. More than bruises upon her skin, the stain of their sinister fingerprints seemed to reach clear to her soul, sullying her inside and out. No amount of soap and water would ever make her clean again, she was sure.

It was little wonder then that Charity shied away from the concern of her friends, pulling back within herself, instinctively using her illness as a protective guard against having to speak to anyone. Even with the doctor and his sister, she would not share her private agonies. Rather, she wrapped her silence about her like a shield against one and all. Often, she would pretend to sleep, merely to avoid enduring another awkward visit.

She was doing so one afternoon as she eavesdropped on a conversation between Doc Nelson and Sue.

"Sheriff Masterson is determined to hang the Indian soon," Charity heard Doc announce. "And half the town is ready and willing to help him do it, with or without a trial."

"But he has no proof that the man is guilty of anything, and Charity hasn't been well enough for the sheriff to question her," Sue was quick to point out, wondering why her heart seemed to leap at the mere mention of Charity's half-breed rescuer. "Besides, you told him that you suspect more than one attacker is responsible for this atrocity. Why aren't he and Marshal Earp trying to find the others, rather than centering all their attention on the single person who helped to save Charity's life?"

"You don't think he had anything to do with the attack?" Doc asked, eyeing his sister curiously, noting the high color in her cheeks.

"I honestly don't know what to think," Sue confided. "Why would this man violate her and kill John, then turn right around and bring them both into town the way he did? It just doesn't make any sense, Andy."

Andy's smile was rueful. "I know that, but I also know the sheriff hates Indians, Sue, even those who are half white. Add to that the fact that our county attorney is out to make a name for himself by getting as many criminals convicted as possible, and that Indian could swear his innocence from now until doomsday, and Masterson would still see him swing.''

"No!" Sue declared almost frantically. "No! Charity knows what truly happened, and she won't let them hang an innocent man. When the sheriff questions her, she'll clear him. You'll see," she maintained in a breathless rush.

"I'm sure she will clear him," Doc agreed, and added in warning, "if she can. You do realize that between the shock and the fever, it's quite possible Charity might not recall much of what happened. As yet, she hasn't spoken a word about that night."

Unshed tears stung at Charity's closed eyelids. Oh, she remembered all right! Would that she could forget! But the facts of that night in hell were etched in her brain for all eternity!

If others wondered why Mano had stopped and rescued Charity that fateful morning, Mano was asking himself the same thing. In his jail cell, he cursed his own stupidity time and again.

Why had he helped the woman? Especially a white woman? What had any of the whites ever done for him? His own father, a white soldier, had deserted Mano's mother before Mano had been born. He'd been raised by his mother's people, the Arapaho. Fortunately, being a half-breed created fewer problems within the tribe than in the white world; but Mano, with his light eyes and curly hair, had still been different.

When the missionaries had arrived in the village, wanting to teach the tribe the ways of the white world, Mano's mother had insisted that he should learn these things about his father's world. She had even sent him away with the old preacher and his wife to live in a town and go to school. Mano's natural curiosity had soon overcome his wariness, and he had lapped up knowledge like a bear at a honeycomb, devouring his lessons with great eagerness.

His schooling had come to an abrupt halt, however, when his benefactor's niece had falsely accused Mano of attempting to deflower her. Mano had protested his innocence in vain, no matter that the woman was a homely spinster several years older than he, and having all the appeal of sour milk.

Wise enough, even at fourteen, to know when his life was in peril, Mano had run. Rather than endanger his tribe, he'd joined up with a renegade band of Comanche for a while. Then he'd spent some time in Mexico with a band of Apache. Finally, much to his own amazement, he came full-circle and joined the United States Army as a scout and interpreter, wearing the same uniform his father had worn so many years before.

When his mother's tribe had at last been forced onto the reservation, he had tried to make things easier for them by serving as an interpreter for both sides. With his army pay, he had supplemented his mother's meager rations until her death during a fever epidemic.

That had been a year past. Shortly afterward, Mano had turned in his uniform, taken his horse and his ten-year pension, and mustered out of the army. He'd been wandering since, drifting aimlessly in search of nothing more or less than his own soul.

Until now. Until a few days ago, when he had foolishly let compassion overrule common sense. Still, superstitious, as many of his mother's people were, Mano could not help but wonder if this had been meant to happen. After all, in saving the white woman called Charity, he'd encountered the one called Sue; and now he knew that she was the doctor's sister, that she belonged to no man as wife. Had fate been blowing in the wind that morning, leading him to this place, this town? To this woman with the cougar's eyes, who called up such a sweet song in his soul?

On the eleventh day of her convalescence, the first day Charity could sit propped up in bed, Doc Nelson finally deemed her strong enough to allow Sheriff Masterson to question her.

"Just for a few minutes, Bat," Nelson warned. "And so help me God, if you upset her and cause her to relapse, I'll nail your hide to the wall. Infection set in a few days ago, and I've just barely managed to save her leg. Another bout of fever, and we could lose her yet."

The tall lawman practically tiptoed up to the bedside, his bowler and cane clutched politely before him. As he gazed down at her, Masterson could not quite hide an involuntary flinch. Charity's once-beautiful face was a mass of multicolored bruises. During her illness, she had lost weight, and now her cheekbones held prominence over the exaggerated hollows of her face. Sue had brushed and neatly plaited Charity's hair into a long braid that hung over her shoulder, but her hair lacked its previous luster, as did her eyes. They stared up at him, solemn to the point of lifelessness, sunk deeply within twin pits in her bony face.

"Charity?" Bat cleared his throat self-consciously. He tugged the chair closer to the side of the bed, then sat and took her thin hand in his.

He jumped in surprise as Charity jerked her hand back from his, his eyes questioning her action.

"She prefers not to be touched," Sue hastened to explain.

Bat nodded, thinking to himself that, after what she had been through, it was little wonder she did not want a man's touch. He turned their talk toward the business at hand. "As much as I regret it, I'm going to have to ask you some questions about what happened to you and John." When she continued to stare up at him with a blank expression, he asked, "You do understand what I'm saying, don't you, Charity?"

Slowly, reluctantly, she nodded. "Yes." The single word came out gruffly, as if her throat had rusted from disuse.

Immediately Bat reached for the water glass on the bedstand, almost knocking it over in his nervousness. "Here," he said, putting the rim to her fever-dried lips. "Maybe this will help."

Doc Nelson rescued the water glass before Charity wound up drenched. "Bat, the water won't help much. Charity's vocal chords were damaged, and her voice may be husky for some time, perhaps for the rest of her life."

Bat's eyes went to the white bandage encircling Charity's throat. "Oh. I'm sorry. I didn't realize."

A heavy silence fell until Bat cleared his throat noisily once again and said, "Charity, do you remember anything about the night of the attack?"

She met his look squarely. "Everything," she squawked, the raggedness of her voice making Bat wince, as if his own throat pained him just by listening to her.

"Can you identify the man?"

"Men," she corrected. "Six men."

"Six?" Bat echoed, his eyebrows rising in surprise. "You're sure?"

For the first time in nearly two weeks, a smile tipped the corners of Charity's mouth, but with mockery, not humor. "I was there," she pointed out.

Heat crept up Bat's neck and into his face. "Yeah, I guess you were. Can you describe any of them?"

As suddenly as that, memory of that hellish night swamped her, making Charity catch her breath. Dots of perspiration broke out on her forehead. Fear made her eyes dilate and her fingers clench in the covers. A whimper escaped her throat, then another and another.

Immediately, Dr. Nelson was shoving past Bat, who was sitting as if frozen in his chair, not knowing what to do. "That's enough, Sheriff. You'll have to leave now."

Andy bent to her, checking her pupils, her pulse, wiping the sweat from her brow. "It's okay, Charity. It's all right. You're safe here. No one is going to hurt you. Do you hear me, Charity? No one will hurt you."

"I still need to question her," Bat insisted, craning his neck to see past the doctor.

"Later. Another day. Can't you see that she's not up to answering your questions yet? Now get out, before I throw you out."

It was quite some time before she calmed enough to recognize reality again; even longer before she quit trembling.

Her own weakness appalled Charity, and she was ashamed of having lost control of herself as she had done in front of the sheriff. She had let fear paralyze her, and in doing so she had become victim to those beasts yet again. As long as she could not control her fear, it was their victory over and over again.

"No!" she cried out, startling herself as well as Sue, who was sitting with her.

"Charity?" Sue asked hesitantly. "What is it?"

Her eyes locked with those of her friend. "I won't let them win! I won't let them get away with this! I just won't!"

"Who, Charity?"

"Those animals! Those swine! Sue, please bring

me some paper and a pencil. Then I want you to go get Sheriff Masterson and tell him I wish to speak with him."

Sue's brow furrowed. "Are you sure, dear? You know what happened the last time."

"I'm sure. At least I have to try. John's murderers must be made to pay, and I'm the only one who can make certain that they do."

The sheet of paper Charity handed Sheriff Masterson a short while later contained the names and descriptions of all six men who had attacked her and John. While she found it much too embarrassing to discuss with him the intimate details of her violation, she had managed to govern her fear long enough to list her assailants and their physical attributes.

"Jeb," Masterson read. "Brown hair, brown eyes, ordinary height, missing first two fingers on his left hand.

"Weasel. Short; thin; squinty, close-set eyes. Thinning hair; looks like his name." A grin curved Bat's lips. "Okay. I guess that pretty well describes the varmint.

"Dandy. Young, mustache, fair-looking, dresses nattily. Nattily?" Bat frowned at Charity, who sat in her bed watching him read, unconsciously tearing at the knotted threads of the quilt across her lap. "What the devil does that mean?"

"Smartly, like a dude or a dandy." She hesitated slightly, then added dryly, "Sort of like you, Sheriff."

"Like me?" Bat wasn't sure if she'd just complimented him or criticized him. "Would you care to elaborate on that statement, please?"

"He had dressier clothing than the others, rather like a gambler, if you will. I recall he wore an embroidered vest, and a gold watch chain."

"You managed to notice quite a bit about these

fellows, didn't you, Charity?'' Of a sudden, his voice was harder, a hint of suspicion in his tone.

She met his piercing look straight on, not wavering, her answer short and forthright. ''Yes.''

''Don't you think that's a bit strange for someone who was enduring such a violent attack?''

''I wouldn't know, Sheriff. I had never been attacked before, and if there is some code of etiquette to it all, I must profess ignorance on my behalf. Was I supposed *not* to take note of what they wore and what they looked like?'' By now Charity's voice was quivering huskily, her hands waving in agitation. ''What is your point, Sheriff Masterson?''

''I believe you have conjured up, in your own mind, descriptions of six men. Perhaps it was merely to satisfy my questions, to get me to stop asking them. Or maybe because you can't recall anything about the person or persons who actually did attack you.'' His tone softened, and he sent her a half-smile. ''There's no shame in not remembering, Charity. Under the circumstances, it would be understandable.''

''Oh, would it?'' Her slim brown brows rose, her nose tilting into the air at a haughty angle that bemused him even as it irritated him. ''Yet recalling those men is not, I take it. In effect, you are calling me a liar, are you not, Sheriff?''

Bat held his hands before him, palms toward her, as if to claim his innocence. ''Now, Charity . . .''

''I am not in the habit of fabricating tales, whether for my own benefit or that of others.'' She paused to draw a painful breath. Her throat was protesting such lengthy speech, and she felt as if she were visibly wilting. This visit, with all its emotional turmoil, had drained her energies more quickly than she had realized. ''I saw those men, Sheriff Masterson. They are as I have described them to you. Now, I would much prefer that you spend your time looking for

John's killers rather than trying to get me to change my story."

"What about the Indian?"

"The one who found me and brought me to town?"

"Yes." Masterson's smile was but a show of white teeth beneath his dark mustache.

"I'm sorry, but I don't recall the man at all."

He let loose a curt laugh. "Yet you clearly recall six others." He waved the paper before her.

Charity's eyes blazed, though her voice remained cool. "I can only assume that I had lost consciousness by then, sir. I repeat—I do not recall an Indian."

"He was not one of the six who supposedly assaulted you and your husband?"

Charity did something she'd rarely done in all her years. She lost her temper. In her attempt to scream at him, her voice sounded like gravel beneath the blade of a shovel, not a pretty sound at all. "There was no *supposedly* about it, Sheriff!" she spat hoarsely. "Even you should realize that! My husband is dead! Shot twice! My unborn child is lost to me—nothing but a bloodstain in the Kansas soil somewhere between here and home! I barely managed to survive, and that only because some Indian who couldn't mind his own business had to take it upon himself to stop and play Good Samaritan!"

Her bunched fists pounded the quilt, her face contorted with grief. "He did me an injustice by preventing my death, Sheriff, but he did not accost either John or me. Now, if you are done badgering me, I would greatly appreciate it if you would leave here and get on about the job of catching the real murderers!"

As she watched the irate sheriff stomp from her room, it struck Charity that she might have been spared death for the sole purpose of seeing John's murderers brought to justice. Surely there was little else left in this world to bring her pleasure. And it *would* be her pleasure to watch those six men die, and her primary goal in life from this moment forth.

5

A full month after the assault, Charity stood next to Sue Nelson in the shade of Ham Bell's livery and stared in dismay at the jumbled contents of her wagon. Her lips quivered, the fingers she brought up to still their quaking also trembled, and her knees wobbled weakly beneath her. Since the day after the attack, the wagon had been stored in the city livery, awaiting her recover. This was the first she had seen it, or her purchases, since that fateful Saturday. This was the first day she had been allowed out of the Nelson's house.

"Oh, my!" she breathed softly, looking as if she might faint. "Oh, dear heavens!" Her eyes were huge in her solemn white face as she slowly approached the open back of the wagon. With hands shaking so badly that she had to try twice to grasp it, she pulled a length of cheery yellow cloth from amidst the tangled mess. As she tenderly brought it to her cheek, rubbing the downy fabric against her skin, her face twisted into a grotesque mask of pain. Small animal moans issued from her colorless lips.

Silently, unobserved, Mano watched the two women from the stall where he was saddling his horse. From the moment they'd first entered the liv-

54

ery, and he'd seen Sue Nelson, his blood had begun humming through his veins, alerting his body to her every breath. Yet even as his every pore yearned toward her, something about Charity drew his attention. She was so beaten, so fragile, as helpless as a baby bird fallen from its nest.

He watched as she reached for something in the wagon. Her trembling fingertips touched a rough plank of dark wood, stroking it reverently. Her gruff voice traveled to where he stood, though her words were not directed toward him. Listening, he was not even sure she was speaking to Sue, who stood next to her, looking on worriedly.

"Johnny was going to make a cradle out of this," Charity rasped. "He was so happy . . . so proud." Her voice broke, and she fell to her knees, her hands clawing at the wagon bed as she convulsed in deep, racking sobs. Her entire frame, thin as it was, shook violently, swaying with the waves of her grief. Yet, as Mano watched from the shadows, he saw no tears form in her eyes, no salty wetness on her cheeks.

He frowned. This was not good. The woman cried out in sorrow, yet no tears came to give her release. Her frail body shook with sobs, but her sorrow was not being eased. Where screams would have helped, only pitiful moans came from her throat. Didn't this woman know that if she were to wail and cry and proclaim her sorrow to the skies, her awful burden of grief would be lightened? Had no one told her? Or was she one of those unfortunate ones whose grief went so deep that she found it impossible to release it?

"Charity, please! Dear one, don't do this to yourself!" Sue was almost beside herself in her efforts to calm her friend. "Come, now. Let me take you back to my house. You can go home to the farm another day, when you are feeling stronger." Her arm came tentatively around Charity's shoulders, as if she was not sure her friend would accept her touch.

Indeed, Charity shrugged the other woman's arm away, even as she pulled the shreds of her shattered dignity about her like a cloak of iron. "I'm going home, Sue. Today. Alone."

"Why can't you at least wait a few days, until I can arrange to come with you? You're still not fully recovered, and if I know you, you'll be trying to take on too much too soon. You need someone to look after you for a while longer, Charity."

Sue noted the stubborn look to Charity's jaw and nodded. "I know you don't like hearing that, but it's the truth. Land's sakes, you've already had a major confrontation with the sheriff today, getting him to release the Indian. Isn't that enough? Besides, if you truly intend to go home, you are going to have to replace some of these ruined supplies first. It appears everything was thrown back into your wagon hodgepodge, and left to rot."

On this Charity had to agree. Whoever had gathered her belongings had done so haphazardly at best, and a number of items appeared to have been ruined, if not by the attackers, then by whoever had retrieved the abandoned wagon and brought it to town. A barrel of flour had broken open, and the contents were undoubtedly wormy by now. Charity would have to buy new. Likewise the sugar; the bag had been slit, and not a crystal was left. The coffee was nowhere to be found, nor the beans. The outlaws must have taken those. Much of her material and yarn was tangled and torn, having been deliberately dragged through the dirt and trampled beneath horses' hoofs.

With effort, Charity steadied herself, forcing herself to review the situation from a safe distance, as if these were someone else's things. As if the soft yellow cloth still clutched in her hand had not once been meant for her baby's night sack. As if the thick plaid flannel would not have found its way beneath the Christmas tree, in the form of a warm new shirt for John.

"I'll purchase the new supplies, and I'll be on my way," she insisted, her hoarse voice taking on a firm tone.

"You still need someone to drive the wagon, Charity. You can't possibly go all that way alone. I hate to say it, but you, of all people, know what can happen in this godforsaken territory! Why, just last week that singer, Dora Hand, was murdered in her bed, killed by a wildly fired bullet! First you, then Miss Hand—why, it's not safe to walk across the street anymore, let alone go several miles outside of town by yourself!"

"I'll go with her."

As Mano's quietly spoken words echoed in the livery stable, it was hard to say who was more startled by his pronouncement, he or the two women who spun around to stare at him. He'd certainly not planned on saying any such thing! Upon finally being released from the county jail, Mano's sole intention had been to collect his horse, his saddle, and his few belongings, and ride out of Dodge as fast and with as little fuss as he could manage.

Or did fate indeed have other plans for him, some vital mission that he must fulfill before his will would once again be his own to command? Damn! What was it about this tiny, battered woman that pulled at him and made him forget all good sense? What was it about her lovely friend that made him want to forget all else in Sue Nelson's arms?

Charity's eyes were huge blue holes in her face, her mouth open in a frightened gasp. Beside her, Sue nearly leaped out of her shoes upon once again coming face-to-face with the man who had rescued Charity.

Before either of them could gather wits enough to scream, and undoubtedly land him right back behind bars, Mano spoke again, quietly and calmly, his words directly at Charity. ''If I was the sort to harm you, I had my chance a month ago. Instead, I brought you to town, where the doctor could tend to you.''

Her eyes suddenly sparkled like blue fire. ''If you expect to hear me thank you for that, you are sadly mistaken,'' she barked. ''You did me no favors, sir.''

''You wanted to die.'' It was a statement, plain and flat.

''Yes.''

''If you had been meant to die, you would have.'' He now applied his thoughts of moments before to her. ''Perhaps you still have some task in life, which you have yet to complete, before the spirits take you to their breasts.'' His words were uttered softly, while his silver-gray eyes held hers, sending their own message of strength and understanding.

A shiver walked up Charity's spine, making the fine hairs on the nape of her neck stand on end. ''Who are you?'' she whispered gruffly.

A half-smile curved Mano's lips, but he merely shrugged and said, ''I am called Mano. I am the man who saved the life you claim not to want. And if you will accept my help once again, I'll see you safely to your home.''

''Why?'' she asked, shaking her head in bewilderment.

He crossed his arms over his chest and gave her a measured look. Something indefinable seemed to pass between them, something only the two of them might comprehend. ''Perhaps I don't want to see you take risks with the life I so recently rescued from the jaws of death. Or perhaps, as in some cultures, having saved you, I now feel responsible for you.''

Later, Sue was to think of this strange encounter

as almost like watching a sorcerer weave a spell, like being on the edge of a magic circle, observing and getting half-caught up in it all, as Mano spun a subtle web of enchantment. It was the most bizarre thing she had ever experienced. In the end, with no more argument, Charity agreed to let Mano accompany her to the farm. She even allowed him to take her arm long enough to help her into the wagon seat.

Somewhere between purchasing supplies and making farewells, Mano and Sue hesitantly introduced themselves. For Sue it was comparable to thrusting her hand heedlessly into a sack, not knowing if she were about to encounter something delightful or have her hand bitten. She only knew that when Charity and Mano drove off together, she felt a hot twinge of jealousy toward her dearest friend, for which she was immediately contrite.

To Mano, meeting Sue on this more personal level was yet another step of blind faith along the long, winding road destiny had mapped out for him. Only the gods knew what lay ahead of all of them. Only they knew how all of this fit together, how it would end—where, and when, and with whom. For now, Mano accepted the fact that he was to help Charity Prindle. He'd saved her life; now, perhaps he was meant to help mend her crippled spirit. He would try.

One of the first things Charity did upon arriving home was to throw everything she owned into a huge pot of boiling water and dye the entire lot black. Since she did this in the big laundry kettle in the side yard, Mano was witness to it all. As he watched her stir gloves, dresses, nightgowns, skirts and blouses, even petticoats into the inky dye, he shook his head and sighed. But when she proceeded to throw in tablecloths and bed linen, hand-crocheted doilies and dresser scarves, and started on the curtains, Mano began to doubt the wisdom of leaving her on her own. The woman seemed to be riding the fine edge of insanity, and God alone knew which way she would fall.

So Mano decided to stay a while; and Charity decided to allow him to do so. Not a word passed between them as they came to this silent and mutual agreement. It just happened. In exchange for his labors and his protection, Charity fed him and provided shelter in the barn for him and his horse.

For the next weeks, Charity tried to hide herself away on the farm, burying herself in work. Despite, or perhaps *because* it had become overgrown with weeds during her absence, her garden still yielded late squash and pumpkin. From somewhere, Mano brought fall berries. These Charity cooked and canned, pushing herself to the limits of her frail physical endurance, forcing herself to busy her hands and to keep her mind carefully blank.

While Mano took care of the horses and did the heavier chores around the farm, Charity tended her milk cow and her few chickens and ducks, and slopped the lone hog soon due to be slaughtered. Fortunately, her neighbor had looked after the livestock in her absence. She cooked, she cleaned, she scrubbed, doing it all by rote, as if in a trance.

During this time, she had four visitors. Doc and Sue came by to make certain she was not overtaxing her limited strength, and were relieved to find that Mano had remained to help her on the farm. In her state of depression, Charity missed the looks of interest that passed between Mano and Sue, though Andy noticed immediately and managed to give the two a few minutes alone before he and his sister had to return to town.

Also with Mano in mind, Sheriff Masterson rode out to check on the rumor that Charity and the half-breed were living together, to tell her of the talk this was causing in town, and to warn her that she was asking for trouble if she let the Indian stay. Pastor Goodhew stopped in to check on her recovery, bringing best wishes from several of the other parishioners, and to invite her back to church as soon as she felt able to attend.

All her life, Charity had found comfort in prayer and in the fellowship of the church. The scriptures and hymns had never failed to fill her with a warm feeling of well-being. But now, words of praise and supplication seemed to lodge in her throat behind a huge knot of anger—anger at God for failing her at a time when she'd needed Him most; for placing her and John at the mercy of those madmen; for taking her husband and baby from her. Mostly, she was angry at Him for leaving her alone and hurting, still living but not alive, existing with a heartbeat but no heart, wandering in a fog of despair with no will to do otherwise.

Guilt ate at her, most of it irrational, all of it very real. Guilt for not having died, for having been raped and sullied, for feeling so angry at God that she could not pray. Two weeks after hiding herself away at the farm, she could no longer stand the weight of it. Despite her shame, despite her feelings of unworthiness, the last Sunday of October found Charity seated with Sue and Doc Nelson in her usual church pew, while Mano awaited her in the wagon outside, refusing to enter this Christian place of worship.

She sat stiffly, her head erect, her eyes directed straight ahead of her, and tried desperately to ignore the whispers buzzing about the church as she waited for the service to begin. Her arrival, as well as her grim demeanor, had caused a stir. This thin, black-draped scarecrow bore little resemblance to the cheerful Charity of just weeks prior.

Beside her, Sue grimaced and reached for Charity's hand in a silent gesture of support as fragments of furtive conversations drifted their way, most of it from other women.

"Not so pretty now, is she?"

"Probably got no more than she deserved. After all, decent women don't get attacked like that."

"She always did attract a lot of attention with those innocent, baby-doll looks of hers."

"I knew that goody-goody act was too good to be true."

"Too bad her poor husband had to pay the price for her flirty ways."

"Now, that's not fair, Gertrude. It wasn't her fault."

"Wasn't it? I hear she's taken up with that Indian now. What does that tell you?"

"I feel sorry for her, and I just thank God it wasn't me, or one of my daughters."

"What will she do now, do you suppose? No decent man will have anything to do with her after this."

Shame and hate rose in Charity's throat, threatening to choke her. Raw hurt tore through her in waves that shook her entire body. While her face flamed, her hands had turned to ice. As the congregation rose to commence the opening hymn, her legs threatened to give way beneath her. Grimly, she locked her knees and prayed for the strength to withstand this unreasonable slander from people she'd thought were her friends.

Perhaps if she hadn't tried to sing, she would have managed the rest somehow. But when she opened her mouth and this horrid, rasping noise poured forth in place of her previously melodious voice, something snapped inside her. The heavy hymnal clattered to the floor as Charity shoved her way past the Nelsons. With movements made awkward by her broiling emotions, she lurched hurriedly down the aisle toward the door. To make matters worse, the organist suddenly ceased playing in mid-song. Voices trailed off into silence. Every eye turned toward Charity's fleeing form.

In the expectant stillness, Sue's call seemed overloud. "Charity! Wait! Please! Charity, don't go!"

Nearly at the door, Charity stopped but did not turn. She kept her back, stiff and proud, toward the congregation. "I don't belong here, Sue," she answered quietly, only the hint of a quiver in her gruff voice. "Where I sought solace, I've been given more pain. In place of understanding, I am offered only gossip and humiliation. I was mistaken to consider these people my friends. You may be sure I won't make the same mistake twice."

With supreme dignity, Charity took the remaining steps to the door. At last she turned and leveled a long, hard gaze at all of them. "Don't bother to come around with lame apologies and so-called Christian concern, which only mask your curiosity. My door will be closed to you."

Silence reigned as the doors banged shut behind her. Then, before the others could muster their thoughts, Sue stood and faced them all, her own eyes blazing with indignation. "How could you do that to her?" she shrieked, tears streaking down her face. "How dare you sit in judgment like that? I've never seen such a bunch of mean, small-minded people! Where is your pity? Where is your Christian compassion? Why, mere weeks ago, not one of you had anything but good to say about Charity. You all considered her a sweet, generous young woman. Have you forgotten so quickly?

"Joe, who cleaned your house and washed your laundry when Helen was due for your baby? Hilda, who helped you plant your garden when you broke your arm? Who baked pies and watched your children and cheered your days with her smile? And the very minute she needs help from you, what do you do but turn away, as if this poor, grief-stricken woman has somehow betrayed you! Now, because of an attack she could not help, you suddenly see her as sullied and unfit to walk among you. Well, let me tell you, if anyone should lower their heads in shame, you should! Not Charity! And I wouldn't blame her if she never spoke to any of you again!''

Head high and cheeks burning, Sue followed in Charity's wake, her brother close behind her.

November found Luke in Dallas, thoroughly exasperated and no closer to tracking down his quarry. Dandy had been through here a month ago, traveling with the same band of ruffians the old drunk had mentioned. No one could say where he'd gone from here. All Luke knew for sure was that the outlaws had come back down to Dallas after spending several weeks cutting a swath through Kansas, attacking people and stealing anything that wasn't tied down. They were suspected of seriously wounding several people and possibly killing a man in Dodge City.

Luke wasn't the only one searching for Dandy and his friends now. The law and God knew how many bounty hunters would also be sniffing after him, but Luke wanted to catch up with him first. He had a personal grudge to settle with the man.

His thoughts drifted back to the previous spring, to Amarillo and the confrontation that had started this single-minded trek for revenge. Luke had gone with a saloon girl to the small house she rented on a side street nearby. They'd been in bed, lustily satisfying their baser urges, when suddenly the door to the one-room shanty had slammed open. Ever vigilant, Luke had grabbed for his gun, leveling it at the man who was standing in the open doorway holding a small derringer. In the lamplight, he recognized the gambler. His name was Dandy, and he'd been playing cards in the saloon earlier that evening.

Dandy had eyed the two on the bed with a malevolent gaze. "You and I had an appointment, Paula," he'd snarled.

In answer, the girl had whined, "You was busy with the game, Dandy. How was I to know it'd break up so soon? A girl's got to make a livin', you know."

Luke, angry at having his pleasure so rudely curtailed, waved the barrel of his Colt. "Get out," he'd growled. "And if you're smart, you'll be more careful about burstin' in on a man like this again. You don't know how damned lucky you are that I didn't blow a hole clean through your head, you stupid son-of-a-bitch!"

With a final glare, Dandy had departed, and Luke had thought that was the end of it. He should have known better. He should have sensed someone lurking in the shadows as he'd left Paula's a few hours later. But the bullet that tore into his back like white-hot lightning had caught him completely off guard. He didn't even hear the sound of Dandy's pistol being fired until after the damage was done. Seconds later, he'd found himself face-first in the dusty street, staring at the pointed tips of Dandy's boots, unable to move let alone draw his Colt.

"Now who's the stupid son-of-a-bitch, gunslinger?" Dandy had crowed, his evil laughter echoing in the night. Still laughing, Dandy had strolled jauntily into Paula's house, leaving Luke to bleed to death mere yards from her door.

But Luke hadn't died. Through sheer determination, he'd clawed and dragged himself to one of the main streets, where he'd then collapsed. The sheriff, on his rounds, had discovered him there and alerted the doctor, who, despite enormous odds, had managed to save Luke's life. Almost a week later Luke regained consciousness and was finally able to tell the sheriff who had shot him, but by then Dandy had left town. Luke had been tracking him since then, and would continue to do so until he found him.

Dandy was one back-shooting bastard who would pay dearly for his unscrupulous deed, and no one would blame Luke for ridding the world of such vermin. In this territory, there were a given set of unwritten laws by which all honorable men abided. You never stole another man's horse, rustled someone else's cattle, cheated at cards, or shot a person in the back. Anyone who did was digging his own grave, and sooner or later someone would throw his worthless carcass into it.

Now, as Luke stepped out of his hotel into an inch of fresh snow, he cursed. A biting wind tugged at the edges of his long black duster, and he pulled the collar high around his neck. "Damn! Of all the rotten luck!" This was what Texans called a blue norther. It swept down from the north, bringing a blast of frigid air cold enough to freeze the balls off a brass monkey, sometimes dumping and drifting enough snow to bury a totem pole. Depending on the severity, the effects could be felt far into the southern reaches of the state, freezing crops and sending man and beast scurrying for shelter.

From the feel of this storm, Luke would be staying in Dallas longer than he'd planned. He also knew that this storm echoed worse weather to the north, with heavy winter snows and almost impassable trails, not only in the mountains but all across the plains. Winter had caught him short, curtailing his travels in search of Dandy. For the first time, he began to wonder if he would ever track the man down.

A few days later, good fortune smiled upon him once more. His prolonged stay in Dallas had reaped unexpected benefits. Through a traveling gambler, Luke learned that Dandy had split from the rest of his band.

"Yeah, I ran into Dandy just last week, up in Wichita Falls. We were in the middle of a game, Dandy and I and a couple of others, when this fellow called Cutter came up and interrupted our play. Crude character, sportin' a knife that looked like it would fell an oak. Anyway, Cutter asks Dandy if he was comin' with them or not, and to make up his mind fast, because the rest of their group was leavin' town early the next morning, and if he wasn't there, they'd go without him. So Dandy says to go ahead, he's tired of beatin' saddle leather day in and day out."

"Did he say anything else, like where he was headin'?"

A smile curled the gambler's mouth. "Not specifically, but he did say he'd be goin' where the sun was warm all day and the cards and the ladies hot all night."

Luke sighed. "That could be any number of places, includin' most of Mexico."

"Not if you have money to spend and a hankerin' for Cajun food and fancy French women," the gambler corrected with a sly grin.

Luke was on his way toward New Orleans before the hour was out.

The snows came, blowing and drifting and cutting Charity and Mano off from the rest of the world for long days at a time. Together, they butchered the hog and hung the meat to cure in the smokehouse. While he watched over her and the farm, Mano kept a quiet vigil, taking care not to intrude on her private sorrow. For this Charity was grateful, and just knowing Mano was there if she needed him made her feel safer.

In silent commiseration, Mano watched and worried as Charity grieved. With effort, he refrained from comment as she continued to lose weight until her bones stood out sharply in her thin face, making her eyes seem enormous within their bruised sockets. As if weighed by her perpetual despair, her lips drew downward at the edges in an austere frown. Lines began to etch themselves onto her brow, and she looked out at the world through wary blue eyes that were suddenly old and dull. Her glorious hair had lost its luster, and her shoulders were often slumped, as if robbed of their mainstay.

Yet, though he kept his own counsel and did not attempt to advise her, many were the nights Mano crept unseen and unheard into Charity's bedroom, only to make certain that she had not succumbed to the temptation to take her own life. And many were the times he heard her cry out in her sleep, her dreams tormenting her with visions of horror.

Just prior to Christmas, the weather cleared enough for Andy Nelson to bring Sue for a visit. They presented Charity with a Christmas gift, mail from back home in Pennsylvania, and a package she had sent for from the catalog. Also included were two fresh-baked loaves of nut bread for Mano, which he accepted with relish, making Sue blush to the roots of her hair.

Both brother and sister were equally appalled at Charity's appearance. Her dull, lifeless hair was pulled back into a severe knot at the nape of her neck, a style which did nothing to flatter her pinched face. She was impossibly thin now, and her dress hung on her bony frame like a black sack, the high, snug neckline covering the scar on her throat. She looked like walking death.

"My God, woman!" Andy exclaimed, gaping at her in dismay. "Have you deliberately been trying to starve yourself? I've seen more meat on an after-dinner chicken bone!''

''Flattery never was your strong suit, Doc,'' Charity retorted wryly.

''And this house!'' Sue added, waving a hand as they entered her parlor. ''I didn't expect to find you'd decorated for Christmas, but this place has all the cheer of a mine shaft! A dungeon would have more light, and probably more color!''

''I am in mourning,'' Charity reminded her curtly.

''That doesn't mean you have to live like a bat in a cave, dear. Lands! It's no wonder people are beginning to say you've turned strange! Even the children are whispering. Just yesterday I heard Jimmy Sneed telling Skeeter Manning that you're a witch; Skeeter wanted to know if you had a black cat. They ended by daring each other to come out here after dark during the next full moon!''

Charity continued pouring their tea, seemingly unaffected by all Sue had to say. ''You might warn them that if I catch them sneaking around my house, their mothers will be picking buckshot out of the seats of their britches. And if I *do* have a black cat, it is only because I was pitching everything into that pot of dye so fast that I might have inadvertently thrown in a cat, too—completely by mistake, you understand.''

It took a moment to register on either visitor that Charity had actually made a joke, be it at her own expense. Andy's guffaw erupted suddenly, echoed by Sue's uncertain giggle. Though Charity did not join in their merriment, her blue eyes seemed to twinkle for the merest of moments—or was that just wishful thinking on their part, simply a trick of the light?

Much to Sue's dismay, since she'd hoped Mano would accompany her friend, Charity declined the

· invitation to spend Christmas with her and Andy. Certainly, Charity was in no mood for festive celebrations of joy and peace and divine love, especially after reading the letter from her sister.

Charity had written previously, telling her folks and John's family of John's death and of losing their baby. Typically, she had minimized her own suffering, partly out of her old habit of not wanting to cause others more pain than necessary, and partly because she simply could not find words to express what she had endured. Besides, rape was something so utterly embarrassing to everyone—something you just didn't discuss readily, let alone in detail, unless it was absolutely imperative.

Now her sister, Zoe, had written back, briefly expressing sympathy for Charity's loss and appropriate concern for her well-being. Included in the short message, however, was the unsettling news that Charity's mother was gravely ill. Though Charity's immediate reaction was to go home at once, the unpredictability of winter weather made traveling any distance nearly impossible. Reluctantly, she realized she could only wait, write, and hope her mother would recover. Perhaps in the spring, she could sell the farm and move back to Pennsylvania.

More depressed than ever, Charity watched the winter days slip by. The holidays came and went, unheeded. January winds whipped into every crack and crevice of the house, piling snow into deep drifts. February dragged its heels endlessly. The first of March brought ice and stronger winds, with gusts enough to sweep a person right off her feet, and make the old house shake as if with palsy. Early on, Charity made up a pallet on the floor in the kitchen and closed off the rest of the rooms in order to conserve heat.

She wrote letters home, saving them until the weather cleared enough to allow Mano to ride into town to mail them for her and collect any news awaiting her. With each trip he made, Charity anticipated some message from Sheriff Masterson about the arrest of John's murderers, but the months went by with no word. She cooked, and she read to pass the time, her mail-order glasses perched on the end of her dainty nose. That the lenses of the spectacles were little more than plain glass, barely magnifying the images seen through them, was not as important as the fact that they helped to hide her eyes and her thoughts from those who might pry.

Since she had little else to read, her Bible became dog-eared, the thin pages falling open to those passages most often read. These days, Charity favored Old Testament verses calling for vengeance and just punishment for evil acts, rather than the more forgiving scriptures of the New Testament. She could soon quote Exodus, chapter 21, by heart. *"Eye for eye, tooth for tooth, hand for hand, foot for foot . . ."*

"And life for life," Charity added in promise to her dead husband and child. "Someday, somehow, I'll see those murdering beasts pay for all they have done. If I have to go after them myself, *I will* see justice done."

6

Spring was in the air; in the smells, in the soft warm feel of it. Birds were singing, flowers were budding, the earth was pregnant with promise, but Luke was in no mood to appreciate these wonders of early April. Like the land, he had waited all winter to begin his mission once again, with renewed energy and determination.

His trip to New Orleans had proved fruitless. Oh, Dandy had been there; the gambler hadn't lied about that. But, within twenty-four hours of his arrival, Dandy had chosen to bed the wrong woman. When her husband had walked in on them, Dandy had barely escaped with his skin. Two witnesses claimed to have seen him sneaking up the back stairs of his hotel with nothing but his flapping shirttails hiding his bare bottom, his pants and boots left lying on the woman's bedroom floor. Five minutes later, he was hightailing it out of town.

Just days behind, sometimes no more than hours separating them, Luke tracked Dandy through Natchez, Vicksburg, across to Montgomery, then on to Atlanta and Savannah. Whether Dandy knew he was being followed, or was just naturally restless, he never stayed more than a couple of days in one place. Of course, this made it all the more difficult for Luke, who had to take time to question people in the towns through which he passed.

Suddenly, inexplicably, he lost the trail in Charleston. It was strange—like walking into a patch of fog smack in the middle of bright sunlight. Dandy was gone, and there simply was no trace of him anywhere. The only thing Luke could figure was that he had friends in Charleston who had helped hide him, or maybe smuggled him aboard an outgoing ship.

After that, Luke had returned to Texas to spend the remainder of the winter in Dallas, thoroughly disgusted with himself for being duped when he'd been so close to achieving his goal. His self-contempt only fueled his determination to resume his quest in the spring, and to conclude it successfully at last. Now, rumor had it that Dandy was back in Kansas, playing the cardsharp and fixing to cheat trail-weary cowboys out of their hard-earned pay. Dodge City was the next stop on Luke's search. With luck, it would be his last.

Standing just inside the sheriff's office, Charity studied the wanted posters tacked to the wall. Included with several others was the yellowing bounty notice, issued six months before, for the six murderers of John Prindle. The amount offered was one hundred dollars each, dead or alive, upon positive identification.

That was what had brought Charity to town on this muddy Wednesday in early April. One of Sheriff Masterson's deputies had ridden out to the farm the night before to tell her that a bounty hunter had arrived in Dodge City claiming to have killed one of the men who had murdered John. She was wanted in town as soon as possible, to identify the body of the dead man and to pay the bounty hunter his fee.

From the minute she had heard this news, Charity had been thrown into turmoil, her emotions rioting wildly. There had been no doubt that she would make the trip into Dodge City. She could not live without knowing whether at least one of those horrid beasts had reaped his just end. She wanted—no, *needed*—to know for sure.

Still, she trembled at the very thought of seeing one of them again. Just to look upon the face of one of her attackers would be like experiencing the attack all over again. Now, moments away from knowing which of the killers lay dead, her stomach was churning, her palms slick, and her fingers like ice.

"You'll get your money, Foley, just as soon as Mrs. Prindle identifies the body." Bat Masterson's voice preceded him into his office, warning Charity of his approach.

The bounty hunter grumbled, "I better not have hauled that stinkin' carcass across the plains fer nothin', Sheriff. When I do a job, I expect to git paid."

Charity stared. She couldn't help it. She'd never before seen a bounty hunter, a man who made his living killing other men. At least not to her knowledge, and certainly not this close. As his stench defiled her shrinking nostrils, Charity hoped never to have the occasion to do so again.

The man's hair hung in greasy globs, dragging past the shoulders of his buckskin shirt, a garment which was surely filthier than it could ever have been on the animal from which it had originally come. His teeth were broken and brown and so rotten that it was a miracle they still clung to his gums. Eyes watering, Charity held her breath and willed her queasy stomach to behave itself.

When he saw her standing there, Masterson frowned. "Ma'am," he acknowledged with a curt nod. "Sorry to drag you into town like this, especially for such a distasteful chore."

"If it means that one of John's murderers has met his death, then it will be well worth any discomfort, I assure you." Almost desperate to escape the enclosed room and the malodorous bounty hunter, she stepped around the sheriff toward the open door. "Shall we get it over and done with?" she suggested. "I assume the body is being held at the undertaker's office?"

Ten seconds after viewing the remains, Charity was reeling out of the undertaker's back room. Gasping and gagging, she could only stumble along. With one shaking hand she held her lace-edged handkerchief over her mouth; with the other she clung to the sheriff's arm and prayed he would soon find a place for her to sit and recover her composure.

As soon as Charity felt the chair beneath her, she pushed his arm away and nearly toppled from the seat as she struggled to find her own sense of balance. On the fringes of her vision, she was aware that Mr. Toppler, the undertaker, and Foley, the bounty hunter, had followed. Mr. Toppler was wringing his hands in concern, his brow furrowed. Foley was scowling too, but mostly from impatience to collect his money and be on his way.

"He . . . he didn't have a face!" Charity choked out, somehow managing to grip the arm of the chair and her stomach as well. "You might have warned me!"

As he knelt beside her, Bat glared at the other two men. "I'm sorry, Charity. I didn't know it myself, or I certainly would have tried to prepare you."

Anger saved her from disgracing herself. "You should have known! It's part of your job to know these things, Sheriff!" she accused. Color flooded her cheeks, mingling with the sickly hue that lingered. Shock and rage warred within her, making her limbs quake.

"If you're done mollycoddling the old gal, I'm waitin' fer my money, and I ain't a patient man, Masterson."

"You'll get your mon—"

"You'll see your blood money when I'm certain that dead man in there is one of John's killers, and not one second sooner!" Fury flared through Charity, lending her strength.

"Well, lady, I guess yore jest gonna hafta take my word fer that, now, ain't ya?" Foley sneered. "Like you said, the man's got no face, and I'm sayin' he's one of the men what killed yore husband."

Pushing herself to her feet, Charity met his superior glare with one of her own. "Think again, Mr. Foley. As the saying goes, 'There is more than one way to skin a cat.' Well, there is more than one way to identify a body, too."

Turning to the undertaker, Charity said, "Mr. Toppler, if you'd be kind enough to assist me, I need to see that body again, please."

"For God's sake, Charity!" Bat exploded, shaking his head in disbelief. "Wasn't once bad enough? Are you deliberately tryin' to make yourself sick?"

She pinned him with a look from behind her eyeglasses. "Having survived the shock once, I believe I am now better prepared, no thanks to you."

With that, she marched wobbily from the room, leaving the men to bring up the rear. At the door of the undertaker's back room, she hesitated long enough to draw a deep breath and will herself not to become ill at the gruesome sight awaiting her on the other side. With teeth gritted together so tightly that her jaw ached, and her back as stiff and straight as an army general's, she grasped Mr. Toppler's arm as added support.

"I'm ready, sir," she murmured, not at all sure she'd ever be ready for this. "Lead on, please."

The second viewing, though not so shocking, was no less grisly, and Charity had to fight an urge to turn and run. Gathering all her cringing courage, she forced herself to examine the lifeless form on Mr. Toppler's preparation table. Through her teeth, she grated out, "His hands. I need to see his hands."

She closed her eyes and swallowed hard on the sick panic lodged in her throat, willing herself not to relive the pain as she called forth everything she could remember about the men who had raped her. Then, slowly, thoroughly, she studied this still, clothed form from head to heel.

A sob, more of relief than anything, broke from her. "That's not one of them, " she breathed, turning to stumble from the room for the second time that morning. "I don't know who that poor, faceless man is, but he is not one of the men who attacked John and me." Charity reached the wooden walkway outside and paused to draw great lungsful of fresh air into her quivering body. Pearls of perspiration dotted her forehead beneath the shading brim of her bonnet.

Behind her, Foley exploded from the building like a riled hornet from a nest. "What the hell are you tryin' to pull, woman?" he demanded. His attempt to grab her arm was foiled as Masterson knocked the bounty hunter's arm aside with his cane.

"Charity, how could you possibly make such a judgment from the condition of that man's body?" Bat asked, trying to defuse the situation before Foley did something drastic.

"I'm telling you, Sheriff, that is not one of the men! I ought to know!"

He tried again. "That night . . . well, the pain and

the shock . . . What I'm trying to say is, it would be enough to confuse anyone.''

"No! I am not some weak-brained idiot, Mr. Masterson! I know what I saw. The events and the faces of that night are indelibly etched in my mind, with a clarity that sickens me, and they will be until the day I die! I will never forget those men, not if I live to be a thousand!

"And you, Mr. Foley," she said, contempt in every line of her face. "You may forget trying to collect from me. If you destroyed that man's face in an attempt to make it impossible to identify him, you cheated only yourself. As stated on the bounty notice, a positive identification must be determined before payment is made. Remember that the next time you try to cheat your way into collecting your blood money."

She was halfway across the street, concentrating on keeping her long skirts out of six inches of mud and not losing her footing in the slippery ooze. Bat Masterson was just behind her, muttering beneath his breath something about mule-headed women.

"Nobody calls Joe Foley a cheat and lives to tell it!" Foley's incensed roar followed them. " 'Specially not a skinny, uppity old biddy like you! You'll pay, one way or t'other!"

When Bat heard Foley cock back the hammer on his buffalo rifle, he spared one brief second to curse his own negligence. Normally, he would have made the crusty bounty hunter leave his weapons in the sheriff's office and collect them again on his way out of Dodge. But his mind had been on other matters, an oversight which could now prove dangerous— perhaps deadly.

"Don't do it, Foley!" Masterson warned, his hand going to his gun as he began to turn to face the man. His gun had yet to clear his holster; Foley's finger was about to pull the trigger of the rifle aimed directly at Charity's back. It was too late to save her, precious seconds too late to prevent Foley from killing her.

Suddenly a shot rang out, and Bat watched in astonishment as Foley yelped and dropped the buffalo gun into the mud at his feet. The bounty hunter's right arm hung limp at his side, blood streaming from a wound just above his elbow.

At the sound of gunfire so close, and coming so unexpectedly, Charity jumped and let loose a screech of her own. Her scream grew in volume as her feet lost purchase in the gooey mud, skating out from under her and sending her skidding into the brown river below her. She landed on her rump with a squish, splashing mud high and wide.

With his own weapon now leveled at Foley, Masterson cast a cautious look in the direction from which the shot had come. On the opposite boardwalk stood a tall man dressed all in black, the smoke still curling from the Colt in his hand. Though his hat was pulled low on his forehead, he was close enough for Bat to see the dangerous gleam in his cool green eyes. At a glance, the sheriff noted the low-slung gun belt, the holster tied low on the man's thigh, the still watchfulness teamed with an almost casual stance. Taken altogether, they were the distinct trademarks of a skilled gunfighter.

Torn between gratefulness that Foley had been stopped, and anger at having been made to look like an incompetent fool by this dark gunman, Masterson glared when the man called out quietly, "Everything under control now, Sheriff? Any man who would shoot an old woman in the back deserves more than a scratch on the arm, but I figured you might need him alive for something."

"I can manage just fine," Masterson spat, not even offering a word of thanks. He eyed the Colt still nestled in the gunfighter's hands. "Town ordinance requires all weapons to be turned in at my office. I want to ask you a few questions anyway, so you can follow me and drop them off now and collect them on your way out of town.''

This drew a soft laugh from the stranger. ''Yeah, I can see how well that plan works,'' he jeered, nodding at the rifle Foley had dropped.

''As soon as you two finish your little chat, I could use a hand up,'' Charity cut in from her place in the mud. Every time she attempted to stand, her feet slipped out from under her. At the moment, she was on her knees, glaring first at one and then the other through mud-speckled eyeglasses. Covered in goo from head to toe, she was truly a sorry sight to behold. She was soaked to the skin, cold, and as mad as a wet hen, not only for finding herself wallowing in the mud, but also for hearing herself referred to as an old woman. Even though she was deliberately projecting a dowdy image, it still stung her feminine vanity.

Her comment drew the gunman's attention. As he leveled those emerald eyes at her, Charity felt a shiver that had nothing to do with cold skip up her backbone. In all her life, she'd never seen a man who so easily projected such arrogant confidence, such an aura of bold strength, all within the space of a look and a heartbeat. Even as it stunned her, there was something incredibly reassuring about him that made her feel almost protected in his presence—safer than she'd felt in months.

A reluctant part of her mind registered his handsome features—the wide, intelligent forehead; the arrow-straight nose; the sharply chiseled cheekbones. White teeth gleamed in a tanned face, showing one slightly crooked eyetooth amid others perfectly aligned. His firmly sculpted lips were curled into a sardonic grin, revealing, of all things, a dimple in his left cheek.

Yet even while a part of her acknowledged his good looks, Charity now knew better than anyone that evil often disguised itself in a tempting package. Besides, she had lived in Dodge long enough to recognize a gunfighter when she saw one, and this man definitely had the look. Her fragile illusion of safety fled on the tainted wings of reality. This man was probably more dangerous than anyone she'd yet encountered. Still and all, the man had saved her life; she supposed that counted for something in his favor, even if he had called her an old woman and was standing there smirking down at her with that disgustingly superior attitude.

While Charity was taking his measure, Luke was doing the same—and was far less impressed with what he saw. The woman kneeling in the mud returning his stare was about as skinny as anyone could get and still remain alive. She looked so much like a scrawny, bedraggled brown-spotted banty hen that he wouldn't have been in the least surprised if she'd started cackling and laying eggs on the spot! Even her voice sounded as if it belonged to a strangled chicken, and an ill-tempered one at that! Beyond her splattered spectacles, perched halfway down her nose, he caught a glimpse of snapping blue eyes.

Despite her obvious anger, she appeared so shaken, so tiny and frail, that an errant urge to protect and defend rose up in him. As he watched, she shivered, bringing forth a startling surge of gallantry he hadn't been aware he possessed. Where these softhearted inclinations sprang from so suddenly, especially directed as they were toward this spinsterish crone, Luke had no idea. He shook his head in self-disgust, and with a sigh of resignation holstered his Colt, trudged reluctantly forward into the ankle-deep mud, and extended a hand toward her. "Ma'am?" he offered.

Just as hesitantly, Charity accepted his hand and let him pull her from the muck, her sallow cheeks reddening at the sucking sound that ensued. How mortifying! Her humiliation grew as he gingerly clasped her elbow and steered her toward the boardwalk, her heavy mud-laden skirts making her lurch unsteadily with each awkward step. More disturbing, however, was the insane urge that suddenly came over her, an absurd desire to lean against the tall gunman, to seek comfort even as her aversion to his male touch quivered through her.

Once safely deposited upon the walkway, more upset than before, she pulled her arm from his hold and muttered a disgruntled "Thank you."

As she brushed ineffectively at her sodden dress, sending globs of mud flying, Luke hastily stepped back, out of range. Though he hid it well, he was stunned by the jolt that had raced through him when their hands had first met. Of course, given the woman's dowdy looks, it couldn't possibly be attraction he'd felt. There was probably some perfectly logical explanation, like the reaction a person got from rubbing one's feet on a rug then touching another object and setting off a spark. It had to be something similar, though his fingers still tingled from the brief contact.

With dismay, he noted that they were also a slimy mess. Frowning, he pulled the neckerchief from around his neck and thoughtfully wiped his hand clean. Then, knowing it would do little good, but somehow feeling obliged, he held the brown-blotched cloth out to her.

With a disdainful sniff, Charity hesitated. Then feeling small and ashamed for behaving in such a haughty manner to a man who had just saved her life, she swallowed her pride, accepted the kerchief, and told him grudgingly, "I suppose I owe you a debt of gratitude. If not for your intervention, that man would have killed me.''

She accompanied her statement with an accusing glare at Masterson, who stood nearby, having dragged the cursing, handcuffed bounty hunter out of the street, about to haul him off to a jail cell. ''If he had succeeded, you, Sheriff, would have been wholly responsible.''

''Now, Charity,'' Masterson began in red-faced denial.

''Don't you 'now Charity' me!'' she screeched, her anger renewed. She waved a muddy finger beneath his nose. ''You lame excuse for a lawman! You nincompoop! You've had six months to find John's killers, and this is the best you can do? I have come to the conclusion, Mr. Masterson, that you couldn't find your behind with both hands in broad daylight!'' Head held high, Charity stalked off, dragging a trail of mud behind her and leaving the three men and several open-mouthed spectators gaping after her.

7

THE incident with the bounty hunter haunted Charity for days afterward. Once more, she had come within a breath of losing her life. Once again, she had been defenseless, with only the gunslinger's fast actions saving her this time. She really needed to become more self-reliant when it came to defending herself. She brooded on this, and the fact that Foley would not be locked away in jail forever. When he was released, would he still want revenge? And what would happen if he did? Would Mano be able to defend her? Would she be forever at the mercy of one man or another?

With a sigh, Charity considered her current position. Though her farm was for sale, at what she considered a reasonable price, she'd had no buyers, and until the farm sold, she couldn't go home to Pennsylvania. Soon she would have to decide whether or not to buy seed, before it was too late to plant. Since Mano had made it plain that he was no farmer and would consider it beneath his warrior's dignity to plow and plant, and since she could not do it on her own, Charity would have to lease her fields. Perhaps Mr. Myers, her nearest neighbor, would be interested in farming her land.

"Just one more man in whom I must entrust my well-being, and hope that he will be honest in dealing with me," she thought with a tired sigh, realizing how much she had come to depend on Mano, not only to handle many of the heavier chores and repairs, but for her own protection as well. Though they rarely exchanged more than a dozen words a day, she'd grown used to having him around, and felt safe just knowing he was there. Now Charity realized that it was time she learned to protect herself from harm. What would happen if she needed help while Mano was off hunting, or busy on the other side of the farm? What if another incident like the one with Foley were to occur, perhaps while she was alone?

"Mano, I want you to teach me how to shoot a rifle," she told him a few days later.

"How to fire one, or how to hit something while you're at it?" he asked.

"Both."

"Uh huh." He nodded, thinking over her request. "Why?"

"So I can defend myself if the need arises, of course."

"Of course," he said in his usual short manner, though she guessed he was secretly laughing at her.

"Then you'll teach me?"

"I'll consider it and let you know."

"Why do you need to consider it?" she argued. "I need to be able to protect myself when you're not here."

He gave a short nod, then asked, "Are you certain you only want to defend yourself, or could it be that you're seeking a way of getting revenge?"

She answered without thinking. "That's ridiculous! Why, even the thought of it is preposterous!"

His answering smile was but a crooked twist of his lips. "I'm not gonna teach you something only to have you use that knowledge to get yourself murdered, woman. I've gone to a lot of trouble to see that you live."

It wasn't as if the idea of killing her attackers herself had never crossed her mind, especially since the law was having little luck in catching them. Still, it remained more wishful thinking than anything else, sort of a fairy-tale version of David and Goliath, with Charity in the starring role as a female David. As she had told Mano, it was entirely absurd even to entertain such thoughts, but just the idea of such sweet revenge was a balm to her soul.

Oh, to be the person to pull the trigger that would put one of those beasts in his grave! One? Well, as long as she was daydreaming, why not dream big? Why not kill all six of the murdering animals! And what she would give to be able to handle a gun the way that gunslinger had when he'd shot Foley! Yes, indeed, wouldn't that be something! Nobody would dare mess with her then!

News came at last of her mother's death, and as prepared as Charity had thought she was, she was devastated to learn of it. It seemed the final blow in a string of losses, and it brought Charity to her knees as even her own injuries had not done.

Her sister Zoe had written that their brother Ted and his wife had inherited the family farm—lock, stock, and rooster. It was only fair, really, since he was the only son, and he had run the farm for their mother since their father's death three years before. Disregarding the mourning period, Zoe would be marrying Nat Warren before the month was out, just as they'd planned before Mother's illness. In essence, her brother and sister had their own lives to live, and Charity realized with a profound sense of loss how little reason she now had for returning home.

For days afterward, she wandered about in a fog of despair. She forgot to sleep, to eat, or even to cook Mano's meals for him. Once, she was planting seedlings in her small vegetable garden plot when a storm blew up. So deeply buried in grief was she that she did not even realize she was kneeling in mud, rain molding her dress to her skin while lightning danced threateningly in the sky over her head. Mano found her and dragged her unceremoniously into the house, tossing towels at her and ordering her to change into dry clothes.

After that, Mano cooked for both of them, sitting across the table from her and watching every bite she took, just to ensure that she ate. It was several days before Charity finally managed to deal with this newest loss and returned to some semblance of normality, or what had passed for normality since John's death.

Then, almost overnight, Charity's despair was transformed into anger. Not a common, flash-in-the-pan anger, but a rage that had been building up inside her since the night of the attack, made stronger by all the tears she could not shed, the relief she could not find. It had been brewing for a long time now, unnoticed, often disguising itself as desolation or depression; but now it was surfacing as a full-blown gale, searching for the smallest reason to break free, ready and waiting to wreak havoc.

Charity was a seething storm on the verge of exploding. Mano could see it in her face, sense it in the tense manner of her movements and speech. Gone was that dull, lifeless look from her eyes. Now, behind the shield of those silly eyeglasses, they gleamed bright with the flame of fury, and something else so familiar to him that Mano could not mistake it in Charity—the urge for revenge!

She was a tempest born of a pain so deep, an agony so great, that only the cleansing fires of vengeance could soothe her soul and save her from eternal despair. Mano was no one's fool; he recognized a woman on the warpath when he saw one. She was a walking, talking keg of dynamite, with a very short fuse—and Mano could not help but wonder who held the match that would surely ignite her wrath.

The moment the man walked past the window of the shoe shop where Charity was having new soles sewn on, she recognized him. He was the same gunfighter who had saved her from Foley. Even at a glance, there was no mistaking him for anyone else. Perhaps it had to do with the peculiar way he moved, so fluid and graceful for such a big man. Perhaps it was his height, or the way he held himself aloof while practically oozing confidence and strength.

Trying not to be too obvious, Charity sauntered over to the door, which stood open to the spring air, and watched as the gunman made his way down Front Street. By standing on tiptoe and craning her neck, she managed to watch until he turned into a store at the far end of the next block. She was certain it was the general merchandise, where a person could buy anything from sheep-dip or saddles to the newest, most expensive Stetson.

"Something interestin' out there, Miz Prindle?" Mr. Mueller asked.

Charity jumped as if prodded with a hot cattle brand and caught hastily at the door frame to avoid tumbling out. "No!" she exclaimed, enough heat flooding her face to steam her glasses. Clearing her throat guiltily, she managed to say more calmly, "No, Mr. Mueller, nothing special."

As she waited impatiently for the bootmaker to finish her shoes, a plan began to form in Charity's mind. Actually, the thought had been there for some time now, but with no foundation for reality. Suddenly, the answer to her dilemma shimmered to life, leaving her almost breathless.

It was a daring idea, exciting and outrageous—if only she could get the gunfighter to agree, if she had the courage to actually ask him. But what did she have to lose? The worst he could do was turn her down.

Charity didn't stop to ask herself the most curious question—*Why him?* For some unknown reason, though there were others just as capable whose aid she might have enlisted, she chose this stranger for her mission. There was something about him, a force that drew her, that set him apart from and above the others, and made him seem the ideal choice. The man personified the word danger, and if that danger did not extend itself to her, he would be perfect for what she had in mind.

By the time Mr. Mueller finally finished repairing her shoes, Charity was in a lather of impatience. But, when she hurried over to the general store, the tall stranger was no longer there. Ready to chew nails in half, she huffed her way onto the broad boardwalk once more. "Well, phooey!" she muttered to herself, scanning the street.

Just as she was about to give up hope, the gunfighter emerged from a laundry halfway down the block and headed up the street in the opposite direction from where she stood. Picking up her skirts, Charity hurried after him, afraid he might turn into one of the numerous saloons before she could catch up with him. If that happened, she feared she would never get to speak with him, for if she didn't lose her nerve by the time he came back out, he would surely be too inebriated to understand what she was asking him.

Ignoring the Alamo, the Long Branch, the Lone Star, and the Alhambra, the man made a beeline for

Hoover's saloon and wholesale liquor establishment, and Charity swallowed a sigh of disappointment. He'd probably spend the rest of the day and night in there, drinking himself under the bar!

Feeling conspicuous in the extreme, Charity loitered outside the hardware store next door to the saloon. For a ridiculous length of time, she stared at the display in the window, furtively watching the entrance of the saloon from the edge of her vision. Wondering how long she could pretend interest in picks and shovels and buckets before someone thought it peculiar and stopped to ask her what was wrong, she let her attention wander, and almost missed her man. He was past her, his long strides taking him into Beatty and Kelley's restaurant before she could react.

Four minutes later, breathless, Charity was seated at the table nearest the tall, dark gunman. A mere three feet separated their chairs. After ordering tea and biscuits, she covertly studied the man through lowered lashes, trying to gather the fortitude to speak to him now that the opportunity was at hand. Nervously, she traced the red-and-white checkered pattern on the tablecloth, her fingers shaking and her mouth gone dry as a desert.

He felt her staring at him. Though he did not lift his gaze from his plate, though he continued to eat without pause, Luke could feel her eyes on him. He'd recognized her the minute she'd sat down. Just as quickly he had dismissed her from his mind— until she'd begun staring at him from behind those funny little glasses perched on the end of her nose. That made him cautious, if not downright nervous.

For years, he'd survived by listening to his instincts, by never ignoring what his finely honed senses were telling him. He'd survived the war; since then he'd survived confrontations with Mexican bandits, Indians, outlaws, gunmen, and a few out-and-out fools, all by paying heed to his instincts. And right now his instincts were warning him to beware of this woman until he knew what she was up to.

Abruptly, without forewarning, Luke raised his head and met her look directly, taking the woman completely off guard. His piercing green gaze bore into her face, trying to see her eyes past the shiny lenses of her eyeglasses. Startled, she gave a weird little yelp and a reflexive jerk, and her teaspoon went sailing through the air to land in Luke's lap, splattering him with tea.

Mortified, Charity just sat there, as if turned to stone—rose-colored stone. She wished in vain for the floor to open up beneath her and swallow her whole, chair and all! Silently he extended the errant spoon toward her, and she could only grimace and mumble, "Oh, God!"

"I should've expected somethin' like this, I suppose, judgin' from our first meeting," came the low, rumbling reply, with more than a hint of laughter in it. With his spare hand, he took up his napkin and began to swipe at his clothes. "Luke Sterling, ma'am, at your service—again."

"Mr. Sterling, please accept my apologies. I'm not usually so clumsy. Truly."

Though he'd heard it previously, and should have been prepared, her voice came as a shock, sending a queer quiver through him. For some reason this time it was oddly compelling, washing over him like a love-husky whisper in a warm, dark room. It sounded so strange, so out of place, coming from a prim little spinster with every square inch of skin between her toes and her chin completely swathed in black.

A dark brow raised, as if in refute of her claim, and he reached forward to place the spoon on the table, next to her teacup. "No harm done."

Picking up his fork, he returned to eating, as if nothing had happened to interrupt his meal. From the corner of his eye, he saw her bite her lip, look down at her cup, then resume staring at him. He barely contained his sigh. Oh, Lord, no! By now his only conclusion was that this homely little mud hen must be smitten with him, all because he'd had the misfortune to be the one to save her life! If he had it to do again, he'd let the bounty hunter shoot her. No, no he wouldn't, not really. But what was he to do now? *Ignore her*, an inner voice advised. That's it, I'll just ignore her, and she'll go away. Good idea!

Except for one thing. It didn't work!

"Psst! Mr. Sterling! Ahem! Mr. Sterling!" The woman was quietly but very persistently trying to gain his attention. "Please, Mr. Sterling, I must speak with you."

Against his better judgment, Luke turned to face her. "Ma'am?" he questioned, that dark brow arching upward again.

"I really need to talk to you," she repeated, glancing nervously about, "but not here. I have a farm a few miles out of town where we could meet. If you agree, of course."

Luke was so flabbergasted that he could barely find his tongue. He'd been sitting here eating, minding his own business . . . "Look, lady, I'm flattered by your interest, but I'm really gonna have to decline your invitation."

As she caught his meaning, Charity's mouth dropped open with such force that she felt her jaw crack. If her face had been red before, now it glowed a brilliant crimson. "Why, you conceited jackanape!" she hissed indignantly.

Frowning, not at all sure he hadn't been mortally insulted, Luke asked, "Is that any kin to a jackass, by any chance?"

"Close enough! For your information, I only want

to hire your services!" Once more, Charity could not believe how handily her own foot had slipped into her mouth.

"I know," Luke replied, barely containing a shudder at the mere thought of bedding this skinny bundle of bones in baggy black. "That's exactly what I was afraid of. The answer is still no." No amount of money would be enough to induce him to make love to this hag! In fact, just thinking about it, Luke was convinced that it would be impossible to work up enough desire toward her to make the deed physically achievable! That queer sizzle he'd experienced at their first meeting had undoubtedly been revulsion, pure and simple.

"I meant your gun, sir!" As he continued to regard her with that odd look, she snarled in that whispery voice of hers, "You are a gunfighter, are you not? Your expertise in that field is for hire, isn't it?"

"Oh! Oh, yes!" Luke's relief was so great that he barely knew what he was saying.

"Fine. Then I'll expect you tomorrow morning, to discuss wages and such. The farm is just west of town about six miles—"

"Whoa! Hold on there just a minute, Miss . . ."

"Prindle," she supplied. "Charity Prindle."

"Miss Prindle, I'll have to know a little more about your situation, before we even get to the matter of my fee. First off, why do you need a hired gun?"

Like a number of other gunmen, Luke made his living by hiring his services out to others. Being fast with a gun didn't always put a man on opposite sides with the law, or on the same level as a common horse thief and one step ahead of the local marshal. Nor was he some hot-headed killer, roaming from town to town looking for trouble and involving himself in gunfights in the middle of the street, as a few popular Western novelists would have folks believe. Of course, most of these writers worked back East, and wouldn't know a gunfighter if they tripped over him! Still, there were gunmen like that, lending credence to the stories, and giving the rest of them a bad name.

Not that Luke's reputation for being fast and accurate on the draw wasn't justified, but most of his work was respectable and well-warranted. The situations varied. Sometimes he hired out to ranchers who were having trouble with rustlers, or to landowners involved in heated disputes over boundaries or water rights, or as a bodyguard to some well-known personage. He'd even ridden shotgun on the train and stagecoach runs, guarding payroll and gold shipments. On occasion, he'd hired on as a deputy marshal, helping to keep peace in rowdy cow towns like Dodge City.

The army had taught him how to shoot; practice had made him fast. For an orphan with few prospects, gunfighting was his route to prosperity. When they wanted the best, they asked for Luke Sterling—and paid accordingly. To date, however, he'd never worked for a woman, and he wasn't about to start now, especially not with this one!

Once more, Charity became conscious of the number of people in the restaurant, and how long she'd been lingering over her single cup of tea and two buttered biscuits. If she didn't want to arouse suspicion, she was going to have to leave. "We can't talk here," she repeated, staring down into her teacup as if fascinated.

Either the lady was reading tea leaves, or she was up to something, Luke thought. After all her previous gawking, now she would not meet his gaze. Something wasn't quite right here. Could someone have sent her in here to lure him into a trap of some sort? After all, who would suspect a prune-faced thing like her of evil doings? On the other hand, she reminded Luke uncomfortably of his childhood image of what a witch would look like. All the poor old bird needed was a wart on her chin with a few dark hairs sprouting from it!

"You can talk to me right here or forget the whole thing," he stated flatly.

"No! I can't! Please!"

He said nothing, merely continued to gaze unblinkingly at her with those relentless green eyes.

"Can I get you some more tea or something?" a feminine voice asked suddenly from over her shoulder.

For the third time that day, Charity nearly leaped out of her skin. "Hannah!" Charity's hands fluttered at her chest as she willed her heart to stay in her body. "No! Nothing, thank you!"

Flustered, she dug into her reticule and nearly thrust the cost of her repast at the befuddled waitress. Then she fled the restaurant as swiftly as her knocking knees would allow, leaving both Hannah and Luke to wonder at her behavior.

8

Luke was relaxing in a steaming tub of hot water in the bathing room connected to the rear of the Dodge House Hotel, puffing contentedly on an excellent cheroot. Habit made him keep his Colt within easy reach, on a low stool beside the tub, even though there was no one else using any of the other seven tubs. For the moment, at least, he had the entire place to himself, while he continued to ponder the oddities of one Miss Charity Prindle, chuckling over his narrow escape of her dubious charms.

He still wasn't sure about her, and that bothered him. Was she merely a strange little duck, a lust-smitten old maid to be pitied? Or was she, in reality, part of some life-threatening trap against him? There was something about the woman that just didn't ring true, but Luke couldn't put his finger on what it was.

Even with his thoughts occupied, Luke heard the quiet, faltering footsteps stop outside the bathhouse door. While he sat naked, up to his chest in hot water, someone skulked stealthily in the hall. His eyes narrowing, his hand reaching for his Colt, he watched the doorknob turn ever so slowly and the

96

door begin to open, inch by creeping inch. With his hand and the gun hidden behind the side of the tub, Luke feigned a relaxation he no longer felt, his head against the rim of the tub and his thick lashes hiding the fact that his eyes were not completely closed. Whoever stepped through that door, he was ready for them.

When a black bonnet over wire-rimmed eyeglasses peeked hesitantly through the crack, Luke nearly swallowed his glowing cigar. Luckily, his eyes did not pop open until she was inside the room, her backside toward him, as she now checked the hallway to make certain no one had seen her enter the room. Surprise, and a healthy curiosity, held Luke silent as he watched her pull the door shut. A chair stood beside the door. Without so much as a glance at him, she quietly retrieved it, and in lieu of a lock, wedged the high back of the chair under the doorknob.

"Just what in tarnation do you think you're doin', woman?" Luke's voice exploded through the still room like a gunshot.

"Aaiieee!" Charity spun around, caught the hem of her skirt on a protruding chair leg, and plopped unceremoniously onto the uptilted seat of the chair with all the grace of a wet rag mop. Both slender hands clutched at her chest above her thumping heart, as if to prevent it from leaping from her body. "You scared the . . . the sugar out of me!" she gasped, spearing him with an accusing look from over the top of her eyeglasses.

"Sugar?" he asked, shifting into a more upright position and replacing his revolver on the stool. A dark brow rose, and one side of his mouth twitched in a picture of blithe disbelief. "Vinegar, more likely. And you didn't do much for my peace of mind either, sneakin' around like that. Now, would you like to tell me what's so dadburned important that you've got to interrupt a man's bath?''

Charity climbed awkwardly to her feet, trying not to upset either herself or the precariously balanced chair. "I need to talk to you privately. I told you that in the restaurant." For the first time since entering the room, Charity looked at him—really looked. Her eyes widened in her thin face; her mouth dropped open. "Oh, my stars and garters! You're naked!"

Luke blinked, his white teeth clamped about the end of his cigar as he jeered, "No kiddin', lady. With observations like that, you should be a Pinkerton detective. And how many people do you know who wear their clothes into the bath with them?"

"No . . . none." Suddenly she was a stammering idiot, every sane and sound thought gone from her head, her disbelieving eyes riveted on the sight of Luke Sterling's bare chest. She looked on in fascination as droplets of water glistened like diamonds amid the cloud of dark curls. Was that dark carpet really as soft and springy as it looked? John's chest hair had been almost blond, and much more sparse.

Luke's amusement turned sour as he watched the skinny spinster's eyes devour him. Suddenly the steaming tub felt a little too much like a cannibal's cooking kettle, and he a tad too much like the anticipated feast. "Uh, lady, this isn't exactly the best place to hold a conversation, you know. You shouldn't be in here. What if someone comes along wantin' to take a bath?" No sooner had the words left his mouth than Luke wondered if that had been her plan all along, to place herself and him in a compromising situation where he might be forced to marry her to save her reputation and his skin.

With effort, Charity dragged her eyes from his chest, and her thoughts to the matter at hand. She half-turned away from him, overcome with embarrassment at her own behavior more than his. Swallowing to dispense a bit of moisture to her parched throat, she waved a hand toward him and croaked, "Could you please cover yourself with a towel or something, Mr. Sterling?"

Under the circumstances, Luke was happy to oblige. God forbid he should stir this old maid's lusts any more than they were already! "Okay, say what you came to say and get the devil out before someone catches you in here! Because I'll tell you right now, I don't care two bits about your reputation, and I won't forfeit my freedom for the likes of you, if it comes to that."

Charity frowned, trying in vain to follow his line of thought. What *was* the man raving about? Oh, well, she didn't' have time to stand about all day chatting, though when she'd first thought to catch him here, she hadn't realized how disconcerting it would be to try to converse with a naked stranger in his bath.

"A little over seven months ago," she began, "my husband and I were returning to our farm when we were attacked by six men. My husband was killed, and I almost died from my injuries. The men got away and have never been found. Sheriff Masterson and his friend, Marshal Earp, have had no luck in tracking these murderers. Personally, I believe if they spent half as much time searching as they do gambling and consorting with loose women, the killers would have been brought to justice long ago. So far, the closest they have come is that bounty hunter who tried to dupe me and collect for the wrong body, and then threatened me for refuting his word. But for you, he would have shot me."

In the telling, her face became contorted with hatred. Pain laced every word, adding gruffness to her voice. "I want those men, Mr. Sterling. I want them dead, and their bodies thrown as carrion to the vultures. I want to spit upon their lifeless bodies." Suddenly, as if aware that she was losing control, she stopped speaking. She stood staring at the wall, her breath coming in harsh gasps, her hands clenched into tight fists at her sides.

Luke watched and listened in amazement. This wasn't at all what he had expected. Actually, he'd expected her to give him some tale about being frightened and needing protection. Also, if she were telling the truth, she wasn't the old maid he had thought her to be. For some reason, when she'd yelled at Masterson the other day, Luke had assumed the man she'd called John was a friend or brother. Now it seemed she'd been married to him— and tragically widowed.

Still, he couldn't help but ask, "Why me? I know you think the town marshal and the sheriff are inept fools, but with Dodge City's reputation it shouldn't be hard to find someone else to help you. Gunmen must be a dime a dozen in a town as wild as this."

"You're right, but so are ruthless outlaws like the ones who killed Johnny. I need to know that I can trust the man I hire."

"And what makes you think you can trust me?"

Her head swung around, her eyes staring at his face as if searching there for an answer to his question. "I don't know. Maybe I'm becoming as crazy as everyone seems to think I am. Or perhaps I'm just tired of waiting for something to happen, for Masterson and Earp to get off their behinds and do something. Maybe it's time I did something about it myself, and I suppose I don't really care any longer if it's safe, or a good idea, or even if any of it makes sense."

Her jaw stiffened stubbornly, and Luke could sense that it pained her to almost beg him for help. "I'll pay whatever is fair. I have some money in the bank, and a small inheritance from my mother."

Luke frowned. He'd have to think about what she'd told him, maybe talk with the marshal to determine just how difficult a job it would be to track these men. He simply had to get a better handle on the situation before he could promise Mrs. Prindle anything, no matter how much she offered to pay. Leaning over, he pulled his watch from the pocket of his trousers and consulted it with a frown. "Meet me back here at the hotel in two hours, and I'll let you know my decision. If I agree, we'll iron out the details then."

"Oh, but you haven't really heard enough of it to decide," she argued, her hands fluttering frantically. "And I can't possibly meet you here again. I've already taken too much of a chance."

"Look, lady, I'm gettin' a little tired of this song and dance of yours. Now, either you want my help or you don't, and if you want it badly enough, you'll be back here in two hours, like I said. Meanwhile, will you kindly haul your carcass out of here so I can finish my bath? This water's about as warm as day-old piss, and my entire body below my armpits is as wrinkled as an old hog's snout."

After their last encounter, Luke wasn't surprised when Masterson gave him a cool reception, especially when he began to ask the sheriff about Mrs. Prindle's attackers. Reluctantly, the lawman relayed the names and descriptions, giving Luke the distinct impression that Masterson thought Charity had invented most of the information. Thus, though they had issued warrants and wanted posters, and conducted a search for John Prindle's murderers, they'd done so blindly, giving little credence to Charity's story. In truth, they didn't know who they were looking for, or how many men had really been involved.

Luke might have been of the same mind had Masterson not listed Dandy's name among the outlaws and given a surprisingly accurate description of the man. In fact, he barely hid his shock and the immediate burst of blood lust brought on by the mention of the very man he'd been hunting so diligently. By the time he left the sheriff's office, Luke was convinced that, contrary to what others might believe, Charity Prindle had not been crazed with shock when she had described her attackers. She had been telling the awful truth, and it was painfully clear that she would receive little aid from Dodge city's infamous lawmen. Little wonder that she had turned to Luke for help, stranger though he was.

Luke had a lot to think about before meeting with her once more. While he wanted only Dandy, for his own reasons, helping her meant going after a half dozen killers, not just one. Still, since rumor had it that Dandy may or may not have joined with the outlaw band again, Luke might be going up against all six regardless.

He needed more details about them, and right now it looked as if the Widow Prindle was the person with the most reliable information. Aside from that, she was willing to pay, and he could always use the money. First he'd talk with her again. Then he'd decide whether or not to help her.

If she had to meet him at the Dodge House, she would do so as secretly as possible. Thus, before the appointed time, Charity discreetly discovered Mr. Sterling's room number. With none the wiser, she crept up the back serving stairs and located his room. Not wanting to alert anyone but the gunslinger to her presence, she disdained knocking. Rather, upon realizing the door was unlocked, she silently let herself into his room—and promptly found her nose flattened by the barrel of his Colt!

"Woman, I don't know how you've managed to live as long as you have. Do you realize I could have blown your blasted head off before I realized it was you?" he ranted. Shoving his gun into the holster slung over the bedpost, he continued to glare at her. "And what in hell do you mean by letting yourself into my room? Last I knew, only chambermaids and whores had access to a man's private hotel room, and then only on request. Of course, after that little episode in the bathhouse this afternoon, I suppose I shouldn't be so surprised, should I?"

Admittedly, her behavior was highly improper, and under ordinary circumstances, Charity wouldn't have been caught dead in a strange man's hotel room, let alone his bath. But these were not usual circumstances; nothing about her life was normal anymore. "I . . . I'm sorry! I didn't think! I just didn't want to attract attention by knocking and making a lot of noise."

Practically nose to nose with her, Luke couldn't fail to see how upset she was. Her face was as pale as the sheets on his bed, and half a dozen freckles stood out across her nose like mud splatters on fresh snow. "Oh, hellfire and damnation!" he cursed softly, grabbing her arm and leading her to the edge of the bed. "Sit down before you fall down!" Again that odd sensation of fire licked at his fingertips.

He released her almost before Charity had time to realize he had touched her, before she thought to panic, or to object to his handling her. Instead, she voiced another, rather inane, objection. "Sir! I can't sit on your *bed!*"

Now her modesty chose to reassert itself! "Fine! Then fall on your blasted face for all I care! As you could see, if you had the sense God gave a flea, there's no chair in the room."

She sat; rather, she perched birdlike on the very edge of the mattress, as if that reduced the imagined offense. Staring up at him, she offered lamely, "You have shaving soap on your ear."

"Yeah, and mush for brains to even consider helpin' you," he countered, taking up a towel and swiping at his ear. "Contractin' to kill six men is no small matter, you know. And there are a number of details to work out beforehand. Such as, what happens if I find only four or five of them? Also, do you want them killed, or simply brought back to Dodge to be tried by a court of law? By the way, I did notice the bounty poster, which leads us to another question: Are you payin' me over and above the bounty? And we still have to negotiate a fee, which might be more than you care to spend." He fired the questions at her without giving her time to answer them, never mentioning his own interest in the men, or his personal plans for Dandy once he caught him.

"Wait! Wait!" Charity stood, her hands waving impatiently. "If you'd just slow down and listen for a moment, there is something I think I should clear up at the start." She took a deep breath and gazed up at him, trying to gauge just how angry Mr. Sterling was going to be when she set him straight. At last, realizing there was no way to ease into the matter, she blurted, "I don't want *you* to go gunning for these men. I simply want you to teach me all I need to know to go after them myself."

Luke stood rooted to the floor, his mouth gaping. Finally, he shook his head briskly, as if to correct his faulty hearing. "That must have been some bad whiskey I drank. I could almost swear I heard you say you want me to teach you to be a gunman—er, gun-woman? Oh, hell! You know what I mean!"

"I do, and I did," Charity assured him. "I want you to teach me everything you can, in as short a time as possible."

He started to laugh; just a couple of deep chuckles at first, which escalated into a rumbling belly laugh.

"Lady, you're as balmy as a bedbug! You've been nippin' the berry brandy a little too much for just medicinal purposes, and the fumes have stewed your brain."

Though she had expected such a reaction, she had hoped against it. Now, unamused, she drew her pride about her like a shield. "I am neither demented nor addled by drink. I realize that what I am asking is a bit unusual, but—"

"Unusual? Unusual?" he hooted. "Unusual is wearin' your boots on the wrong feet cause they fit better that way; unusual is havin' a genuine fondness for skunks. You're beyond that. You're downright strange—'teched' in the head, as they say."

"I am willing to pay well for your expertise as my teacher."

"Uh uh." He shook his head. "I might go after those men for you—for a price. But there's no way I'm gonna teach you to be a female gunslinger. Why, I'd be the laughingstock of the territory—right behind you, of course."

He eyed her curiously. "What I'd like to know is why you'd even consider such a blamed fool thing. Why didn't you just ask me to track down those fellas for you and kill them, like I thought you were goin' to?"

"As you yourself pointed out, Mr. Sterling, who is a woman to trust? How would I know that the men truly were dead? What proof would I have, other than your word, that the deeds had been done and the contract fulfilled? You could easily cheat me, with none the wiser. As my dear mother was fond of saying, 'If you want to be certain that something is done right, you must do it yourself.' I'll see those men dead, with my own eyes, and, if I have anything to do with it, by my own hand, if it is the last thing I do in this lifetime."

"It may very well *be* the last thing you do, Miss, uh, Mrs. Prindle," he hastened to point out.

"So be it, then. At least I will have tried, which is more than anyone else has done so far."

"Damn it, woman, where are your ears? I've told you I'll go after those men for you. I know you have no reason to believe me, but I don't lie. I do a lot else that'll probably send me to hell one day, but I don't lie and I don't cheat."

"And I don't care. Don't you see? This is something I have to do, if I am ever to have any peace for my soul. Those animals killed my husband! They killed my baby!" Charity stood there, her hand clamped over her wayward mouth. She stared at him, horrified at what she had let slip.

"Your baby?" he echoed softly. The sheriff hadn't mentioned this, and the thought made his stomach churn. If Luke had one vulnerability, one tender spot in his otherwise tough hide, it was for small children, perhaps because he had been so ill-treated himself and wanted better for all the other children in this misbegotten world. "How old was your child?"

Charity just stood there shaking her head, refusing to remove her hand from her mouth, lest she blurt out something else as revealing. Her eyes were huge, and bright with the sheen of unshed tears.

His patience, which he was not well-noted for to begin with, gave way. "Damn it all, woman! Do you want my help or not?" He jerked her hand away from her lips, his fingers like iron bands about her wrist. "Tell me! How old was your baby?"

"It . . . it wasn't b-b-born yet!" she wailed, her eyes growing even larger in her ghost-white face. She tried; she truly tried to hold the terror at bay, but the memories were overwhelming her all at once. Even as she told herself to be reasonable, to believe that this man meant her no harm, she could not regain even a false calm. If only he would let go of her hand, maybe then she could think straight again.

She couldn't seem to get enough air into her lungs! There was an odd buzzing in her head. At the edges of her vision, the world was growing dark, forming a swirling tunnel, threatening to suck her into its spiraling maelstrom. "Please! Please!" she whimpered hoarsely. "Let me go! Don't hurt me!"

He caught her before her unconscious body hit the floor. Concern clouded his emerald-green eyes as he placed her gently on his bed. "Poor little mud hen," he murmured, feeling an unbidden surge of compassion for the agonies she must have endured.

He couldn't help wondering if her attackers had merely beaten her so severely that she had lost the baby, or if they had raped her. Certainly, she was far from attractive, not at all the type to inspire lust in a man. Of course, there was no accounting for taste. Her husband had obviously found her comely enough to get her with child.

And she had lost them both, husband and child, at the hands of brutal murderers. Lost what must have been her sole chance at happiness, for she appeared to have wanted the child. At the least, she wanted to avenge its death, and that of her husband, which in itself set her above most of the women Luke knew.

Homeliness aside, no one deserved to have her life devastated so completely, so ruthlessly. Why, it was a wonder she was as sane as she seemed; and little wonder that she wanted revenge so badly. He could even understand her need to deal personally with her attackers, rather than to leave the foul deed to others. In her place, it was what he would have done.

She had labeled them correctly when she had called them animals—for men, real men with an

ounce of decency about them, would never purposefully harm a defenseless woman, especially not
one who was carrying a child. Any brute who would
do such a thing deserved to be hunted down like
the beast he was; then killed very, very slowly, so
that he would have time to feel the same pain he
had inflicted upon his victim, so that he had time to
reflect upon his sins and the end to which they had
led him. That Dandy was one of them only made
Luke twice as determined to catch him.

Dampening a towel in the washbowl, Luke removed her eyeglasses and stroked the cloth over her
face. His movements were uncharacteristically awkward as he tried to revive the poor lady, but he
wasn't used to aiding fainting females. As she began
to stir and mumble indistinguishably, Luke focused
his attention more fully. His gaze scanned her face,
willing color to her pale flesh, silently pleading with
her to open her eyes. Strange, how the lines in her
face had relaxed as she lay unconscious. Why, for a
moment there, she'd looked almost young. And
when her thick lashes fluttered open, what a pretty
blue her eyes were without her eyeglasses hiding
them, if one discounted the deep purple circles beneath.

Mentally, Luke gave himself a stern shake, wondering if he were losing his mind. Since when had
skinny old crones appealed to him? Lordy, but he
really was going to have to stay away from that rot-
gut whiskey they were peddling downstairs.

Charity groaned, bringing a hand to her spinning
head.

"Are you all right, Mrs. Prindle?" Luke asked so-
licitously.

In her befuddlement, she began to panic once
more, attempting to rise from the bed. "No, no, you
lie right there until you're feelin' better." Recognizing the fear on her face, Luke used his most calming

voice, the one that always seemed to work on the most fractious horse. "Everything is going to be just fine. Believe me."

When she lay there, all stiff and still, as if waiting for the most unbearable pain to begin, Luke could scarcely stand it. "Look, lady, I'm not gonna hurt you. I've decided to help you. You have my word on it. Now, will you please stop lookin' as if you expect me to hit you at any moment?"

"You . . . you're going to help me?" Charity asked hesitantly, as if afraid to really believe his words. "You'll teach me how to shoot?"

Luke sighed heavily and nodded. "Yes," he conceded reluctantly, wondering why he didn't just go after Dandy and his cohorts and bring proof back to her when the matter was finished. It was ridiculous to agree to this scheme, and valuable time would be wasted trying to teach her skills she probably couldn't learn. "I'll no doubt regret it as long as I live, but I'll teach you that, and more, if you're capable of learnin' what you'll need to know to go after your husband's murderers."

"Oh, I'll learn all right, Mr. Sterling. Don't you worry about that for a moment." Then her face clouded again. "I really don't want everyone in town to know about this, if you don't mind. It would only create more problems than I wish to deal with just now."

"Then how do you propose we handle this matter?"

"If you could move out to the farm for a spell." At his darkening look, she hurried on. "You can bunk in the barn with Mano."

"Mano?"

"He's the Indian who found me and brought me in to Doc Nelson's. He lives out at my place now, and helps with the heavier chores." As she accepted her eyeglasses from him and put them back on, she frowned thoughtfully. "If you truly dislike Indians, I suppose we could make other arrangements. Come to think of it, I don't think Mano is going to be too thrilled to meet you, either."

"I'll respect his ways as long as he agrees to do the same for me," Luke told her. "Anything else?"

Regardless of the fact that she was still half-lying on his bed, his pillows propped at her back, Charity dared to look him straight in the eye and say, "Yes, Mr. Sterling, there is. Whatever we decide upon as a fair fee, your payment will be rendered fully in cash—not in favors, if you take my meaning. I will not be part of the bargain in any way. Is that fully understood and agreed upon?"

He stared at her with incredulous disbelief. At last finding his voice, he blurted the first thing on his mind. "Lady, have you taken a good look in a mirror lately? As nags go, you look like you've been rode hard and put away wet! I've seen forty miles of bad road that look better than you!"

Lips pursed, Charity told herself she was vastly relieved to hear this, though it hurt oddly to hear him put into words what she already knew to be true. Wasn't this what she wanted, after all—to be undesirable to any and all men? "Then I can trust you to keep your baser urges in check?" she prodded.

"Yes, ma'am!" he replied too enthusiastically, rubbing her pride more raw.

Then those green eyes of his took on a devious gleam as he said, "I might warn you, though, before you agree to this scheme, that this isn't gonna be some sort of picnic, for either one of us. I intend to earn my pay, which means I intend to work you hard. And I have a few rules of my own, some of which you may find a little hard to swallow, so if you want out now, just holler before it's too late."

"What kind of rules?" she asked, beginning to feel unsure of herself.

"Basically, it all boils down to one major issue," he informed her with a wry smile. "As long as I'm your teacher, I'm in charge. You may be paying me to teach you, but in my classroom, I'm the boss—the only boss. What I say goes, and I won't stand for a lot of complainin' or lame excuses. Is that fully understood and agreed upon?"

"Perfectly."

"Good! I'm so glad we got things straight between us from the start," he said, his tone deliberately mocking. "Now, let's discuss how much all these lessons are gonna cost you, shall we?"

9

"**Y**ou *do* ride, don't you?" Luke had waited until Charity and Mano had left town in the wagon, catching up with them a few miles from the farm. His question was directed toward Charity.

Her delay in replying, as well as her sheepish look, were answers in themselves. "Not really," she hedged.

"What does that mean? Either you ride or you don't!" he snapped back.

"Well, when I was a little girl, back in Pennsylvania, I used to ride our old mule when Pa wasn't using him."

Luke rolled his eyes toward the heavens and sighed heavily. This was going to be more difficult than he'd considered. Of course, that might be a blessing in disguise. If the Widow Prindle had too much to learn, by the time she eventually learned it all, her desperate urge for revenge might have withered and died on the vine, so to speak. That, or perhaps after the first futile attempts, Luke could convince her to let him go after the outlaws himself.

"You can't go chasin' after murderers in a wagon, that's for sure," he told her. "You'll have to learn to ride, first off."

112

From Mano, who sat hunched on the wagon seat next to Charity, the reins in his able hands, came a grumbled, "Shouldn't be chasin' after them anyhow. Shouldn't be hirin' gunfighters, either." The Indian had been surly at best since Charity had told him that she had hired Luke and why. He'd done nothing but mumble and glare at both Luke and Charity with those bright, condemning eyes. "Stupid idea."

Luke privately agreed with the half-breed. This was the dumbest thing he'd ever agreed to do. Usually, 'No' was one of the easiest words in Luke's vocabulary, the most ready on his tongue. And once he'd said no to something, he held firm to his decision, rarely changing his mind. Why hadn't he said that simple, wonderful little word to this woman? What was keeping him from doing so now?

"Will you teach me how to ride, then?" Charity asked him.

Loner that he was, Luke was not accustomed to consulting or including other people in his plans; yet somehow he sensed that he should try to enlist Mano's support, if only to prove to the Indian that he was not some ogre out to take all of the widow's money, or to lead the poor lady astray with his wicked ways.

This last should be evident to just about anyone with one good eye, but who was to say? Maybe to Mano, Charity Prindle was a raving beauty. Perhaps the man was naturally jealous of anyone who came too near her. Obviously, Mano felt protective of her, for whatever reason—perhaps because he'd saved her life not so very long ago and didn't want to see her risk it in the near future. This, at least, Luke could understand.

With all this in mind, Luke suggested, "You probably should be askin' Mano here to teach you. Unless I miss my guess, he's a better judge of horseflesh than I'll ever be, and probably a lot more patient, too." Luke's sharp gaze probed Mano's bland face, trying to get some measure of the man. "Besides, it's a well-known fact that Indians are excellent riders; isn't that right, Mano?"

"Sure is, Sterling." The grin that stretched Mano's lips made Luke suddenly nervous, and the glint in those silver eyes told him that Mano knew it and was secretly laughing at him. "We're also real good at knowin' when someone is blowin' a lot of meaningless smoke signals around. In other words, white man, if you're willin' to stoop low enough to kiss my ass, shine my boots instead. In the long run, it'll gain you more favor."

"Mano! Really! Such language!" Charity was mortified, and she couldn't begin to imagine what Luke Sterling must be thinking. She could only hope that Mano hadn't offended him to the point of changing his mind about instructing her. "Please forgive my friend, Mr. Sterling. I'm sure he didn't mean any offense."

"Bullshit!" Luke's answer was succinct, if crude, accompanied by a grin to match Mano's.

"I beg your pardon, sir?" Charity gasped in outrage.

She might as well have been speaking to herself, for her two escorts seemed to be immersed in some mysterious, silent battle of male supremacy, and paying her no heed at all. Without a word, they were waging some sort of war of wills that completely baffled her, even as it irritated her.

What really made her angry, however, was that even when they each nodded, smiled tightly, and finally decided to stop staring holes through each other, she was as confused as ever. Whatever it was they had settled between themselves, both seemed satisfied with the result, while Charity was still trying to figure out what the devil was going on.

* * *

Within a few days, Luke had settled in, and Charity's lessons had begun in earnest. Each morning, she awoke, dressed, and hurried downstairs to prepare a huge breakfast for the three of them. Though her own appetite was next to none, Luke insisted that she eat almost as much as the men.

"You're skinny as a rail," he told her bluntly. "Hell's bells, woman! You and Job's turkey could sit side by side on a telegraph wire, and I'd be hard put to see either one of you! If you don't want your gun, your horse, or your enemy to land you smack-dab on your arse-end, you've got to get a little meat on your bones, and some muscle in those puny little arms of yours."

His eyes traversed her black-clad frame from head to toe, and he shook his head, adding, "And do somethin' about that hair, will you? Loosen that knot some, so it's not skinned back so tight that you all but stretch your eyelids off. Besides distortin' your vision, it makes you look dowdy as hell." As an afterthought, he added, "Too bad we can't do away with those god-awful eyeglasses, since they're gonna get in the way."

Charity didn't know whether to laugh or scream at him. If only he knew just how much she had suffered and how hard she had worked to achieve this spinster-witch look he so obviously disliked! She gave him what scarcely passed for a smile and replied tartly, "Such flattery, Mr. Sterling! With so silver a tongue, it's a wonder you don't make your way in the world with words, rather than your gun. However," she went on, seeing his eyes narrow at her warningly, and knowing her verbal darts were hitting their mark, "neither my hair nor my eyes are your concern."

His smile was every bit as insincere as her own as he answered in kind. "Oh, I beg your pardon, dear lady, but they are! You can't shoot what you can't see, and you can't see right with your eyes strainin' like that. It distorts your vision, and it'll throw off your aim. And that isn't even countin' the headaches you must get from all those pins pokin' into your scalp."

That he was correct made her even angrier. "Is there anything else, Professor?" she mocked irritably.

His grin was wicked and handsome, and she wanted to slap it from his gloating face. "I can't think of anything at the moment, but I'll be sure to tell you the minute somethin' comes to mind."

Luke decided that the first order of business was for Charity to learn to ride. Therefore, much to her dismay, part of each day was devoted to riding lessons. To save herself, Charity could not recall her father's old mule being nearly as tall as this horse, or having nearly as many teeth! Though Mano had grudgingly consented to help by choosing a gentle, amenable mare for her to learn upon, Charity was still just a wee bit afraid of the animal, and they all soon knew it, including the horse!

"You have to let her know who's master—or mistress, in this case, I suppose," Luke instructed. "If the animal knows you're afraid of her, you might as well give up, stay home, and stick to your knittin'."

"She tried to bite me when I put the bit in her mouth!"

Luke insisted that Charity learn to saddle and care for her horse, as well as to mount and ride it.

"It's part and parcel of the whole," he informed her. "Just because you're a woman, and small, makes no difference. You can't rely on someone else bein' on hand to saddle your horse for you. You need to learn to do these things for yourself."

She began with saddling her mare a half dozen times, under Luke's eagle-eyed supervision. At long last, she was deemed ready to progress to mounting.

"It's fairly easy," Luke stated. "First take the reins in your left hand." He watched as she did as he had instructed. "Now place that hand on the horse's withers and grab the saddle horn with your right hand. Place your left foot in the stirrup, pull yourself upward, and swing your right leg over the horse's back and into the opposite stirrup."

He positioned her hands and feet for her, feeling her stiffen as soon as he touched her. This he attributed to the fact that he was a gunfighter, though she hadn't yet shown as much fear of him as others often did. Then again, perhaps her wariness had more to do with the attack on her than with him personally. His own reaction, not unlike that of being stung by a bee, bothered him more. With a mental shrug, he proceeded to try to boost her into the saddle.

"Mr. Sterling!" she cried out, alarmed at suddenly feeling his large hand intimately cupping her bottom. "What do you suppose you are doing, sir?" she demanded. Her haughty retort was completely ruined as she lost her balance, her foot slipping awkwardly from the stirrup as she fell clumsily at his feet.

"I'm helpin' you to mount your mare, ma'am," he responded with that maddening grin of his. "You have to be *in* the saddle before you can learn to ride. There's no other way to do it."

"I beg to differ."

"Oh?" He cocked his eyebrow at her for the tenth time that day. It was an annoying habit that Charity was fast coming to detest.

She let loose a sigh of exasperation. "I know I have to get onto the horse. I'm not altogether ignorant, you know." She chose to disregard his dubious expression. "I merely meant that I would prefer to ride sidesaddle, as has been the accepted form for women for centuries. I simply cannot sit astride the horse in skirts.''

"And I won't teach you any other way," he announced firmly.

"I beg your pardon?" Now it was Charity's brow arching delicately upward in her face.

"You can beg whatever you want, and it still won't change a thing, lady. You'll learn to ride astride, or not at all. Ridin' sidesaddle is for sissy-pants Easterners who want to trot their fancy high-priced horses around the park once or twice and not get their clothes wrinkled or work up a sweat. You're gonna be doin' some mighty hard ridin', chasin' after those murderers, and the best way to stay in the saddle is to hang on with all you've got, and that means with both legs and a couple of elbows!"

"But my skirts!" she protested.

"Get rid of them."

"What!" Her outraged shriek brought startled squawks of protest from her chickens in the side yard.

"Look, either tuck your skirts around your thighs, or split them down the center and stitch them, like some of the ranch women are doing these days. That, or wear a pair of boy's britches. It's all the same to me, Miss Charity. Do whatever suits you best, but make up your mind that you're gonna be ridin' with one leg on either side of your horse, and your backside square in that saddle.''

Before she even fired a gun, Luke insisted that she familiarize herself with her weapon; first rifle, then pistol. She learned to load and unload it; to dismantle it, clean it, reassemble it. Then she did it over and over again, naming the parts as Luke pointed them out, until she was ready to pull her hair out, and Luke was finally satisfied with her.

Only then did her actual lessons on how to aim

and fire begin. At breakfast, Luke informed her that he and Mano had set up a practice target behind the barn. "We decided that was the safest place," he explained, sharing a look with Mano. "Even if you miss the target, at least you won't chance hittin' the horses."

Charity did not share their amusement, especially when she saw the target. The men had piled bales of straw into a small mountain, then attached a huge canvas to the front side of it.

The canvas looked vaguely familiar. "Where did you get that?" she asked.

"It was folded into the bed of one of the wagons."

She shook her head. "We can't use that. It's a cover for the grain when it's harvested, to keep it dry until we get it to the mill."

"Well, I guess you have a choice to make then," Luke drawled, chewing on a piece of straw and leveling that cool green gaze at her. "Either you want dry grain, or you want to learn to shoot. Which is more important to you?"

Casting a glare at him, and another look at the huge target, she asked mockingly, "Are you sure it's big enough?"

Mano chuckled. "It was either that, or build a new barn and graduate you down to the outhouse as you improve. This was easier."

"And safer," Luke added with a wry grin. "With the looks the lady's been givin' me lately, she'd wait until I was in the outhouse to pepper it with bullet holes."

First, Luke demonstrated what he wanted her to do. With an unloaded weapon, he showed her how to hold it, how to steady and aim it, how to cock the hammer back and pull the trigger. In the process, his large hands were continually coming into contact with hers, and each time they did, Charity gave an involuntary start. Since the attack, Doc Nelson and Mano were the only men to touch her, and then rarely.

She tried to ignore Luke's touch, telling herself it was necessary, but when he grabbed her hips from behind, to correct her stance, she couldn't contain a startled scream. Heart pounding, she jerked away from him, shaking violently in reaction. The pistol fell from fingers gone suddenly numb. Behind the lenses of her spectacles, her eyes were wide and dark with renewed fright as she stared up at him—waiting fearfully for his next move.

"Oh, for cryin' out loud, woman! I'm not gonna bite you! And I wish to hell you'd stop jumpin' like a scared rabbit every time I touch you! Damn it all, but you sure can make a man feel as low as a piss-ant, even when he hasn't done anything to deserve it!"

"I . . . I'm sorry!" Charity stuttered. "I just can't seem to help it sometimes. Ever since those men . . ." Her voice trailed off pathetically.

Luke sighed, sympathy overriding his anger. His growing compulsion toward compassion was becoming an irritating habit, but there was something so damned vulnerable about the woman! Which in turn prompted a peculiar desire to protect her.

"I realize that," he told her, "but I can't teach you how to aim properly without touchin' you. I have to show you how to hold your weapon, how to stand and position your hands and your elbows, how to hold your head and sight down the barrel." Since his own gut always tensed now in anticipation of those odd, shocking sensations at each contact with her, he privately thought it would benefit them both if he *could* instruct her without having to touch her, but it was literally impossible to do.

"I'll do better. I promise."

She tried. She truly tried to do everything he

taught her. She practiced with the rifle until her
shoulder was so sore and bruised that she could
hardly move it without crying. Finally, thankfully,
she learned to position the weapon in the correct
manner, to avoid having it kick back at her when
fired. Handling Luke's pistol was another matter altogether. The Colt was heavy and awkward in her
small hands. In the beginning, it took all the strength
in her arms to hold it out before her and attempt to
steady it. Now she understood why he was constantly urging her to eat.

As large as it was, just hitting the target was a
major feat at first, and she fast came to admire and
envy Luke's remarkable skill with a gun. As long as
it was within range of his firearm, the man could hit
anything. He had eyes like an eagle and amazing
reflexes, and it all seemed so ridiculously easy for
him, and so terribly difficult for her.

If it hadn't been so frustrating, and so imperative
that she learn, her first fumbling lessons might have
been laughable. She looked and felt like a bumbling
fool, especially when she inadvertently caught the
flange of skin between her thumb and finger in the
hammer hinge of the pistol. It was three days before
the tender, swollen skin healed enough to continue
her lessons, but she learned to pay closer attention
after that. There was enough pain involved in learning to ride and shoot without causing herself more
through her own clumsiness.

When she was finally hitting the canvas with reg-
ularity, Luke decided a smaller target was in order.
He retrieved half a dozen grain sacks from the barn
and tacked them up to the straw barrier. Then, as if
to impress upon her the seriousness of her goal, he
painted the outline of bodies on them.

"Pretend they're the men you're gonna kill," he
instructed baldly, his eyes probing closely for her

reaction to his words. "They're about the right size."

Feeling as if she had just been dunked in a vat of ice water, and knowing her face was ghostly pale, Charity gritted her teeth and took careful aim. For each of the six men who had raped her, she envisioned a face imposed on a gunnysack. A familiar feeling of rage filled her, making her hands tremble and the barrel of the gun waver dangerously. With effort, she brought her emotions under control and fired.

With each repeated report of the Colt, an anguished moan of grief issued from deep within her. When the lesson was finished, the burlap sacks were riddled with holes, and Charity was drained to the depths of her soul.

Once again, Luke felt like the lowest of beasts.

"Again." The order came briskly, in that nononsense tone Charity was fast coming to hate. Luke stood there looking like some high-and-mighty potentate, all calm and cool, his arms folded across his chest. In comparison, Charity felt like a garden grub, perspiration dripping in rivulets from every pore. Her hair was straggling from her bun, and her spectacles had the annoying habit of riding to the end of her nose. For the hundredth time that day, she took aim and fired, imaging Luke in the sights of her gun.

"You're firin' wide to the left. Correct it.

"Concentrate, dammit! You're rushin' your shots.

"Once more.   —

"Again.

"Are you gonna listen to me, or do you want to call it quits now, and forget the whole thing?" he taunted.

She returned glare for glare. "I'll quit when those men pay for what they did, or when I'm in my grave, whichever comes first."

"Then practice, dammit! And make it count for somethin'!

"That's not the way I taught you. Do it right!

"Again.

"By God, we're gonna be here till midnight, but you're gonna get it right if it kills you!"

On and on it went, until Charity wasn't at all sure that these endless, miserable lessons would not be the end of her. As he had warned, Luke was a hard taskmaster, relentless in his pursuit of perfection. How often had she wanted to toss the gun down, run off, and have a good cry? How often had she fantasized about turning the weapon on him when he yelled at her? Or running him down with her horse? Except for the fact that she had yet to work up to a gallop, of course.

Winning a mere scrap of praise from him was tantamount to a miracle, though all the more cherished when it came. By now, she was hearing his harsh commands in her dreams, but even this was a welcome relief to the terror of the nightmares that still plagued her sleep. When she was so tired at the end of the day that she was ready to drop in her tracks; when her brain ceased to function for all the new things he was constantly insisting she learn; when she ached in places she hadn't even known she possessed; when a hot, soaking bath sounded heavenly, but she didn't even have the energy with which to haul and heat the necessary water—then he bluntly reminded her that she was the one who wanted to acquire these skills so foreign to her.

She was the one who wanted revenge so badly— who wanted to learn to kill.

For his part, Luke was learning patience—the hard way. Never before had he attempted to teach anyone else the skills he had learned long ago. When he had agreed to teach Charity, he hadn't fully realized how trying it would be. Time and again, he had to bite his tongue to hold back sharp comments, and all too often he found himself barking at her anyway.

With the knowledge that he was dealing with a lady, one who had been though hell not long ago and was bound to be even more sensitive as a result, he tried to hold his cursing and criticisms to a limit. But every time she seemed to deliberately disregard his advice, the colorful phrases seemed to spill out of his mouth. Invariably, she would turn those round shiny lenses and condemning blue eyes on him, and he would feel like a worm; and invariably, it would happen all over again a short time later.

But she never cried. She griped and muttered and got mad as all get-out, but she never shed a single tear, and Luke had to wonder at that, even as he came to admire her more and more each day. For such a tiny thing, she had more than her share of guts, and stamina beyond anything he would have imagined. He was pressing her hard, and he knew it, and he had to wonder why she hadn't taken a broom handle to his head before now; but she had to learn fast and well, and the longer it took, the farther Dandy and the others would be from their reach.

"You want me to do what?" Mano exclaimed incredulously, eyeing Luke as if he'd just crawled from beneath a rock.

"You heard me. Charity is ready to progress to moving targets now, since I doubt her quarry will simply stand still and let her shoot them. Unless she's willin' to have all her dinner plates shattered to bits, we're gonna need some cow chips."

"And you want me to run around like some squaw and collect them? Well, think again, mister. If you need 'em that bad, gather 'em yourself."

"Do you have a better idea?"

Mano gave the matter some thought. Then he grinned, his teeth showing white in his dark face. "Yeah. I'll be back."

He strode off toward the house, returning half an hour later with a huge platter of burned hotcakes. It seemed that while he objected mightily to anything that might demean him in his own mind, Mano had no objection to cooking when it was necessary.

Staring at the charred pancakes, Luke frowned and shook his head. "Just what is all that?"

"Your targets," Mano retorted with a superior sneer. "They're hard, heavy enough that the wind won't carry them away when you toss them, and easily made when you need more. And it keeps all of us from havin' to run around pluckin' cow manure out of pastures."

Though Luke admitted it reluctantly, not wanting Mano to get a swelled head, it was an ingenious idea, and fit the purpose perfectly. With Charity in tow, and Mano following to assist, they headed for the open field behind the barn.

"All right," Luke said to Charity, "first I'll show you how it's done. Watch carefully." As Mano threw the first target into the air, Luke followed its path and fired. The hotcake burst immediately. Mano tossed another. This time, Luke shattered the target, then proceeded to fragment three of the broken pieces before they hit the ground.

"You expect me to be able to do that?" Charity gasped, stunned by his speed and accuracy, even though he'd already had his gun in hand at the start. From the look on Mano's face, he too was duly impressed.

"Hit it once, on the first try, and I'll be satisfied," came the wry reply. Luke handed her the gun. "Now, the trick is to lead your target. Anticipate where it's gonna be by the time your bullet reaches it."

Charity sighed, knowing in her heart that this was going to be the hardest lesson yet. If she could do this, she could do anything. And never again would she have to rely on others for protection.

Resignedly, she readied her weapon and prepared herself for another long, tiring day.

Now that Charity was becoming adept at handling a gun, it was time to get her used to wearing it. For this, she required a gun belt, holster, and weapons of her own. Taking it upon himself to acquire these items, and a few others she would need both now and once they were on the trail, Luke made a quick trip into Dodge City.

While his numerous purchases weren't questioned, his sudden reappearance in Dodge City was, most particularly by Marshal Earp and Sheriff Masterson. Sworn to uphold the law and keep the peace in Dodge, they liked to keep an eye on drifters, gunmen, and any potential troublemakers. Why was Sterling back in Dodge now? Had someone hired him, and for what purpose?

"Last time he was here, he was askin' a lot of questions about John Prindle's killers," Masterson commented thoughtfully. "You don't suppose Charity hired him to go after them, do you?"

Wyatt shrugged. "You could always stop by her place and find out."

"Maybe I will. Next time I'm out that way."

As Luke rode down the lane leading to the Prindle farm, he took a good look around him, and had to wonder what it must feel like to call such a place home. He'd lived on this earth for thirty years, and had never had a real home, never even stayed in any one place for very long at one time since he'd run away from the orphanage.

His gaze took in the acres of farmland Charity's

neighbor had already tilled for her, and he shook his head. No, if this were his land, he wouldn't farm it. He didn't think he'd make much of a farmer. If this property were his, he'd run cattle on it, maybe even raise a few horses.

That was his 'someday dream,' the reason he put every dime he could afford in a bank account in Dallas. If he lived long enough, and saved enough, someday he'd be able to buy land and see his dream come true. Maybe. If he didn't manage to get himself killed first. God knew, the life expectancy of a gunfighter wasn't long, and as lucrative as it could be, it wasn't the easiest profession from which to retire. There was always someone out there ready to prove he was faster on the draw, wanting to challenge him even when he didn't want to be challenged.

Sometimes, like now, Luke wondered why he'd ever gotten into gunfighting. Then he reminded himself that he really hadn't had much choice, other than possibly staying in the army. Yet even there, as young as he'd been, his skills with a gun had been earning him a reputation. If he'd stayed, there probably would still have been someone challenging him; only then, he'd have either wound up in an army prison, been hanged for being forced to kill someone else, or seen a court-martial, none of which held much appeal.

Taking that into consideration, Luke supposed that things had worked out for the best, since he seemed destined to make his way in the world with his gun. Of course, this latest job, working for Charity Prindle, was a little out of his ordinary line. He wondered if she had any idea what she was setting herself up against, or if she realized yet that he would never consider letting her go after those six outlaws on her own. If she went at all, she'd be going with him, and he'd do his damnedest to see that she came to no harm.

But how could you keep a person so bent on revenge from being hurt? How did you impress upon them that killing another human being, no matter how evil or deserving of death, was something that would stay with you for the rest of your life? That it wounded your soul and ate at your being like a worm carving its way to the center of an apple? That it crippled your very spirit, turning you into a hardened, lonely shell—like Luke Sterling.

How could he tell Charity all this, especially when he was every bit as set on revenge as she was?

10

"**W**HAT is all this?" Charity asked, eyeing the packages heaped upon her kitchen table. The rifle was the only thing not wrapped in paper and string.

"It's all yours, so you might as well satisfy your curiosity," Luke drawled, pouring himself a cup of coffee from the pot which was always kept warming on the stovetop. Turning a chair backward, he seated himself and propped his arms across the back, waiting to see her reaction. "Open that one first," he prompted, pointing to the most oddly shaped bundle.

Hesitantly, Charity did as he bid. Inside, she found a gun belt, too small around to fit Luke properly, and hanging from it a holster and a Colt revolver, similar to the one he wore. "These are for me?" she questioned, her gaze flying to his. "And the rifle, too?"

He nodded. "I can't keep lending you my weapons," he explained gruffly.

Boots were in the next package she opened. Though she hadn't actually given it much thought, she could see that they would be much better for riding than her shoes. Still, she couldn't help but ask, "How did you know my size?"

"I traced the soles of your shoes."

Immediately, she was suspicious. For weeks now, she had sensed someone in the house, in her bedroom, while she slept. "When?" she questioned warily.

"The other day, when you got them muddy and left them on the back steps. Why?"

After that, she couldn't very well tell the man she suspected him of creeping into her bedroom at night. "Just wondered."

A smart little Stetson, a slicker, vest, and neckerchiefs were next revealed. Again, though she hadn't yet considered purchasing these items, she realized that they were all necessary to her venture, to help her weather the elements as she traveled.

All but the neckerchiefs. Had he seen the scar on her neck, though she always tried to keep it hidden? Had Mano perhaps mentioned it to him? Just the thought of the ugly reminder of her night of terror made her voice more raspy than normal as she asked, "What are the bandannas for?"

"To keep the dust out of your throat when you're ridin', and the sun from blisterin' your neck."

"Oh." Once more, he had a logical explanation that had nothing to do with any invasion of her privacy, and until she learned differently, she would have to accept his word as true. She was becoming increasingly uncomfortable, however, with the fact that this man had gone into town and purchased apparel for her. It simply wasn't done! Though she fully intended to reimburse him for the entire cost, she could only hope he had been secretive in buying them, so that no one would suspect that these things were meant for her. Her reputation wouldn't stand much more tarnishing.

Upon opening the final package, Charity found

real reason to take exception. "Explain, please, Mr. Sterling," she told him in her coldest tone. "The rest I can understand. These things"—she gestured toward the denim trousers, the shirts, and the split riding skirts—"are entirely unfitting and unnecessary, most especially those scandalous britches!"

He'd anticipated her reaction, particularly since not one item was black. The shirts were shades of blue and tan, while one shirt was denim blue and the other a fawn color. "There's nothin' wrong with the skirts," he countered calmly, determined not to let her ruffle him. You've already been wearin' your own. These are just sturdier, more fit for ridin' than the ones you tried to remake from your old dresses. The cloth is heavier, and there's less of it to get tangled up in your saddle. And I bought the shirts because I didn't know if you had any in your closet to go with the skirts and pants."

"Yes. What about the pants, sir? Can you offer some reasonable explanation for those, also?" she continued haughtily.

His cool green eyes speared her, freezing her in place as he spoke. "If you intend to wear a gun, and learn to draw it with any speed, you have to tie the holster around your thigh. Since I was unsure just how well this would work with the skirts, I bought the britches as well. If you find you can make do with the skirts, fine. Wear them instead. Aside from getting the best performance out of you in your lessons, I really don't care."

Only slightly mollified, she answered stiffly, "I do hope you were discreet in making your purchases."

"I tried to be, though I did get some strange looks over the skirts. I hope it was obvious that they aren't my size," he added mockingly, "or my reputation as a gunfighter won't be worth a damn from here on out."

"If you'll tell me how much all of this cost you, I'll pay you back immediately."

He rose and ambled toward the door. "Just add it to my fee, Miss Charity."

He was almost out of the door when he added, "And don't let me catch you tryin' to throw those new clothes into a pot of black dye."

The next day, they were back to her lessons, both of them still smarting from their encounter the previous afternoon. She was still miffed at Luke for taking the liberty of buying clothes for her, then daring to tell her what to do with them. In turn, Luke was equally put out with Charity for not having had the courtesy to thank him for seeing to her needs. She hadn't even thanked him for the Colt, which he'd so carefully selected.

Consequently, Luke was much tougher with her today, working her extra hard, and making her practice the same things over and over again, even when she did them correctly. Nothing seemed to satisfy him, and he was much more surly than usual. She'd already gone through a platter of Mano's infamous charred hotcakes, and despite her gloves, blisters were forming atop the callouses she'd previously earned. Bone-tired and sore, she was primed for a fight by the time Luke decided to change targets unexpectedly.

"Since you seem so all-fired proud of yourself, let's try somethin' a little more difficult, shall we?" he suggested sarcastically, plopping a bushel of wrinkled fall apples on the ground near her feet.

She stared at him in disbelief. "You've got to be kidding! Apples? You honestly expect me to shoot at apples?"

"And hit them," he added with a smirk.

Charity exploded. "That's it! That's the final

straw! You can take those apples and do whatever you please with them, but I'm finished!"

"Quittin' on me, Widow Prindle?" he taunted.

"Yes! Until you behave like a reasonable human being, if that's at all possible for you! In fact, since I know how to shoot now, I don't believe your services will be required any longer. I'll have your money waiting for you by the time you've packed and are ready to leave. Thank you, and good-bye, Mr. Sterling."

Her words stung. Ignoring the fact that she'd just fired him, Luke taunted, "You call the little you've managed to learn shootin'? I'll show you shootin', lady." He scooped four small apples into his palm and tossed them into the air all at once.

Reflexively, Charity's eyes followed their flight. Before her disbelieving gaze, she saw all four explode in rapid succession, to the accompaniment of Luke's gunfire.

"Need more convincin'?"

Across the way, a wild honeysuckle vine had climbed the far corner of the barn. With the two shots left in his revolver, Luke neatly clipped two blossoms, severing the delicate stems but leaving the fragile petals intact, without so much as a bruise.

"That's shootin'. That's what it's gonna take to go up against your husband's killers. You're nowhere near good enough. Like it or not, you still need me, though you'll probably choke on your pride admittin' it."

Surprisingly, Luke found he liked being needed by her. Though he didn't understand it, it satisfied something inside him, and he wasn't ready to give that up over some stupid argument. Besides, he was comfortable here, he rationalized. He could number his friends on one hand, but he was fast growing to like and respect both Charity and Mano; and for a lone wolf like him, that was a rare thing.

Charity, despite her name, was not feeling as benevolent just now. Spitefully, she screamed back at him, "You're nothing but a pompous bore, Luke Sterling! Get off my property! Now!"

"Make me," he countered stubbornly.

"Don't push me, mister!"

"You need me," he repeated.

"Like hell I do!"

"Like hell you don't! Even if you do somehow learn all I'm tryin' to teach you, there's no way on God's green earth I'll let you set out after those murderers alone. If and when I deem that you're ready, I'll be goin' with you."

"You think so?"

"I know so."

"I can't afford your fee for tracking down six men," she pointed out stiffly. "I can only pay you what we agreed for teaching me."

"I don't want your money, and I sure as hell don't need your death on my conscience."

"It's not your fight," she reminded him.

"Yes, it is. I've been after Dandy for over a year now," he admitted gruffly. "When Masterson listed him as one of the men you'd accused, it occurred to me that if I'd caught up with him sooner you might never have been attacked. How do you think that's made me feel, especially since I've gotten to know you?"

She stared at him in openmouthed amazement. "Is that why you believed me when the others didn't? Is that why you agreed to help me? Because you feel guilty? Responsible?" Her anger was forgotten now, pushed aside by the shock of what she was hearing. "Luke, that's crazy! There were five others in that band of killers. Who's to say it wouldn't have happened anyway, even without Dandy as part of it?"

Then, as if what he'd said had just fully registered, she asked, "Why didn't you tell me about Dandy sooner? Why are you looking for him?"

As he answered, Luke's voice was as cold and emotionless as a grave, sending shivers up Charity's spine. "He shot me in the back last spring and left me for dead." Ignoring her gasp, he continued mockingly. "That was his mistake. He should have made sure he'd killed me, because now I'm gonna kill him. But I'm gonna make damned sure he's facin' me when I do it, because I want him to know who's endin' his miserable life."

"Why?"

He gave her an incredulous look. "Why?" he echoed. "You actually have to ask why I'm gonna kill him?"

"Don't be thickheaded. Even *I* know that it's totally dishonorable to shoot someone in the back— not that I can't see Dandy doing something that low-down. I'm asking about the circumstances leading up to it. Why did he shoot you?"

Luke wasn't about to tell Charity that it had all started over a saloon girl's invitation to her bed. "We had a slight disagreement, which I mistakenly assumed was settled. Not only did I underestimate Dandy, but I let my guard down at the wrong time— an error I won't make a second time, I assure you."

That put a halt to Charity's objections, if not her questions. Truth be told, she was vastly relieved to know that she would not be heading off on her own, since Mano had already agreed, reluctantly and with much grumbling, to stay behind and keep an eye on the farm. It was comforting to realize that Luke would be beside her every step of the way to guide her and aid her if she faltered. Not that she doubted her own resolve, but from the first just having Luke near made her feel braver, more secure, as if he were somehow lending her his strength. Irrational as it was, he'd become her talisman against evil, her flesh-and-blood symbol of protection and courage.

For her first attempts at drawing and shooting, they practiced once again with still targets. Atop several bales of straw, Luke had lined a row of empty bottles and broken jars she could no longer use for canning.

"Later, when you've mastered this, we'll go back to movin' targets," he told her.

Try as she might, and as easy as it looked when Luke demonstrated, she simply could not coordinate her hands and eyes for a smooth draw. Her movements were awkward, jerky; as a consequence, her aim was thrown off. Half the time, her pistol got caught partway out of the holster; and when she did manage to pull it free and fire, the bottles too often remained standing along the straw bales, like jeering sentinels on a castle wall.

"Well, I think we can safely assume you're never gonna be a stunnin' success at the fast-draw." Luke stood and shook his head at her. They'd been practicing her draw for days, and she was almost as slow now as she'd been at the start, though his own skills were being honed sharply in the process.

"It looked so easy," Charity complained with a frown.

"Don't fret. You'll get the hang of it soon. Of the two, accuracy usually counts for more than speed, anyway. You can be as fast as lightnin' and still get killed if your aim is lousy. At least you can hit what you aim at most of the time."

"Yes, but only when I don't have to worry about getting my gun free of the holster first. When you told me a lot of learning to fast-draw was in the wrist action, I thought there would be no problem. I thought it would be as easy for me as handling a whip."

Luke gave her a curious look. "Whip?" he echoed. "Are we talkin' about a buggy whip?"

"Sometimes," she told him with a nod, "but more often a loose horse whip or even a bullwhip. They're longer and heavier, but once you get used to them, you can snap the head off a chicken in the blink of an eye."

He was giving her the strangest look, and she couldn't for the life of her fathom why.

"Are you tryin' to tell me you know how to use a whip that well, or are we talkin' about someone else, or whips in general?" he asked, weighing his words carefully.

"You don't believe me, do you?" Charity couldn't decide if she was offended or amused. "Fine. I guess I'll just have to prove it to you." She marched off toward the barn, determination in her stride and a gleam in her eye.

She emerged from the barn with a braided rawhide whip. "You ready for chicken dinner again? Because if I kill them, you have to eat them. I can't afford rash wastefulness."

He grinned at her, his attitude that of an indulgent parent with a precocious child. "Sure, lady. Show me your stuff!"

Rather than enter the chicken pen, which was too small an area to work well with a whip, Charity let a couple of hens loose to run in the barnyard. The poor birds had barely breathed freedom when Charity sent her whip singing through the air. Once, twice in rapid succession, and the chickens were dashing about minus their heads, just minutes from the cooking pot.

Luke stood in openmouthed amazement. "I'll be blistered!" He whistled softly. "Where in tarnation did you learn to do that?"

It was Charity's turn to gloat, and she did it with aplomb. "My brother taught me when we were children. It started as a lark, out of boredom, but I soon found I had a talent for it, and it was such fun! It also made getting apples from hard-to-reach branches much easier and a lot less hazardous,'' she said with a wry chuckle. "I do believe it's the only skill I ever achieved that did not meet with my mother's approval, especially when her chickens kept mysteriously disappearing."

He gave her a considering look. "Can you do that with other targets, or is it limited to chickens and apples?''

"Hmph!'' she snorted, her hands on her hips. "What a Doubting Thomas you are!'' She strode to where they had set up the bottle targets. One, two, three sharp cracks of her whip, and three of the bottles tumbled in rapid succession. Another gliding arc, and the remaining three were swept away in one smooth action.

"Does that satisfy your curiosity?'' she asked with a slight smirk.

"Some of it. I'd still like to see more, so I can get a handle on just how good you are with that thing. One thing's for sure. You're a darn sight better with a whip than with a gun.''

"I agree, but a whip has its limitations, you know. It can't be used as accurately in small, enclosed areas. It's too apt to catch on something and throw off your aim. Then, too, it only has a reach of a few feet. In my case, I can only handle about seven or eight feet of whip with steady accuracy. Anything longer is too awkward and heavy for me. A bullet can go a lot further, a lot quicker.''

At his urging, she further demonstrated her unique ability. In quick succession, she snapped the buttons from the shirt her garden scarecrow was wearing; the cotton fabric remained undamaged. She snuffed the flame on a candle, neatly trimming the wick at the same time. She lassoed a bale of hay from the barn loft and brought it tumbling down with little effort.

When he remarked favorably, still dumbfounded at her ability, she explained, "It's mostly being able to judge the distance from your target, consider angles, time the snap, and control your wrist action. Depending on what you hope to accomplish, you can hit something sharply, with a hard, stunning lash; you can wrap the rawhide around the object and pull it toward you, like you would if you had roped it with a lariat; or you can barely tap your target, just a ticklish little flicker. Also depending on your intentions and ability, you can bind, cut, welt, bruise, choke, or hold your object."

"Or victim," Luke added astutely.

She nodded once in acknowledgment. "Or victim. However, as I pointed out, the whip has its disadvantages. I still have to be able to shoot. I just wish I could learn to be quicker on the draw. I need all the advantage I can get."

Luke agreed wholeheartedly. Even with him along to help protect her, she would, indeed, need all the advantage she could muster. With this in mind, Luke talked Mano into teaching Charity a few tricks with a knife. And while they were at it, maybe Luke himself could pick up a pointer or two from the Indian.

Despite her minuscule size, it turned out that Charity was much more adequate at close-range encounters than at throwing the weapon, once she'd accustomed herself to the necessary bodily contact. Her aim with a knife was equaled only by her fast-draw, both outrageously awful! As if to make up for her lack of skill in this direction, she was fast on her feet, extremely agile in close combat, and great at ducking past Mano or Luke's guard time after time to "plant" her blade.

Along with other things, Mano taught them both how to fight "Arapaho style," as he'd been taught as a boy. Though Charity had gained some weight in the past few weeks, and had a wiry strength that both men soon came to respect, she was still scrawny by most standards. Mano taught her how to take advantage of her smaller size, how to use leverage in place of muscle, to use her legs and feet to knock her opponent off balance when he least expected it.

In turn, Charity showed Mano and Luke how to scratch, claw, bite, pull hair, and perform the popular fake-serious-injury-lure-your-opponent maneuver, perfected during her childhood fights with her brother and sister. Many a time, she lured Luke into defeat, her self-confidence growing by leaps and bounds. It soon became a contest between them to see who could gain the advantage over the other, using fair means or foul.

For Luke this training was pure torment. It was impossible not to touch each other in some way, however lightly or briefly; and no matter how often it happened, despite Charity's haggard appearance, for Luke it was always, inexplicably, like being thrown into a bed of thorns. His skin prickled and burned in a manner that was suspiciously akin to being attracted to her. He simply didn't understand it. For all her previous problems, Charity seemed to be adjusting better to the constant handling than he; while he became particularly adept at making certain that nothing more than hands and feet, and an occasional elbow or knee, collided with her—which was quite enough as it was.

On the other hand, unlike Charity, Luke took to knife-throwing like a duck to water, quickly mastering the techniques Mano demonstrated. Since it came so easily to him, he simply could not understand why Charity was having such difficulty.

"Hell's bells, Charity!" he complained loudly. "You can pluck a chicken bare, feather by feather, with that blasted whip of yours, but you can't hit the broad side of a barn with that knife! It makes absolutely no sense at all! Your arm is still going forward, your wrist is still turnin'! What's so blamed hard about it?''

''It wouldn't be so hard if the pointed end would stay straightforward! Pooh! At this rate, the best I can hope for is to knock my enemy silly with the dratted handle!''

''Pooh?'' Luke echoed, his mouth puckering about the word in an effort not to laugh. Mano turned his back, his shoulders shaking suspiciously. ''Pooh? By any chance, is that somethin' related to bird droppin's? Which, by the way, your chickens are up to their scrawny necks in.''

''And whose fault is that? You have me so busy I don't know which way is up anymore!''

''That way is up,'' Luke told her, gesturing heavenward. Instinctively, she looked toward the sky, just as Luke had hoped she would. In doing so, she left herself open for his surprise attack, and the next thing she knew, she was flat on the ground, face-first.

''That was a dirty trick!'' she complained loudly, spitting grass from her mouth.

''But effective,'' Luke hastened to point out. ''Just don't ever let your enemy do the same thing to you.''

''With friends like you, I don't need enemies,'' she grunted, levering herself to her feet.

Somewhere inside, in the vicinity of Luke's heart, something warm expanded at the knowledge that this plucky little woman considered him her friend. He knew there were few people she trusted these days, and he was particularly honored to be included in that select group.

''Oh, no!'' Charity's wail of dismay brought him out of his private thoughts. She was holding her eyeglasses, which were twisted like a piece of barbed wire, one lens completely shattered.

Normally, when they knew they were going to be practicing their wrestling tactics, Charity left her spectacles off, to avoid breaking them. When he'd tackled her, Luke hadn't given her glasses a thought. Now he regretted his carelessness. Without them, Charity probably wouldn't be able to hit a blasted thing, and their shooting sessions would be suspended until a new pair could be obtained.

"Charity, I'm sorry. I didn't think about your eyeglasses."

"It's all right," she told him with a resigned sigh.

"No, it's not. How are you gonna target-practice when you can't see?"

"I can see just fine," she admitted reluctantly, sheepishly.

"Sure you can," he scoffed. "And I'm the King of England."

"Well, Your Majesty, put this in your crown and wear it," she retorted smartly, disgusted that she now had to confess that the glasses were no more than a useless decoration. "The lenses were nearly plain glass, and I can see just as well without them. Better, in fact."

Frowning, he stared at her in complete bafflement. "Then why the hell were you wearing them?" he growled. "You must have known they make you look like an old hag."

"So you've said. More than once." She was getting really miffed now.

"Well?"

"Has it ever crossed that feeble mind of yours that perhaps I want to look like an old hag?" Her eyes blazed up at him. Without all that glass to distort and shield them, they were incredibly big and blue, like a perfect summer sky, heavily fringed with a thick curve of dark lashes and snapping with emotion.

"You were hidin' behind them," he said softly, incredulously.

"Yes."

"What now? How do you intend to hide now?"

"I don't intend to hide," she told him proudly, drawing herself up to her full, haughty height of five feet nothing. "I'm learning to fight back. That's why I hired you."

11

THE first time Luke saw Charity in her new blue denim britches and shirt, he nearly choked on his tonsils. Holy Hannah! The woman had legs! The longest, most fascinating legs he'd ever seen! Swallowing hard, he tried to calm his clamoring body, even as his disbelieving eyes devoured her. Beneath those sheltering, voluminous tents of black cloth she called mourning dresses, the Widow Prindle had concealed a delicious little body, thin though it was, and with more curves than a snake with a twitch! And every one of those curves flowed alluringly into another, creating hills and vales that almost begged to be explored. Even her new riding skirts had somehow succeeded in disguising her hidden charms, which, considering his peculiar responses these days, had probably been a blessing.

Now, as she stopped in front of him, Charity tugged self-consciously at the bandanna about her neck, hoping it would stay in place to hide her scarred throat. She felt next to naked in these boy's trousers. Surely, they were never meant to fit this tautly about one's derriere! Or were they?

For the first time, Charity realized that, while she'd never consciously noticed it before, Luke's

144

denim trousers fit every bit as snugly as hers, as did Mano's. Perhaps they actually were designed to cling closer than one's own shadow! But, my lands, it was absolutely shameless the way the material stretched so revealingly across the front of a man's groin, literally emphasizing his bold masculinity! And she was awfully afraid that her own behind was outlined every bit as faithfully!

"Are you ready to begin practicin'?" Despite hastily clearing his throat before speaking, Luke's voice still came out sounding as husky as hers, only much deeper, like a rusted church bell.

Charity's brow furrowed as she considered returning to the house and changing into one of her split skirts, though they were all in desperate need of laundering, which is why she'd finally resorted to wearing these pants.

Noting her frown, and wondering about it, Luke asked, "Is there some problem I should know about?"

"No. Yes." Charity shook her head in indecision. "Well?"

"I'm not sure about these britches," she finally confessed. "I think you must have misjudged the size."

Just when he'd finally managed to drag his mind off of her marvelously long legs, she had to remind him! Lord, he could fry in hell for all eternity for his lascivious thoughts! "They're supposed to be fairly snug, you know," he managed to inform her, "so that they don't snag and tear as easily as loose britches. In fact, a lot of cowhands and drovers actually shrink their denim pants to fit better."

"They do?" Charity wasn't at all sure she believed him. Nor was she sure she liked that glow of frank appreciation in his bottle-green eyes!

"Sure! Why, I've known a few who wear their denims while they take a good dunkin' in a water trough, and then they lay out flat in them until they're dry.''

''The men or the trousers?'' she asked skeptically. ''Dry, you mean?''

She nodded.

''Both,'' he said. With a teasing grin, and skimming his eyes over her sweetly curved body, he told her, ''You know, they claim your denim pants aren't too tight unless your eyes start to bulge when you wear them.''

''Then mine are fine,'' she decided. ''But yours must be several sizes too small!''

From just inside the open barn door came a snort that didn't sound like a horse, and Luke was willing to bet his saddle that the rude noise had come from a half-ass Indian who answered to the name of Mano. One of these days . . .

Luke had one boot planted firmly on the bottom step of the kitchen porch before his mind registered what his nose was already telegraphing. Yuck! Boiled beef and cabbage! There was no way on earth he'd ever fail to recognize that smell, or ever look forward to the meal it presaged. To him it would always represent those disastrous days at the orphanage—Thursdays, to be exact—each and every Thursday of his life for ten long years.

One whiff, and Luke was a child again, alone and adrift, aching for just one person who would care, one solitary soul who could understand and sympathize with a sad, lonely little boy. There had been no one. For years and years. No one to care when he was yanked from his chair, his thin little legs whipped with a switch until they were covered with red welts. No one to weep for him when he was sent to bed, beaten and hungry, and made to eat the same supper he'd refused, now cold and congealed, the next morning. No one to hold his tummy or bathe his face when the greasy meal made his stomach revolt.

Even now, years later, Luke could feel his stomach being to turn. Sweat broke out on his brow. He didn't need a mirror to know that his face had lost most of its color, and now looked and felt like putty. On instinct, he swiveled and started back the way he'd come, away from the house.

"Luke!" Charity's raspy voice cut through the early evening air, aimed at his retreating back. "Where are you headed? Supper is on the table. Come and eat it while it's hot."

Fifteen years fell away from him, as if they'd never been. In his mind, he could hear echoes of the matrons who had run the orphanage with greedy hands and stony hearts.

"Look, brat, you'll eat or starve, and one less mewling mouth around this place would be a relief!"

"You get your behind back up on that chair and eat, or I'll whip you until the blood runs down both of your legs, and that's a promise, boy!"

"The likes of you don't deserve lobster and pheasant, you uppity little bastard, so eat what's set in front of you and be grateful you got that!"

Luke's hands were clenched into tight fists at his sides, and he had to swallow hard on the nausea that threatened still. As he swung around to face Charity, years of suppressed rage glowed from his eyes. "I'm not eatin' that slop!"

Taken aback, Charity could only stare at him in surprise. "Luke,—" she began, only to be cut short.

"I *hate* beef and cabbage! And nobody is ever gonna make me eat it again!" He turned his back to her and stalked off in a huff. His words drifted back to her. "Not at breakfast, neither! Nobody! Ever!"

"Well, I never!" she exclaimed softly, a hand on either hip as she gaped after his retreating figure. "You'd have thought I tried to poison the man!"

Mano appeared at her elbow, a wry grin splitting his face. "I take it he doesn't approve of the supper fare."

"Well, I surely didn't expect I'd have to consult with him before deciding what to cook for dinner!" Charity sniffed. She flounced back into the kitchen, letting the door slam shut behind her. "He can eat his blasted saddle for all I care!"

Later, when she'd had time to think about it, Luke's reaction still seemed extreme. In her mind, Charity replayed his exact words, and had to wonder at how pale his face had been, almost as if he were actually ill. Why would anyone react so strongly to eating beef and cabbage, for heaven's sake? Even if he truly loathed it, for whatever reason, he could have politely informed her that he didn't care for that particular meal, instead of throwing a tantrum like a rebellious little boy!

She found herself wondering what he'd been like as a boy, but the thought boggled her mind. She found it difficult to imagine him as anything but the man he was today. Still, once upon a time, he *had* been small; and obviously, someone much bigger or with much more control had forced him to eat beef and cabbage, a fact he resented to this very day.

For some strange reason, Charity's heart was suddenly touched by the image of a little boy with dark hair and green eyes being made to eat a supper he detested. In her mind's eye, she could see him sitting in a chair much too large for him, his chin barely clearing the table edge, his eyes shimmering with unshed tears, his lips tightly pursed to keep them from trembling.

And when he had stubbornly refused to eat his supper, had they then made him eat it for breakfast, instead? Is that what his words had meant? she wondered.

Charity shuddered. What sort of parents had he

had? Were they merely very strict, or had they mistreated him? For some unknown reason, she wanted to believe that they had just been stern. She couldn't bear to think that he'd had a miserable childhood. Perhaps because, if her own child had lived, she'd have done anything to make his world safe and happy.

If her child had lived, she'd have played with him every day, and baked cookies for him, and saved the ripest, reddest apples just for him—and though she would have cooked good, nourishing meals for him, to make him grow straight and strong, she'd never have forced him to eat anything he truly disliked. She would have been such a good mother! If only . . .

A short while later, Charity made her way toward the barn, carrying a linen-covered basket. Mano was nowhere in sight, but at the end of the row of stalls, on a bale of straw, Luke sat waxing his saddle. A wry smile teased at her lips as she recalled wishing that he replace his dinner with this very saddle, and now here she was trotting his supper out to the barn for him, like some clucking mother hen!

When he noticed her, Luke did nothing. He merely sat there, waiting, one dark eyebrow quirked in question.

Without ceremony, she plunked the basket down at his feet. "Your supper," she told him tersely.

He frowned. "I told you—"

"I heard what you said. I'm not deaf." Without another word, she turned and left as quietly as she had come.

With all the eagerness of someone about to open a basket of snakes, Luke cautiously peeled back the edge of the linen, holding his breath against the expectation of the stink of cooked cabbage.

For long minutes he simply stared into the basket, his mouth slightly open in mute amazement. Inside, wrapped in a napkin, were several fluffy golden biscuits, still steaming from the oven. Wedged carefully into a corner, flanked by boiled potatoes, was a small bowl of browned gravy. In the opposite corner, supported by a serving of crisp baked apples, was a jar of hot, black coffee.

Luke swore softly, shaking his head in disbelief at this unexpected act of kindness. Why had she done this? If he'd been paying for his meals, he would have expected it, of course. But he wasn't, and he couldn't understand why she would go to all the extra work and bother to prepare a separate dinner just for him, especially when he had so rudely refused the meal she had previously cooked.

God! When was the last time someone had cared whether or not he'd gone hungry? When had anyone gone out of their way to please him or see to his comfort, without doing so out of fear or because they were being paid well? He couldn't remember when—if, indeed, there had ever been such a time.

"I'll be!" he murmured with a crooked smile, reaching for a warm biscuit and marveling quietly at the glow of gratitude he felt. "Charity Prindle, you're quite a woman under that prickly hide of yours."

Charity pitched the last of the chicken feed in a spray across the hen yard, latching the door behind her on her way out of the pen. To herself she wondered when, if ever, she would get into a decent routine again. With all her practice sessions, her farm chores either had to be done very early in the morning or after supper. Then there were always household chores to do whenever she could find the energy and squeeze them in between everything else. Never before had she let dishes go unwashed after a meal, or had laundry wait so long between washings, and she couldn't remember the last time she'd dusted the furniture or cleaned the parlor.

At least Mano was here to help, and now Luke had taken to doing odd jobs around the place, as if to make up for all the time the lessons took from her day. One morning she awakened to the sound of hammering, and found Luke replacing a rotting floorboard on the back porch. Another evening he and Mano straightened the barn door, which always wanted to hang crooked. He'd fixed the kitchen window, which tended to stick after every rain, repaired a wobbly leg on her table, and had nailed several loose shutters back into place. All small things, but annoying; repairs Johnny would have done if he'd still been alive.

Charity's gaze strayed toward the apple tree where Luke was busy hanging a feed sack filled with straw from one of the lower limbs. This was his latest idea for a target. Holding onto a rope tied around the bag, he would give it a sharp tug, sending the target swinging. On a signal from Luke, Charity was supposed to draw her gun as quickly as possible and shoot the bag. Or, sometimes she turned her back to the target, then drew, turned, and shot at Luke's command.

Squinting against a brilliant sunset that she was too weary to appreciate, Charity wandered nearer, wondering if once again Luke had deliberately chosen to use feed bags because they were so similar in size to a man's body. It seemed he was constantly trying to impress upon her the fact that she was learning these skills in preparation for taking another person's life, and when the time came, it would not be a sack full of straw in her sights.

With these thoughts foremost in her mind, she looked up at him soberly and asked, "What's it like to kill a man, Luke? I know you've tried to warn me, but you've never really come out and said what it's like. I need to know."

He stared at her silently for so long that she began

to wonder whether or not he would answer. Finally he nodded. "Yes, I know you do, but I'm not sure a million words could ever make you fully understand. I think it's one of those things you have to experience on your own before you really know how it feels. Sort of like tryin' to imagine how it must feel to be a bird and fly; or what it's like to give birth or to die.

"You see, Charity, I can teach you how to aim straight and true, how to pull the trigger with a sure, steady pressure, how to judge speed and distance for accuracy. I can teach you everything there is to know about guns and shootin'—but I can't teach you how to kill. Or how it feels when you do. No one else can do that for you.

"And by the time you learn that particular lesson in life, it's too late to try to back up and change your decisions. It's done and it can't be undone. You can't pour blood back into a dead man's heart and make him live again. You can only try to live with yourself and your own conscience from that moment on, and for a lot of people that's nearly impossible. So be sure, lady. Be real sure you can handle the guilt before you pull that trigger and end someone else's life.

"On the other hand, if you're facin' the business end of someone else's weapon, and you really don't have much choice about it, don't waste time tryin' to decide what's right and wrong. Shoot first and save the questions for later, or you might not live long enough for regrets."

Charity regarded him solemnly, her face lined with sorrow. "I'm very familiar with regrets," she informed him flatly. "I live with them daily. You just teach me the necessary skills, Mr. Sterling, and trust me when I tell you that when the moment comes, I'll be ready, willing, and able to send each of those six men to an eternity in hell."

"You can't be sure of that. I've seen men twice your size, and as determined as the devil, suddenly freeze at the most crucial moment—and I've seen them forfeit their lives because of that last-second hesitation, their reluctance to spill another person's blood."

"Perhaps they didn't have as much reason for killing as I do," she suggested in that sandsoap voice of hers.

He shook his head, the gesture both an admission of defeat and of regret. "Contrary to what you might have heard, revenge isn't always sweet, Charity." His leaf-green eyes regarded her gravely for a long moment. "It can be as bitter as bile."

"You're speaking from personal experience, I suppose?" she asked.

"Of course."

"How many men have you killed?"

"I suppose you mean as a gunfighter, not in war. Either way, the answer is the same. More than I care to recall."

"And do you have regrets?"

"More than I care to count."

Now Luke figured it was his turn to ask the questions. "What was your husband like?"

Taken by surprise, Charity gave a start. Then, as if just realizing how personal her own questions had been, she decided to answer him. "Johnny was a good man, honest and kind and gentle," she answered gruffly. "And not at all weak. Farm work is harder than most folks realize, and it takes a strong man to do it, especially by himself."

As she spoke, her thoughts turning back to happier times, she was unaware of how soft her features had turned and how misty her big blue eyes had become. "His family owned a farm near ours back in Pennsylvania, and he and I grew up together. I can't remember a time when I didn't want to be his wife, or when I didn't love him."

"You miss him a lot, don't you?"

"He was my best friend. There was nothing I couldn't tell him, and he always seemed to understand. It sounds crazy, but even now, I'll think of something I want to share with him. Then I'll recall that he's not here any longer to talk with. Sometimes I wake in the night, and wonder why he's not lying next to me in our bed, or I'll hear a sound and go to call out to him. That's when I miss him the most, I think, when I forget for a moment that he's gone; and then I remember and the pain is all new again."

The softness was gone from her face now, replaced by grief, a sorrow deeper and truer than anything Luke had ever witnessed. It touched a part of him he'd thought long dead, bringing with it a poignant ache. Yet even as he regretted that his prying had brought Charity more distress, he couldn't help the small twinge of envy he felt toward her husband. In life, the man had been fortunate to be loved in a way Luke had never known. Even in death, that love lived on in his widow's heart. To Luke's way of thinking, and despite the poor fellow's untimely murder, John Prindle had been a lucky man.

"I'm sorry, Charity," Luke said softly, not knowing if his words were for her or for himself.

"So am I," she rasped, eyes burning with tears that would not fall.

12

CHARITY scarcely had any time for the small comforts of life—like crisply ironed laundry, tending to her vegetable garden, keeping an eye on the baby chicks and ducklings that had recently hatched, or just paring her toenails before they turned into talons. She had to grab her opportunities when she could manage a few spare minutes, and the necessary energy.

Which was why she was hastily washing her hair at sunrise, in the icy water from the kitchen pump, not even bothering to heat the water on the stove. With the men due to arrive for breakfast before long, and the morning meal still to cook, she was feeling especially rushed for time. She was bent over, her soapy head wedged awkwardly between the lip of the pump and the bowl on the counter, ready to rinse her hair, when the pump handle broke off in her hand. It simply snapped off, dropping like a rock and dragging her arm with it, and whacking her in the head with the force of a hammer.

She cursed—long and hard. She cursed as she threw the broken chunk of cast iron out the kitchen window, which happened to be closed at the time. Glass shattered satisfyingly. She cursed as she

155

danced a jig around the table, cupping one hand to the throbbing lump on her skull and swiping soap from her stinging eyes with the other. She cursed when she couldn't find her towel, then when she found it soaking wet on the floor. She cursed as water and itchy bubbles ran down her neck and shoulders and back, soaking her thin camisole and plastering it to her skin.

And when she had run out of ordinary curses, for ordinary, everyday, aggravating things, she cursed Johnny. She cursed him for dying. For leaving her alone and lonely. For not taking her with him. For not fighting harder, or lingering longer, or being here now to fix the bloomin', blasted, damned pump handle!

Luke found her huddled on the kitchen floor, trembling violently, pounding her fists on the floorboards, and cursing gutturally at the top of her voice. "Damn you, Johnny! Damn you! Damn your hide! I hate you! I hate you! I hate you! Oh, God! I love you! I loved you so much! Blast you to hell and back again! Oh, Johnny! Oh, damn!"

Great racking sobs shook her fragile frame, and at first Luke was sure she was crying her heart out. But when he knelt beside her and tried awkwardly to comfort her, not a tear dampened her lashes. While soap and cold water streamed down her cheeks and neck, her eyes remained painfully dry in their red-rimmed sockets.

Her body lurched and heaved terribly, but just as Luke tried to pull her into his arms, Charity jerked to her feet and stumbled across the kitchen. Shoving Mano out of the doorway, she nearly fell down the porch steps, and ended by sitting on the second one and emptying her stomach over the side.

Behind her, Luke exchanged a worried look with Mano. "What the hell is going on?" he asked softly, tersely. Twin creases formed above his nose as he eyed the broken window and the watery mess in the kitchen.

Mano merely shrugged and said simply. "Her pain is building inside, and it needs to find release. She mourns, but she hasn't cried."

Luke was aghast. "Not even at his burial?"

"She was in her sickbed when they buried him, too near death to be at his graveside."

"Surely she's wept since then, sometime; in the middle of the night, or when no one's around to notice."

Mano just shook his head. "No. No tears. No relief; and no healing." He glanced at Charity's bedraggled form, still hunched over the side of the steps. "Only suffering that doesn't ease the way it should."

"And it's been seven months?"

"More like eight now."

Luke voiced what both of them were thinking. "It's not natural."

Mano merely nodded in mute agreement.

On a sigh of helpless exasperation, Luke hissed, "Well, isn't there anything anyone can do to help? Surely, she can't go on this way much longer. My God! She's skin and bone! Her eyes look like two burn holes in a blanket! She's bein' eaten alive by grief and hatred. Blast it all, she was even cursin' him for dyin'!"

"That's the first normal thing she's done, other than want revenge against her attackers."

"Normal? You call hatin' him for dyin' normal?"

"Think about it, Sterling. He left her. She lived. She's had to go on living and suffering and bleeding from her soul. Where he's gone, her husband feels no pain. She envies him this. Their unborn child lives with him. He can see the babe, touch it, know it. She cannot, and the knowledge cuts deeply into her heart.

"She loves him; she hates him. She grieves for him, yet she envies him. She yearns for him, but cannot reach across the emptiness to find him. She cannot die; she cannot live. She cannot weep; she cannot laugh. In this life there are two faces to everything, two mouths which must be fed. Charity must learn to give to both sides, to turn in both directions. To not bend, is to break; to not yield, is to suffer undue pain."

"If you know all this, can't you help her? Before she succeeds in killin' herself? Can't you explain it to her?"

"She wouldn't listen to me, any more than she would listen to you, or to her friends in town. She is determined to close her eyes, and with them, her heart."

"There must be someone who could make her listen, and show her that what she's doin' to herself is wrong."

Mano hesitated, deciding. "There is one thing I've thought of, but she may not agree to it."

"What? At this point anything is worth a try."

"Among my mother's people, the ones you know as the Arapaho, there is a man who is very old and very wise. He is the tribal shaman, the Diviner of Dreams. Perhaps he could help her, if he's still living, and if we could get Charity to agree to see him."

"Do you know where to find him?"

Mano's mouth turned up in a sneer. "Those confined to the reservations are not hard to find. They sit in one place and wait to die." His silver eyes cut to Charity, who sat limply on the stairs. "It's what she does, in her heart."

"You saddle the horses and pack what gear you think we'll need. I'll throw some of Charity's things together and inform her that we're leavin'."

"You might have a fight on your hands. She's a

stubborn woman, and I can't see her willingly agree-ing to this," Mano warned.

"Oh, she'll agree," Luke promised darkly. "If she still wants revenge on her husband's killers, and my help, she'll agree."

Using the pump in the yard outside, Charity was rinsing the soap from her hair when Luke ap-proached her.

"I need to talk to you."

Her head half under the water, she mumbled something that sounded like an agreement, and Luke had to be satisfied with that for the moment. He waited impatiently for her to finish, watching ab-sently as she leaned to one side, gathered handfuls of gleaming blonde hair, and began to wring the ex-cess water from them.

Suddenly it dawned on him what he was staring at. The morning sun was shining down upon her wet head, turning the long, streaming strands into gold. Wet, it was a rich, dark golden hue, and it hung straight and thick to her waist when she finally stood upright and turned to face him. Dry, left free of re-straints, it would be absolutely beautiful! Why didn't Charity do something soft and charming with it? Why did she deliberately make it as dull and unat-tractive as possible? Was this another means of hid-ing, like her eyeglasses had been?

"I can have your breakfast ready in half an hour or so, if you and Mano will come up to the house then. I'm sorry about the delay." Crossing her arms over her chest in an effort to shield her chilled breasts and the damp black camisole from his view, Charity made no other reference to her strange fit of just minutes before, other than to add, "I suppose I must see about getting the pump handle and the window repaired." Luke had the distinct impression she would prefer to forget the embarrassing incident had ever occurred.

He had opened his mouth to tell her of their impending trip to the Arapaho reservation when the sight of her bare throat drove all other thoughts from his mind. Always before in his presence, she had worn high-necked dresses or bandannas that covered her neck. Luke supposed it was for modesty's sake that she did so—now he knew differently.

Through no volition of his own, Luke's long fingers reached toward her. As if frozen, her eyes huge and wary, Charity watched and waited, unable even to breathe or to blink, as his calloused fingers touched the vivid scar circling her throat. Before her eyes, Luke's features contorted in fury. His eyes blazed beneath lowered brows, his nostrils flared, his mobile lips flattened to a thin, angry slash.

Reacting to this abrupt and unexpected anger in someone she had come to trust, Charity panicked. "No!" Her lips formed the word, the single syllable vibrating through the flesh beneath his fingertips, but no sound emerged. When she tried to take a step backward, away from him, his hand wrapped around the back of her neck and stopped her slight movement. His thumb brushed in gentle, repeated strokes over the ugly gash.

"Who did this to you?" he demanded, grating the words from between clenched teeth.

She could only stand before him and quiver violently.

If possible, her helpless quaking angered him more. "Was it one of them, Charity? Was it one of the men who killed your husband?"

She managed a weak nod.

Luke wanted to be sick. "Tell me."

Her eyes searched wildly past him, around him, and finally settled on his again, as if begging him to release her. "Tell me," he repeated firmly, evenly.

"He . . . he c . . . c . . . cut m . . . m . . . me!" she stammered. Several deep, shaky breaths later, with Luke's steady gaze gently coaxing, as if he willed the words from her body, Charity admitted softly, "He kept me from Johnny. He held me; hurt me. He laughed."

"Did he violate you?" Though she had said that the men had killed her husband and her unborn child, Charity had never made it clear just how she had lost the baby. Mano, if he knew, had never volunteered the information. Suddenly Luke needed to know. Had the shock of seeing her husband murdered, of having her throat sliced, been enough to make her body reject the child? Had her attackers beaten her, thus causing the miscarriage? Or had it been worse, as Luke suspected? Had one or more of those bastards raped her?

Again, she nodded, speech failing her. Beneath his thumb, he felt her struggle to swallow and realized with a start that his fingers had tightened unconsciously around her throat. Deliberately, he loosened his hold, but did not release her entirely as yet. "Was he the only one?"

Now she shook her head, shortly, sharply. "No." Her teeth clamped over her bottom lip to stop its quivering.

He waited, his emerald gaze compelling an answer. "How many of them forced you, Charity?"

"All of them. All of them. All of them!" What started as a whisper ended as a hoarse shout. "All six, each in his turn! They all had me, Sterling! Is that what your twisted mind with its sick curiosity wants to know? Are you satisfied now?"

Her eyes were closed, as if holding back tears, but none seeped through her clenched lashes. After what Mano had said, Luke doubted there were any tears hidden there, and he wished there were. Her stiff neck strained against his restricting hand, while her own hands had come up to push against his chest.

"I'm sorry." After what she had lived through, after what he'd practically forced her to confess, his apology sounded woefully inadequate. "Charity, I'm so sorry."

Her eyes popped open, wild and glowing with a thousand tangled emotions. "Don't pity me, Luke!" she demanded. "Don't you dare pity me! Teach me, help me, lend me your skills and your knowledge, but keep your worthless pity."

"I will help you, Charity," he assured her earnestly, reminded of why he'd wanted to speak with her in the first place. "I want to help you, and so does Mano. That's why we're leavin', just as soon as you can get dressed and ready to ride."

"Leaving?" she asked, confused by his seeming change of topic. "Why? For where?"

"Trust me, Charity. It'll be fine. I promise you."

She was instantly wary. "Trust you?" she echoed. "When I trusted you to teach me to ride, I wore blisters and sore muscles for weeks; likewise with the shooting lessons. That same blind faith cost me my eyeglasses. And after you'd sworn to be discreet, you rode into Dodge and bought riding skirts and pants for me, disregarding the risk to my reputation. What is it likely to cost me to trust you this time?"

His smile was a little sad and a lot puzzling as he removed his hand from her neck and trailed his fingers through the silken strands of her hair, watching them fall like spun sunshine. His answer did nothing to ease her mind, as he murmured, "Some tears, I hope—and a few ghosts."

"Mano, I don't want to do this. Luke? Luke, don't make me go through with this. I'm scared. I'm really, truly scared." Charity divided her attention and her comments between the two men walking on either side of her, escorting her to the old shaman's tipi. Suddenly she knew what it must feel like to make that final walk to the gallows.

"Buck up, Charity. You don't want the old fellow to think you're afraid of him, do you? You might hurt his feelin's." This from Luke, who wasn't about to show her how unsure he was about all this himself.

"Hurting his feelings is the least of my worries right now, Sterling!" she returned with a hateful look for his distinct lack of sympathy.

"Now, Charity, you know he won't hurt you. He's a healer. I thought you liked him when you met him the other day; and the two of you talked for half the day yesterday, and you weren't this nervous when you came from his tipi."

"Yes, but this business of peyote seeds and dreams. It really has me spooked! What if something goes wrong, and I never wake up again? What if I get caught in one of these dreams and can't get out?"

"It's only sleep; just a few, harmless dreams," Mano assured her.

Luke patted her shoulder awkwardly. "And how could you not wake up? That's silly!"

"Easy for you to say!" Charity snorted inelegantly. "You're not the one who is going to be helpless in the hands of that old witch doctor!"

"Hell's bells and little catfish!" Mano exclaimed, forgetting himself and his Indian demeanor for the moment. He glanced hastily about to see who might have heard. "What ever else you do, please don't call him that again, to his face or to anyone else. He's the tribal shaman, sort of like a religious priest, not a witch doctor!"

She wrinkled her nose up at him and challenged, "Can you honestly stand there and tell me he doesn't dabble in a few mystical, perhaps magical, definitely unnatural practices every now and again?''

When Mano remained silent, refusing to answer, Charity nodded. ''That's what I thought,'' she said tersely, feeling both astute and spineless.

''Now, Charity, pull that lip in before you trip on it. Mano and I have both promised to be right there the whole time.'' Her lower lip, the one now protruding in an alluring pout, was really quite bewitching, Luke noticed suddenly. Why was it that every time he turned around, he was finding something more to admire about her, something else fetching or almost pretty, something edging on downright attractive? First her eyes, then her legs and her hair, now her mouth. Not to mention the lady's spunk!

''Will you hold my hand, Luke?'' Pleading eyes turned up to his. ''And if I should die, will you see that I'm buried next to Johnny?''

He stopped dead in his tracks and pulled her to a halt. Taking hold of her arms, he nearly shook her. ''Now you listen to me, lady! No more talk like that! Do you hear me? I'll hold your blasted bony hand if it'll make you feel better, but no more talk about dyin'! Or don't you intend to live to see your attackers brought to justice—*your* justice?''

''Charity's justice?'' she mused, a half-smile crinkling the corners of her eyes. ''Yes, that has a certain promising ring, doesn't it?''

''Widow's justice,'' Mano suggested softly, reverently. ''From the wickedest workings of a woman's mind.'' A chilling breeze swirled about them, suddenly and from nowhere, then was gone—as if Mano's words had invoked the spirits, awakening them from their slumbers and summoning their attention.

Luke shivered; Mano frowned in concern; Charity's smile held hidden mysteries.

* * *

The dreams! Charity had never experienced such vivid dreams! The colorful, distorted images floated around her, not in her head, as she might have imagined, but all about her—surrounding her. Everything seemed so real. No, more than real. Bigger and louder than normal. There was even a sense of smell! She'd never smelled anything in any of her former dreams; at least she didn't think so.

It all started out very nicely, with drifting images of her childhood. She saw herself as a child—no, somehow she *was* that child again, all sunshine curls and huge blue eyes. Lands! Now she was eight years old again, stuck in the branches of that old apple tree, tears running down her cheeks as she waited for Zoe to run back up to the house and get help. Oh! There was Zoe, dawdling, a nasty smirk on her face, with no intention of bringing help for Charity. Why, she could actually hear her sister's jealous thoughts!

And there was Mama, calling for her and looking worried because it was getting dark and Charity was nowhere to be found. Zoe got a whipping that night, for forgetting to tell anyone where Charity was; Charity got a spanking too, for climbing the tree in the first place and scaring Mama, and for tearing a hole in her dress.

Oh! There was Johnny, when he was younger. His image was as clear as crystal and twice as dear to her now. He was all of fifteen, and full of himself. And there they were, sitting on the banks of the creek beneath the shading branches of the trees. They were fishing, and Charity had her mouth screwed up in distaste as she baited her hook with a squiggly worm. With no forewarning, Johnny leaned over and kissed her. The worm fell into her lap, forgotten.

And then Charity found herself standing before

the altar in her old church, dressed in pristine white and almost sick with nerves. Beside her, Johnny was trying his best not to betray his own anxiety. Behind them, friends and relatives smiled and sniffled as they watched the two young people recite their wedding vows. It was a bright and shining moment, full of promise, full of love.

Foreboding came over her, and Charity stiffened. Gone were the brilliant colors, swept away by a thick, swirling gray mist that made her shrink into herself and shiver with fear. "No!" she cried out, both within the realm of her dream and out of it. How strange that she could be both places at once, that even as she cringed from some impending evil, she could hear the shaman instructing her in his serene, singsong voice, and could feel Luke's fingers tighten upon her own in a gesture of comfort and reassurance.

And how odd that she no longer needed Mano to interpret the shaman's Indian speech. Somehow, remarkable as it was, Charity could suddenly understand his every word. Ah, the wonder of dreams!

Suddenly, out of the mist, a face sprang out at her! "Aaaah!" Charity's shriek of terror and the man's awful laughter echoed in her own ears. The shaman's words came faintly. "Control the image, little one. Make it do what you want."

The image of Cutter's laughing face contorted almost as soon as Charity willed it gone. Before it dissolved entirely, she saw her attacker's throat, neatly sliced, his bloodless face above it.

The other killers followed, forming a circle around her and performing some macabre dance. Where their bodies should have been, Charity perceived only shifting forms, like sheer curtains blowing in a breeze. But their faces loomed at her, larger than life. She recognized each one of them. Instinctively, she tried to shy away from them. Her voice had deserted her, leaving only pathetic whimpers.

"Destroy your enemies, woman. With your mind, destroy them." She heard and obeyed the shaman's command.

One by one, the faces melted away, but not before altering in some way first. The handsome Dandy was no longer attractive; now his countenance became gruesome to behold, all puckered and bloody. The one called Jeb had a hole in the center of his forehead. And Whitey's face was bruised and swollen almost beyond recognition. Bronc's features were twisted, as if in the throes of torment.

The dream scene shifted. Now Charity writhed with pain, her screams of agony tearing through the night. Once more, she was reliving that terrifying attack, that nightmare that had no end! It was so real! Oh, God! The pain!

"The pain is in your mind. These dream men cannot harm you," the old man's voice told her. "See these men, look closely for flaws and weaknesses. See what they wear on their bodies, the color of their eyes, what horses they ride. Notice anything unusual about them."

Even as he spoke, the pain faded, her screams ceased. Now, as if the entire episode had been frozen in time, she viewed it with numbed feelings. She had thought she remembered that night so clearly in her mind that she would never forget a single torturous moment of it. Now she saw what her pain-blurred senses had missed. Small details that would help her in her search for these men.

Jeb, the man who had first caught her, the one with two fingers missing on his left hand, also had a white, diamond-shaped birthmark on his neck. How had she missed that? And Dandy had a wart on his buttocks, one nobody would notice unless his britches were down. He rode an Appaloosa, a distinctive horse which should make him easy to track. Cutter seemed particularly enthralled with his knife, handling it like a lover, even talking to it when no one else was around to notice. He was ugly, and probably more crazy than sane.

Weasel had one eye that turned in toward his thin, crooked nose. Anywhere he went, Whitey would be noticed and remembered for the wide streak of white hair in his otherwise dark head.

Bronc's saddle was as unique as a signature, black leather trimmed in Spanish silver. Now, in this queer, painless state, Charity carefully noted the design. If she never found any of the others, she wanted to find Cutter and Bronc. She wanted them all, all six of the murdering bastards, but she would track Cutter and Bronc for the next fifty years and to the ends of the earth, if that is what it took to repay them for that night in hell.

Without warning, the dream stole command from her. The pain was so unexpected, so intense, that it robbed the air from Charity's lungs. She arched up soundlessly, helplessly, and the last thing she knew before she slipped into blessed oblivion was the sight of Bronc's leering face above hers, and the rake of his spurs ripping her tender flesh.

13

$\mathcal{J}$T seemed the natural course of things for Charity to wake to the sound of Johnny's voice. This was the way it had happened before, on that wretchedly long night, the night he had died and left her alone in the middle of all that pain and darkness. But it wasn't dark now. Why not? And the expected pain was not there. Or was it lurking just out of sight, waiting to catch her unawares once more?

Again, Charity heard Johnny's voice softly calling her name. She turned her head and found him sitting near her. But he was not tied to the wagon wheel, he was not injured and dying—and he was not alone. In his arms, he held a baby swathed in a pink blanket. In the infant's bright, downy hair was a tiny pink bow.

"Isn't she beautiful, Charity?" Johnny asked, smiling at her. "Her name is Faith." At this, he shrugged self-consciously and added, "It sort of fits her somehow, you know?"

She knew, yet still she had to ask, had to hear it from her husband's lips. "Who . . . whose child is she, Johnny?"

"Why, ours, of course. She looks so much like you, Charity. She has your hair, and your mouth."

"Am I dead now, too? How did I get here?" Charity sat up and looked around at the soft white light glowing all about them. There was nothing else to be seen—no grass, no trees or sky, no walls. "Where *is* here, anyway?"

Johnny shook his head. "No, Charity, you're not dead. Somehow you called to me and Faith in your dreams, and somehow we came to meet you here. I don't understand it any more than you do, but I'm glad it happened. I've often wished you could meet your daughter. I wanted to say good-bye properly."

Tears stung her eyes. "You left me, Johnny Prindle! You left me out there on that prairie all alone! It's a wonder I didn't get eaten alive by wolves before Mano found me."

"I didn't want to leave you, Charity," he said reasonably, patting the baby on her back when she began to fuss. "I just didn't have much control over it, you know?"

"And now?" she asked, her chin jutting out at him. "Do you have any control now? Can you come back? Can I come with you and the baby? Can we live somewhere together again and be a family, the way it was supposed to be?"

Johnny shook his head regretfully. "No, Charity. I died; Faith died; you lived. You must go on living without us. But we'll always love you, and we'll be here waiting for you whenever you do join us."

Her arms reached out, her hands shaking. "May I hold her, Johnny, just for a while?"

He smiled and passed the babe into her waiting arms. The newborn infant was so light, so tiny that Charity could scarcely believe she was real. But she was warm and soft and fit so perfectly into the curve of Charity's arm. Her eyes were open, and she stared up at Charity with Johnny's warm brown eyes. Her mouth formed a perfect bow, the rosy lips small and faultless. One little fist waved outside the blanket. Charity sat enchanted for the longest time.

At last, she spoke again. "You know, Johnny, there have been times when I've almost hated you for leaving me. I've missed you so much and I've been so lonely for you. Somehow I knew that you and our baby were together, and I was so jealous that you could be with her when I could not."

"We missed you, too, Charity. Already I'm teaching little Faith about her mother, telling her what you were like as a child. By the way, I think you'll be glad to hear that I saw your mother the other day."

In the back of Charity's mind, she realized that this conversation bordered on being insane. No one, at least no one in his right mind, talked with dead husbands and children—not even in their dreams! "Is Mother all right, Johnny? And you, are you whole and happy? Does Faith have everything she needs?"

He shook his head and smiled again. "That's my Charity girl, always putting someone else's needs ahead of her own. We haven't a care in the world; it's you who needs to look after herself. You're too thin."

As if he heard some sound that she could not, he turned his head and listened. Then he reached out to take the baby from her. "We must go now, Charity."

For a moment more, Charity clutched the warm, sweet bundle close. Then reluctantly, she gave her over to her father. "Can I come too, Johnny? Please? After all, I seem to have made it this far, somehow."

He shook his head and bent to kiss her cheek, damp and shining now with tears. "That's not possible, Charity. You've got to go back and live your own life to its proper end. I don't know what lies ahead for you, but I hope you'll have another love, other children. You really should try, you know. You can't give up on living, and on loving, because we can no longer be together.''

Charity was stunned, and hurt. ''Wouldn't you care, Johnny, if I found someone else to love in your place?''

''Dearest, we had our love, and it was as sweet as honey. I'll never regret a moment of it, except for leaving you. But our time together is gone, and I wouldn't want you to grieve endlessly. Let your heart heal, Charity. Let me go, as I've had to release you. Hold me only as a sweet, comforting memory. Cry for me, and for Faith, and then go on and find others to take our places—and we'll be glad for you, that you're not alone and unhappy.''

''But, Johnny . . .'' Already he was beginning to fade away, he and the baby, right before her disbelieving eyes. ''Johnny! Don't do this to me again, John Prindle. Do you hear me? Don't you dare leave me alone again!''

From the mist, his voice came softly. ''Go back, Charity. I no longer belong to you, nor you to me. Go back to living.''

By the time Charity's dreams ceased and she lay sleeping a normal, natural sleep, Luke felt as if he'd been tied into knots and dragged through cactus. He felt wrung dry of emotion and energy, and more than a little sick. Beside him, Mano, for all his stolid Indian image, looked a bit green about the gills himself.

It was as if they had journeyed back with her in her dreams, sharing her pain and her loss, feeling them with her. Indeed, they almost had, for as she had thrashed and screamed and talked in her unconsciousness, she had described what she had been seeing and hearing and feeling. What Mano had only guessed, he now knew. What Luke had never known, he did now, and understood her hatred all the more. Understood and shared it.

He'd felt her pain, shared it as closely as any man was capable of understanding this kind of woman's pain. At times, he'd been close to tears himself, just listening to her frantic cries; and his rage had built steadily all the while.

"Mano, did that animal really take his spurs to her, or was she only dreamin' that he did?"

"The dream was true, Sterling. She has the scars to prove it."

Luke swallowed the intense hatred that threatened to choke him. "If she still insists on trackin' down those men and killin' them, I'm goin' with her. I just thought you ought to know."

"I figured you would."

Ever so gently, Luke eased his tortured fingers from her paralyzing grip. All through the ordeal, she had clung to his hand with desperate strength, never once letting go, not even as she envisioned holding her child. Flexing his numb fingers, Luke raked his other hand wearily across his face. He felt a hundred years older than when he'd first entered this tipi.

He wondered if Charity would recall her tears, if they had given her any relief. Would this drastic measure of reliving everything so vividly through dreams help her, or would it only make her more bitter? And what was this craziness of speaking with her dead husband, of holding her unborn child, now apparently a thriving infant in her father's care? Talk about drunken dreams!

Tenderly, still supporting her limp body in his arms, Luke wiped the last, glistening tears from her lashes. "Sleep, you poor little darlin'," he whispered. "Sleep and heal. Lord knows, you sure can use it."

* * *

It was mid-afternoon of the following day before she awoke at last. Between fits of tears, Charity kept telling herself that all those vibrant, lifelike images she recalled seeing, all those horrible things she had relived, were only dreams. Even as her tears fell like rain, even as she choked on sob after sob, she told herself that only some of it had ever really happened. Only the remembrances of the attack. All the rest had been a result of the peyote. Surely, that was it. What other explanation could there be?

Still, it had seemed real at the time, sitting there talking with Johnny, holding their baby. Oh, that sweet, darling infant girl, so tiny and perfect, so precious! Faith! Her daughter! And to think that Johnny had named her that, after the talk they'd had about names. What was it he had said? That it seemed to fit her somehow? Well, it would, if things were really as they seemed, if Faith were living among God and His angels.

"Charity, old girl, you're as crazy as a loon to even consider believing what you think you saw," she told herself sternly. "You did not talk to Johnny. There is no way such a thing would ever be possible. There is no way of knowing whether your unborn child would have been a boy or a girl, let alone that her name was Faith."

Still, the feeling of having held her daughter in her arms lingered, bringing with it a particularly poignant emptiness. Her mind held a vivid portrait of a tiny rosebud mouth, of miniature fingers, of downy blonde hair.

And Johnny, her beloved Johnny, telling her to go!

The pain came, fresh and new, in devastating waves, and with it torrents of tears. Her loss was multiplied until Charity thought surely she would simply break into a million jagged pieces and cease to be. The agony was unbearable, her heart rending within her breast. She wailed, she cried, she beat the ground with her fists until the sides of her hands were black and blue. She wept quietly; angrily; brokenly; loudly. And then she cried some more. She sobbed until her whole body ached and her eyes were swollen nearly shut.

It seemed that once the dam had burst, there was no holding back the salty floodwaters. Then, just when Charity finally brought herself back into shaky control, when the sobs had been reduced to hiccups and she peered blearily out from slits between her swollen lids, she found it. She'd been lying on her stomach, her head cradled on her arms. Now, as she levered herself up, the bodice of her shirt gaped slightly, just enough for her to catch a glimpse of pink.

Her heart began to race wildly, even as her mind shouted out a warning. With shaking fingers, she reached down and plucked the tiny, shiny pink ribbon from where it had fallen down the front of her shirt. Tears blurred her eyes, but she didn't need to see to know where this scrap of cloth had come from. It still smelled like Faith, exactly like her small baby daughter, seen but once and now lost to her all over again.

Mano had been correct all along. Charity had needed to mourn, to grieve, to release all that pent-up sorrow and anger. The trip to the reservation and the old shaman had proved a success. The peyote-induced dreams had provided that final prodding, that extra push in the right direction that had served to act as Charity's release.

Over the past three weeks, since their return from the Arapaho reservation, Charity's appetite had returned and she had begun to fill out. Her collarbone no longer protruded so drastically; nor did her shoulder bones stick up like bed knobs. Gone were the pathetically skinny arms and bony hands.

The process was so gradual that she didn't see it in her black-draped mirror, or as she was dressing in the morning light. Certainly, she hadn't noticed the roses in her cheeks or the added sheen to her hair, or that her clothes no longer hung from her bones like rags.

In the small measure of peace and calm she had gained from the shaman and the dreams, Charity had unconsciously let herself begin to relax, to let down her guard without truly being aware of it. She slept better now that nightmares had ceased tormenting her at night. Her emotions weren't constantly riding a sword's edge. She worked just as hard around the farm, yet at the end of the day, she often had a smidgen of leftover energy. She cooked, she cleaned, she practiced shooting and riding, she gardened, and sometimes she went for whole hours without thinking of Johnny and the baby.

She was healing and not even noticing.

Still, there were times when she grew reflective, and very confused. The dreams had given her much to think about, not the least of which was that there actually seemed to be an afterlife, just as she had always been taught. Johnny and her mother and her baby daughter all lived there! On the heels of that joyous idea came reluctant denial. To believe that would be to accept that she had actually talked with Johnny; and to think it had truly happened would be to admit to an unbalanced state of mind.

Yet . . . if it had been all her imagination, where had that bit of ribbon come from? It was enough to make a person's mind come unhinged. Oh, but wouldn't it be nice to believe it really had happened? Wouldn't it? And who was to say it hadn't, after all? Who really knew what magic that old shaman possessed, with his peyote and his garbled incantations?

Charity reached up to touch the tiny ribbon, tucked securely in the pocket of her blouse. A smile etched her lips, a tear glistened in her eye. Yes, wouldn't it be lovely to believe?

She was awfully quiet at times, and Luke couldn't help but wonder what was going on in her mind. Though she hadn't suggested otherwise, and still practiced long and hard, was she having second thoughts about going after those six men now that a lot of her anger had been released? Had her need for vengeance eased along with her grief? Would she be content to let him, or the law, handle the matter for her now?

"No, Luke," she told him when he asked. "I haven't changed my mind. If anything, I am more determined than ever. While the dreams have given me ease from my nightmares and much of my pain, they have also served to point out to me anew how much I have lost at the hands of those murderous beasts."

"But you're just startin' to heal, Charity. Is it wise to tear those wounds open so soon? To rake up all that pain again, by confrontin' those men yourself, when I could just as well do it for you?"

"Perhaps not wise, but necessary. Accepting my loss and being able to forget it are two very different things, you see. All the anger and resentment are still within me—and the god-awful fear. How can I ever hope to get on with my life if I'm constantly looking back over my shoulder in fear that someday, somehow, those men could suddenly reappear? At times I feel like a small child who needs reassurance that the boogeyman isn't lurking under the bed. For me, evil wears a face now, six specific faces, and I'll never be completely free of the terror until I know that those men are forever gone, banished to ever-lasting hell.''

"They aren't the only wicked men alive," Luke pointed out. "Eliminatin' them won't make the world a perfect place. It won't make everything all safe and wonderful."

"I'm not asking for perfect, Luke," she tried to explain. "I just want to make it a little better—for myself and any other unfortunate man, woman, or child those animals might decide to attack. I want to go to sleep at night knowing I'll never have to see their faces again, that I'll never hear those voices or feel their hands on my flesh." A violent shiver coursed through her at the remembrance of it all. "I need to know that there is no earthly chance of running into one of them on the street one day. Or having them suddenly show up at the farm in the dead of night. And having someone else deal with them is not going to allay those fears for me. This is something I must witness for myself, do for myself, if I'm ever to have any true peace in my soul."

"Your soul," he repeated softly, drawing her gaze to his and holding it. "Have you considered the damage that killin' those men might do to your soul, Charity? The price of vengeance might be more than you can pay."

"I suppose that's something I'll discover for myself soon enough," she suggested. "Until last fall, violence was never part of my life. Nor was revenge. My nice, comfortable little world shattered then, and I doubt I'll ever be that secure or naive again. I don't expect to enjoy extracting my revenge. Maybe I won't even gain much satisfaction from it. It may sicken me immensely. But it is something I must do, regardless of the consequences."

If Mano hadn't seen fit to let the information slip, Charity would never have known that Luke's birthday was two days away. When she asked him how he had come by the date, Mano gave her a sheepish grin and confessed, "The man talks in his sleep."

"What?"

Charity was dumbstruck, sure that Mano was merely teasing, until he added, "Yeah. I heard him mumbling to himself one night and my curiosity got the best of me. I started askin' him questions, and you could have knocked me over with a feather when he actually answered me." At her condemning look, he grumbled, "Well, you know how close-mouthed he is about his past."

"Like someone else I know," she commented dryly. "Are you sure he was really asleep? Maybe he was just playing along and having his own joke on you."

"Naw, he was asleep," Mano assured her. "Believe me. He told me things he wouldn't dream of sayin' if he was awake."

"Like what?" she couldn't help asking.

"Things we have no business knowin' until he wants to tell us," he admitted shortly. "But I can tell you that he doesn't have a family, he likes chocolate cake, and his favorite meal is chicken-fried steak with gravy and biscuits."

Never let it be said that Charity Prindle couldn't take a hint! Luke's birthday supper was going to be chicken-fried steak, gravy, potatoes, and stewed tomatoes. There would be fresh garden peas, and biscuits so fluffy they practically floated off the platter.

For dessert, there was a triple-layer chocolate cake slathered with thick fudge icing, guaranteed to make your tongue and tummy dance in delight. Charity baked the cake the night before, long after the two men had retired to their beds in the barn. She wanted it to be a surprise, and she certainly couldn't count on Luke staying out of her way or giving her enough time to herself to manage it during daylight hours.

The routine went as usual, with chores, a riding lesson for Charity, shooting practice, and the newly added tracking lessons from Mano. All through the morning and afternoon Charity couldn't help glancing at Luke from time to time, wondering why he gave no indication of this day being any more special to him than any other. Surely the man had not forgotten his own birthday!

At last the supper hour arrived, and the men, freshly washed, took their places at the table. Upon seeing his favorite meal on the table, Luke inhaled appreciatively and smiled. He waited politely for Charity to finish saying grace, which had become her habit once more following their return from the reservation. He tasted the food, seeming to linger over it a bit more than usual, and complimented Charity grandly on her cooking skills. Much to her delight, his compliments were not merely politely spoken words, for he accepted second helpings of everything.

"I don't know when I've enjoyed a meal more." Luke sighed, finally pushing himself back from the table. "I generally don't make such a pig of myself, but everything tasted so good."

Mano exchanged a wink and a smile with Charity, bringing a wondering frown from Luke. He said nothing about it, however; merely carried his dishes to the kitchen sideboard for washing, as was his habit, and helped himself to another cup of hot coffee from the stove.

"I hope you saved room for dessert," Charity said quietly. "I made it especially for tonight."

Luke groaned and patted his tight stomach. He truly was full, but he didn't want to disappoint Charity. "I'll give it a try," he promised, sitting down again.

Almost as if they had practiced their moves beforehand, Charity went into the pantry for the dessert, and Mano stationed himself near the kitchen lamps. As Charity reentered the kitchen, Mano turned down the wick on the lamps. Only the faint illumination from the candles glowed in the room as Charity placed the cake squarely before Luke and said, "Make a wish and blow out the candles, Luke."

"What's going on?" he asked, completely befuddled. It took him two tries to set his coffee cup safely aside. "What is all this?"

Charity's face was soft in the candlelight, her smile both excited and tender, her eyes aglow. "A little birdie told me that today is your birthday. Was he wrong? When is it?"

Luke's brows drew together. "June seventh," he replied hesitantly, wondering how in the devil she'd found out.

"Well, then, my birdie was right."

He just sat there looking at her rather awkwardly, so she prompted him further, "Come on, Luke. It's not as if we're going to make you tell us how old you are. That's why I put only ten candles on the cake, because I didn't know how many were supposed to go on."

Still, he hesitated.

"Luke? Please? The candles are melting pretty fast, and you're going to have wax all over the top of your cake. And don't tell your wish out loud, or it won't come true."

He looked into her candlelit eyes and saw the gentle caring. At that moment he would have jumped off a thousand-foot cliff if she'd asked him to. "Okay," he conceded.

He made his wish, then blew out all the candles in one big puff.

Charity quickly removed the candles and cut huge

slices of cake for each of them. Serving Luke first, she teased, "I'd love to know what you wished for."

When he opened his mouth to tell her, she waved her hands excitedly and exclaimed, "No! No! Don't tell me! It won't come true if you tell!" Then, with a sly grin, she said, "But if I were to guess, you wouldn't really be telling, would you?"

As they ate their cake, she and Mano made outlandish guesses at what Luke's wish might have been.

"A harem!"

"A pet rhinoceros!"

"A cancan skirt!"

"A three-legged racehorse!"

"Frog's hair!"

"Hen's teeth!"

Charity's cheeks ached from laughing so much. It had been a lifetime since she'd enjoyed herself like this.

Finally, she deemed it time to present Luke with his gifts.

"I'm sorry it couldn't be fancier," she told him as she handed him the small wrapped package. "If I had had more forewarning, I would have had more time to sew."

As it was, she had performed a small miracle. Inside the layers of paper lay a black cotton shirt, its yoke, pocket flaps, collar points, and cuffs tastefully decorated in gray-blue piping. He was silent for so long, his fingers gliding back and forth over the material, that Charity started to think he didn't like the gift.

"It's black, of course. Seems I dyed every stitch of cloth in the house in that vat of dye. You're just lucky I managed to find that gray piping buried in my sewing basket. It escaped the dye pot, somehow." She was chattering like a mindless magpie.

She knew it, but couldn't seem to stem her words. "I hope it fits. Of course . . ."

"Charity."

"If it doesn't, maybe . . ."

"Charity."

"I can still alter it . . ."

"Damn it, Charity! I'm tryin' to thank you for the shirt, if you'll shut your flap-trap long enough!"

She blinked to a halt. "You are? You do? Do you really like it?"

"Yes, I like it just fine. In fact, it's probably the nicest shirt I've ever had." By now his neck was red, and color was creeping into his face. "You sewed this yourself? For me?"

"Of course I sewed it for you! Who else is having a birthday today, you great goose?"

With gruff self-consciousness, Mano presented his gift to Luke. It was a leather belt, hand-tooled in Arapaho designs for good fortune.

Luke was stunned and grateful. "No one's ever done anything like this for me before," he told them both.

"Oh, pish-posh!" Charity exclaimed, dismissing his statement for polite fibbing. "If that were true, then you must have been raised in a cave all your life."

Luke stiffened, his lips thinning into a straight line. "No, just an orphanage, until I was fourteen. Then I ran away to fight in the war." He said it so unemotionally, his words so flat and hard, that they hit Charity all the harder.

"I'm sorry!" she gasped in dismay, aghast at her blunder. "I didn't know."

"You didn't? That comes as a surprise," he said mockingly, "since you managed to find out when my birthday was. Just how did you discover that, if you don't mind my askin'? And don't give me that cock-and-bull story about some 'little birdie,' either.''

Mano looked distinctly uncomfortable, and after all he'd done for her Charity wasn't about to tell tales on him. She was certain Luke would not appreciate Mano's method of gathering information.

''Haven't you ever heard that old adage about not looking a gift horse in the mouth?'' she asked him stubbornly.

Her dart hit its mark. Bowing to defeat, Luke decided not to press the issue. Did it really matter, after all? These two people were his friends. They'd gone to a lot of effort to give him the first birthday celebration he'd ever had, and he just wanted to sit back and savor it.

14

"**T**ROUBLE comin'," Mano declared dryly. First to hear the sounds of approaching riders, he stood next to the kitchen door, watching with narrowed eyes and silently bemoaning the fast-cooling supper he'd barely begun to eat. Immediately, Luke and Charity left their places at the table and joined him.

"Who is it?" Charity asked, her teeth worrying one edge of her lower lip. "Can you tell yet?"

Mano nodded and grimaced. "It's Masterson, and he's got Marshal Earp with him, so I suppose it's more than a social call. They've probably found out that you're living out here with two men, and intend to warn you how dangerous both of your boarders are."

"That or arrest me for unseemly behavior for a widow," she joked lamely. "I suppose it's too much to expect that they've come with news of those murderers."

Without a word, the two men formed a protective barrier between Charity and the lawmen, who were now entering the farmyard; though why they thought she needed protection, she could not guess. She tried once, unsuccessfully, to shove them aside and go around them to greet her uninvited guests. Failing that, and recognizing that neither was going to move an inch, she ducked swiftly and slipped beneath the long arm Luke had braced against the door frame.

It was a tight squeeze, and in doing so, Charity's breasts were crushed against Luke's ribs. She froze, her breath lodged in her throat; her eyes, wide with shock and fright and something even more disturbing, locked with his. Her heart hammered so hard against her own ribs that she wondered if it meant to leap from her body.

Luke was wondering much the same thing as his startled gaze held hers and began to warm in direct relationship with his quickly heating blood. Even through his shirt, and her dress, he could feel the pebbled tips of her breasts poking into his flesh like piercing brands. He could see the answering emotion in her eyes, that tiny flash of desire almost immediately overwhelmed by fear, and had a moment to be grateful that she was caught at his side and not directly facing him, where his swelling manhood would be undeniably evident and possibly pose a threat to her peace of mind.

It was a unique situation for both of them, for even when they'd practiced fighting Indian-style, Luke had been careful to avoid this sort of intimate contact with her. Though she wasn't as skittish as she'd been at first, he usually tried to make certain she was forewarned before touching her, bracing himself as well. This time it had come as a complete surprise to her, and to him.

Her face was paling, and that sprinkling of freckles over her nose was becoming more pronounced with each passing second. If she didn't breathe soon, she'd likely faint at his feet, Luke realized with a start. He stepped back, just enough to allow her to slip past him and regain her fragile illusion of safe distance.

Charity's lips trembled on a shaky breath as she sought to ease the ache in her chest and regain a semblance of emotional balance. Meanwhile, her physical balance was still in jeopardy—for sheltered from view beneath her skirts, her knees were literally knocking together, and the whimsical thought popped into her mind that if her knees were tinder, she'd be a raging ball of flame right now. As if she hadn't barely escaped that same fate just moments before, crushed against Luke Sterling's muscled chest, staring up into those compelling green eyes!

Those eyes were even now snaring hers once more, silently asking her to trust him as he said softly, soothingly, ''Charity, I would never harm you. Please don't fear me. I'm not a threat to you. You believe that, don't you?''

She nodded, although judging from the way her heart was still leaping about in her chest, like an eight-legged frog trying to go in all directions at once, she wasn't quite so convinced that Luke didn't pose a very real threat to her. Emotionally the man was becoming a definite hazard. Charity wasn't sure exactly what kind, or why, or how, but something was happening; and she wasn't at all certain she was prepared to deal with it.

''Charity?'' Her name being called out pulled her back to the present, reminding her that they were standing at the kitchen steps. Drawing her eyes from Luke's, she turned to face the scowling lawmen. Sheriff Masterson wore an especially dark look. He had been the one to address her.

Slowly, as if just coming out of a trance, Charity nodded. ''Sheriff, Marshal Earp. What brings you out this way?''

Bat fired back a sharp query of his own. ''What is this gunslinger doing here, Charity? Just what is going on?'' Bat divided his attention and his comments between Charity and Luke, who was standing directly behind her on the small porch.

Luke didn't care for Masterson's tone. His eyes blazing, he was moving toward the top step, and Masterson, before he realized what he was doing.

As he stepped even with Charity, she caught his arm with both hands, firmly pulling him to a halt. ''No, Luke. Let me handle this. Please.''

''Seems we had this same conversation a few months back when Mano came to stay at the farm,'' Charity reminded the sheriff, her eyes narrowing and her mouth drawn into a thin, straight line as she stared the lawman straight in the eye. ''It's gettin' old, Sheriff Masterson, your nose in my business, when you have criminals running free who need catching.''

''Now, we were just worried about you, that's all. When we learned that Sterling was staying out here, we got concerned that he might be up to no good.''

''Yeah,'' Wyatt was quick to add, ''and with only the Injun to protect you, we thought maybe you might welcome some help right about now.''

''Luke Sterling *is* my help, and my extra protection, gentlemen.'' Charity made her announcement with smug satisfaction, thoroughly enjoying the displeasure so evident on Masterson's face.

Even so, Luke nearly startled a shriek out of her when he snaked his arm around her waist and pulled her close in front of him. ''Trust me,'' he whispered into her hair. That, and the way his fingers came up to tenderly stroke her flushed cheek, left an altogether different impression on those who watched from too far to hear his murmured words.

''Oh, so that's the way the wind's blowin','' Wyatt snickered, shifting in his saddle.

Pure astonishment held Charity speechless as Masterson voiced the same conclusion. ''It seems

I've been mistaken, Mrs. Prindle, in thinking you needed more time to recover from your grief and the violation of your person,'' he told her stiffly. His mocking blue gaze roved over her with deliberate disdain, taunting the tall man who stood behind her, still holding her to him.

Later, Charity intended to rake Luke Sterling over hot coals for making her appear so wanton and embarrassing her like this. Maybe she'd even boil him in oil, after she'd drenched him with honey and staked him over an anthill! For now, she figured she had few choices—either play along with Luke's deception and turn it to her own advantage, run screaming into the house and refuse to ever show her face again, or kill every man between here and the nearest convent, where she would seek solace.

Irrationally, she chose the former, her decision made when Masterson sneered and said, "I should have listened more closely to all the talk in town and not worried about your welfare, Mrs. Prindle. After all, they say a cat always lands on its feet."

"I didn't ask for your concern, sir," Charity retorted. "Furthermore, it takes a lot of nerve to sling mud at my reputation, when all the while you're living in the same house with a known prostitute and paying the rent!"

The shock on his face made her want to laugh. "How did you know about Annie?"

She shot him a full-blown smirk. "As you said, Sheriff, you should listen more closely to the talk going around town. All of Dodge has been snickering up their sleeve at you for nearly a year now. If you don't believe me, ask anyone. Ask your friend, the marshal."

"You deserve to be horsewhipped!" Pointing an accusing finger at Luke, Charity shouted at him in that unique smoke-and-cinders voice that sent tremors tripping up his spine.

"Me?" he asked innocently, backing away from her and ruining his attempt at righteousness with a wicked grin that emphasized the deep dimple in his left cheek. "What did I do?"

Matching him step for step, she stalked him across the yard, wagging that finger at him like a potential weapon. "You know what you did, you snake! I should pin your ears back and sew them fast to your head!"

Luke winced as she continued to march him backward across the barnyard. "I should truss you up and tickle the soles of your feet with a feather until you plead for mercy! I should skin you alive, inch by inch!"

Here she stopped and thought a moment. "I wonder if Mano knows how that's done properly—and if he'd be willing to teach me." Then she shrugged. "Oh, well. If he won't, I'll learn by trial and error, won't I?" By now, there was an evil glint in her bright eyes. "I can always start by pulling the hairs from your nostrils, one at a time."

The part about tickling with a feather didn't sound too bad to him, revised, of course. In fact, the more he considered it, the more intriguing it became—but pulling nose hairs? Now, that was entirely too cruel!

Throwing up his hands in self-defense, Luke exclaimed, "Now, Charity! I can explain, if you'd just give me a chance."

"You bet your Stetson you'll explain, mister! You did everything but swear on a stack of Bibles that you and I were sharing a bed! You deliberately besmirched my reputation, and I'll know why, or else!" Here, Charity was stretching the truth a little herself, for her name had been bandied about Dodge City ever since the attack. She felt justified in her comment, however, since not a word of that awful gossip had contained a grain of truth.

Luke had already heard a few dazzling examples of Charity's idea of "or else," and that was enough to convince him. If there was more, he wasn't up to hearing the continued listing until he'd braced himself a bit. "I really didn't mean to give that impression," he began. "Not at first, anyway. You were standin' to my right, and a little in front of me, if you'll recall, and that put you in exactly the wrong place if I'd had to draw my gun. You were blockin' my aim, Charity. I just wanted to move you to a more convenient spot, but I couldn't very well say that, could I?"

"That's it?" Fury lingered in her snapping azure eyes. "That's your entire explanation?"

"Well, no," he hedged. "I figured the two of them were here to fish for information, probably thinkin' you'd hired me to go after those killers for you. I didn't think you'd want them sniffin' out the whole truth of the matter. So when they jumped to the wrong conclusion, I saw it as the perfect smoke screen. People tend to see only what they want to, Charity, and if they think we're merely lovers, they'll be less apt to stumble across our real plans. The last thing we need is those two stickin' their noses into everything."

"Well, did you have to go to such extremes?" she asked in exasperation, her temper cooling just a bit. "You've made me look like a tart! I don't deserve that, though when you boil it all down and start pinning sins on a person, I suppose fornication is mild compared to murder. I may not be the fallen woman some folks would like to believe, but here I stand, planning to kill six men."

It was Sunday, and Charity had decided to cook chicken and dumplings. She made a bargain with

Luke. "If you and Mano can catch two hens for me, not my laying hens either, and kill them and pluck them, I'll probably have time to pick some strawberries and make a couple of fresh cream pies for dessert."

It was too tempting to pass up. The deal was made, and Charity headed for the strawberry patch, basket in hand. Luke went to corral Mano into helping him catch and clean those chickens.

A few minutes later, hearing a tremendous ruckus coming from the chicken pen, Charity's curiosity got the better of her. As she crept around the back of the house, so the men wouldn't catch sight of her, she stifled a giggle. From all the cackling and cursing she heard flying through the air, she could fairly well guess what she would see.

She was not far wrong. Chickens were jumping and flapping wildly in all directions, with Luke and Mano in hot pursuit. The air was thick with feathers and vile language, the squawking almost deafening.

"I got 'im! I got 'im! Hell! I missed him!" For a moment, it looked as if Luke had one of the slippery fowl cornered, but the hen eluded his grasping hands and flew right through his hair to escape. Though he managed to duck in time to avoid her sharp claws, his hat went spinning off his head and landed amid a wet glob of feathers.

Mano, on the other hand, had slipped in some fresh chicken droppings, and was now belly-down in the dirt. Luke made another grab at a passing bird, tripped over Mano's outstretched legs, and landed in a magnificent belly flop beside his cohort. "Oh, shit!" he groaned on a whosh of air from his lungs.

"That's about it," Mano agreed, picking up one palm and staring at the unsightly goo dripping from it. "Yuck! How does Charity stand these stupid, stinkin' birds?"

"Better yet, how does she ever catch them?"

"She probably waits until they go to sleep, then snatches 'em off their roost."

"You think so?"

Mano nodded. "Sure, but we can't let her show us up. Suppose we try sneakin' up on 'em? You from one side, and me from the other, workin' together."

"Sounds good to me."

Round two began. Again the chickens won. Though Mano's strategy sounded good, it had a few flaws. Hen after hen escaped them, until the last one scrambled away so abruptly that Mano and Luke bumped heads as they lunged for the bird.

"Ouch!"

"Dad-blast it!"

"Damn, you have a hard head!"

By now Charity was laughing so hard she could scarcely stand. Tears of mirth raced down her cheeks. Her ribs ached, and peals of her merry laughter rang in the air.

Luke stopped rubbing the knot on his head and listened in disbelief. Mano, too, seemed to freeze in place. As one, they turned to face her.

It was hard to maintain an indignant attitude when her delighted laughter was so precious and rare. It was worth gold, so surely it was worth a little humiliation. Still, she *was* laughing at *them!*

"You . . . you . . . you two looked so fun . . . ny!" She hiccuped, pointing a quaking finger at them. Then off she went in another fit of hilarity. "Why didn't you try the chicken catcher?" she asked between gales.

"The what?" they repeated after her like dim-witted twins.

"The chicken catcher." Still clutching her ribs, Charity went to the corner post of the gate to the pen. Hanging there, in plain sight, was a long iron rod, curved back upon itself at one end. "You hook this around their legs, and lo and behold, they're caught!"

Luke's glower made stormclouds look tame. "Why didn't you give us that handy bit of information about half an hour ago, pray tell?"

"Yeah," Mano grumbled. "You know I don't know anything about farmin'."

"Oh, that wouldn't have been half as much fun as watching the two of you practically chasing your own tails," she guffawed. She paused to catch her breath and ease the stitch in her side. "Honestly, I thought one or the other of you would know how to go about catching the hens, or at least have seen me do it."

"Uh, huh," Luke said in obvious disbelief. "I think you just wanted a good laugh at our expense." His gaze raked her face. There was definitely an impish twinkle in those summer-blue eyes. Then, as if for the first time, Luke took a really good look, and found himself suddenly speechless.

"Luke?" The puzzlement was clear in her voice. "Is something wrong? You're staring."

He knew he was making her nervous, but he just couldn't help himself. The transformation in her, from the dowdy widow he'd first met, was astounding! No longer did her cheekbones jut out so severely that they overshadowed the rest of her features. Though her huge blue eyes still dominated her face, there were no purple circles beneath them to detract from their loveliness. Healthy color bloomed in her cheeks and skin, her hair shone with new luster, her eyes danced with life.

Charity shifted nervously. Even Mano watched askance as Luke finally found his tongue. "When did you become so beautiful? How did you do it while I wasn't watching?"

Her expression was that of a frightened doe that

had suddenly caught scent of the hunter. "Beautiful?" She forced the word up through a frozen throat. Her eyes widened, her teeth worrying her bottom lip.

As she stared back at Luke with a strangely wounded look on her face, she reluctantly acknowledged of the changes that had crept up on her without her realization. The Charity standing before him now was a near match for that pretty little innocent she used to be, that naive woman-child of mere months ago. Most of the features were the same, if a little more careworn and stern. If there was something more wary, more solemn in her eyes; if her mouth turned down more wearily; if her face seemed a bit wiser, it was only to be expected, given all she had endured.

"Yes, beautiful," Luke repeated softly.

As his hand reached out to brush her golden hair, Charity stepped backward, almost falling in her haste to elude his touch. "Don't!" she cried. Her heart beat frantically in her chest.

Luke frowned, shaking his head as if denying what he was now witnessing. "Charity, I've held you while you cried. I've been both friend and teacher to you. We've fought and laughed together. You know I won't hurt you."

"You held me? When?"

"In the old shaman's tipi. Don't you remember?" He was treading shaking ground here, and knew it. Her dreams were a touchy subject with her. She was unsure of how much she had revealed, and was too embarrassed to ask.

"I remember you holding my hand during the dreams. I remember waking afterward and crying, but you weren't with me then."

"No, not then. Before. Charity, I know it all. So does Mano. We sat there with you and witnessed it all through your words, your screams."

Charity dared a swift look in Mano's direction. he merely nodded, his expression stern.

Her hands flew to cover her burning cheeks. "Oh, God! How awful!"

"I agree," Luke told her. "Oh, not that we know. Hell, we'd guessed most of it anyway. I mean, it's awful that you had to go through all that; awful that some men behave like animals; that innocent people like you and Johnny get caught in their way."

"I'm so ashamed that you and Mano had to hear all that!" She bowed her head and swallowed hard.

"Don't you dare take that attitude with me, Charity Prindle!" Luke's sharp tone pulled her gaze back to his. His emerald eyes flashed a warning. "You've done nothin' to be ashamed of, lady, and you know it! I know how angry you get when someone even hints that any of it might have been your fault, so don't pull that meek, hangdog face now. Stand up straight, hold that beautiful head up high, look the world straight in the eye, and tell anyone who doesn't like it to kiss your bu—"

"Luke!" she shrieked in dread anticipation.

"Buttons," he finished with a roguish grin that brought his dimple into prominence. His eyes danced with merriment as he watched flags of red reappear in her cheeks. "Why, Charity! You nasty little gal! What did you think I was gonna say?"

Now her own bright eyes dared his. "Exactly what you had in mind to say and didn't!"

"Luke is right, Charity," Mano put in. "Walk with pride." With a chuckle, he added, "A runt like you needs all the height she can get! Now, the two of you can catch those blasted birds. I have nobler things to do with my time—like talkin' to my horse." Whistling a jaunty tune, he sauntered off toward the barn.

Luke had to laugh at her indignant expression. "You are pretty short, you know." Then he said soberly, "Tell me why you backed away from me when I went to touch you." His eyes searched her face as he awaited her answer.

Her expression darkened. "You know why. I don't like being touched."

"Charity, I thought you were comin' to trust me. In all this time, have I ever given you cause to fear me?"

"No, but you didn't think I was beautiful then."

"And now that I realize how lovely you are, I'm gonna suddenly turn into some ravenin' beast and attack you? Come now, Charity. Do you really believe that?"

"I don't know. I only know that it makes things different somehow."

Again her teeth worried that lower lip, drawing his attention to it, making him suddenly want to taste it himself. She saw the desire flare in his eyes, and her own widened at the realization. He understood her unrest immediately. "Don't worry, Charity. I'm not some weak-minded animal who can't control his urges. I'm a man in full command of my own actions."

Luke could only pray that he was telling her the truth as he stepped closer and took her chin in his fingertips. At this moment, he wanted to kiss her more than he could ever recall wanting anything else. His other hand eased its way to the flat of her back, preventing her retreat. "One kiss, darlin'," he crooned softly. "That's all. Just one little kiss."

Charity stiffened in anticipation, her eyes growing wider and wider as his face came nearer, nearer, then blurred out of focus as his mouth softly brushed hers. His breath was a warm whisper forming her name. His lips moved lightly, feathering and tickling over hers, but even as she recognized his gentleness, her lungs seemed to freeze within her breast. Her heart was pounding madly, making it even more difficult to breathe! She broke out in a cold sweat, trembling violently, a silent scream rising up inside her.

Just as the panic became a living thing, just as Charity feared she might faint from lack of air, Luke raised his lips from hers. Realizing how shaken she was, he kept his arm about her to steady her until she was capable of standing alone once more. Her quivering hand rested on his shirtfront, directly above his heart, and beneath her palm she could feel his heart thundering every bit as hard as her own. Emerald eyes stared down into hers, adding to her turmoil. Those eyes spoke loudly of unfulfilled desires, of longings tightly reined.

"I know you're scared, Charity." He spoke softly, as if not to frighten her away. "I know you want to run and hide from this, but I also think you have more spunk than that. I'll try to be patient and not rush you. I promise I'll never bring you pain—only pleasure, if you let me. Someday soon I want to hold you, to kiss you—to make love with you, when you're ready to let yourself go that far."

For a fleeting moment, before he'd touched her, Charity had dared to hope that, just this once, her trust in him would be enough to conquer her fears. And afterward, there had been a scant instant when she'd wished the reality of the embrace hadn't been so frightening, when she'd regretted not being able to respond to him differently. But the images of agony burned into her brain and body had been too powerful to be so easily defeated.

Fighting through the lingering fear, Charity whispered shakily, "You're right, I am scared. Horrified. The moment I feel a man's hand upon me, my blood turns to ice. I get sick inside, and I want to crawl away and bury myself far from the pain. I want to scream with terror. That is as plain as I can say it, as truthful as I can be with you. I honestly don't know if there will ever come a day when I won't be frightened half to death of a man's touch—even yours."

"I know they hurt you," he answered low. "I know you can't help flinchin' away when I touch you, that you don't mean to do it. I understand that, and I think, in time, it will go away. If you allow it. If you want it badly enough. If you try hard enough and long enough. All I'm askin' is that you let me help you try. Let me help you heal."

It took supreme effort to turn and walk away from her. With every step he took, he felt her eyes burning into his back.

15

As he stood in the dark shadows at the edge of the barn, Luke's eyes were drawn toward the lighted kitchen windows. At this very minute, Charity was in there, naked and up to her neck in hot water. He knew that for certain, because he'd been the one to haul the buckets inside for her so that she could take a bath. Now he was lurking about like some randy goat, puffing away on a cigar and letting his own imagination torture him with images of her nude, water-glistening body.

Luke sighed, and gazed up at the star-filled sky, as if searching for a sign—or help. Deep inside, something told him his troubles were just beginning. It wasn't just lust that was eating at him. If it were that simple, one rousing trip to the nearest cathouse would solve all his problems. At least it would relieve some of his tension.

No, his feelings toward Charity were more complex than this burning desire in his gut. Somewhere along the line, he'd come to really like the lady, which was as much a surprise to him as discovering a lovely face and form hidden beneath all that grief and widow's garb. He'd never, in all his years, found a woman he truly liked and respected—until now.

And that scared the devil out of him! Probably every bit as much as he had frightened her with that chaste kiss he'd forced on her the other day. Since then, she'd been as skittish as a cat in a room full of rocking chairs, casting leery looks at him from huge blue eyes. And though that single kiss had been more innocent than he could recall sharing with any other woman, his desire for her had grown.

Given the ordeal she'd survived, Luke could well understand her fears; but understanding didn't mean he liked the situation, or accepted it. For some reason, her intense fright only made him want to help her overcome it. He wanted to be the one to restore her faith in men. At the same time, he had this incredible need to protect her from anything that could hurt her—including herself.

What had started out as pity toward her was now respect. Her grief had touched him, as had her steadfast loyalty to her dead husband's memory. It still amazed him to meet a woman who had truly loved her man, as Charity so obviously had. Too, he had to admire the way she never wavered from her goal of avenging John's murder, how she worked long and hard to prepare herself to meet that ultimate challenge. Her faithfulness and honesty were in direct contrast to everything he'd ever believed about women.

Then there were those unexpected, caring gestures of hers, like the day when she'd brought a special supper to the barn for him after he'd made such a horse's ass of himself; and that surprise birthday celebration. His perceptions of her had taken another turn then. He really didn't know quite what to make of his confused feelings toward her, or what to do about them. He only knew he enjoyed being with her in a way that was far different from anything he'd known with other women. He felt a need to help her in any way he could. And he wanted her with an urgency that bordered on desperation.

A flicker of movement drew his attention back to the kitchen window, and Luke nearly swallowed his tongue as he saw her bare silhouette outlined briefly, clearly, on the window shade. The image was gone in an instant, but his body had already responded with alacrity.

"Damn!" he murmured, tossing the cigar to the ground and grinding it viciously beneath his boot. "Maybe I'd better think about takin' that trip into town after all. She's scared enough already without havin' me pantin' after her like some slobberin' dog."

One glance toward the front of his britches, and she'd read his thoughts as if he'd shouted them. He certainly didn't want to frighten her any more than she was already. Not now. Not when he needed to prove to her that he could be trusted to keep his own desires in check. And these days, being anywhere near her was enough to make his blood boil.

Charity was in the kitchen alone, fixing breakfast and expecting Luke and Mano at any moment. Only half-awake this morning, she had to force herself to concentrate on the bacon hissing and spitting in the pan before her, or she was sure to burn it. As it was, she'd already boiled the coffee over and dropped an egg on the floor.

She was so busy concentrating on her cooking that her sleep-fogged mind failed to alert her to the slight squeak of the kitchen door—or to the footsteps creeping stealthily behind her. Without warning, a burly arm clamped tightly around her neck. The point of a knife poked warningly into her ribs.

Her startled shriek only halfway to her lips, Charity froze. Even before he spoke, in some remote corner of her mind Charity knew this was not Luke or Mano testing her. Icy droplets of fear dotted her forehead as she stood motionless, waiting, praying that this breath wouldn't be her last.

"I come for my money, you old biddy!" The growl came close to her ear, and Charity thought she might faint from the stink of his breath. "Nobody cheats Joe Foley out of what's due him!"

Just knowing who it was helped. Charity's mind began to function again, her training overriding her fear. Her hands and arms were free. Before she had time to wonder if this maneuver would work or get her killed, she brought one hand up to the arm that ringed her neck. The other reached behind her own head to grab a handful of Foley's greasy hair. Twisting, she bent sharply forward, folding herself from the waist, knees bent as Mano had taught her. At the same time, she used her elbow to deflect the knife. Better a cut arm than a punctured lung, any day!

Abruptly, the unsuspecting bounty hunter found himself tossed over the tiny woman's head. He landed on his back, the air gushing from him as he hit the floor with a thud. The woman's wild scream still rang in his ears. Before he could catch his breath or gather his wits, pain stabbed through his fingers; his knife fell from his numb grasp. Then the steel of his own weapon kissed his bare throat, and Foley had to fight the urge to swallow, lest he hurry his own way to hell.

"Move, and you die!" she hissed, her voice as cold as a winter wind. "If you even blink, it will be the last thing you ever do."

They stayed frozen for what seemed forever, the bounty hunter sprawled on the floor and Charity poised over him with the knife blade at his throat. Foley's eyes were watering with the effort not to blink by the time boots pounded up the porch steps and into the kitchen. Charity never moved at the sound, never looked up from the man's mean eyes, did not ease the knife away as Foley had hoped, thus giving him another chance at her. She sat just as she was, daring him to try something, looking almost disappointed when he didn't.

"Charity!" Luke's roar nearly shook the rafters.

"Mr. Foley decided to give us a surprise visit this morning," she rasped from her place on the floor.

She waited until Luke had his Colt leveled at Foley's chest, then slowly removed the knife and backed away from her victim. Grabbing the edge of the table, she pulled herself shakily to her feet. "He was a mite put out when I refused to pay him, and now he's come to try once more to collect, as he so pointedly put it, 'what's due him.' "

Then the whole, terrifying situation hit her, and she was shaking so badly that her teeth were almost chattering. When Mano stepped close to comfort her, she shied away, her eyes as wide and wary as those of a spooked filly. An agitated movement of her hands told them she wanted this man out of her house.

"What do you say we give the man 'what's due him' then, Mano?" Luke suggested, his eyes spitting green fire. A fury such as he had rarely known raged through him, that this animal had dared to threaten Charity. Grabbing hold of the front of Foley's filthy buckskin shirt, Luke yanked him to his feet and gave him a rough shove toward the door.

Mano turned to follow, then asked instead, "Are you all right now, Charity?" She nodded, but did not answer. "Are you sure?" he pressed. Again that nod, as if she were afraid that if she opened her mouth she would begin to scream and never stop.

"Don't come out to the barn for a while." Silently, her eyes questioned him. "Believe me, you don't want to know," he told her. Beneath his stolid features lurked the same anger she'd seen on Luke's face. "Just stay up at the house, and unless your life is threatened, don't come near the barn."

Charity never knew what they did with Foley. She didn't ask, and neither Mano nor Luke volunteered any explanation of what went on in the barn that day. Without being told, she knew the bounty hunter was dead. Since the moment Luke had marched him out the door, she hadn't seen a sign of Joe Foley; but his horse now occupied a stall in her barn.

Charity had passed the first true test of her ability to meet an enemy and use her training. Though she'd been shaken by the encounter with Foley, she hadn't panicked, as Luke had feared she might. She was as ready as she'd ever be to go after John's killers.

The following day, Luke told her that he was going into town. "I've got to get supplies and have our empty ammunition cartridges reloaded at Zimmerman's store. We'll be headin' out day after tomorrow."

"In that case, I could use a few things from town myself," she said, trying to ignore the way her heart had begun thudding at Luke's announcement that it would only be a matter of hours before they began tracking their quarry.

Nodding agreeably, Luke said, "Make a list, and I'll get them for you."

He was fairly certain Charity would not want to be seen with him in Dodge. There was no telling how much damage to her reputation had already been incurred from Masterson's visit to the farm. None of her friends had visited since then to inquire about her, and the last time Mano had gone to town for supplies, he hadn't gleaned much information along those lines, though he'd made it a point to stop at the doctor's office to relay greetings from Charity.

"I'd rather go with you," Charity surprised him by saying. "There are some things I need to buy for myself, things I don't want you purchasing."

Luke grinned, his dimple flashing. "Ah, but I wouldn't mind selecting your unmentionables, sweet Charity."

She politely declined, hiding the smile that tempted her own lips at his teasing. "No, thank you. I think I can manage well enough on my own."

In the end, all three of them rode into Dodge City together. As they made their way down the streets at an easy pace, Charity felt curious eyes turning their way. This was the first time she'd worn her split riding skirts away from home, and she was particularly conscious of the fact that she was riding astride. Well, gossips be damned! If they wanted to talk, let them! Though she was certain her face must look as if someone had set it on fire, she adopted a casual attitude, surprising more than a few people with her polite greetings, and garnering more pleasant replies than she'd hoped for.

At one point, old Mrs. Spencer toddled out to the edge of the street, pointed her cane at Charity, and called out in a wobbly voice, "Nice to see you lookin' so good, Charity. Quite an improvement over the last time I seen ya."

When they turned onto Front Street, Mano left them, telling them he would meet them later at the Dodge House restaurant. Charity agreed without question, privately wondering if he was off to find Sue.

Luke was about to ask if Charity could manage her errands safely on her own, thus freeing her from his presence, when she surprised him again by asking, "Where do we go first, Luke? Do we hitch the horses and walk from here?"

When he just stared at her rather stupidly, she prompted, "Well?"

"Uh, Charity," he muttered, feeling extremely uncomfortable, "are you sure you wouldn't rather do your shoppin' on your own? Maybe you shouldn't be seen associatin' with me so openly."

"Don't be silly! That was just when I wanted to hire you secretly and not have everyone know about it. Since Sheriff Masterson has successfully blown that plan to the winds, I don't see any need for sneaking around, do you? Besides, we don't owe explanations to anyone. Let them die of their own curiosity, for all I care."

"Then you don't mind bein' seen with me?" he questioned, that peculiar note sounding in his voice again, and tugging at something in Charity's heart.

"Of course not. Why should I?"

"Lots of reasons, two bein' your reputation as a widow lady and mine as a gunfighter."

Charity sighed. "You know, Luke, since the attack I've started to learn a few things about people and reputations and gossip. A good name is a wonderful thing to have, but it's not everything, and it's not always lasting, no matter how perfect you try to be. Gossip can spoil an unblemished reputation irreparably, through no fault of the owner of that spotless life. Once it's tarnished, that ideal glow is forever gone."

"Your point?" he prodded.

"My point is, my spotless reputation was destroyed last fall. It cannot be redeemed and shined to its former angelic sheen. And, frankly, I don't give a royal damn. People can either accept me and care for me the way I am, whether I be saint or sinner, nice or nasty—or they can let me be. Friends don't stop liking you just because you develop a few faults, or behave oddly, or do a few things wrong, or they aren't really friends, are they?"

She didn't wait for a reply. "What I do is my own business, as long as it doesn't cause anyone else any harm—except those deserving of it," she qualified. "And who I choose for friends is my business alone. I consider you and Mano my friends, and anyone who doesn't like it can just . . ." Here she paused, gave him an impish grin, and concluded smugly, ". . . kiss my buttons!"

It took a moment for her words to register. Then he threw back his head and laughed. "Really feelin' your oats today, aren't you, Charity?" On impulse, he offered his arm to her, and when her small hand nestled willingly there, he could have burst with pride. Together they strutted down the street, defying anyone to challenge them.

He helped her choose her new saddlebags. While she dithered over bolts of cloth and ladies' underdrawers and such, he selected tobacco and did some private shopping of his own in another section of the store. Together, they decided on the best leather wax for waterproofing their boots, saddles, and saddlebags, and bought oilcloth for her bedroll.

While he went on to Zimmerman's, Charity dropped in at the lawyer's office and had him legalize a copy of a will she had written up. It stated that if she should die, her farm was not to be sold, or the proceeds divided between her brother and sister. Rather, the farm was to be equally divided between Mano and Luke Sterling, if both survived her. If only one survived, the farm would be wholly the other's, to do with as he wished. If neither man survived her, the property or its profits were to be used for the betterment of orphans, under strict supervision to ensure that the funds were not mismanaged by disreputable persons.

Sue joined the three of them for lunch, and Charity informed her small gathering of friends what she had done. She wanted Mano and Luke to be prepared, and Sue to know about it in the event that anyone objected. At present, only the three of them protested, especially Sue, who had just now learned of Charity's intentions to go after the killers.

"Oh, Charity, how can you even think of doing such a thing?" she exclaimed in genuine dismay. "You're going to get yourself killed!"

"I hope not, but that's why I wrote out the will," Charity conceded.

"Well, that was wasted effort on your part," Luke put in. "I didn't teach you everything I know just to sit back and watch you die. Besides, I don't know what the hell I'd do with a farm!"

"Neither do I," Mano muttered, frowning at her.

"You could always sell it."

"And you could learn to shut your mouth before I paddle your behind for bein' so blamed stupid and stubborn," Luke warned, though he was inordinately pleased that she would include care for orphans in her will.

His blunt command earned a startled look from Sue, which she abruptly transferred to Charity. Mano just sat there grinning.

"There's that silver tongue again," Charity chided, all sugar and sand. "Sterling certainly seems to be the right name for you, doesn't it?"

16

THE first rays of the rising sun were painting the plains soft hues of pink and gold as Charity and Luke rode out of the farmyard together. They were on their way at last, all the last-minute arrangements for their departure having been completed.

Charity hadn't slept much the night before, and when she'd come down to breakfast Luke had commented on the circles under her eyes. "You look like you've been dragged through a knothole backwards," he'd told her frankly. Then, eyeing her speculatively, he'd asked, "Havin' second thoughts, Charity?"

Third, fourth, hundredth thoughts, was perhaps more accurate. Worries had plagued her throughout the endless night. Was she truly ready for this? Would Mano be able to keep the farm running smoothly in their absence? Was she off on a fool's errand, trying to track down six killers and wreak revenge?

As much as she was coming to trust Luke, was going off alone with him like leaping from the frying pan into the fire? After all, he'd warned her that he desired her, that he wanted her. How long would he respect her wishes and her fears? Moreover, she'd had the most disturbing dream. In it Luke had been making love to her and, incredulously, she had actually been encouraging his passionate caresses, literally begging for more!

In the end, her soul's demand for justice had won out over all her lingering anxieties. Coupled with an odd excitement and a heretofore untapped thirst for adventure, it spurred her on. Not that she was gleefully looking forward to confronting her attackers face-to-face and killing them, but she firmly believed the world would be as relieved as she was once it was rid of these vermin.

Surreptitiously, she touched the tiny pink ribbon in her breast pocket. It had become her personal charm for good fortune and continued faith, just as Luke was a source of security and courage.

They were to begin their search just south of Dodge City, and follow the cattle trails into Texas, on the chance that the band of outlaws was once again thieving along that route. In each small town and every cattle drive they encountered, they would ask questions, hoping for information leading to the six men they sought.

"It might take weeks, maybe months, before we find even one of them," Luke warned her. "We may end up chasin' our own tails."

"I don't care if it takes years," she informed him, swallowing a yawn and pulling herself upright in the saddle. "I haven't waited this long, or worked this hard, to see those animals get away. I'll eat beans and sleep on the ground and ride this horse till she drops, but I won't give up until they've all paid with their life's blood."

"Fine. I just wanted to remind you of what you have ahead of you, because you and that mare will probably both have calluses on your backsides before we're through."

* * *

They spent that night on the prairie, camped out under the stars. It was the first time Charity had slept outdoors since the attack, and she was more than a little nervous. All her life, even on the trip west to Kansas from Pennsylvania, she had always had some type of roof over her head at bedtime, even if it meant sleeping half-upright on the hard bench seat of a noisy, dirty train.

She sat as close to the fire as possible, though the heat from the campfire was almost too hot on this warm, clear June evening, and tried to ignore the sounds of the night creatures stirring outside the small circle of light. Shadows seemed to dance just beyond her vision. Every sound was magnified. Every inch of her flesh itched as if something were crawling on it. Her stomach felt queasy, and she knew it wasn't merely from their simple supper of beans and bacon.

For the tenth time in as many minutes, she scratched. A spark flew from the fire, and she flinched. One of the horses stomped, and she nearly leaped from her skin.

Across the small fire from her, Luke watched and sighed. The flickering flames revealed the pallor of her face and the fear building in her huge blue eyes. "You're as jittery as a June bug in a hot skillet," he told her. "You want to tell me why?"

Even his soft voice made her jump. "I don't like sleeping outdoors," she confessed, shooting a frown at him.

"You'll get used to it."

She shook her head and swallowed hard. "I don't think so." Reluctantly, she added, "The only time I spent the whole night outside was the night Johnny died."

"You'll get used to it," Luke repeated gruffly, wanting to offer comfort but knowing that now was not the time. Just now she needed to face her lingering fears and conquer them headlong. She needed to build her inner strength, not give in to weakness. "We'll be sleepin' out more often than not."

He watched as her teeth began to gnaw her lower lip, and fought the urge to pull her into his arms and kiss her until she forgot her fears, forgot everything but him.

"If we keep the fire burning, will the animals stay away?" she questioned, her voice sounding very small.

"More than likely." *At least the four-legged variety*, Luke added silently to himself.

"What about snakes?" she questioned with a shudder. "They seek the heat, don't they?"

He smiled. He couldn't help it. "I don't think you have to worry about snakes just yet, Charity. The ground hasn't warmed up enough for them to be active at night."

"Oh. Well, good."

"If you're really that nervous about it, you can always share my bedroll with me," he offered roguishly, grinning at her.

"And trade one kind of snake for another? No, thank you," she retorted. Mentally, she weighed the dangers and decided she'd rather chance sharing her blankets with a rattlesnake than a man—any man.

A full day of riding and the lack of sleep the night before finally took their toll. Even her sore muscles and the lumpy ground beneath her bedroll were not enough to keep her eyelids from sliding closed. The last thing she heard before sleep claimed her was Luke's soft whisper. "Go to sleep, Charity. I'll protect you." She had no choice but to trust that he would.

Since their trip to the Arapaho shaman, Charity's nightmares had diminished. No longer did she live in fear of those dreaded visions invading her dreams. Tonight was the exception. Tonight, with strange sounds all around her, with the breeze wafting across her face like stealthy fingers in the dark, she dreamed.

She watched, trembling, as the men crept up on her as she lay sleeping. Their hands reached out to touch her. So many hands—dirty hands—dripping blood from their fingertips. A scream rose in her throat and froze there, threatening to choke her. Her body refused to register her mind's commands to move, to jump up and run from the danger. Rough fingers grabbed her, bruising her tender skin, tearing at her hair. They loomed over her, threatening shadows without faces. But she didn't need to see their features to know who they were, to see those leering grins.

Then one of them leaned closer, his breath fanning her cheek, and she braced herself for the searing pain to come. The scream rose from deep within and tore loose, erupting in the night. At last her limbs obeyed her will, and suddenly she was kicking and clawing with all her might, her only thought to free herself from these dark demons.

"Charity! Charity! For God's sake, woman, wake up! It's just a dream, darlin'. Just a dream."

She didn't know how long he'd been calling out to her, but Luke's voice finally penetrated her terror. Desperately, blindly, she reached out to him, wanting to believe his words, but caught between sleep and consciousness, afraid of what was real and what was not. Her screams dwindled to hoarse whimpers, her breath coming in harsh gasps, her entire body trembling uncontrollably.

As he continued to speak, softly now, trying to calm her, she gathered the courage to lift her tear-laden lashes. Relief flooded her as he filled her vision. But just as quickly, her eyes darted swiftly past him, searching for the shadowy forms that had filled her dreams, seeking proof that they truly were not there, lurking, waiting to pounce from the darkness.

"It's okay, Charity. You're safe. Believe me."

A final shudder shook her, though the quaking did not abate entirely. Shame brought a rush of color to her cheeks. "I'm sorry!" she rasped. "It was the dream again."

"I know."

Suddenly she became aware that he was holding her close, realized that she had literally thrown herself into his arms, begging safety. Embarrassed more than ever, she attempted to push back from him, but he refused to let her go. His big hands lightly stroked her hair as he murmured, "Shhh, little darlin'. Just stay still. I'm not gonna do anything but hold you until you feel safe again."

"Will I ever feel safe, while those murderers run free?"

It was a question neither of them could answer and Luke didn't try. He merely held her, willing her trembling to cease, rocking her in his warm embrace.

When she'd finally calmed, he eased both of them onto the bedroll, snuggled her close against his chest, and covered them with her blanket. Though she voiced no immediate protest, he felt her stiffen. "Go back to sleep, Charity. We've got a long day ahead of us, and we've got to make an early start."

"The fire's almost out. Shouldn't you put some more wood on it?" she asked hesitantly.

"It's all right for now."

"Are you sure?"

"Positive. Besides, haven't you ever noticed how much brighter the stars seem without any other lights around? Look at them up there, twinklin' like diamonds scattered on a blanket of black velvet."

Charity couldn't remember when she'd last taken

the time to appreciate the splendor of the starlit sky. Now, lying with her head pillowed on Luke's broad shoulder, she stared upward in awe. Truly, it was a marvelous sight, one of God's most magnificent wonders. "They are beautiful," she conceded.

His arms were warm, incredibly gentle for all their strength, his shoulder wide enough to cradle her head quite comfortably, as if it had been created for just this purpose. The steady beat of his heart beneath her fingertips was subtly soothing. With a final shaky sigh, she let herself relax fully against him.

That small gesture of trust brought a smile to Luke's lips. "See that bright one there?" Her gaze followed his pointing finger. "That's the North Star. Sailors and travelers use it to guide by. Now follow the line of stars from it. See how they form a dipper? They call that the Little Dipper."

His voice droned on, lulling her with its deep resonance. "There are others that form lions and bears and such, so I've heard, but I've never been able to pick them out or make much sense of them. To me, they always look like somethin' else. See there? Doesn't that look like a lady's lace shawl? And there, that looks like a king's crown, don't you think?"

By the time he pointed out a dragon, she was fast asleep in his arms. With a satisfied sigh of his own, Luke closed his eyes and drifted into a light slumber, secure in the knowledge that her smallest stirring, or the slightest noise that did not belong to the night, would awaken him.

If Charity had thought Kansas flat and devoid of trees, Oklahoma was worse by far. Miles and miles of nothing but dry prairie stretched before them, saved from ugliness only by the spring flowers now in full bloom. This was Indian territory, and she could well understand why the United States government had deemed it worthless and deeded it to the hapless tribes.

While Kansas was fast becoming a wheat farmer's dream, Oklahoma had not as easily lured the plow to its realms. As yet, only the hardiest souls had attempted to reap harvests from this section of the plains. Towns were few and far between, and then it was almost inappropriate to call the seedy collection of saloons and shacks towns. Each was merely a rest stop along the cattle route from Texas to Dodge City, a place for a cowhand to buy a meal, a bed, a bottle, and a woman for a night and be on his way with the next sunrise.

In Charity's estimation, the cowhands were being robbed. Any camp cook worth his salt could produce a better meal than the dirty little eateries in these tumbledown villages. The beds were bug-infested, and she suspected the town harlots were little better. The only decent bargain was the whiskey, and even it was watered down.

"Is Texas like this?" she asked, her nose wrinkled in disgust. She and Luke were eating supper in a tiny café near their hotel, the only hotel in the tiny town of Sharod. She'd ordered stew, but she wasn't certain just what the greasy mess on her plate actually contained, and she was afraid to ask.

Luke's steak was so tough he could scarcely chew it, and what he supposed were potatoes were charred beyond recognition. "Parts of Texas are pretty barren, yes," he answered. "But Texas is a darn big place, darlin', and it has everything from cotton to cactus. Dependin' on where you go, you can find mountains, desert, swamps, or seacoast."

With a gesture toward the muddy liquid that passed for coffee, he said, "You should have them put a shot of whiskey in that. If nothin' else, it might make your food set a little better in your stomach."

Though she declined, his suggestion had some

merit, especially when she considered that she'd had to clean the remnants of someone else's meal from her fork before she could use it. Didn't Doc Nelson sometimes use whiskey to sterilize his instruments?

"I hope the next town at least has a bath," she complained. "You'd think someone in this godforsaken snake pit would own a tin tub I could rent. My horse smells better than I do."

He sent her a grin across the table. "I think I'd have noticed if you smelled that bad, though we could both do with a good scrubbin'. We should be comin' up on the Washita River sometime tomorrow, and if the cattle don't have it all stirred up, we can clean up a bit there, maybe wash out a shirt or two."

This was the closest either of them had come to mentioning the fact that since her nightmare, Charity's bedroll always butted up next to his whenever they had to sleep out in the open. Though she usually fell asleep with several inches separating them, never inviting his touch, sometime in the night he always gathered her into the warm, sheltering curve of his body, offering his shoulder as her pillow.

After all these months without Johnny, and all she'd endured, it was disconcerting to awaken in Luke's embrace. Perhaps most perplexing was that it also felt so right, so good, like coming home after a long absence. Without a word between them, they would rise and start their day as if it were perfectly normal for a man and woman to share a bed with neither benefit of vows nor carnal intimacy.

Tonight, however, they were staying in Sharod, and she would have her own bed in her own room next to his. When they'd finished eating, he walked her back to the hotel, checking her room and the lock on her door before leaving to make the rounds of the town's drinking and gambling establishments. "Keep your gun handy, and don't let anyone in but me," he warned. "I'll be back as soon as I can. I'll knock three times on the wall when I'm in for the night."

It was their signal, so that Charity would know he was back and not worry if she heard noises coming from his room. Luke would knock three times on the connecting wall, and she would answer with two of her own, to reassure him that she was all right. Though he was usually gone for hours, she rarely slept until he returned, regardless of how tired she was.

It wasn't fear for her own safety alone that made Charity so tense during these lone vigils, though she felt uneasy by herself in these small ugly hotel rooms that all looked so drab. It was not knowing exactly where Luke was, or what trouble he might have encountered, that troubled her most. In the short time they'd been traveling together, she'd become used to having him near, and she didn't know what she would do if anything happened to him now.

She told herself it was silly to fret over him. The man was a gunslinger, and fully capable of protecting himself. He'd done so for many years on his own, without her to act the mother hen. Still, she couldn't help remembering what he'd said about Dandy shooting him in the back. It irritated her that Luke neatly sidestepped further inquiries about the incident, and she couldn't stop worrying that something like that might happen again. Just sitting, waiting, and wondering was a tremendous trial to her patience. She'd much rather be out there with him, fully aware of what was happening at every turn.

Tonight was no exception. As Charity waited anxiously, the minutes ticked by slowly, each hour stretching into eternity. She sat rigidly on the straight-back chair, her nerves tightly strung, her Colt within easy reach. Fully dressed, she sternly refused the dubious comfort of the lumpy bed until he returned. Only then would she douse the dim lamp, strip down to her camisole and pantalettes, and allow herself a few hours of restless sleep.

Despite her efforts, her eyelids were drooping when she heard the heavy tread of boots halt outside her door. Abruptly alert, her heart pounding, she snatched up her gun, aiming it toward the door. Caution kept her silent. If it were Luke, he would call out to her, but never before had he approached her door without first signaling on the wall.

As she watched, the doorknob turned. The warped boards of the door creaked as they took the would-be intruder's weight. When the lock held, thunderous knocking accompanied the rattling of the knob, and a drunken voice whined, "Come on, Lucy, honey. Watcha doin'? You ain't s'posed to lock yer customers out."

Moments later, a woman hissed loudly, "Jess! You ornery critter! You're knockin' on the wrong door! Get yer carcass and yer money down here, b'fore you git shot fer wakin' ev'rybody up!"

As Jess stumbled down the hall in search of his pleasure, the breath whooshed out of Charity's chest. Her entire body wilted like day-old lettuce, and her hand trembled as she carefully set aside her Colt once more.

Meanwhile, in a rowdy saloon just down the street, Luke was nursing a shot of whiskey and casually questioning the bartender about his recent customers. As was his habit, his gaze constantly swept the smoky room, noting everyone who entered and left through the bat-wing doors—and those who wandered upstairs, returning a short time later minus the few dollars charged by one of the haggard barmaids for a few minutes of pleasurable entertainment.

This was his tenth stop of the night, with little to

show for his efforts, if he discounted the invitations of several 'ladies of the evening' to spend the night in their beds, offers which he had promptly declined, with scarcely a smile to soften his refusal. Of course, he wisely saved the rejections until after he'd smoothly determined that none of them knew anything of value to him.

With a grunt of disgust, he downed the last of his drink and shouldered his way through the swinging doors. Once again the nightly rounds of barrooms and gambling houses had been a waste of time. He was tired, it was late, and he knew Charity would be unable to rest until he returned to the hotel.

It was an odd but not unpleasant feeling to know that someone would be waiting up for him. Although they would be sleeping in separate rooms, and although her thoughts would no doubt center on whether he'd gleaned any useful information— rather than on his personal safety—it made him smile to think that she would be there when he got back. It was small compensation for not having her next to him on his bedroll, for being forced to wait to hold her in his arms once more.

By the time Luke finally returned, Charity had worked herself into a fine state. Returning his knocks with hearty thumps of her own, she then marched into the hall and pounded on his door. "Sterling. We have to talk. Now," she demanded, pushing him aside when he answered her summons, and striding past him into the room.

He questioned her actions with an amused quirk of his eyebrow. "Missed me that much, did you?" he taunted. "I'm flattered."

"Don't be," she snapped. "I'm thoroughly vexed right now, and I don't mind telling you that I'm sick of waiting around like a faithful dog and worrying myself into a stew while you traverse saloons and amuse yourself each evening with cards and drink.

And cheap women," she added, glaring at the smear of lip rouge on his jawline.

He dared to grin at her. "Jealousy becomes you, darlin'."

"This has nothing to do with jealousy," she huffed, facing him like a banty hen itching for a fight. "It has to do with the fact that I sit twiddling my thumbs, doing very little to aid our cause, a venture that is primarily my concern, I might remind you. From now on, wherever you go, I go too, be it a dance hall, a barbershop, or a gambling hall."

"Or a bathhouse?" he suggested wryly, reminding her of the day she'd been so determined to speak with him that she'd trapped him in his bath. "Charity, most of those places are barely safe for men, let alone a woman. You'd chance puttin' yourself in the same danger you encountered at the hands of those six murderers. They aren't the only beasts roamin' the earth; there are plenty more just like them who would relish a temptin' little morsel like you."

"I realize that. I'm not stupid. And I didn't learn to shoot merely to sit around and let you take all the risks. I'll carry my gun and the knife Mano gave me."

"No."

"Yes. I'll even disguise myself, if that will help ease your mind."

"Forget it."

"I'll make myself so ugly even you won't want to be seen with me," she said, "but I refuse to spend another endless night wondering what is happening and worrying myself witless."

"You really don't have an ounce of sense if you think I'll take you into those places with me," he argued.

"Fine. Have it your way. I'll go by myself then. Just don't be surprised when you look up from your poker game and see the 'Widow Prindle' at your elbow.''

''Don't press me on this, Charity, or I'll be forced to lock you in your room at night,'' he threatened.

''I'll scream the roof off until someone comes to let me out,'' she warned.

''Not if you're gagged and trussed up like a Christmas turkey,'' he answered with a smug smirk.

They stood glaring at each another in a showdown of wills. Finally she said softly, ''Some man tried to get into my room tonight while you were gone. He mistook my room for another woman's. You do realize that if he'd succeeded, they'd be mopping his blood off the floor and I'd probably be sitting in the sheriff's office right now.''

At her words, spoken so calmly, he envisioned the scene that might have ensued. Righteous anger vied with jealous rage, making his blood run cold in his veins. In that moment he knew he'd kill any man who dared to touch her.

''Think about it, Luke,'' she told him, noting his clenched fists and the angry set of his jaw. ''The risk of danger is there, whether I'm here alone or at your side in some saloon. Wouldn't it be better for both of us to know exactly where the other is at all times?''

With that, Charity left him to his thoughts and returned to her own room to make up a list of the items she would need to purchase for her suggested disguise. Included in the growing column, written in her delicate script, were several items that would send Luke's eyebrows straight into his hairline—among them 'net stockings' and 'satin garter.'

17

THEY crossed the Red River into Texas just north of the town of Wichita Falls. Again Charity was doomed to disappointment as she eyed the muddy water. A bath would be impossible. She was beginning to doubt she would ever be clean again.

Noting her crestfallen expression, Luke told her, "If we keep a steady pace, we can be in Wichita Falls in a couple of hours. You can get a bath there for sure, though I can't help wishin' the area around the falls wasn't such a favored site for campin'."

"Why?" she questioned.

He grinned devilishly. " 'Cause then we could bath there, standing stark naked under the rush of water."

"You're joshing me."

"Nope." He shook his dark head, still smiling, his green eyes agleam.

"Naked? In the daylight? Right out in the open?" Shock laced her voice.

"Yep."

"You're indecent! Absolutely decadent!"

"I'm a man who likes his pleasures, sweetheart," he told her smoothly. "And someday you'll experi-

224

ence all of those pleasures with me. Mark my words, Charity.''

''Is that a threat?''

''No, it's a promise. One I mean to keep, to myself and to you.''

Though Wichita Falls was only three years old, it was already a thriving town. It had a bank, several stores, the inevitable numerous saloons, and three hotels. Best of all, Charity was at long last able to order up a hot, steaming tub of bathwater. The hotel owner's wife also offered her the use of her laundry room, for which Charity was thoroughly grateful.

Luke left her in Martha Whiting's capable hands, with a warning not to leave the hotel until he returned. Delaying his own bath, he rode a few miles outside of town to the site where several cattle drives were currently camped.

Meanwhile, Charity and Martha struck up an immediate friendship. With the older woman's delighted assistance, Charity managed to acquire most of the items for her saloon girl costume—all without stepping foot from the premises. In her younger years, Mrs. Whiting had worked in a tavern and had kept a few of her favorite outfits.

After briefly explaining her quest for Johnny's murderers, Charity found Martha in full agreement with her need for the disguise. ''You certainly can't strut into a saloon dressed like an average upstandin' female, that's for sure, dearie. They'd rush you right out again, for fear you'd start sermonizin' and ruin their good time. Only loose women and barmaids are allowed to see such goings-on. If you want to stay long enough to gather any information at all, you're gonna have to fit in with the rest of the gals. 'Course, I imagine that handsome gunslinger you're travelin' with might have a few things to say about your plans. Or have you already discussed them with him?''

"Lands, no! And you're right. No doubt he'll have a glorious fit, so I'm not going to say a word to him until I absolutely must. In fact, if the chance presents itself, my best bet will be to time my first exhibition at a critical moment, when there is simply no opportunity to change back into my usual attire. Then he'll be forced to go along with my idea.''

"Good luck, sugar," Martha offered with a chuckle. "You're gonna need it.''

By the time Luke returned, Charity was innocently helping her new friend wash the dinner dishes.

"Charity, did you get everything done?" Luke asked in lieu of a proper greeting.

His voice held an undercurrent of excitement, and his face was unusually animated. His eyes glowed like emeralds in the sunlight. His stance was one of barely restrained energy.

"You've heard something?" she questioned softly, hope and excitement burgeoning within her.

He nodded. "We'll be headin' for Albuquerque in the mornin'." The slight shift of his gaze toward Mrs. Whiting told her that he would say little else until they were alone.

"Will we have time to stock up on our supplies before we leave?"

"We'll have to take time. There's some mighty rough territory between here and there, and not much in the way of civilization. The stores are closed for the night, but first thing in the morning we'll make our purchases and be on our way.''

Luke lingered over his supper while Charity helped Mrs. Whiting finish the kitchen chores. Then the two of them bid the woman good night and sauntered with admirable calm up the stairs. The door to Charity's room had scarcely closed behind them when Charity rounded on him. "What did you hear?" she asked breathlessly.

"Jeb is supposed to be stayin' in Albuquerque. Seems he met up with his brother there and decided to split from the rest of the band, at least for the time bein'."

"Any word on the others?"

"No, but when we find Jeb, he might know where they are."

"But will he tell us?"

"Oh, he'll tell us, if it's the last thing he does," Luke assured her in a deadly tone that sent cold shivers up Charity's backbone.

Desolate. Barren. Hot. Dry. All aptly described the land through which Luke led them. There were no towns, no telegraph poles, no railroad tracks, not even a stage line going in their direction. Just flat, endless prairie as far as the eye could see. After two weeks of hard riding, traveling from sunup to sundown until Charity felt sure her tailbone was becoming part of her saddle, the prairie finally gave way to desert.

Though she was fascinated by this change of scenery, her trepidation was clear to see, and Luke was quick to reassure her. "Two days at most, Charity, and we'll be across it and headed into the plateaus. This is only a small extension of the desert further south, like the offshoot of a lake. We've got plenty of water, so there's nothin' to worry about."

Charity had wondered why Luke had bought extra canteens before they left Wichita Falls. Now she knew. They'd filled each to the brim before leaving the last river behind them.

Now she asked, "Are you sure we won't get lost out there?" She'd heard horrible tales about people losing their way in the desert and dying slowly of thirst, sometimes mere miles from precious water.

"I've been through here before. I know where we're goin'."

True to his word, Luke did seem to know the way, though to Charity the sand and cactus all looked the same in every direction. And though she'd promised herself to trust him, she didn't draw a decent breath until the low plateaus appeared on the western horizon.

Her uncertainty, and her complete reliance on him, served Luke well on their solitary trek. With each passing day, her trust in him was growing stronger. Perhaps her lingering fear of snakes, or a need for comfort, aided his cause; now, instead of bedding down slightly apart from him, to be pulled into his embrace only after she was fast asleep, Charity crept willingly into his arms each evening. No longer did she flinch at his touch, though she did tense at the murmured endearments he whispered into her ear and the occasional nibbles he took on her nape.

Holding her close to him throughout the night and having to restrain his natural urges was sweet torment for Luke, but one he willingly endured. Though they bedded down fully clothed, he soon memorized every tantalizing curve of her body. By the end of that first week, he could have recognized her by smell alone, a scent that was solely hers and utterly beguiling, like a silent siren's call to his tortured senses. At odd moments, just the sound of her sand-on-silk voice was enough to send gooseflesh racing along his skin, desire flaring instantly.

For her part, Charity was fast becoming accustomed to sharing a bedroll with Luke. Certainly, it was cozy, and his chest made an excellent pillow. When the desert nights turned cold, the heat radiating from his big body warded off the chill. As long as he made no unwanted advances, she was content with the arrangement. Warm and safe, she slept better than she had in months.

Most nights, as he held her cuddled to him, they lay talking softly and gazing at the stars until sleep claimed them. But the night they huddled together beneath the blankets and oilcloth as a thunderstorm raged overhead and poured rain all around them would live in Luke's memory forever.

They'd arrived at the foothills of the mountains just east of Albuquerque, their destination within easy reach the next day. Both were tense in anticipation of locating the first of their six quarry. The very air about them seemed to vibrate with a similar restlessness as clouds scurried across the heavens, building steadily throughout the late afternoon, driven by the wind. Spears of lightning lit the dark sky, and thunder reverberated in a growling drumroll.

They rode as long as they could before stopping, searching in vain for shelter from the storm. The low scrub brush offered little. The best they could find was the lee side of an outcropping of rock. There they spread their bedrolls as close to the slight overhang as possible, using one length of oilcloth beneath their blankets and one overtop, making extremely cramped quarters and providing slim hope of remaining dry.

The first huge drops of rain were already pelting the thirsty earth, sending up puffs of dust, by the time they hurriedly finished unsaddling and staking the horses. Fortunately, they were not completely drenched by the time they sought shelter, though their meal consisted of strips of dried beef, stale biscuits, and warm, tin-flavored water.

By now, the rain had become a deluge, showering a wind-whipped spray over them. Damp and chilled, they shucked their boots and crawled beneath the shield of the small tarp, where Luke gathered her shivering body close to his, her backside to his front.

"We're lucky we made it this high up before the storm hit," he told her quietly, his warm breath fanning her hair. "At least here we won't be caught in a flash flood."

Charity hadn't even considered that, and the thought sent another quiver through her. Misinterpreting her reaction, he said, "You're cold. You really out to wiggle out of those wet clothes before you get sick."

"No." Her refusal was accompanied by a shake of her head, her hair tickling his nose. "My spare clothes are in the saddlebags." And the saddlebags were well beyond her reach.

"Charity, we're talkin' about your health," he stressed firmly. "Now, either you shimmy out of that skirt and top, or I'll remove them for you."

"You wouldn't dare!"

"If it means keepin' you from catchin' your death, I'll dare more than that," he warned darkly. "Besides, it's not like I've never seen a woman in her underwear before, and it's darker than the inside of a goat under here, so I wouldn't even see that, more'n likely."

"But you'd know that's all I had on."

Her soft, shaken reply hit him hard in the gut. In his mind, he again saw her silhouette briefly outlined on that window shade, and he swallowed hard on the desire the image brought with it.

"Knowin' and doin' somethin' about it are two different things," he reminded her and himself.

It all boiled down to how much she truly trusted him. Long moments passed before he felt her arm shift upward toward the buttons of her shirt. As he held his breath, waiting, his heart thundered loudly in his ears.

One by one, Charity's trembling fingers pushed

the buttons free of their holes, and with each one she felt as if she were taking another step closer to the brink of a crumbling ledge. When the last one was undone, she struggled to pull the tails of her shirt from the confining waistband of her riding skirt.

"Let me help you."

Luke's gruff voice sent fresh tremors through her, but she did not demur as he helped ease the wet cloth from her shoulders, tugging it down her arms until she was shed of it altogether. His cool fingers grazed her bare flesh, raising gooseflesh in their wake. The skirt was next, and once she'd dealt with the fastenings, he pushed the sodden material downward, his hands faithfully traversing the curves of her scantily clad bottom, her thighs, her bare legs, all the way to the soles of her feet in one long, smooth caress.

Catching her breath, torn between alarm and an unbidden surge of feeling that vaguely resembled yearning, Charity bit her lip. A cry rose in her chest and stayed there, waiting in suspense for his next move.

It was not what she expected. When his long fingers quit her quivering flesh, they rose to attack the buttons of his own shirt.

"Wh . . . what are you doing?" she asked, on the edge of pure panic as his upper torso contorted with the effort to rid himself of his shirt in the tight space.

"I'm removin' my shirt. You're not the only one who's wet and uncomfortable." A whimper escaped her, and he added wryly, "Don't go into a fit. That's all I'm gonna take off. Just my shirt."

His shirt alone was too much for her peace of mind, especially when he settled back and pulled her tightly to him once more. Charity could feel the furring of hair on his arm where it came to rest in the curve of her waist. His thick, springy chest hair teased her through her thin chemise. With every breath, it tickled and nudged at her back.

Suddenly the air inside the blankets seemed inadequate, steamy with the scent of damp wool and warming flesh. With every labored breath she could smell him. An errant thought flew into her brain, and she wondered if he could smell her, too. Quickly she banished the unsettling thought, struggling to regain some small measure of calm in this awkward situation. Repeatedly, silently, she told herself that Luke would not harm her, that she had nothing to be upset about. They would both simply go to sleep, and by morning the storm would be over and they could resume their normal routine.

When his lips feathered across her bare nape, Charity started violently and nearly shrieked aloud. "Don't!" she squawked.

Ignoring her protest, he anchored her firmly in place. His mouth traversed her naked shoulder as he whispered, "I've never felt skin as soft as yours. It's like touchin' warm silk."

"Luke?" It was a mewling plea that tore at his heart.

"Shhh, darlin'. It's all right."

His hand came up to tangle in her hair as he loosened the pins that held it in its untidy knot. "Your hair is like waves of sunshine," he crooned, spreading the heavy tresses about her shoulders, burying his face in the silken mass and inhaling deeply.

Gradually, easily, his lips drifted from shoulder to neck to jaw, ending their exploration at the corner of her quivering lips. Shifting for easier access, he looked down at her, trying to see her face in the deep gloom of the covers. "Let me kiss you, sweetheart. Just one sweet kiss to dream on."

Taking her silence as consent, he moved his mouth unerringly over hers, and as his lips touched hers,

Charity wondered if the thunderous pounding was the storm raging all about them or the sound of her own heart about to explode in her chest. In self-defense, her hands came up to push against his broad chest. But as his mouth plied hers ever so gently, her fingers lingered there and, with a will of their own, wound themselves into the soft thatch of curls. His tongue nudged her lips apart, tracing their sensitive inner curve with liquid heat before darting between her teeth into her mouth, like a bee in search of honey.

As the sudden, unexpected move startled her anew, Charity's teeth involuntarily closed down on his tongue, hard enough to warn him off. Abruptly, he drew back.

Charity stiffened, recalling the last time she'd bitten a man as his tongue had thrust into her mouth. Fear became a living thing as she anticipated Luke's reaction, fully expecting the violence she'd reaped before. Trembling, too frightened even to call out, she waited for his fist to pound down against her face, her breath coming in sharp, panicked spurts as she cringed away from him.

It took several seconds for her to realize that he was chuckling, that the shaking beneath her fingertips was his chest as he laughed softly. Then, to her further surprise, he murmured, ''All right, then. You kiss me, darlin'. You control it. Bring your lips against mine and take it just as slow and easy or as bold and brazen as you want.''

For Charity this was a novel approach indeed and as her fright began to abate, oddly appealing. Both nature and upbringing had made her unassertive. During her short marriage to Johnny, she'd often invited his attention with sweet smiles and loving glances, but she'd never initiated advances toward him. Johnny had always been the one to begin their lovemaking, the one in charge of setting the pace of their passionate embraces.

Now, here was Luke giving her leave to do whatever most pleased her. Here and now, she had the choice of rejecting him or kissing him, and she knew in her heart that he would honor her decision either way. In consideration of his day-to-day behavior toward her, she had to admit to herself, finally and absolutely, that he wasn't like those other men. In fact, he wasn't like any other man she'd ever known.

Tentatively, so slowly that Luke thought he was imagining the movement, her mouth edged upward. Gently her lips brushed his with a touch as light as butterfly wings. Through supreme effort, he forced himself to stay still, to let her assume complete control. Only his lips responded to the light pressure of hers, and only at her direction.

When her lips had investigated his to her satisfaction, when he made no move to resume power over her, Charity grew bolder. The tip of her tongue crept out to whisk lightly across his lips. His resulting groan sounded to her ears more like a growl, and she froze momentarily. But when he stayed still, she again let her tongue play over the contours of his warm, inviting lips, exploring them hesitantly.

Just when Luke feared he might die of torment, when his lips ached for the feel of hers, her mouth melted fully onto his. As he had done, she urged his lips apart. Their breath mingled. Carefully, her tongue snaked into his mouth, finding his.

This seemed to startle her as much now as it had when he'd kissed her, for she jerked back almost before the slight touch was completed. Then, as if compelled by powers beyond herself, she reached out and did it again. Slowly, not wanting to frighten her, Luke let his tongue tangle with hers in a languid kiss that sent sparks of desire spiraling through his bloodstream. In some far corner of his mind that still functioned, he was certain that this was the sweetest, most beautiful moment of his entire life. He was also thankful that the angle of their lower bodies was such that Charity could not tell how her kiss was affecting him.

Charity was experiencing sensations she'd never felt, even with Johnny, feelings she'd never dreamed existed, that both excited and frightened her. Reason, what reason she still possessed, told her it was mostly her imagination, teamed with the fact that she'd been a widow for nearly a year now. Urges, both familiar and new, came rushing at her from all directions. Her blood was clamoring in her veins, her skin tingled from head to toe, her head spun like a child's toy top until she could scarcely tell up from down.

As the strange emotions became too much to bear, she tore her mouth free of his, panting as if she'd just run up a mountainside. A lifetime seemed to pass before she regained her senses. Feminine curiosity broke through at last, the first she'd felt in a long, long time, and she whispered hesitantly, "Did you like it at all? The way I kissed you?"

"Honey," he replied on a grumbling laugh that sounded every bit as shaken as she felt, "if I'd liked it any better, my hair would have curled." As it was, his toes were tight knots in his socks.

With a satisfied smile, Charity snuggled her face into his chest and sighed softly. Within heartbeats, she was fast asleep.

Such relief was a long time coming for Luke. Tightly entombed in their tiny shelter, Charity's warm, near-naked body taunting his, he held both heaven and hell in his arms. The storm wore itself out as he lay sleepless; and ever after, whenever he smelled wet wool, he knew he would be reminded of this night and all its blissful agony.

18

THEY reached Albuquerque by mid-afternoon of the following day, and just two hours later were as frustrated in their efforts as they'd been since the outset. Jeb was no longer there.

"He and his brother lit out about a week ago," a waitress informed them.

"Do you have any idea where they went?" Luke pressed.

"You might try down around Socorro. There's some to-do about more silver bein' found around there, and those two seemed mighty excited on hearin' it."

With Socorro just sixty miles south, along the Rio Grande, Luke and Charity didn't even bother to stay the night in Albuquerque. They simply loaded up on supplies and rode out.

It was early evening, exactly two days later, when they arrived at the mining town, after first passing a veritable sea of tents. The rumor of fresh silver strikes had reached many a hopeful ear, it seemed. The saloons were starting to come to life for the night, sending a cacophony of tinny piano music past their swinging doors and into the streets. Men by the dozens were streaming through those doors, as if whiskey were going to be outlawed at any minute and this was their last chance to taste it. Charity had never seen such chaos.

Getting one hotel room for the night, let alone two, proved nearly impossible. After an hour, Luke managed to rent a tiny room above one of the saloons, and it came dearly.

"I don't like this, but it's the only thing available," he complained, wincing as the piano player hit several sour notes, the noise so loud it sounded as if the piano were in the same room with them.

He left, returning a short time later with a plate of supper for her. "You eat and freshen up. I'm gonna scout around a bit and see if I can find our friend and his brother. This is just the sort of place to do it, too. Not that I think those two are up to minin' for their silver. That'd be too much work. More'n likely they're out to steal someone else's."

"If you find him, come and get me," Charity told him firmly. "Don't you dare call him out yourself."

"Now, Charity," he began.

"Don't you 'now Charity' me, Luke Sterling. I have a score to settle with that snake, and I won't have you cheating me out of it."

He agreed, reluctantly, and left her with a terse reminder to lock the door behind him, and not to leave until he returned.

He was back almost before she was ready.

Luke walked three steps into the room and stopped cold, staring in disbelief. He looked at her, then back at the door, as if hoping that he'd accidentally entered the wrong room. The woman standing before him was Charity, but not the Charity he'd left just a short time before.

She was dressed in shiny red satin, the ruffles of her skirt ending not far below her knees, where a black crinoline underskirt peeked boldly out. The bodice was cut low across her breasts, the skimpy shoulders flowing into full, flounced sleeves that trailed halfway down her upper arms. Her long legs were now encased in dark net stockings, her dainty feet in strapped black high-heeled slippers. A fluffy black plume adorned her hair, which she had piled in haphazard curls atop her head. Loose tendrils wafted down her nape, as if in invitation of a man's touch. About her neck, covering her scar, was a red satin band. Rouge stained her cheekbones and luscious lips, and her blue eyes appeared huge and bright against their darkened lids and lashes.

In Luke's opinion, Charity's own natural loveliness needed no enhancement. Given the choice, he preferred her God-given beauty to this blatant display of painted flesh, though she did look stunningly sensuous, enough to set his pulse thundering in his ears and blood pounding hotly in his groin.

"Well, say something!" she snapped at last, breaking the awful silence.

He said the first thing that came to mind. "You look like a harlot!" As he inhaled his first decent breath since entering the room, he added nastily, "And you smell even worse. Holy hell, what did you do, take a bath in the stuff?"

"Just about," she answered, not at all provoked. "To tell the truth, I wasn't sure how much to put on, since I've never worn anything but lemon verbena or a touch of lavender toilet water. I want to appear as authentic as possible."

"As authentic as what?" he barked, already guessing her answer. "And why?"

"Like one of those girls downstairs, of course, so that I can blend right in. Since my widow's disguise is obviously not appropriate in saloons, I had to create another."

"Just where the devil did you come by that getup?" he asked with a frown.

"I bought it from Mrs. Whiting."

"The hotel keeper's wife in Wichita Falls?" Luke stared at her in astonishment, recalling the kindly, rosy-cheeked woman who had appeared the perfect picture of a contented housewife." "And where would she get that sort of clothing?" he questioned.

Charity came close to gloating. "She used to be a barmaid," she declared with a superior look.

"You're joshin' me."

"Nope. She hung up her garters in exchange for an apron when Mr. Whiting proposed marriage to her. But land's sakes, did that nice little lady have stories from her past!"

"You'll have to tell me all about it sometime, but for now, get changed." There was no mistaking the authority in his command. "I'm not takin' you anywhere dressed like that. And be quick about it, because I've found Jeb. He's in a saloon right across the street."

"Oh, my stars!" Now that the moment was nearly upon her, Charity was suddenly unsure what to do next. Rushing up to him, she grabbed Luke's arm, tugging him toward the door. "Luke! Let's go!" She changed her tune in mid-stride. "Wait! We've got to form a plan! Oh, Luke! Help me! My mind has gone berserk! I can't think straight!"

"Will you calm down?" he grumbled irritably. "You're actin' as crazy as a bedbug!"

"Well, think of something!" she screeched. "We can't just march in there and gun the man down! Or can we? What kind of law do they have here?"

Luke shook his head at her ridiculous suggestion. "No, Charity. The best thing would be to provoke him into a fight, with him makin' the challenge, but I can't see a man askin' a woman to step out into the street for a showdown. I guess we'll just have to watch until he leaves the place and catch him out in the open."

Walking to the solitary, grime-coated window, Luke rubbed a spot clean with his sleeve. "I can stand lookout from here while you change into your regular clothes."

As she still hesitated, he growled, "Go ahead. I promise not to watch you—this time."

With her mind finally starting to function properly again, Charity had other ideas. "Wait, Luke, I have a better plan. Why not lure him out, with me as the bait? The man is a rutting pig, and if he sees me dressed like this—"

"He'll recognize you and smell a trap," Luke interrupted shortly.

"It was a dark night almost a year ago," Charity reminded him, "and Jeb didn't have half the incentive to remember me that I have for remembering him. Besides, you barely recognized me yourself."

"Say we do lure him out," Luke said, playing along with her for the time being. "What then?"

"Well, if I make him think I've changed my mind and prefer you, maybe he'll get jealous or mad enough to challenge me."

Luke felt obliged to point out the fallacy of her scheme. "He'd call me out, darlin'. Not you. He'd want to get rid of the competition so he could have your sweet body all to himself."

"Well, shucks!" Charity was momentarily stymied. "Maybe I could call him names or spit at him or something. Then, if he turned his anger on me, I could shoot him."

Luke grinned at the image forming in his mind. "I hate to be the one to tell you this, but you're gonna look pretty damned silly struttin' into that saloon, dressed like that, with a gun belt around your waist."

"I'll wear it strapped to my thigh, under my skirts," she countered swiftly. "And I can tuck my knife into the garter on the other leg." She lifted the bottom edge of her skirt just high enough to allow him a quick glimpse at a red satin garter trimmed in black lace decorating an endlessly long, trim leg.

"Oh, Lord!" he groaned, swallowing hard. He had to admit that her idea held some merit. If Jeb was half as hot for her as he himself was right now, the man would follow her anywhere, with his tongue hanging down around his knees.

"Okay," he conceded, for lack of another workable plan. "We'll try it. But be careful, Charity, and don't stir up more trouble than the two of us can handle."

Charity's plans started to unravel right from the start. First of all, Luke was not about to let her waltz into the crowded saloon on her own.

"With your luck, you'll have every man in the place sniffin' your skirts within minutes, and you're apt to start a riot. That won't get Jeb where we want him.

"Besides, if the owner of the place sees that he has a new girl workin', one he hasn't hired, I can tell him you're with me. My personal good luck charm at the card tables or some such nonsense. Otherwise, he's likely to be plenty put out with you."

"Why would he be?" Charity asked naively. "It's not like he has to pay me or anything."

Luke just rolled his eyes to the heavens and tried to explain as simply as he could. "Darlin', the saloon owner gets his share of his girls' nightly earnin's, whether it's made servin' whiskey or doin' somethin' more private."

They entered together, Charity clinging to Luke's arm like a decorative, painted doll. Actually, she was very thankful for his assistance when she found that walking on the spindly high-heeled slippers was precarious at best, not at all like her usual footwear.

Without his aid, she feared she might topple onto her face in a flurry of skirts and make a grand spectacle of herself! And Luke's broad grin told her he was well aware of her predicament. Blast his hide!

Strolling up to the bar, Luke ordered drinks for both of them, while Charity stared about in wide-eyed amazement. Over a hundred men, and a scant handful of women, were squeezed together in a room that would have comfortably accomodated half that number. Jostling and elbowing their way to the bar and around the tables, men laughed and cursed and yelled, spilling as much liquor as they consumed. Their boisterous voices blended with the screech of the piano, which was being played with more vigor than talent. The potent smells of liquor, cigar smoke, and unwashed overheated bodies combined in a nauseating odor, while overhead a blue haze hovered like a malignant cloud.

It was as revolting as it was fascinating to behold.

"Here," Luke said, thrusting a mug of foaming beer into Charity's hands. She stared at it as if it were a creature from a foreign land, her delicate nose wrinkling in distaste. With a laugh, he leaned close to be heard over the din. "Just sip at it now and then, but for God's sake don't drink enough to addle your senses. And wipe that frown off your face. You're supposed to be a fallen woman, remember, darlin'?"

Blue eyes blazing daggers, she sent him a sugar-sweet smile that should have melted his socks. "Where is he?" she whisper-yelled.

With a slight jerk of his head, Luke indicated the rear of the room. Then, his gaze never leaving her face, he watched for her reaction as she slowly scanned the tables. Could she identify her quarry after all this time?

He knew the very instant she'd spotted Jeb. All the color drained from her face, leaving only two enormous blue eyes and rouge-reddened cheeks and lips arched in a macabre smile, stark against skin as white as flour. As her slight body began to weave, he snaked an arm around her waist and gathered her close, his own body absorbing her violent quiver.

"Don't you dare faint on me, Charity Prindle!" he hissed into her ear. "You told me this is what you wanted. Now prove it!"

For several seconds more, she stood frozen. Then, without a word, she raised the beer mug to her trembling lips and gulped a third of it straight down.

Frowning, Luke yanked the mug from her mouth. "Hey! I warned you to take it easy with that!"

She blinked up at him, gave a small unladylike burp, then wiped the foam from her lips with dainty fingers. Drawing away from him, she stood straight as an arrow at his side. "I'm ready when you are, Sterling," she croaked in a voice that sounded like a shovel grating over cinders.

Once more her gaze sought Jeb, at the back table where he was playing cards with three other men. His mud-colored hair straggled over his collar in lank, greasy strands, and he looked as if he'd neither bathed nor shaved in weeks. Dirt streaked his face, and his clothes were rumpled and grubby, one shoulder of his shirt ripped at the seam and hanging haphazardly. As she watched, he took a gulp of beer, slopped it down his bristled chin, and swiped the foam away with the back of his hand. His sneering smile displayed a crooked row of yellowed teeth.

Just the thought of this foul swine touching her, his slobbering mouth over hers, was enough to make Charity's skin crawl. That this piece of slime had dared violate her body! Dark rage settled into the marrow of her bones, freezing her heart.

"Well, are we gonna stand here all night, or make him notice me?" she asked, suddenly impatient to have done with it.

Luke caught her arm. Judging from the hate in her eyes, he wouldn't have been surprised if she meant to march right up to Jeb and shoot him where he sat. "Hold your horses, honey," he instructed. "I'm waitin' for an openin' at his table. As soon as one of the others drops out of the game, I'll step in. Might as well see if we can't lighten his pockets while we're at it. That ought to sour his mood; then you can make him feel better by flirtin' with him."

"Lucky me!" she retorted waspishly through gritted teeth.

They stood, waiting and watching, Charity growing more anxious by the minute.

A big, dirty miner approached her, grinning at her with thick lips and rotting teeth. "Ain't seen you around here b'fore. You new?" His opening approach was further ruined when he scratched at his ribs and let loose a foul belch that threatened to wilt the plume atop Charity's hair.

"She's with me," Luke growled, his green eyes narrowed in warning. Dressed all in black, as he'd been when Charity had first seen him, Luke looked every inch the formidable gunfighter. Inebriated though he was, the miner was still sober enough to recognize more trouble than he wanted to tangle with. He backed off in a hurry.

But the longer they stood there, the more notice Charity attracted. In rapid succession, four more men approached her, to be turned away just as brusquely. Through it all, Charity stood silent, letting Luke deal with each man while she tried valiantly to hide her revulsion behind a false smile. Her old fears were fast growing, threatening to choke her. Only fierce determination and Luke's solid presence at her side held them at bay.

At last, just when Charity thought she couldn't bear it any longer, one of the miners at Jeb's table decided to quit the game. With seeming nonchalance, Luke led Charity forward.

"Mind if I join you fellas?" he drawled, seating himself as if taking their agreement for granted. Though they frowned, none of the remaining players objected openly. As had the others, these three obviously recognized him for a gunfighter and were reluctant to cross him. They simply glowered, first at Luke, then at Charity, who stationed herself to one side and slightly behind Luke's chair.

One of them finally grumbled, "It's your money, mister."

As the cards were dealt, Luke grabbed hold of Charity's hand, brought her icy fingers to his lips, and sent her a roguish wink. Placing her hand on his shoulder, he said for all to hear, "Now, you stay right here, darlin'. I don't want my good luck gal wanderin' off."

His comment brought raised brows and knowing laughter, serving to lighten the tension around the poker table, just as he'd hoped it might. Only he knew that Charity's heightened color was due to more than the rouge staining her cheekbones.

Standing there, practically face-to-face with one of the men who had raped her, Charity felt as if her blood had turned to ice. He was seated directly across the small table from Luke, and every time she raised her eyes, she met Jeb's leering look. The muscles of her face were as stiff as stone, while her knees trembled so violently that she had to lean against Luke's side to stay upright. As he picked up his cards, merely the sight of Jeb's fingers, grime encrusted beneath his nails, was enough to sicken her as she unwillingly recalled the feel of those hands grasping her shrinking flesh and tearing at her clothes.

She knew she had to get her emotions under control, and quickly. She didn't dare let Jeb see her animosity. She was supposed to be friendly toward him, if not downright alluring. But it was next to impossible to smile at a man she hated with every fiber of her body and mind.

Sensing her difficulty, Luke tugged on her arm, making her bend to him. On the pretext of kissing her painted cheek, he whispered. "If you can't manage a decent smile, a pout will do. It might make him think you're bored with me and want a change of partners, but quit glarin' holes through the man. Pull yourself together, Charity, or forget the whole stinkin' idea."

She pouted. As the card game dragged on interminably, she fidgeted. By playing games in her mind and imagining Jeb dead at her feet, she even managed to dredge up a few smiles for him.

Meanwhile, the men went on with their gambling. Luke was winning steadily, whether by design or luck, Charity didn't know. Conversely, Jeb was losing, possibly because his mind and his eyes kept straying toward Charity's amply displayed breasts. When fresh drinks were ordered, Luke pointedly neglected to order another beer for Charity. Rather, he offered her small sips from his own mug, another effective tactic to draw Jeb's attention toward her. Each time Luke raised his glass to her lips, Jeb's gaze would follow. When her tongue slipped out to lap a fleck of foam from her lips, Jeb's tongue reflexively licked at his own. Luke barely restrained a derisive laugh.

At one point, one of the men said, "Thought your brother would be here tonight, Jeb."

"Naw. Harlan's too busy humpin' his brains out, which is probably where I should be, considerin' the cards I've been dealt so far. Shit! If I was to see a queen pop up in my hand right now, I'd more'n likely come in my britches!"

Charity's quick gasp at Jeb's uncouth comment almost gave her disguise away.

Luke covered her lapse by inquiring indolently, "Got the hiccups, honey? Here." He offered her a warning look and another drink of his beer.

"Speakin' o' women, Jeb, you still got an itch for that little redhead runnin' the laundry tent?" another player asked.

"Yeah. Thought I might take me a stroll down that way later, if nothin' more int'restin' turns up." A smirk curled Jeb's lips as his hot gaze traversed Charity's curves, like iron filings drawn to a magnet.

The beer curdled in Charity's stomach.

"I got the idea Wilma was less than impressed with your charms," the third miner put in. "Didn't she threaten to throw you, clothes and all, into her washtub the last time you offered to take her to bed?"

The men laughed. Jeb sneered. "That don't mean nothin'. We all know the gals what squawk the loudest about not wantin' it are the ones who squeal the longest once you stick it to 'em, and beg for more when you're done."

Charity's stomach turned over.

" 'Course, they always want to get paid, too, like they was the one doin' you a favor, not the other way 'round. Money-grubbin' bitches, all of 'em!"

"Talkin' 'bout bein' robbed, did y'all hear about Bill Wilson?" the man to Luke's right asked. "He got jumped last night and cut up real bad. Whoever done it stole everything but the thread out o' his pockets!"

A sly glint entered Jeb's eyes. "He know who it was?"

The miner shook his head. "A man don't talk much with his throat slit."

The spark of satisfaction that flitted across Jeb's face was quickly hidden, but Charity saw it and cringed inwardly at the stark evil it had revealed. She covered her revulsion with a shaky smile in Jeb's direction.

Toward the end of the game, Luke took Charity completely off guard when he abruptly pulled her onto his lap. Fortunately, her startled yelp was interpreted as surprise as she tumbled into his arms, skirts flying. Above the laughter, Luke announced in a loud, slurred voice, "Game's almost over, honey. Why don't you amuse yourself by countin' my winnin's? Then you and me can go back to my room and play more int'restin' games. We'll see how much of my money you can sweet-talk me out of tonight."

Stunned, Charity wondered, just for a moment, if Luke truly was drunk. As she wriggled in an initial attempt to remove herself from his lap, his fingers tightened in warning around her waist.

"Stay still," he hissed quietly into her ear, his tongue sending shivers across her skin. "Just play along. Our fish is hooked. All we have to do now is reel him in, slow and easy."

Her startled gaze flew to his, then veered toward Jeb. Luke was as sober as a judge, and Jeb, for all his pretended amusement, was either furious or jealous, just as they'd hoped. Though the man's lips smiled, his eyes smoldered with a look that was all too frighteningly familiar. She'd seen that same look on his face one other night, a hellish night she'd remember vividly until her dying day.

With renewed determination to rid the earth of this murderous dog, Charity threw herself into an act that should have landed her a leading part in any theater performance. If all went well, there'd soon be one less bloodthirsty bandit to prey upon unsuspecting victims. Winding her arms around Luke's neck in a wanton display, she cooed, "Are you sure you haven't had too much to drink, sugar? It'd be a real shame if you fell asleep before the party got a good start.''

After the tricks he'd pulled on her all evening, it was almost funny to see the way Luke's eyes widened in surprise, then narrowed. ''I think I'm up to it,'' he drawled with a drunken smirk, ignoring the ribald chuckles of his fellow players.

''Deal me out, fellas,'' he said, drawing Charity to her feet and gathering his winnings. ''I think the lady's feelin' ignored, and her invitation's too good to pass up.''

Together they headed toward the door, Luke making a show of staggering unsteadily, his arm slung across her bare shoulders, while Charity lurched alongside on her high heels, pretending to take his weight. From the corner of her vision, Charity saw Jeb shove back his chair, abandoning the game, his gaze following them.

''He's coming,'' she murmured.

''Good. That's what we want. And I hope others notice, too. It never hurts to have witnesses to testify that the other man started the fight, and you had no choice but to finish it.''

They cleared the doorway and stepped into the street, just beyond the lights of the saloon. There, Luke stopped and pulled her into his arms, entwining her own around his neck. ''Kiss me, Charity, and make it look good,'' he ordered. ''He's watchin'.''

God help her, but when Luke's lips took hers, she almost swooned. It was like being branded with a hot iron. Shock rippled through her, tearing the breath from her lungs, scattering her thoughts like dry leaves in the wind. As his lips plied hers with expert insistence, darts of fear speared through her, mingling with a dark desire that sprang up suddenly, shockingly, heightened by the wild excitement of the danger so near at hand.

Just as abruptly as the kiss had begun, it ended. Jerking his lips from hers, Luke glared at Jeb, now standing just a few feet from them. "You want somethin'?" he growled.

"Yeah," Jeb answered boldly, leering once more at Charity's heaving bosom. "I wouldn't mind havin' me a little of that myself, 'specially since she's been sendin' me more smoke signals than a squaw with an itch."

"Is that so?" Luke said, drawing his words out slowly, still playing the part of a man whose senses were dulled by drink. Turning to Charity, he asked, "You want him, honey?"

"Sure do, sugar," she purred. Like a flame suddenly doused with water, her voice went cold. "I want him dead."

Jeb's eyes went wide in surprise at her sudden turnabout. "Why, you teasin' little whore! You been flauntin' those tits and battin' those eyes at me all night!"

"Now why would I do that, Jeb?" she taunted softly. With one hand, she gathered her skirts and tucked one side out of the way, baring most of her right leg and the holster secured high on her thigh.

Jeb's eyes bulged, his gaze turning wary as he gaped first at her, then at Luke, and back again. "Wh . . . what's goin' on here?" he stammered.

"You still want me, Jeb? Come and get me. If you have the guts. Or are you only interested in raping helpless women and killing their husbands?"

Her soft tone did not blunt the force of her words. Jeb jerked as if she'd struck him. His eyes narrowed, trying to see her features better in the half-light. "Who are you?" he asked hoarsely.

Her answering laugh was eerie. "Don't you remember me?" she goaded. "Why, Jeb! I'm sorely disappointed in you. I'm the woman you and five of your filthy friends attacked last year just outside of Dodge City. Does that ring a familiar bell with you? I'm the woman who's going to kill you, just the way you killed my husband. Say your prayers, Jeb, if you think they'll do you any good, because you're about to meet your Maker. Better yet, beg me for your worthless life, the way I begged all of you that night.''

"Lady, you're crazy!'' Jeb licked his lips nervously. "You've got me mixed up with somebody else.''

She shook her head. "No, Jeb. I remember you all too well, but don't feel alone in this. You're not the only one I intend to kill. I want the other five, too. In fact, there are a couple I want worse than you. It might make me feel more kindly toward you if you tell me where I can find them.''

"I don't know. I tell you, you're talkin' to the wrong man,'' Jeb insisted.

"You're a poor liar, Jeb. Where are they?''

"I don't know, and I wouldn't tell you if I did.''

"I'd think that over real carefully if I were you. I could always shoot you up some before I kill you. Maybe shoot off a toe or two first and work up from there. That could be mighty painful, and I imagine it would bring your failing memory back real quick, don't you?''

Beads of sweat broke out on Jeb's forehead and trickled down his face. "You're bluffin'! I ain't never seen no woman that good with a gun.''

"There's a first time for everything, Jeb—and a last.'' Charity stepped back, her fingers hovering over the walnut grip of her Colt. Fear and uncertainty flared suddenly within her, but the challenge had been made; she had to follow through with it now. And she was scared. So utterly scared that she had to grit her teeth to keep them from chattering. Her knees had turned to pudding. Her stomach was doing crazy flip-flops. Her palms were perspiring, while her fingers felt like icicles. She flexed them slightly, urging blood into them, praying she wouldn't drop her gun or catch it on the holster as she had so often in practice.

Taking a deep breath, she released it slowly, trying to make the calm she portrayed a reality, willing her hands to still their trembling, focusing her total concentration on her opponent.

"Well, Jeb? Are you going to go for that gun you're wearing, or are you going to stand there and let me shoot you down in the street like the mangy dog you truly are?"

"What about him?" Not daring to take his eyes from her, Jeb's head jerked toward Luke.

"Luke has nothing to do with this," Charity told him. "This is entirely between us. Just you and me."

"She's right, Jeb," Luke put in quietly. "I'm just here to watch and make sure it's a fair fight—for now. But I should warn you. I'm fond of the lady, and if you somehow manage to kill her, instead of the other way around, I'll be obliged to challenge you myself."

"Now, can't we settle this some other way?" Jeb whined. "I've got some money. Maybe . . ." Even as he spoke, attempting to distract her, he went for his gun.

Charity's hand flashed forward, Colt drawn and aimed, just as her heel twisted beneath her, throwing her off balance. Her cry of alarm was drowned out by the sounds of dual gunfire, her finger plying the trigger as she tumbled to the ground.

19

$\mathcal{A}$s he watched her fall, Luke's heart stopped beating. Reflex had him drawing his own weapon, turning it toward Jeb. It was then that he realized Jeb, too, had fallen. He lay flat on his back in the dusty street, the dim light from the saloon showing a single bullet hole right between the eyes.

Before he could step toward her, Charity was sitting up, staring at Jeb's body in shock and bewilderment, her Colt still in her hand. "My God! Oh, my dear God!" she cried out.

People were pouring into the street from the saloons as Luke bent over her, gently gathering her trembling body into his arms, his eyes and hands searching frantically for wounds. "Were you hit, Charity? Are you hurt?"

"He's dead, isn't he?" she sobbed. "Did I do that? Did I kill him?"

"Dammit, Charity! Forget about Jeb! Answer me! Are you hurt?"

"N . . . no. I don't know. I don't think so." She turned her face into his chest and began to wail. "Oh, God, Luke! I think I'm going to be sick."

"Not here, you're not," he ground out, lifting her into his arms and standing. "If you're bound to puke your guts up, at least wait until I get you someplace more private to do it.'' Anger was fast replacing fear, his relief so great he didn't know what he wanted to do first, kiss her or beat her.

Elbowing his way through the milling crowd of onlookers, he strode swiftly across the street, intent on reaching their room before Charity made good her threat. He gave their door a vicious kick, sending it crashing open as he stomped to the bed and tossed her unceremoniously onto the lumpy mattress.

Belatedly, he recalled the fact that she'd never given him a proper answer as to her injuries. Quickly, he lit the lamp and began tugging at her clothes.

"Luke! No! What are you doing? Stop!'' Screeching and kicking, Charity tried to swat his hands away.

"I'm checkin' for injuries, you twit. Now stop thrashin' around and let me do it.''

"I'm not hurt,'' she exclaimed, then quickly qualified her statement as her ankle gave a sharp twinge. "At least I'm not shot. But I think I twisted my ankle when I fell, and it's starting to throb like the very devil.''

She couldn't have surprised him more if she'd told him she'd grown two heads. Stunned, Luke stopped trying to rip her clothes from her and simply stared at her, speechless. "You twisted your ankle?'' he repeated, dumbfounded.

Then he started to laugh, great barks of rolling laughter. "You twisted your ankle!'' he roared, as if it were the funniest thing he'd ever heard.

When his laughter dwindled to a huge grin, he again gathered her close, burying his face in her tumbling hair. "Oh, Lord, Charity! When I saw you fall, I almost went crazy. I don't think I've ever been so scared in my whole life as I was right then.''

"I wasn't doing so good, either," she admitted softly. Then, as his words brought everything fresh to mind, she shuddered. "Luke, I heard two shots. One was mine, I know. Where did the other one come from?"

Pulling back slightly, he frowned down at her, wondering at her question. "From Jeb's gun, of course. Where else?"

"I wasn't sure. I thought maybe it was yours." She fell silent, mulling it over, then asked soberly, "I killed him, then? It truly was my bullet that went into his brain?"

"Yes."

"Oh, God!" she muttered again, more a prayer than an oath. Her face, which had gradually been regaining its normal color, turned pale again. She started to shake and couldn't stop. Within seconds, her teeth were chattering in her head, both she and the bed wobbling like a bowl of pudding as reaction set in. Then she began to cry, great gulping sobs that seemed to tear loose from somewhere deep inside her.

Luke cradled her in his sheltering embrace, his big hands soothing up and down her heaving back. "I know, darlin'. I know," he crooned. "It's never easy, no matter how it comes about, no matter how justified." He held her long after she'd hiccuped herself to sleep, wondering if she'd awaken them both with nightmares. He'd tried to prepare her for the aftermath of killing someone; now all he could do was offer sympathy and comfort, and hope that the events of this night would not haunt her forever.

The first thing Luke asked the next morning was, "Do you want to quit now, Charity, and go home? I'll understand if you do. I'll even hunt the others down for you, free of charge."

"Why would you do that?"

"Because we're friends."

"Friends don't take advantage of each other, Luke. I'd never ask you to do such a thing for me on the basis of our friendship."

"The offer stands. Last night was just the beginnin', darlin'. It's not gonna get easier as we go along. Takin' another person's life isn't somethin' you get used to with practice, like playin' the piano."

She laughed humorlessly and shook her head. "I want to go on, Luke. Yes, I was terribly upset, and I suppose it won't be the last time, but I'm fine now. Truly. When necessity demands, I can be a very strong person."

"Stubborn's more like it," he retorted, relieved to note that her normal color had returned, along with a spark of defiant determination in her eyes. "You're sure?"

"Positive."

"All right," he conceded. "Then I reckon our next step is to try to find Jeb's brother. Maybe he'll be able to tell us where to start lookin' for the other five."

Charity agreed. "First, I have something else I want to do, though." She talked Luke into taking her to the edge of town, where she began plucking stalks of weeds and dead flowers.

Luke looked on in confusion. "You gonna tell me what the hell you're doin', or am I supposed to guess?"

"I'm picking a funeral bouquet for Jeb," she told him simply.

Certain his hearing was failing him, Luke shook his head. "You're doin' what?"

"You heard me."

"Well, I've got news for you, darlin'. You're pickin' the ugliest mess of weeds I've ever seen."

She smiled sweetly. "I know."

Back in town, she marched straight to the undertaker's, where she left the bouquet and a neatly penned note to be placed in Jeb's demurely folded hands. The note read: *May you rot in hell*, and was signed, *Widow Witch*.

Luke again shook his head, amazed at the temerity of this woman. "You know, of course, that the undertaker will tell one and all about this."

"That's my intention. I'm hoping the other five will hear about it. I want them to wonder which of them I'll find next, who will be next to be buried with my calling card and widow's weeds."

"You're gonna earn yourself a reputation you'd be better off without," he warned. "Believe me, Charity, I know. You have no idea how many men I've faced who wanted nothin' more than to see if they could outdraw me. Men I'd never met before, who'd heard about me and thought they were faster, or better, and ended up dyin' over some stupid notion of gainin' glory. But dyin' isn't glorious, especially over somethin' as asinine as that."

When they left the undertaker's, she surprised him again by asking, "Is there a church nearby?"

Luke's mouth fell open. "Don't tell me, after what you just did, you want to pray for his soul."

"No. I'm going to pray for mine."

"Regrets?"

"Not that I killed him. Only that by doing so, I have put my mortal soul in jeopardy, and probably ruined any chance I had of joining Johnny and my baby in the hereafter."

He took her to the old Spanish mission that had been founded centuries before, when Socorro was no more than a peaceful Piro Indian village.

As it turned out, they didn't have to search for Jeb's brother. He found them. The man was waiting for them as they left the mission.

"You the one who calls herself the Widow Witch?" he growled, stalking up to her with hate glazed eyes. "You the one who gunned my brother down in the street last night?"

Luke sent her a look that plainly said, *I told you so.*

With a sigh, Charity stiffened her backbone in preparation for another confrontation. "If Jeb was your brother, you have my sympathy. But you should also know that he was a murdering thief, and deserved worse than what he got."

"Keep your sympathy for yourself, 'cause you're gonna need it. You killed the only kin I had left. I wanna know why."

"He killed my husband, he and five of his rampaging friends. Maybe you've heard of them." She went on to list the remaining names, noting the signs of recognition registering on his face at three of the names.

"I have no grievance with you," she added quietly. "It was Jeb I wanted, and the others. You know who they are. I know you do. Just tell me where I can find them, and I'll be on my way."

"On your way to hell, maybe," the man snarled. "If it's an eye for an eye you believe in, then you owe me, not the other way 'round."

Exactly as his brother had done the night before, Harlan drew for his gun. This time, Charity did not stumble. Her aim was true as she drew her Colt and fired, the shot kicking the gun from Harlan's hand, sending it flying out of reach.

"I don't want to have to kill you, mister," she said, "but if you make me fire again, I'll aim for your heart. Now, tell me where my husband's murderers are."

"I saw only three of 'em, up in Albuquerque when I met up with Jeb," Harlan muttered, glaring at her. "I never heard of this Bronc, or Dandy neither."

"Then tell me about the others," she prompted. "The three you met."

When he dared to smirk, deliberately withholding further information, Charity slowly cocked back the hammer and leveled the barrel at the center of his chest. "You have to the count of three, and you have a choice. Either you tell me what I want to hear and walk away, or they can plant you next to Jeb in the cemetery." Her cold, unwavering gaze held his, letting him know she wasn't bluffing.

Harlan found his tongue. "Cutter said somethin' about headin' down around El Paso. That's all I know. Honest. He told Jeb to meet him there if things didn't work out here. Said they could always slip across the border into Mexico if things got too hot in the States."

"Were Whitey and Weasel going to El Paso with him?" Luke wanted to know.

"They didn't say, and I didn't ask."

Luke nodded. "Much obliged. Now, turn around and start walkin'. Fast. Don't bother pickin' up your gun. You can get it later. And don't let us see your face again while we're in town. Not if you want to stay healthy."

When Harlan was beyond hearing, Luke looked at Charity and grinned. "That was some mighty fancy shootin', lady. Almost as good as last night, though I still don't know how you managed to put that bullet square between Jeb's eyes the way you did."

Charity considered lying to him, to make him feel better, but she just couldn't do it. Her teeth worried her bottom lip as she debated the best way to tell him. In the end, she simply blurted out the truth. "I was aiming for his heart before I fell. As it is, it's pure dumb luck that I hit him at all, let alone where I did. I think I need to practice walking in those blasted high-heeled slippers before I go out in them again."

Charity had never seen the blood drain from a

man's face as fast as it did from Luke's, or rush back so quickly and vividly. "If you ever pull another stunt like that, I swear I'll blister your bottom raw!" he roared. "You scared the livin' daylights out of me, and now I learn that wasn't the half of it! Hell's bells, Charity! You're enough to drive a preacher to drink!"

Rather than follow the westward bend of the Rio Grande through southern New Mexico to El Paso, Luke decided it would be faster to cut straight through the desert, south to the Texas border. Charity was doubtful. This route ran directly through an arid area called the *Jornada del Muerto*, which, translated to English, meant the Journey of Death. The name itself gave her the shivers, let alone the thought of traveling through it for several days.

"It might be shorter, but will it really save time?" she argued. "It certainly won't be easier, for us or the horses. And the river route is bound to be safer."

"Stop being squeamish, Charity. I know you detest the desert, but it will only be for a few days. We have to get to El Paso while there's still a chance that Cutter will be there."

Reluctantly, she agreed. Now here they were, three days into their journey, surrounded by sand and cactus and the most intense heat Charity had imagined this side of Hades. It rose in waves over the parched land, hovering to create shimmering mirages of lakes and rivers that beckoned always out of reach.

With little else to do, they exchanged stories of various happenings in their lives, gradually coming to know each other better. While Charity naturally spoke most about her childhood in Pennsylvania farm country, Luke told her mainly of his travels since becoming an adult. He recalled a few humorous tales from his days in the army during the war, then described people he'd met and situations he'd encountered as a hired gunman.

Rarely did he mention his own childhood, or what his life had been like at the orphanage, though Charity repeatedly nudged him toward the subject. The way he deftly maneuvered around answering, she deduced that it must have been a very unhappy period for him, and though she had no wish to bring forth painful memories, she couldn't help being curious. With her persistence, she finally managed to make him lose patience.

"Damn it, woman!" he exploded, glowering across the small space separating them as they rode side by side. "Will you please let it be? Not everyone was as fortunate as you were, with a lovin' family and a storybook childhood. Okay?"

"No, it's not okay!" she retorted, giving him glare for glare. "Something about that time in your life is eating at you to this day, and I think if you'd just talk about it, you might resolve it. You remind me of one of those big African birds I've read about that go around hiding their heads in the sand, thinking they're safer that way."

"Ostriches," he said wryly, supplying the name that eluded her.

She nodded. "Right. The only trouble with them is, while their heads are hidden, the rest of them is vulnerable to attack. Think about that for a while, Mr. Almighty Gunslinger."

"Seems to me, the only one attackin' me is you, Widow Prindle," he shot back. "Most people are smart enough to know when to keep their mouth shut and not ask stupid questions."

"That's just because most of them are afraid of you, and I'm not."

"Keep it up, and you're gonna be," he warned with a dark look.

"Horsefeathers!" She dismissed his threat with a

crinkled nose and a haughty huff. "Besides, fair is fair, Sterling. If you can hear all my most intimate secrets laid bare and bleeding, then I'm entitled to know a few of yours."

"Oh, so that's your reasonin'," he snorted. "And here I was thinkin' you were just the most blamed nosy female this side of the Mississippi."

"And you're the orneriest, most stubborn cuss God ever set breath into! Just because you didn't know your father and mother is no reason to—"

"I knew my mother," he cut in sharply. "She was a coldhearted, selfish bitch. A graspin', greedy whore who gave more thought to her next lay than she did to her own son. Is that what you were itchin' to hear?"

She gaped at him in openmouthed amazement, appalled by his raw hatred. "Luke! How can you talk that way about her? No matter what she did, she was still your mother!"

"Cats are better mothers than she was, or could ever hope to be."

"That's still no reason to call her a wh . . ." Charity's voice trailed off in embarrassment.

Luke's laugh was as bitter as gall. "Shit! You can't even say the word, and I've had to live with the fact all my life. I'm not just name-callin' here, sweetheart. The woman opened her legs for any man who paid her price. The truth is, she spread her favors so thin that when I was born she didn't even know who to name as the father." He speared her with a frosty look. "Know what that makes me, darlin? A bastard. A genuine bastard."

"No!"

"No, what, Charity? No, I'm not a bastard? She wasn't a whore and a lousy mother? Guess again, honey."

"But . . . but surely she loved you."

Again came that curt laugh laden with spite.

"Sure. She loved me so much she dumped me off at the orphanage when I was four years old. She lit out of there like her tail was on fire, with nary a fare-thee-well, and I haven't seen hide nor hair of her since. Which is probably best for both of us, I reckon, 'cause if I ever do chance across her path, I'll more'n likely strangle her and end up swingin' for it. How's that for fairy-tale endin's, Charity?" he mocked.

She stared at him with tear-glazed eyes, not knowing what to say. Pity and anger welled up inside of her, anger at his mother for abandoning him and at Luke for being so blunt and sarcastic and hateful in the telling. "You're twisted with hate, Luke Sterling!" she blurted out. "No wonder you're such a nasty, despicable . . ."

"Bastard?" he offered gruffly.

"Oooh!" she shrieked, thoroughly put out with him. Wanting only to rid herself of his odious presence, she kicked her mare into a gallop, swiftly putting space between them.

"What's the matter, Charity?" he called after her. "Wasn't my story to your liking? Don't you want to hear more of the grisly details of my youth?"

When she kept riding, not sparing him so much as a backward glance, Luke spurred his own mount into a run. "Charity! Damn it, Charity! Whoa up! You're gonna kill your horse, runnin' her like that in this heat! Come back h . . . Aaargh!"

His strangled cry made her curb her mare. Casting a quick look back, Charity gaped in horror. Horse and rider lay writhing on the sand; the horse trying to gain his feet, while Luke grappled with a strange, scaly-looking lizard that had its jaws locked firmly around his upper arm. Cursing and yelling, Luke tried to shake it off, but the animal held tight. From where she sat, Charity could see blood already staining Luke's shirtsleeve.

"I'm coming!" she screamed. "Oh, Lord! I'm coming!"

Racing pell-mell back to him, Charity drew her Colt, desperately trying to draw a bead on the hissing creature, but as Luke and the thing, whatever it was, struggled violently, she feared to fire lest she hit Luke by mistake. Frantic, she tossed the gun aside and reached for her whip, coiled across the pommel of her saddle. With barely time enough for a muttered prayer, she sent the leather singing through the air. For just a heartbeat, it snapped taut, and when it fell slack the creature's body had been neatly severed from its head.

Vaulting from her saddle, Charity stumbled toward where Luke lay with his eyes closed tightly, his teeth grating together on a moan as he tried to pry the animal's teeth loose from his arm. Even in the throes of death, its massive jaws maintained their grip.

Frightened half witless, Charity swallowed her fear and reached out to help him. "No!" he yelled, his eyes snapping open to blaze up at her. "Don't touch it!"

"But Luke!"

"No, I said! Damn it, Charity! For once in your life, do as I tell you. It's poisonous."

At last the huge jaws pulled free, leaving Luke's flesh clinging in shreds to rows of razor-sharp teeth. Shaking, tears streaming down her pale face, Charity knelt beside him. "What can I do? How can I help you? Oh, God, Luke! How poisonous is that awful thing? What on earth was it?" Her eyes wandered involuntarily toward the large coral and black lizard-like corpse.

His free hand holding his wound, Luke struggled to sit upright. "It's a Gila monster, and it's about as venomous as a rattler, I suppose." He groaned. "Hell, I don't know! I've only seen one a couple of times before, and they always ran off. If my horse hadn't thrown me right on top of this one, he'd probably have done the same. Just my damned luck!''

''Oh, Luke! I'm sorry! It's all my fault! If you hadn't been chasing after me, none of this would have happened! Now, what do we do?''

''We clean the wound as best we can and bind it,'' he said.

At that moment, Charity would have sold her soul for a doctor. With no medications on hand, not even a flask of whiskey, she helped him squeeze as much of the venom as they could from the wound. He refused to let her suck the poison out, afraid she might swallow some of it. ''One of us is gonna need a clear head,'' he told her.

They drenched the wound with water from one of the canteens, Luke warning her to use their precious supply sparingly. Then they bound his arm tightly with strips of cloth torn from her spare shirt.

As soon as his arm was tended, Luke insisted they ride on. ''As near as I can figure, we're about two days north of Las Cruces. That should put Fort Seldon to our southwest, no more than thirty miles. We'll have to try for it. Stayin' here sure won't do us any good.''

''But can you ride?'' she fretted.

''For now. If it gets to where I can't, I want you to strap me to the back of my horse and lead me in, if you have to.''

''Luke! We're in the middle of the desert! Everything looks the same, whichever direction we turn.''

''Just head southwest and keep goin' till we get there. If nothin' else, we're bound to hit the Rio Grande again, and some sort of settlement.''

''Luke, I'm scared!''

''Yeah?'' he answered with a wry laugh. ''Well,

so am I, but we haven't got much choice, darlin'. Now let's get movin'."

To compound matters, Luke's horse had pulled a muscle in its foreleg when he'd stumbled into the hole. The animal was lame. Luke and Charity were forced to ride doubled on her mare, which would further slow their progress.

Not that it mattered much, to Charity's way of thinking. As long as Luke was lucid, they had a chance, but left to her guidance, they'd never reach Fort Seldon. It might as well have been a thousand miles away, for all the good it would do them. As they plodded onward through the blistering sand, she feared they were bound to die out here in this vast wasteland, with nothing but cactus and scorpions and Gila monsters to witness their sad demise.

20

FOR a while Luke was almost normal, though his left forearm pained him when he moved it. Seated behind Charity in the saddle, he curved his arm across her lap for comfort, letting his hand rest provocatively near the juncture of her thighs. In his right hand he held the reins, this arm riding her rib cage and occasionally brushing the undersides of her breasts as the horse plodded over the rough sand.

Charity wasn't sure if the contact was intentional or accidental, and she certainly wasn't about to broach the subject, only to have him mock her. As it was, she was becoming intensely aware of just how intimate their position was. On either side of her, his long firm thighs were aligned with hers, her bottom snuggled tightly against the front of his britches. From calf to shoulder, their bodies were practically molded together, like two warm wax figures melting together.

With his head tilted slightly to one side, to accommodate the hat she dared not remove or risk sunstroke, his every breath tickled her ear. Trying to readjust to a more suitable position in the saddle was a dire mistake. No sooner had she begun to wriggle than she felt his manhood stir to life, nudging at the cleft of her buttocks through their clothing. Her eyes went wide, and she immediately sat stock-still.

Despite the pain he was enduring, Luke chuckled, the sound reverberating through her. "Cozy, isn't it, darlin'?" he teased.

"Crowded was the word that came to my mind," she fibbed glibly.

"Little liar. Still, I'd stop squirmin' around like that if I were you. It'll be a lot less temptin' for both of us."

They rode in silence for a while, though Charity could almost feel the grin that curved his lips so near her temple. Each time she inhaled she could smell him, an alarmingly delicious mixture of male sweat and bold masculinity. When his teeth nibbled the rim of her ear, she almost leaped free of the saddle.

"Stop that!" she hissed, the entire left side of her body sprouting chill bumps.

"Just testin' to see if you're still awake," he taunted.

"Well, behave yourself and keep us heading in the right direction, because I have to tell you I'm completely lost out here. If we have any hope of reaching that fort, it will be your doing, not mine."

"Yes, ma'am," he quipped on another laugh.

He wasn't laughing for long. Before another hour had passed, he was leaning more heavily against her back, his breathing becoming more and more labored. Under the blazing sun it was hard to tell, but Charity thought his skin felt hotter too.

"Luke?"

"Mmmm?" he asked groggily.

"Luke, do you want to stop and rest for a while?"

"Uh, uh. 'Fraid if I get off this horse, I'll never get on ag'in."

"Luke? Are we still going the right way?"

"Mmm, hmn."

"Are you sure?"

"Yeah. Sun's to the west of us. Gonna set in a couple of hours."

Charity felt like a fool for asking such an obvious question. If she hadn't been so nervous, she would have been able to determine that for herself. Still, rather than comfort her, his answer further dismayed her. The sun would be setting soon, and night on the desert was almost as cold as it was hot during the day. Traveling on in the dark would be hazardous indeed, but could they afford to stop?

As Luke had pointed out, once he dismounted, he might not be able to climb back onto the horse again, and Charity doubted she possessed enough muscle to boost him into the saddle, even if he were aware enough to help. In addition, stopping for the night would present an entirely different set of problems. Foremost was the fact that it would delay their arrival at the fort by several hours, costly hours that could mean the difference between life and death for Luke. And she would have to find some way to build a fire for light and warmth, a chore Luke had always claimed before.

The question of whether or not to stop was resolved shortly before dark, when Luke suddenly toppled to the ground, dragging her with him as he fell. Fortunately, her startled horse did not bolt, perhaps because the poor animal was too tired.

As she'd suspected, Luke was burning with fever, out of his head with it. When she tried to wake him, he simply mumbled incoherently, swatting feebly at her. Weary, frantic with worry, Charity wanted nothing so much as to lie down where she was, close her sun-bleared eyes, and perish peacefully in her sleep. But that was the coward's way out, and she couldn't let Luke die if there was any means of keeping him alive.

Hauling herself to her feet, Charity ground-tied the horses and unsaddled them. Then, with the last rays of daylight streaking the sands purple and pink, she scouted the nearby area for anything that might burn, keeping a wary watch for snakes and Gila monsters. She found something that resembled a dead cactus, dried and bristly, and several clumps of sagebrush, which she lugged back to their make-shift camp.

Next, she unrolled their bedrolls, tugging and pulling until she finally managed to drag Luke's inert body onto it. Leaving him there for the time being, she located the sulphur matches, threw the dry brush into a pile, and lit it. It flamed up immediately, though she knew it would soon burn out. She desperately needed something else to put with it, something that would burn through the night. Remembering that two of their canteens were formed of wood covered with canvas, she quickly transferred their contents into two empty metal canteens, trying not to spill more than a few drops of the precious liquid. Only the good Lord knew when and where they would find more water. With the heel of her boot, she crushed them, then tossed them onto her small campfire.

Her guardian angel, or Luke's, must have been whispering in her ear, for Charity suddenly recalled that their saddles were made of wood, too, overlaid with leather. It was the only thing she could think of that might burn until morning. Without a moment's hesitation, though she was fully aware that cowhands and most other Western men considered their saddles their most prized possessions, she dragged Luke's saddle into the fire. He could always purchase another one; he couldn't beg, borrow, or steal another life, if she somehow managed to save this one for him.

While the fire blazed, she boiled a few strips of

dried beef in water, stirring and mashing it until she'd created a broth. With some difficulty, she forced the thin brew down Luke's parched throat, succeeding only by laying his head in her lap and stroking his neck until he swallowed reflexively. Already his skin was dry and crinkled, his raging fever fast depleting his bodily fluids. After dampening a strip of cloth, she dabbed at his face, trying to cool his flushed flesh. He was so hot that her cloth dried nearly on contact.

Upon unwrapping the binding from his wound, she found it red and angry. Frantic, certain it was becoming infected, she poured water over it, as near to boiling as she thought he could stand. Then she dabbed at the ragged bite until it looked clean again. Debating the wisdom of her actions, aware that if he were awake Luke would forbid her doing so, she hesitantly put her mouth to the wound. Gathering her small store of courage and praying for more, she repeatedly sucked the poison from his arm, as should have been done before. After carefully rinsing her mouth, she heated a knife blade to glowing, seared the torn edges of his injury, and rebound it. Throughout all of her torturous ministering, Luke barely flinched, this alone telling her how severely ill he was.

She'd done all she could for his wound. Now, somehow, she had to ease his fever. Knowing she had little choice and hoping he wouldn't awaken in the midst of it, Charity removed his clothing. The only movement he made to stop her was when she loosened his gun belt. Even in the throes of delirium, he instinctively wanted his weapon close at hand.

Piece by piece, her fingers trembling so badly she could scarcely manage the fastenings, she peeled his sweat-drenched clothes from him. As she tugged at the buttons of his britches, she averted her eyes and murmured shakily, "Please don't wake up now, Luke, or I'll never be able to go through with this!"

By the time she'd yanked his trousers free, her face was as flushed as his. "This is silly!" she chastised herself. "The man is sick. You are the only one here to help him. Now, quit being such a ninny and get on with it."

Though she'd been married to Johnny for a year, Charity had never before viewed a man's naked body in its entirety. Modest, God-fearing folk that they'd been, she and her husband had retained a sense of decorum even in the privacy of their own home. Never had they dressed or undressed or bathed within sight of each other. When they'd made love, it had always been at night, the lamps out, with Charity gowned in her long nightdress and Johnny fumbling beneath its yards of cloth. Now, for the first time in her life, Charity was seeing a man as God had created him—naked, vulnerable, and incredibly beautiful to behold.

She was stunned. Sitting back on her heels, every other thought flew from her mind as her eyes traversed Luke's long, lean form. His lower body was just as hairy as his top half. Dark hair bristled on his muscled legs and a thick thatch of it cradled his resting manhood. Even his toes were lightly sprinkled with it. Of their own accord, her hands crept forward to touch the springy mat on his chest, her fingers threading through it. Sweet heavens, it was as soft as it appeared!

Her hands wandered, fingers wide-spread, to measure the width of his broad chest; running lightly over his ribs, his shoulders, his arms; feeling the latent strength beneath her touch. As he moaned and began to thrash, she jerked back, suddenly remembering that she was supposed to be tending him and appalled at the disgraceful way she had been ogling him when she should be trying to bring his fever down. Shame flooded her, even as a sinful thrill lingered deep inside.

Tempering her wayward thoughts, she took up the wet cloth and proceeded to swath his body with it, head to toe. Soon, there was no part of him she hadn't touched, and with every stroke she could only admire him more. Even his feet were handsome, and in sleep his manhood presented no threat. Truly, he was the most beautiful man! As her hands learned the textures of his flesh, her mind began to accept the wondrous marvel God had performed when he had fashioned man.

The dry desert breeze turned cold, aiding her now in her efforts. Before long, Luke began to tremble violently. Though she pulled him as close to the fire as she dared, and piled all their blankets and oilcloth tarps over him, he still shook with bone-rattling intensity.

"Oh, Luke! What am I to do now?" she asked fearfully, expecting and receiving no answer from her delirious patient. Not knowing what else to do, she crawled under the blankets with him, cuddling his quivering body close to hers, just as he had done when she'd been chilled in the storm. By turns, all through the long night, he alternated between fits of fever and chills.

He mumbled and ranted for hours, rambling on and on. Unwittingly now, Charity heard it all—all the terror of a four-year-old being brutally abandoned by his mother, begging her not to leave him; the horror of those long years at the orphanage, at the mercy of despicable strangers; the anguish of war; the torments of his chosen life as a gunfighter; the relentless loneliness that ate at his soul like a canker.

All the while, she held him, crooned to him, prayed for him, wept for him the tears he would not grant himself. When exhaustion finally claimed her, she fell asleep with his head nestled gently to her breasts, her fingers unconsciously clutching the tiny pink ribbon, her small emblem of faith and hope when all seemed lost.

"No. Don't go." The hand lying on the curve of her hip tightened, holding her in place with more strength than Charity thought he could still possess after the night just past.

"Luke, we have to get up now," she answered softly, trying to slip from his grasp. "The sun is up, and we have to find shelter from it." When she received no answer beyond being pulled more tightly to his fiery flesh, she shook him slightly. "Luke? Did you hear me? Can you understand what I'm telling you?"

"Stay," he muttered, his head wobbling on her chest. "Stay."

It was useless. Charity couldn't even be sure Luke knew who he was talking to. In his fevered mind, was he once again that four-year-old child, begging his mother not to leave him? Or was he asking her, Charity, not to go? Beyond a few muttered words, she could not rouse him further.

For several minutes more, she lay there, giving him the security of her presence. Then, gradually, she eased him onto his back and pulled her aching body to its feet. Though it was early morning yet, the day's heat was already building. Soon it would be intolerable, as blinding and suffocating as the heart of hell. They had to escape it—but how? Clearly, Luke was in no condition to travel, especially during the burning heat of the day. If they rode at all, it would have to be at night. If he lived that long . . .

With bleary eyes, she scanned the surrounding terrain. Dried brush and cactus and never-ending sand met her weary gaze. Had she the energy, she would have sat down and cried. Instead, a crazed laugh bubbled up. "I can't afford to cry," she admitted to herself with a wry smile. "That would be a waste of water."

Spying a cluster of taller cactus not far away, she went to investigate them, her dulled mind throwing aside the need for more sleep as she contemplated how to survive in this desolate place. With nothing but her own inventiveness to guide her, she had soon rigged up a tiny makeshift tent by draping the tarps from their bedrolls over the higher arms of the cactus. Nearby, she did the same with the saddle blankets, making a small patch of shade for the two horses.

Using the blanket Luke lay upon as a travois of sorts, she tugged and yanked until she managed to drag him under the shelter of the oilcloth-draped cactus. Then she collapsed beside his unconscious body, panting and drenched from her labors. Knowing she could ill afford to rest yet, she forced herself to boil another small batch of broth from the dried beef, willing herself to be patient as she tended to Luke's needs first, then the horses', and finally her own.

Over and over, she promised herself, "If I ever get out of here alive, I'm going to sell the farm and move to someplace cool and green and wet, where they haven't even heard of sand. I swear I will."

When their water supply was dangerously depleted, when she dared not use more of it to cool Luke's raging fever, she once more resorted to desperate measures, not at all sure of the result or hazards involved, yet knowing she must try something. With her knife, she whacked off large chunks of cactus, carefully extracting the meat from inside. Praying she wasn't about to do him more harm than good, she rubbed the moist, gooey globs across his flesh, repeating the procedure again and again as the milky substance seemed to bring some relief and no obvious adverse reaction.

Unable to resist, she stripped to her camisole and underdrawers and applied a generous amount of the juice to her own thirsting skin, reveling in the immediate cooling it brought, if only temporarily. With no one else around to notice, and Luke still out of his head with fever, Charity debated long and hard with her own conscience before allowing herself to remain clad only in her undergarments, taking care to stay in the limited shade of the steamy tent she had created.

Throughout the long, sweltering day, she alternated between bathing Luke and dozing briefly. At intervals, she forced broth between his dry, cracked lips, doubting it did much to counter the fluids he was losing through his fever. When he ranted and raved, she held him, crooning soft, meaningless phrases of comfort. His nudity ceased to concern her, his health and her own taking precedence.

At last, driven by a commanding thirst the likes of which she'd never known, Charity took a final, reckless step, fully aware that she might be putting her life in irretrievable peril. All afternoon she'd warred with herself over the wisdom of it, but the milky juice of the cactus beckoned like a beacon in a stormy night. Fear clawed at her as she lifted a small piece of cactus meat to her lips. An even more imperative need forced her to sink her teeth into the fleshy substance, compelled her pursed lips to suck the moisture from it.

The juice trickled over her tongue, dripping down her parched throat. Tasteless. Sticky. Wet. When her stomach failed to reject the offering, when her tongue did not flame or swell, she dared another taste, and another. Numbly, she sat and awaited her fate. Two hours later, her senses remained undulled, her stomach without cramps, her fair skin clear of warning blotches. If anything, she felt stronger, more alert. She ate more. Again she waited.

Finally, knowing she had tested it as best she could, she mashed the fibers into a milky gruel. Heart in her throat, she fed it to Luke, spoonful by spoonful, praying all the while that she wasn't giving this brave, handsome man the equivalent of poison.

Then she lay down with him, cuddling him to her breast, her slender fingers stroking his dark head. "Oh, Luke!" she beseeched as he lay so hot and helpless in her arms. "Please get better! Please don't die! I don't know what else to do to help you."

She awoke sometime later to a purple twilight and a cool evening breeze sweeping gently across the land. Immediately aware that something was different, it took a moment for her sleep-fogged brain to register the fact that Luke's fever had broken. His cheek and her camisole beneath it were damp with sweat, but the rest of his skin was cooler to the touch. Though he mumbled unintelligibly and failed to waken when she shook him gently, his breathing was less labored now. Not knowledgeable about illnesses, she could only hope that he was recovering rather than dying.

Either way, it was time to move on. Neither they nor the horses could last much longer here without water. With more determination than energy, Charity prepared a final, meager meal of cactus and beef broth for them. Somehow she managed to dress them both, struggling to pull Luke's clothes over his long, limp limbs.

As she packed their dwindling supplies and saddled her horse, she wracked her brain for a way to get Luke's unconscious body mounted atop a horse, for try as she might she could not waken him. Since his horse still favored its wounded foreleg, they would have to ride double again on her mare, and it would be best to try to get him astride, rather than strapped over the animal's back.

In the end, she simply sat on the ground between Luke's spread thighs, lashed his long legs to hers, tugged him up into a sitting position behind her and tied a length of rope around both of their waists. She pulled his arms around her chest, and tied his wrists together. It took several exasperating tries just to maneuver herself and her burden to her knees; longer to lurch awkwardly to her feet. Behind her, leaning heavily upon her small frame, Luke was dead weight.

Step by unsteady step, weaving precariously and almost toppling both of them onto their faces, Charity approached the waiting mare. Urging the confused animal to her knees, Luke in tow like a looming giant shadow, Charity dragged herself, and him, into the saddle and coaxed the wary mare to her feet again.

"Good girl," she praised, patting the horse's neck as she struggled upright under the double burden. "Now, just get us to safety, and I promise you all the green grass and water you can hold."

They rode all night and into the following morning. It wasn't until sunrise that, with a sigh of relief, Charity was sure they were headed in the right direction. She'd merely been guessing their way in the dark, praying she was heading them west toward the river and not deeper into the desert.

The poor mare was lagging now, her hoofs almost dragging through the sand. Charity was faring little better. With Luke leaning heavily against it, her back felt as if it were about to break in half. Fortunately, his fever had not flared again, but not once had he gained full awareness. Throughout the night, he had groaned and muttered, almost tossing them both to the ground when he suddenly began to thrash. It had taken all of her strength to hold them upright, all of her patience to try to calm him when he became restless.

Half-asleep in the saddle, Charity blinked with surprise when the mare suddenly displayed renewed liveliness. There was a definite spring to her step as she neighed loudly and broke into an abrupt trot, almost jerking the reins from Charity's numb fingers. Luke's stallion, on a lead behind them, trotted alongside, his nostrils flared wide.

"What in the world?" Charity wondered aloud, hanging on for dear life as she and Luke were bounced about. As she attempted to control her mount, the horse fought her, and she finally gave in and let her have her head.

Then, on the horizon, she caught a glimpse of green. Certain she was imagining things, she hardly dared to hope it could be true. Not until clumps of grass began to mingle with the sand did she truly begin to believe. One small tree, then another. A flowering bush. Thicker grass. A whole line of trees. Then, before she could gather her wits, the horses plunged down a tree-lined slope and stopped—knee-deep in water!

21

TOGETHER, she and Luke tumbled head-
long into the warm muddy water of the Rio Grande.
Charity came up sputtering, struggling for balance
as her wet clothes and Luke weighed her down. As
nothing heretofore had done, the water revived him
somewhat, at least to the point where he was par-
tially aware of what was going on and less of a hin-
drance as Charity fought with the knots that kept
them lashed together.

Laughing, crying, she dragged him toward the
shallow bank, where they both collapsed. "Oh,
Luke! We made it! We made it! Isn't it wonderful?"

"Where are we?" He moaned weakly.

"I don't know," she confessed on a wobbly sigh
of relief. "All I know is that we're out of the desert
at last, and we have shade and water. That's all that
matters now, that and you getting better." She
turned toward him, her eyes solemn as she studied
his face. "Oh, Luke! I was so afraid for you! The
longer your fever went on, the more certain I was
that you were going to die."

"I don't remember much of anything."

"Of course not. You've been unconscious for most
of three days," she informed him.

"And you took care of me." A small smile curved his lips, though he could scarcely garner enough strength to lift his eyelids. "You saved us both, darlin'."

"Since I almost got you killed to begin with, it was the least I could do. If not for me, you would never have been bitten by that horrible creature. I'm so dreadfully sorry, Luke, for all you've been through because of me." Tears glistened, making her eyes shimmer like blue stars.

With shaking fingers, he reached toward her cheek, his hand falling short. "Don't cry, darlin'. It's gonna be all right. Just hang in there a little while longer, until I get my strength back."

"Promise me you won't die, Luke," she said, choking back a sob. "Promise me."

"Now why would I go and do a fool thing like that when I have a real, honest-to-goodness live angel lookin' after me here?" he joked lamely.

"Promise." One huge teardrop rolled down her face, making a thin, clean streak on her dirty face.

"I promise." Abruptly, he lost the battle with weariness. As his lids slid closed, he muttered, "You look like you fought with the devil and lost, darlin'."

"No, I won," she assured him softly, a smile lighting her face. "I won."

Though muddy and warm, the river water was nevertheless more precious to Charity than all the gold in the world. After days of worry, of scrimping on their water supply, she now reveled in it. While Luke slept, she bathed from head to toe, lingering in the tepid river until her skin pruned. She filled the canteens to brimming, then laundered their spare clothing and blankets, spreading them out on the sun-dappled grass to dry. Afterward, she led the horses back into the stream and sponged them down, washing the salt and sand from their dusty coats.

Unraveling a length of rope, she fashioned a fishing pole from one of the tough strands, a broken branch, and a bent hairpin. Luke awoke to a brilliant sunset and the tantalizing aroma of frying fish and freshly brewed coffee.

"At the risk of breakin' my promise, I think I must have died and gone to heaven," he said, his stomach grumbling hungrily in chorus with his rumbling voice.

Charity's eyes flew to meet his. "You're awake," she breathed. Crawling to his side, she eased his head into her lap and offered him a sip of coffee from her cup. "How do you feel?"

"Like death warmed over," he grumbled. "I'm as weak as a babe, and as filthy as sin. Whew! Is that me that stinks so bad?" he added, wrinkling his nose.

"Well, now, it certainly isn't me," Charity countered. "I had a nice long bath while you caught up on your beauty sleep, so it has to be either you or the fish."

A smile creased the corners of his eyes. "Just my luck to be nappin' while you romped naked in the water. That's a sight I'd have given my saddle to see."

"Uh, Luke," Charity stammered, "you don't have a saddle any longer. I burned it."

"You *what?*" His head bobbed up from her lap, only to fall back again. He glared up at her, daring her to repeat herself.

"I had to, Luke. It was the only thing I could think of to use for fuel for the fire. There isn't too much to burn out there in the desert, you know."

"What about *your* saddle?" he asked irritably. "Did you burn it, too?"

"No," she admitted ruefully. "It didn't come to that. But it might have," she added.

"Is there a reason you chose my saddle to burn first?" he griped weakly.

"Your horse was lame. I figured if we had to ride my mare, I'd better save my saddle for last. I wasn't sure yours would fit her as well. I'm sorry. I did my best, given the circumstances."

"I know you did," he said. "Don't mind me. I never could abide bein' sick. It makes me as grouchy as an old bear."

"You'll feel better after you've had a decent meal and a bath."

Against all complaints that he could manage on his own, she proceeded to feed him, again with his head propped in her lap. "You gonna wash me, too?" he teased, his green eyes aglint with humor.

"I might at that," she countered smoothly, taking him by surprise. "It won't be the first time, you know. Who do you think did it for you while you were raging with fever?"

"You?" he croaked.

Her smile was both serene and taunting, a strange and alluring combination. "Yes, me."

"All over?" To her delight and his dismay, Luke felt a rare blush rising to his cheeks.

"Right down to your fuzzy little toes," she answered with a grin.

"Well, I'll be hornswoggled!"

"Maybe."

Despite her brave words to the contrary, now that he was aware, and on the mend, Charity had hoped that Luke could tend to his bathing on his own. But when she had to help him to his feet and guide him gently into the nearby bushes to attend to more private needs of nature, she had to admit he was far too weak to wash himself without risk of drowning.

Now, as he lay supine and waiting, it was his turn to grin like a cat after a canary and her turn to blush.

"What's the matter, darlin'? Losin' your nerve now that I'm awake?" he taunted.

"Why don't you just close your eyes—and your mouth—and let me get on with this?" she suggested gruffly.

"Because this is somethin' I've gotta see to believe, sweet thing. I wouldn't miss this for all the tea in China."

"Keep it up, and I'll stuff this soapy cloth into that sassy mouth of yours," she warned, brandishing the rag like a weapon.

He chuckled. "Now be nice, Nurse Prindle. I'm just a poor weak man in need of tender, lovin' care."

Silently, every moment an agony of suspense for each of them, Charity worked the buttons of his shirt from their holes, and was not surprised when her fingers fumbled at the task. Her knuckles brushed the dark hair on his chest, and she jerked back as if burned.

Indeed, Luke felt as if he had been burned, branded by her light tough. He waited, silently, watchfully, as she gathered her courage and reached out to finish ridding him of his shirt. Though she tried to accomplish this without touching him again, it was impossible to do. Again and again, her fingers seared his skin.

Taking up the sopping washcloth, Charity bathed his face, his neck and arms, his back, his broad hair-furred chest; never once meeting his searching gaze, silently willing him to lie still and silent beneath her ministrations. Yet she could feel his eyes upon her, questioning, compelling. With a will of their own, her hands caressed him through the cloth, delighting once more in the contrast of silk-soft matting and firm muscle.

Luke bit back a groan of tortured bliss.

As she bent to tug his boots from his feet, her back to him, the silence strained uncomfortably between them. "You need a shave," she offered hoarsely, her voice whispering over him more huskily than ever.

He gave a noncommittal grunt that could have meant anything.

Coming back up, she let her hands hover over his belt buckle, trembling. Small, pearly teeth worried her lower lip. With a breath so deep that she might have been preparing to launch herself from the crest of a steep waterfall into perilous rapids, she loosened the buckle and dealt swiftly with the remaining fastenings of his britches. As her fingers brushed his yearning flesh, one small knuckle dipping accidentally into his navel, Luke's breath hissed between clenched teeth.

Feeling as if her chest were going to explode, Charity gulped for air and yanked at his demin pants at the same time. They pulled free, landing her at his feet, his britches in her hands, her eyes riveted to his manhood.

For all the times she had previously bathed him, all those times he'd remained unconscious and unknowing, she was still unprepared for the sight that now met her gaze. Before, in fever and sleep, his manhood had remained flaccid, limp and unthreatening. It was not so now. At this minute, it was alive, rigid, and throbbing, like a rattler primed to strike.

"Charity, look at me," he commanded softly.

"I am!" she squeaked in dismay and disbelief.

If the moment hadn't been so serious, he would have laughed. "Look at my face, darlin'," he corrected.

Swallowing hard, she forced her eyes to his. They were glowing like brilliant gemstones in the night, reflecting the flickering light of the campfire and glimmering with passion and understanding.

"Honey, I'm as weak as a newborn colt. I couldn't hurt you if I wanted to, which I don't. But I do want you, and that's somethin' I just can't hide, as much as you might want me to."

"I know." Her voice still came out sounding like a rusted door hinge. She cleared her throat, willing strength to her trembling limbs as she picked up the discarded cloth and knelt at his knees. "I know," she repeated, reassuring herself.

Like a skittish filly ready to bolt at the slightest movement or sound, she began at his feet and worked her way up his legs. Now it was Luke who trembled as her slight touch drew ever nearer to the fount of his aching need.

"Can . . . can you finish now?" she stammered softly, her voice quivering as she offered him the damp cloth.

"I really don't think so," he admitted, clamping his teeth tightly together.

"Oh."

Eyes averted, she reached out to wash the only part of him left unbathed. At her merest touch, his male member jerked, as if she'd startled or hurt it. In turn, Charity flinched violently, letting out a tiny yelp. Luke stiffened and ground out a muffled curse.

As she started to yank her hand away, his fingers clamped around her wrist, holding her in place. "No. Touch me, Charity. Know me. Please."

"I already know you," she whispered.

"Not like this."

Under the gentle, insistent guidance of his hand, her fingers lingered, slowly discovering the secrets of his arousal, learning the feel of tempered steel gloved in velvet. A deep moan rose from his throat.

"I'm hurting you!" she protested, again trying to pull away.

"No. Yes. I ache with wantin' you, darlin', that's all.''

Along with everything else, this was a new and startling revelation to her. That he would admit to such a thing, yet make no move toward her, only emphasized what she already knew deep in her heart. Beneath that rough, tough exterior lay a tender, vulnerable man.

As she knelt beside him, her hand still cradling him intimately, something wondrous was born within her. With every beat of her heart, it blossomed more fully to life, flowing through her with amazing warmth and ease.

"I think I want you, too."

Her words were little more than a whisper, but he heard them as clearly as if she'd shouted them in his ear. They vibrated through him like a quivering arrow, darting straight for his heart.

"Then take me, sweetheart," he murmured low, his eyes gleaming up into hers. "I'm at your tender mercy."

"How?" She met his gaze with a look of innocence and eagerness that tore at his soul.

"First, you should take off your clothes, honey. Either I'm a little underdressed for the occasion, or you're wearin' entirely too much. And I need to see you. I want to feast my eyes on you."

Blushing prettily, she removed her shirt and boots. More hesitantly, she rose, unbuttoned her skirt, and let it drop at her feet. Then she stood there, uncertain of what to do next until he prompted gently, "All of it, Charity. Right down to that silken skin."

"I've never done this before," she admitted tentatively, her fingers making knots of the ribbons on her camisole as she attempted to unlace them. "I've never undressed in front of a man while he watched me."

"You were married."

"Yes." The camisole fell apart, baring her creamy, rose-tipped breasts to his view, making his mouth water for the taste of them.

"Didn't you ever undress for your husband?"

"Not in front of him. And he never undressed before me, either. Until you, I'd never seen a man completely unclothed." Her underdrawers fluttered to the ground, and she stood before him, naked and uncertain.

Luke wasn't sure which shocked him more, her shy admission or the sight of her standing before him like some small, divine goddess.

"Come here, love," he instructed, his voice harsh with desire. As she put her small hand trustingly in his, he pulled her gently down to sit atop his firm belly, her legs straddling him. He urged her forward until the tips of her breasts brushed the dark hair of his chest. Her eyes went wide, blue as a midsummer sky and dancing with delight and wonder.

"Kiss me, Charity. Steal my breath away, and give it back again."

She did just that, and more. Perhaps it was the feeling of being in charge that held the fright at bay this time, the fragile illusion of holding dominance over the situation and the man, if only for a time. Whatever the difference, Luke was profoundly grateful for it, but not half as thankful as Charity.

It was with blessed relief that she let her mouth find his without having to fight paralyzing fear. As her lips caressed his, softly at first and then more boldly, her heart was pounding rapidly, but with growing excitement rather then mad terror. Her breath came short and fast, not in panic but in anticipation. The slight tremor that quivered through her was a shimmer of sheer pleasure as the hair on his chest teased the sensitive tips of her breasts, tickling them into hard pebbles.

Her tongue crept between his teeth, tangling with

his in a long, slow dance of desire that sent stars swirling in her head. Beneath the palms she had braced upon his shoulders, she felt Luke's heart thumping wildly in rhythm with her own. As the kiss deepened, he moaned and brought his arms around her, urging her closer to him, but did nothing more to assume command over their embrace. As his warm, calloused hands stroked gentle, sensual patterns over her bare back, she arched beneath his touch like a cat stretching itself in the sunlight, then slid more fully over him, her own fingers sliding up the column of his neck to thread into his crisp dark hair.

Dizzy with desire, she broke the kiss at last, gulping for breath and trembling in his arms. "Oh, Luke!" she breathed. "Luke!" Her lips wandered lightly over the unshaven bristles on his cheek. Her tongue dipped out to test the pulse beating rapidly at the base of his throat. Her teeth nipped softly at the curve of his shoulder. Now that she'd allowed herself to taste him, it seemed she couldn't get enough of him. Burying her nose in the dark curls below his throat, she inhaled deeply, reveling in the smell of soap and warm male flesh and another scent that was distinctly his own.

She was driving him mad with desire, and it was all Luke could do to let her have her way with him, when everything in him wanted to roll her beneath his yearning body and bury his aching flesh in hers. Every kiss was a spear of pure fire, every tentative touch like white-hot lightning. His hands drifted smoothly over her back, lingering in the delicate arch. Then, before he could help himself, they skimmed over the curve of her hips to cup her satin-skinned buttocks, pressing her womanhood more firmly against the taut muscles of his belly.

Without warning, a fierce, pagan throbbing, like the beat of native drums, started hammering at that secret place between her legs. Instinctively, Charity rubbed her lower body against his, seeking to ease the sensual ache there, even as she crushed her chest into his, weaving erotic furrows in the dark matting with the twin peaks of her tingling breasts.

"God, Charity!" he groaned. "You're so hot, so sweet. All I can feel is you! All I can smell!"

She claimed his lips once more, their tongues entwining, lips gliding and meshing in fervent search for more and better splendor. She'd never felt this way before, so wild, so frantic, so engulfed with strange, sensuous longings, caught in the powerful clutches of delicious desire. In its own way it was as frightening as the old fear had been, but in a way that made her yearn for more, and more, and yet more.

The pulsing between her thighs grew ever stronger, a moist heat gathering there. Her body writhed on his, their flesh slick now with a fine sheen of passion. Her brief embarrassment died quickly beneath the flames of passion licking through her.

Tearing her mouth from his, she gasped, "Please! Please, Luke! Help me! Show me!"

In answer to her plea, his long, strong fingers clamped around her waist, lifting her, lowering her, guiding her slowly onto his throbbing shaft. Inch by inch, the muscles of his arms bunched with the effort, he eased her gently downward.

"Brace your palms on my chest, darlin'," he rasped. "Take as much or as little as you want, as slow and easy as you need to."

In effect, he was telling her that she was still very much in control of their lovemaking, that they would proceed according to her wishes and needs. Even now, in the midst of delirious desire, she was thankful, for as she felt the tip of his manhood pressing for entrance into her body, a swift stab of fear raced through her. For one terrible moment, all she could recall was the rending pain the last time a man had taken her, the blood and terror of being mauled by lusting, groping beasts.

Sensing her sudden fear, feeling her tense abruptly, he set out to calm her. "Easy, darlin'. There's no rush," he crooned. Bending her down to him, he nuzzled her neck, her ear, his warm lips and breath tickling and teasing.

The moment passed, his compassion overriding her fright, and with a trembling sigh, she relaxed against him once more.

Long, lazy kisses brought desire rushing back, intensified tenfold. Lifting her slightly, only enough to create space between their upper bodies, Luke brought his dark head to her breasts. His wet, hot tongue traced intricate patterns over the milky globes and lapped at the rosy crests, making them pout for more of his tender touch. She murmured softly, and he gladly complied, taking one nipple inside his burning mouth, suckling it until she whimpered in longing, twisting her body to offer him the other for his pleasure and hers.

When she was aching with need, wanting him so badly she thought she might die of it, he guided her into place above him once more. "Be gentle with me, darlin'," he warned with a soft chuckle. "You're takin' advantage of a recovering invalid, remember."

His teasing remarks brought a smile to her lips, a light laugh bubbling from her throat. The last traces of fear fled her eyes, leaving them bright and clear and filled with joy. Slowly, with his aid, she settled herself onto him, feeling her body stretch to accommodate him, feeling herself filled with him. A half-shocked, blissful moan escaped her parted lips, mingling with Luke's soft gasp as he felt himself cloaked in her satin sheath.

When she'd taken the length of him with no discomfort, Charity simply sat there, luxuriating in the feel of him deep inside her. Their eyes held for long heartbeats, celebrating her victory over all the old terrors, anticipating the splendor to come.

Then she rose, slightly at first, moving tentatively as if testing unknown limits. It was the sweetest torment he'd ever known. Shudders coursed through him, making him both strong and weak at once.

With each silken stroke, she gained confidence, grew bolder. Her thighs clasped his tightly as she rode him, hands braced upon his thundering chest. Her hair came loose from the knot at her nape, fluttering down to cloak them both in a golden cloud.

Content to let her set the pace, he sought her breasts, cradling them tenderly, toying with the blushing tips as they rose and fell before his avid green gaze. Waves of rapture washed over him, through him. The chords of his neck stood out as he strained to hold back his own pleasure until she'd gained hers.

Charity was floundering in a sea of passion, tossed and pulled by turbulent tides, sure to drown in this torrent of sensations over which she had no power. Yet it was so wondrous, so stunning, that she had no wish to survive it. She was caught up in tumult, rising higher and higher toward the crest of something strange and awesome, racing toward a place she'd never gone before.

He felt the first silken pulsations of her impending release, recognized them and felt her stiffen over him, a look of shocked amazement on her flushed face. "Don't fight it, sweetheart," he ground out. "It's the nearest thing to heaven we'll ever know."

Then the spasms shook her. On a glad cry, she threw back her head and let rapture take her where it would. Luke followed, clutching her tightly to him as ecstasy erupted with a force that rocked his very soul.

An eternity later, they drifted into calmer waters. With soft sighs and gentle kisses, they bathed in the golden aftermath.

"I never knew it could be that way," she whispered shakily, shyly, her head pillowed on his shoulder.

"To tell the truth, neither did I," he admitted, sated to a state of numb satisfaction.

"If I wasn't bound for hell before, I am now," she added softly.

Immediately, he felt his calm dissolving. "Care to explain that, darlin'?"

"Beautiful as it was, it was still wrong."

"There was nothin' wrong about it," he grumbled, fighting an urge to give her a good shake. Turning his head, he lifted her chin, making her meet his eyes. "It wasn't sinful or shameful, no matter what you've been taught to believe. Pleasure isn't evil, Charity, and I'll be damned if I'll let you ruin what we just shared by feelin' guilty over it. It was good and right and wonderful. And if you dare say otherwise, I'll gladly blister your round rump till you have to walk all the way to El Paso."

A glimmer of a smile curved her lips and glinted in her eyes, and he thought he read gratefulness in their sea-blue depths. "For someone who was feeling so puny just a short while ago, you sure are getting sassy. Are you sure you're up to walloping me?"

He chuckled and grinned at her. "Probably not just yet, but I will show you what I'm up to, darlin'."

With that, he hauled her up and over him once more, and as his lips took hers in a mind blurring kiss, she felt his burgeoning manhood brand itself against her thigh.

22

THE next morning, when Luke found out Charity had sucked the venom from his wound, he was livid. "You little idiot! Do you have any idea what could have happened if you'd had just one small cut in your mouth? Or your lips? Or your tongue?" His voice rose in volume until he was roaring at her.

"Well, I didn't, so—"

"You still might have swallowed some of the poison. Then where would we have been? Both of us helpless on that damned desert!"

"It wasn't my idea to travel through that 'damned desert' in the first place," she reminded him heatedly. "And I did get us out of it, didn't I?"

"That you did," he conceded with a brusque nod. "And I'll be forever grateful. You saved my life. But do you realize what you risked? Do you have any idea how blasted lucky you were? If you ever endanger your own life to save mine again, I promise I'll kick your butt from here to tomorrow!"

"What is this fascination you have with my backside?" she grumbled, wrinkling her pert nose at him. "Every time you threaten me, it has something to do with my posterior."

294

Her comment brought a reluctant grin. "Yeah, I know. I reckon it started the first time I saw you in a pair of those tight denim pants of yours. I almost swallowed my tongue. I couldn't believe what a sweet little bottom you had, firm and sort of heart-shaped, and just the right size to fit my hands."

Her mouth flew open, working helplessly for several seconds before she exclaimed on a half-laugh, "Luke Sterling! You lecherous old man!" Through her surprise, her eyes twinkled with merriment.

"Old man, am I?" he repeated, a glint of roguish humor in his own bright gaze, his previous anger forgotten. "Old man? Should I prove to you just how much life this old body still has in it?"

He was stalking her, grinning devilishly, eyes gleaming and nostrils flared as if to catch her scent as she backed slowly away from him. "I think you need a few more lessons, lady mine."

"What. . .what kind of lesson?" she asked breathlessly, fighting back a silly giggle. "Guns? Knives? Fast-drawing?"

"Uh, uh." He shook his head at her, cocking that dark brow upward in a gesture of pure male arrogance. "First, a lesson in controllin' that runaway mouth of yours. Then a lesson on age and men and lovin'."

"In that order?" she taunted, laughing openly now.

He grabbed for her, pulling her into his arms. "Lesson number one," he murmured, his mouth swooping down to capture hers.

His lips were firm and warm and sweet, and Charity had to agree, in those first few moments when she could still think coherently, that it was an effective way to stop a person's speech. Her lips conquered by his, her tongue involved in more pleasurable pursuits, she couldn't have uttered more than a moan if her life depended upon it.

Her shirt was unbuttoned, his hands seeking to free her breasts from her camisole, before Charity became aware of anything but his lips moving seductively over hers. In a reflexive move to stop him, her fingers rose to clamp about his wrists. "Wh . . . what are you doing?" she gasped, tearing her mouth from his.

"I'm undressin' you, darlin'," he drawled. "Then I'm gonna make love to you."

"Here? Now?" she squeaked.

"Right here. Right now," he confirmed.

"But we can't! Luke, it's broad daylight!"

She sounded so thoroughly scandalized that he had to laugh. "Charity, honey, there's no one around to see us but the horses and a few birds, and they won't tell anybody."

She swatted at him. "I was right about one thing, at least. You may not be old, but you certainly are a lecher!"

Once more he silenced her the best way he knew how. Again, she succumbed to his charms, knowing only the feel of his mouth on hers; his hands dealing swiftly with their clothing; the warm sunlight beating down upon her naked flesh; the soft breeze blowing through the trees. The tickle of grass on her bare back and bottom as he lowered her gently to the ground and covered her body with his.

His hands caressed her with infinite tenderness. Gooseflesh rose in the wake of his wonderful, wandering mouth as he peppered her body with kisses, beginning at her face and working his way slowly downward, inch by tantalizing inch. Her world turned upside-down.

Then, abruptly, he stopped, his hand frozen on her thigh. Before she opened her eyes, she felt the rage coursing through him, felt his fingers tighten convulsively on her leg. The fire in her veins turned to ice as she lifted her lashes and saw the horrible look on his face.

"Luke?" Her voice shook with confusion and dismay as she questioned him.

Her small, wary plea seemed to call him back from his dark thoughts, making him aware of how badly he was frightening her. With trembling fingers he traced the long, jagged scars running the length of both thighs, the scars he'd known she carried but hadn't seen until now, the puckered flesh he'd overlooked the night before by the soft light of the flickering fire, when passion had ruled his senses.

"Charity!" His low cry was gruff with emotion, filled with anger and compassion. "Oh, little darlin', how you must have suffered!"

She tried unsuccessfully to push his hands away. "Don't. Please, don't look at them. They're so ugly! So awful!" A sob broke loose, tears trickling down her cheeks, and his heart tore in his chest.

"No. Nothin' about you could ever be less than beautiful, love. But it does make me want to find the man who did this to you, who dared to mark your lovely body this way. If it takes years, I'll never stop searchin', until he's been made to pay for this, in full measure."

Then he did the most amazing thing! He put his lips to her scarred flesh and kissed her there, his mouth traversing the length of each scar, as if by doing so he might erase the pain she'd endured, could expunge it from the very depths of her mind and soul, as if it had never been.

And suddenly, magically, she felt beautiful again, whole again for the first time since the attack, treasured above the most precious of jewels. Joy, astonishment, disbelief flooded her being. Her heart sang. Her soul ached. Her mind cried out with gladness. Tears pooled in her eyes and stung her throat. "Oh, Luke! Luke!"

As he rose above her, tenderly joining their bodies as one, she chanted his name like a prayer—a prayer of thanksgiving and love.

El Paso reminded Charity of Dodge City, only larger, noisier, and dirtier. Like Dodge, it was a cow town, but it was also a border town and thus a convenient crossing to and from Mexico for numerous bandits, murderers, and general riffraff. In addition, El Paso was a thriving center for some of the finest Mexican leather goods, which enabled Luke to easily purchase a fine new saddle, and eliminated the need for them to ride double.

Discreet questioning in the proper places soon unearthed news of Cutter. Brutish braggart that he was, he hadn't bothered trying to hide his whereabouts. He was still in El Paso, evidently feeling safe and content, spending most of his time drinking and whoring and intimidating everyone.

It didn't take long to discover that Cutter had worn out his welcome at all of the best brothels in town. Word had spread like wildfire that his preference for using his knife was not limited to male opponents or to merely frightening women into submission. The man enjoyed cutting people and, one and all, these working ladies were terrified of him.

"He carved up one of my girls so awful that she almost bled to death before the doc got here," one madam told them.

The image of Cutter wickedly wielding his blade made Charity flinch with the memory of her own pain at the man's hands. "And the law did nothing about it?" she surmised.

"What law?" Sadie snorted. "The piles of cow dung that pass for the law in this town take one look at a bastard like Cutter and all but piss down both legs."

"You can't refuse him entrance, I suppose?"

Sadie laughed sourly. "You kiddin', honey? I've hired two of the biggest brutes I could find, just tryin' to keep enough order around here so he'll think twice about hurtin' any of my girls too bad again, and they still come cryin' to me with cuts and bruises. At least no one else has needed the doctor for any of her injuries, but I have to pay my girls twice the usual rate to put up with his abuse. They're all scared half to death of him. But we also know that if he doesn't get his pleasure here or at one of the other brothels, he'll likely attack some poor innocent on the street."

"Yes," Charity agreed wanly. "That's exactly what he'd do. He's done it before."

Sadie cast her a speculative look. "That why you're lookin' for him?"

Charity simply nodded.

"Maybe we could work together," Luke proposed. "Get Cutter out of your hair for good."

Sadie's eyes lit up. "Sugar, you manage that, and you'll see the happiest bunch of whores in all of Texas. Just tell me how we can help."

"First, we have to make sure Cutter doesn't suspect anything. That means that you and your girls have to keep quiet about any plans we make. The next time Cutter comes by, we'll lead him right into our net."

"Luke, I hope you aren't thinking of using one of Sadie's girls in this scheme you're hatching," Charity said. "I imagine they're nervous enough these days, wondering which of them Cutter will choose next, without the added burden of being deliberately used as bait. One slip of the tongue, one wrong move, and the whole thing could explode in our faces, at her expense. It's too much to ask, and too dangerous." Charity adopted her most obstinate expression, then added, "Unless we make certain that *I'm* the woman he seeks out."

"That's the most asinine thing you've said yet," Luke assured her. "Hell's bells, Charity! He's bound to recognize you!"

"Jeb didn't," she countered quickly. "And I'm sure Sadie has lots of ways to make me look different."

Sadie nodded agreement. "By the time I get done with her, even her own mother won't know her."

"That's all well and good, but what's gonna make Cutter choose Charity over one of the other girls?"

"Boredom," Sadie answered with a knowing grin. "Let word get out that I've got a new girl workin', and Cutter'll be beating a path to Sadie's Sin House faster than a jackrabbit with his tail on fire."

Luke still wasn't ready to agree. "I don't know, Charity. You had a hard enough time actin' a convincin' saloon girl. How in tarnation are you gonna play a whore without givin' the game away?"

"By reminding myself every minute how much I owe that demon from hell," she stated coldly, yanking the neckerchief from around her throat, ignoring Sadie's gasp as the distinctive scar was revealed. "I want to send him back there forever, into that viper's pit from which he crawled."

That very day, news spread that there was a new filly in Sadie's stable of harlots—fresh, pretty, and eager to please. By design, all offers from other interested customers were graciously declined, as Charity and Luke anxiously awaited Cutter's arrival. It was almost eight o'clock before he showed up, early by bawdy house standards, since the midsummer sun was an hour from setting, but late enough for Charity's nerves to be fraying rapidly. Her hands were clammy, her head pounding.

"Brace yourself, honey. Here he comes," Sadie whispered in her ear.

"I came to see this new gal ya got," Cutter announced loudly, his voice making the downy hair at Charity's nape stand on end.

Pasting a bright smile on her face, she turned to face him, one hand posed jauntily on her hip.

"This is Cherry," Sadie said, introducing her by the name they'd chosen earlier.

Cutter laughed, obviously enjoying the joke almost as much as Sadie had when she'd first derived it. "Is she?" he asked wryly.

"Depends on how much you're willin' to pay, Cutter," Sadie quipped.

His cold, mean eyes traversed Charity's scantily clad body, devouring the ripe breasts pushed high and proud above the lace trim of her black satin corset, skimming downward past the matching bloomers to her shapely stocking-clad legs.

"See something you like, mister?" Charity drawled huskily, barely keeping the quiver from her voice as she met his snakelike gaze. She was betting wildly on her sudden intuition that Cutter might be tiring of women who openly feared him, that he wouldn't be able to resist one who didn't, one he could purposefully and viciously bring to heel until he broke her spirit and made her plead for mercy.

"You ain't heard of me yet, have ya?" he boasted.

She deliberately taunted him further. "I don't believe everything I hear."

He laughed again. "Well, seein' is believin', girlie. How about you and me goin' upstairs, and old Cutter'll show you a few tricks you ain't learned yet."

As Charity tossed her head, the ostrich plume bedecking her curls bounced pertly. "Fine with me, but I bet I have more tricks up my sleeve than you do."

"You ain't got no sleeves," he pointed out with a leer. He studied her more intently, his eyes narrowing. "You look sorta familiar, like I seen you somewheres b'fore," he said slowly, almost suspiciously, causing Charity's heart to skip several life-giving beats.

"I . . . I been around some," she managed to choke out with a shrug. Taking his arm, hoping he couldn't feel the trembling of her frozen fingertips, she guided him toward the stairs. "You ever been to St. Louis?"

Twice on the way up the steps, she almost tripped. When Cutter looked at her oddly, she gave him what she hoped was a convincing laugh. "Good thing I'm not as clumsy off my feet as I am on them, isn't it?"

"Yeah, well, we'll see," he grumbled.

Upon reaching her door, Cutter drew his knife from its sheath, pulled her to his side, and growled, "Okay, open it."

Swallowing the sharp terror that speared through her, knowing she still had to play her role believably, Charity retorted smartly, "You know, I was going to do just that, since I don't usually make a habit of tryin' to walk through walls."

"Shut up!" he barked, giving her a rough shake. "If you want to live past the next couple of minutes, that room had better be empty, 'cause if it ain't, yours'll be the first throat I slit."

With windows facing east and the shades tightly down, the room was shadowed but not dark. When nothing seemed amiss, Cutter yanked her forward, slightly ahead of him, warily keeping his blade ready. Three steps across the threshold, Charity stopped without warning. As Cutter barreled into her, she twisted to one side, clasped his wrist tightly with both hands, tangled a foot behind his, and with one calculated jerk sent him tumbling to the floor.

Before he could rise, Luke emerged from behind the door and leveled the long barrel of his Colt at Cutter's chest. "Drop the knife," he commanded, his voice as menacing as the look on his face.

The weapon clattered to the floor; Luke kicked it

out of reach. "Now the gun belt, nice and easy. No, use your left hand. Raise the right one over your head and keep it there."

Cutter glowered but did as instructed.

"Good. Now get up real slow. Make one wrong move, and it'll be your last, Cutter."

While Luke was disarming Cutter, Charity shimmied into a skirt and blouse, exchanged her high-heeled slippers for boots, and buckled on her own gun belt. "I'm ready, Luke," she announced quietly.

"What's this all about?" Cutter demanded.

"Judgment day," Charity answered calmly, though her stomach still felt as if it were somewhere around her knees. She aimed her own pistol at him. "Move. We're going down the back stairs so we won't disturb any of Sadie's customers, though from what I've heard of your escapades in El Paso, you could yell your fool head off and no one would care enough to help you."

"Where we goin'?" Cutter sounded nervous now.

"Someplace a little less crowded, where Charity can kill you at her leisure," Luke said, prodding him along.

They led him from the house, Luke taking the lead, Charity guarding him from behind. Through a maze of deserted back streets and alleyways they went, finally halting at a remote spot near the edge of town.

"This is far enough," Luke told him.

"Turn around, real slow," Charity added, "and meet your destiny."

Cutter faced her with a snarl. "You won't get away with this. I got friends."

"I know your villainous friends," Charity broke in. "They're next on my list of prey, all but Jeb. He was the first to taste my vengeance. Now I want to know where the rest of them are—the other four who attacked Johnny and me and left us to die on the Kansas prairie. Remember me yet, Cutter?''

"Yeah, you're that farmer's wife from up Kansas way, aren't you? I knowed we should'a killed ya. Hell, the way you was bleedin' I thought we had.''

Charity offered him a frosty smile. "You should have made certain of it, you and your band of rutting murderers. Because now it's my turn, and I won't make the same mistake. First, though, you're going to tell me where I can find the others.''

"I ain't tellin' you nothin'.''

"Yes, you will. Fast or slow, willingly or not, it's your choice, but the longer you delay the more pain it will cause you.'' Charity uncoiled the whip hooked to the left side of her gun belt and shook it loose. It straightened with a snap, slithering in the dust between them. With slight movements of her wrist, Charity sent it writhing like a serpent before Cutter's wary gaze.

Standing to one side, Luke watched and waited, a silent sentinel ready to defend his lady if it became necessary. He scarcely saw Cutter's hand move, so swiftly did the outlaw draw the knife from somewhere inside his trousers. It was there suddenly, unexpectedly, long and lethal, the setting sun glinting off its finely honed edge.

As Cutter drew back his arm, poised to throw the weapon straight at Charity's heart, Luke reached for his gun. The Colt was just clearing leather when a sharp crack split the air, echoed by Cutter's yelp of pain. The knife flew from his bloody hand and landed several feet beyond the man's reach. Before him, Charity stood calm and confident, a sneer curving her lips.

"That wasn't very smart of you," she taunted, eyeing his lacerated fingers. "Even if you have another weapon hidden, you couldn't use it now.''

Like the cornered animal he was, Cutter snarled. "You bitch!"

"Witch," she corrected smoothly. "In Socorro, where I killed Jeb, they know me as the Widow Witch. By nightfall, all of El Paso will have heard of me. Care to guess why, Cutter?"

When he disdained answering her, she told him. "I leave a calling card and a bouquet of dead weeds on my victim's corpse. Does that make you feel better, knowing that you'll go to your grave with a small memento from me? It's only fair, after all, since I'll go to mine with one from you."

With her spare hand, she tore away the decorative ribbon that banded her throat, baring the scar to his view. "This is the least of the reasons I'm going to kill you, you realize. But first, tell me where to find your murdering partners."

"I'll die before I tell you anything," he boasted.

"You'll wish you could," she promised in return.

Her whip lashed out with an evil hiss, slashing and snapping, slicing into Cutter's flesh time and again, shredding his clothes to tatters. Despite Luke standing guard with his gun drawn and ready, Cutter tried to run, desperate to escape. The smooth leather sang its siren's song, wrapping around him like strong arms, dragging him back for more of its punishing caresses, more biting kisses.

Within ten minutes, such a short time yet so endlessly long, Cutter was blubbering and whining, spilling out names and places as fast as he could talk between shuddering sobs. On his knees before her, he begged for his life.

"Beg God for leniency for your soul," she replied. "He'll listen more readily than I."

Despite his injuries, Cutter suddenly dived for his knife. His fingers had barely touched the handle when Charity's whip sang out for the final time, banding in tight circles around his neck. When it finally released its hold on him, Cutter lay lifeless in the dirt, the last bit of breath squeezed out of him.

As Charity slowly gathered the loosened leather into a neat coil once again, Luke looked down on Cutter's body, noting with some amazement that though the man had choked to death, there was a fine slice across his throat—a replica of the one he'd bestowed upon Charity just one year past.

He sought her gaze and found that she, too, looked stunned. In a voice so low he had to strain to hear her words, she moaned, "Good God, Luke! What kind of awful creature am I becoming?"

According to Cutter, Dandy was on his own these days, working the gambling halls along the Texas gulf coast. Luke deemed Galveston the most likely point to begin their search. Thus, they headed overland once more, with San Antonio as their most immediate destination.

Charity was not pleased to find herself traversing dry, barren terrain once again. Left to her choice, they would have continued following the Rio Grande and its moderately green banks, regardless of the added time it would take. She and Luke argued long and hard before she finally gave in to him.

"Yes, it's dry, but not like the desert we rode through before," he told her. "There are rivers and shrubs, even an occasional tree and short grass."

Halfway to San Antonio, Charity knew Luke had stretched the truth almost to breaking. The rivers were few and nearly dry from the summer's drought, the grass almost nonexistent, and trees as rare as hen's teeth. Even in the mountains it was dry and dusty. The only sizable river was the Pecos, and it, too, was now behind them.

"Drat you, Luke Sterling!" she grumbled, removing her neckerchief and swiping at the film of sweat and dirt on her face and neck. "This is absolutely the last time I let you talk me into following your lead. I want Dandy every bit as much as you do, but a couple of days longer, in relative comfort, surely won't make that much difference. Cutter was still in El Paso; what makes you think Dandy won't be in Galveston, or one of the other towns along the coast?''

''Because I've been trackin' the man for over a year now,'' Luke reminded her. ''He's as slippery as a greased pig and twice as wary. It's almost spooky the way he seems to know when I'm gettin' too close. I can be hours behind him and he disappears like smoke on the wind. I'm gettin' damned tired of catchin' his scent, only to come up empty-handed.''

With a sigh, she resigned herself to the relentless sun and miles of throat-scratching dust. There was just no talking to the man at times like this, when he had his mind dead set on having things his way.

They were about five days from San Antonio. Charity was riding alongside Luke in a heat-induced stupor, when she suddenly noticed that the sun wasn't nearly as bright as usual. The wind was picking up, and all about them the sky had taken on an eerie, yellowish-brown cast, blending with the horizon until she could not distinguish land from sky. To the southwest, a threatening cloud was building, close to the ground. Yet it didn't resemble a normal stormcloud.

''What's going on?'' she asked, noting the deep frown creasing Luke's brow.

''Dust storm,'' he stated tersely, his eyes roving the land before them. ''And it looks like it's headin' straight for us. We'd better find shelter, and quick.''

Even as he spoke, the wind grew in strength, gusting and blowing sand and dirt into whirlwinds, swirling it into their faces and down their necks. ''Lower your hat over your face and cover your mouth and nose with your bandanna,'' he yelled over to her. ''Put your slicker on and pull your collar up as tight as you can get it around your neck.''

Though she was sure she would swelter inside her slicker, she did as he instructed, feeling grains of dirt grinding between her skin and her clothes as she struggled awkwardly into the waterproofed garment. The wind threatened to tear it from her grasp before she managed to wrap it around her. Faster than she, Luke leapt to the ground, grappling with a shirt he yanked from his saddlebags, battling gale and fractious horse as he tied the cloth around his stallion's head. From her saddlebag, he grabbed her black petticoat as cover for her mare.

Befuddled, she screamed over the whine of the wind, ''They'll suffocate! They won't be able to see!''

''They can't see now!'' he roared back. ''At least this will keep the worst of the dust from their eyes and nostrils!'' She realized then that he was right. Without some protection from the flying sand, the horses would choke on it as it collected in their noses and throats.

As they rode on, fighting their way through the dense curtain of dust, she wondered if she might meet a similar fate. Even with the scarf tied up over her nose and looped over her ears, granules filtered under it, over it, through it. Tears poured from their stinging eyes, the screen of their lashes doing little to filter the fine dirt. It pelted their skins through layers of clothing, grinding and rubbing as if they were being scrubbed raw with a hard bristled brush. It found its way into their ears and grated between their teeth as they struggled to breathe. It coated their throats.

Charity couldn't begin to imagine where they would find shelter on this barren plateau. If a mountain had loomed before them, she would have run blindly into it.

Providence must have been guiding their steps. There was no other way to account for their stumbling upon the cave in the midst of nowhere. Luke spotted it first, or she might have ridden past it, never knowing it was there.

Grabbing her mare's reins, he shouted above the roar of the storm, "There!" He guided them both, horses and all, into the dark entrance and several feet beyond.

Walking through the gates of heaven could not have been more welcome. Now that they were surrounded on three sides by solid rock, the sound of the storm subsided to a muted whine. The wind scarcely reached them here, the dirt no longer biting its sharp teeth into their flesh.

Pulling the scarf from her face, Charity started to take a deep breath, her first in more than an hour, only to choke on the dust lodged in her throat. Cough after rasping cough shook her, until she had to lean forward and hang on to her saddle horn for enough support to remain astride the animal. Next she knew, Luke had pulled her from the saddle and was thumping her on the back. When the spasms eased somewhat, he lowered her to the hard ground. His hand, bearing the canteen, appeared before her.

"Take a mouthful, but don't try to swallow it," he commanded her. "Swish it around in your mouth and spit it out. Then, when you have most of the dirt washed away, drink slowly. Don't gulp it down, or you'll start chokin' again."

She had to fight an urge to do the opposite of what he instructed. All she wanted was to feel the tepid, tin-tasting fluid coursing down her parched throat. Finally, leaning heavily on his shoulder, she caught her breath. "Are we safe now?" she croaked out.

"I think so, as long as we stay out of the wind."
As if his words had angered some primeval storm
god, a gust of wind blew far into the cavern, showering them with grit. "Maybe we'd better move further into the cave," he suggested, brushing dirt from
his watering eyes.

Making his way back to the entrance, he tugged
at a small scrub bush, trying to yank it from its precarious hold in the earth. After several attempts, it
came loose, roots and all, and he dragged it back to
where she waited. "We can tear this apart and wrap
some cloth around it for a torch. It won't last long,
but it's the best we can do."

He was wrong about one thing. Their torches
lasted much longer than they would have expected.
The roots were covered with some sort of black substance, thick and slippery with a vile odor, which
when touched with the flame of a match, burned
magnificently. Applying Luke's original idea, they
wrapped their spare shirts around the roots, soaking
them with the dark, oily fuel and using them to light
their way into the dark recesses of the cave, each
step taking them deeper and deeper into the unknown.

23

$\mathcal{I}$T was a strange, dark world unlike anything either of them had ever experienced, lit only by the shadowy, flickering flames of their torches. Not far inside, the floor slanted abruptly downward. The passage narrowed, forcing them to abandon their horses, but by now Luke was curious enough to want to go on without them, at least for a short distance. Imagining snakes and bears and all manner of creatures lurking in the gloom, Charity was less enthusiastic. But since she found the prospect of staying behind, alone, even more intimidating, she reluctantly followed in his footsteps.

"We'll take our ropes, just to be safe," Luke proposed, leading the way. Agreeing readily to any measure that might make this venture less dangerous, Charity also checked to make certain her whip was still looped to her belt and her knife in its sheath. And just in case, knowing how Luke tended to get them into situations in which they were without water, she slung a canteen over her shoulder.

The further they went, the more damp and cool the cave became, the walls and floor taking on a sheen of moisture that gleamed in the torchlight. The passage widened again, allowing Charity to walk alongside Luke now. Though she still couldn't see more than a few steps ahead, this gave her more courage than viewing only the breadth of his back.

"Look at this!" Luke exclaimed softly, touching his hand to the wall. His fingers came away dry, after stroking what appeared to be a frozen trickle of water—rose-colored water.

"Fascinating," Charity said waspishly, rubbing gooseflesh from her arms. She still didn't like this place, and wasn't at all sure whether her prickling flesh was due to simple apprehension or the chilled air. She stepped away from him, tugging at his sleeve as she did so, not really watching where she was planting her feet, eager only to conclude this gloomy tour and get back to the entrance once more, storm or no storm.

In the blink of an eye, her boots slipped out from under her. As she fell, she pulled Luke down with her. Suddenly she was sliding on her backside, barreling downward at breathtaking speed, Luke right behind her, the two of them swooping recklessly along a wide, steep, slick trough. She landed with a thump, Luke careening into her and spinning them both around in dizzying circles. Together, they skidded for several more feet before coming to a stop against a mound of ice.

But it wasn't ice at all. It was a growth of some sort, sprouting from the floor of a huge room filled with similar mounds, all in different shapes and colors. More of these strange growths hung from the roof of the cavern. Still more seemed to line the walls and floor in streams of color. It was a most magnificent sight to behold, and neither of them could quite believe their eyes. It was as if they had dropped down the rabbit hole of Lewis Carroll's child's tale of *Alice's Adventures in Wonderland*.

For one of the few times in her life, Charity was struck speechless, sand and grit forgotten, her eyes

as big as dinner plates as she gaped about her in
wonder. Beside her, Luke was likewise dumbstruck.
They sat surrounded by glimmering, twinkling gem-
stone formations, as if they'd fallen into some mystical fairyland—or a giant's playroom strewn with
glowing, odd-shaped glass blocks.

Some were so clear they could see right through
them. Others resembled flavored ice. Spirals danced
down the walls, reminding Charity of unicorn horns.
Some shapes were as thick as a horse's belly, some
impossibly thin and delicate, some intricate drapes
of the finest embroidered lace. Every shade of the
rainbow, every color they'd ever imagined, winked
at them, as if splashed from an artist's dropped pal-
ette, transforming gloom into glitter. Many radiated
an odd light of their own, illuminating the entire
room in a soft glow, a fortunate turn of events since
both Charity and Luke had lost their torches in the
fall and their makeshift lanterns still burned in the
upper passageway, out of reach.

"I'm dreaming all this!" Charity whispered at
length. "I must be!"

"Then I'm havin' the same dream, darlin'," he
murmured, his softly spoken words bouncing back
at them from the shimmering walls, setting a nearby
spiral to trembling.

"What is this place? It's like a bejeweled castle, or
some bizarre enchanted forest. Only instead of trees,
there are . . . well, whatever they are, they're the
most beautiful things I've ever seen."

She was so awestruck that Luke couldn't help but
encourage her illusions. "Does that mean I get to be
a prince, and save the fair princess from an evil
witch?" he said, chuckling.

"I *am* the evil witch, foolish man!" She giggled
playfully.

"No, you're definitely the princess. You're much
too lovely to be an honest-to-goodness witch." He

caught her jaw in his hand, bringing her face closer for his inspection, gently brushing granules of sand away. "No warts, no hairs sproutin' from your chin, no long crooked nose. Just unbelievably smooth skin and the most delectable lips God ever fashioned on a woman."

Just before his lips closed over hers, she whispered, "And you're the most handsome prince a woman could ever want, Luke Sterling."

He kissed her then, enfolding them in a fantasy world all their own. His touch was pure magic, instantly bedazzling her. Their clothing seemed to melt away, as if by the wave of a sorcerer's wand. Then she was naked in his warm embrace, besieged by desire, an all-too-willing captive, engulfed in splendor within and without.

Wandering, exciting hands brushed the last of the sand aside, as they intimately explored each other's bodies. Touch by touch, kiss by tantalizing kiss, the spell was woven, entrancing them both, sucking them into a star-studded whirlpool of delight. Bewitched by her scent, her taste, Luke's mouth ran rampant in search of her most potent secrets.

And found them.

His tongue teased, seduced, turned her quivering body to hot, molten wax, malleable to his touch alone, making him feel as powerful and mighty as the most acclaimed wizard. The heat of her response set his own passions flaring to miraculous heights. Her soft mewlings and sensual cries of wonder inflamed him further, as he brought her to completion with soft strokes of his lips and tongue.

Ripples of rapture still engulfed her as he brought his body over hers, joining them with one smooth thrust. He was in her, around her, a part of her, and with each plunge he lost more of himself to her, until he couldn't tell where he left off and she began.

Paradise was a heartbeat away, in all its glory. Ecstasy came rushing toward them on fiery wings, sweeping them up beyond the clouds, beyond the sun, where joy was pure and sweet and endless. And when they could bear no more, they descended slowly, riding the gentle curve of a rainbow of dreams to the golden comfort of each other's arms.

As Charity's lashes drifted lazily open, she beheld once more the spectacle of wonders that had spawned this marvelous moment. It was as if they had been embodied within the heart of a jewel. If she lived forever, she could never envision more dazzling majesty, a time or place more perfectly beautiful. She would cherish this memory forever.

Getting out of their underground fantasyland proved a bit more difficult than discovering it. After first investigating the huge room from end to end, exclaiming over its marvels with childlike delight, they found that the only way out was the way they'd entered. Charity blessed Luke's foresight in bringing their ropes, and she watched anxiously as he lassoed a protruding chunk of rock near the top of the slippery chute they'd slid down.

"Now, let's hope it will hold our weight," he stated.

At his prodding, she went first, but her clumsy attempts failed her. Despite all her vigorous training, she did not have the strength in her arms to pull herself upward on her own.

"All right." He grimaced, eyeing the rope and the rock thoughtfully. "I'm gonna try it alone. When I make it to the top, tie the end of the rope around your waist and I'll pull you up."

He planted a swift kiss on her worried brow. "Wish me luck," he said.

She did more than that; she prayed for all she was worth. Though there was little chance of him injuring himself if he fell, if this attempt failed they might spend the rest of their short existence in this palatial prison, dying of starvation amidst overwhelming splendor. It was not how she wanted their lives to end.

He made it. Just barely! Once he'd achieved the rock, he had to stand upon it, stretching to his full length, to reach the upper edge of the passageway. He'd scarcely secured a handhold when the rock crumbled beneath his feet, sending a cascade of jagged chunks rumbling down at her. Her shriek of alarm brought a shower of more delicate formations toppling from the high ceiling of the lower chamber, and she had to leap nimbly aside to avoid being buried under the falling pieces.

"Charity! Are you all right?" he hollered down, causing yet another small avalanche.

"Shhh!" she hissed. "The place is crumbling all around me!"

At his whispered command, she unearthed the lost end of the rope and tossed it up to him. Swiftly, she tied the other end around her waist and gave a sharp tug as signal that she was ready. Slowly, steadily, he hauled her up the steep incline, yanking her the last few feet, bringing her tumbling into his waiting arms.

Quickly, silently, lest the entire structure collapse around them, they made their way back to their horses, then to the mouth of the cave. Outside, the sun was shining once again, the storm past, as if it had never occurred. For the first time in many a day, Charity welcomed the blinding rays and sweltering heat, much preferring the limitless sky and open land to the glorious confines below.

Still, with the immediate danger now behind them, her mind was free to dwell on the magnificent wonders they'd chanced upon, and the breathtaking love they had shared in the glow of a strange, magical place that would never again be revisited except in her dreams.

His thoughts traversing similar paths, Luke mounted his horse. As he settled into the saddle, something poked uncomfortably into his leg. Bending, he plucked a chunk of glimmering stone from the top of his boot, where it had lodged. The egg-sized gem shimmered a pale blue-violet, its depths catching the sunlight and sending it back in sparks of purple.

A secretive smile curved his lips as he tucked the jewel safely into his saddlebag, saying not one word to Charity about this precious keepsake, a dazzling reminder of a rare and brilliant enchantment.

San Antonio was a unique blend of Spanish, American, and German cultures, a fascinating place that Charity would have adored exploring for a few days. But Luke was like a horse heading for the barn door, eager to reach Galveston and Dandy, and nothing short of death was bound to slow him. In fact, their journey was about to be made easier from here, and quite a bit faster. A railroad line ran from San Antonio through Houston, then a smaller line spurred down to Galveston. They had tickets for the first train out, with a scant two hours to spend waiting.

Splurging on a hotel room they barely got a chance to use, Charity spent nearly half of that time soaking up to her neck in a steaming bath. In the interest of saving time, Luke joined her with an ornery gleam in his emerald eyes and a roguish suggestion that they wash each other.

"You are a truly wicked man, Luke Sterling," she told him, her fingers swirling patterns of soapy bubbles through the thick dark hair on his chest. "Absolutely debauched."

"You wouldn't want me any other way." He

grinned, content to let her have her way with him, savoring every spine-tingling movement of her hands as they leisurely explored his wet, slippery body.

He was both right and wrong, she mused, keeping her disturbing thoughts to herself for now. The more she came to know him, to appreciate him, the more she was certain that she would want him any way at all. Charming. Bossy. Tough. Gentle. It didn't seem to matter. Bit by bit, day by day, he was stealing her heart away; and there didn't seem to be a thing she could do about it.

Friend. Lover. Teacher. He was invading every aspect of her life—and it felt so right, so good, to have him there.

It was also a novelty to enjoy the sensual freedom of touching him this way. To run her hands so intimately over every part of his big, muscled body without fear, without guilt or shame. To openly, lovingly learn him with hands and mouth and her own flesh sliding over his. To feel confident in her feminine powers over him, to caress him and feel the quivers running through him at her touch. To know that she was bringing him pleasure, building his desire, making him yearn for her until he groaned aloud and reached out to claim her.

By the time they turned in their key and headed for the railway station, their room was awash with water and wet bedsheets. Behind them at the hotel desk a man was complaining loudly to the manager of water dripping from the ceiling of his room. Not normally a betting person, Charity would have given odds that his room was directly beneath theirs. Giggling, squeaky clean and glowing from more than soap and water, she pulled Luke, freshly shaven and grinning from ear to ear, from the hotel.

She was still chuckling, supremely relaxed and revived, as they loaded their horses aboard the train and made their way to their seats. To her further delight, Luke had managed to get them a semiprivate compartment, rather than seats in one of the public cars of the lesser-priced section. Here, the bench seats were nicely padded, with curtains over both the outer window and the closed aisleway door.

When the whistle sounded loudly and the train began to chug slowly from the depot, no additional passengers had yet joined them. Either the people who had bought tickets for this compartment had missed the departure, or no one had wanted to spend the extra money for more private travel. After waiting a short while, and finding themselves still quite alone, Luke rose and calmly locked the door. At her mute question, one dark brow spiked upward; one emerald eye winked suggestively.

"Again? Here?" she squeaked, knowing the answer even as he tossed his Stetson on the seat opposite her.

"Why not?" He grinned. "We're as snug as two bugs in a rug in here, with nothin' to do for the next six hours but while away the time." Her hat landed next to his with a soft plop. Their bandannas and shirts joined the rapidly growing pile of discarded clothing.

"You could teach me to play poker," she suggested archly, shivering with delight as his fingers played with the ribbons of her camisole, his knuckles brushing the exposed tops of her breasts, one hand snaking teasingly into the deep crevice of her cleavage.

"Now, why would I want to waste valuable time doin' that?" he asked, his broad, tanned back now toward her as he pulled her boots free and tossed them to the floor.

"Well, you've taught me almost everything else," she pointed out.

His smile was devilish to behold. "Not quite."

"What about the porter?"

"What about him?"

"He might stop by for some reason."

"And find the door locked and go discreetly about his business elsewhere."

"He'll know!"

"He might guess. Does that really bother you?"

"No. But aren't we going to eat sometime today? Traveling with you, I need to keep up my strength."

"Later."

It was hours and several blissfully fulfilled fantasies later when, replete at last, they joined their fellow passengers in the dining car. As she satisfied her growling stomach, Charity felt her face burn brightly at the memory of the wicked, wonderful things Luke had done to her body, the unmentionable things he'd taught her to do to his. Their loving had been wild and passionate, savage and tender, with neither of them holding anything back. She'd never known it could be so mad and magnificent—but now that she did, she would never willingly settle for anything less.

Upon alighting from the train in Galveston, the first thing Charity noticed was the salty tang in the air. Even the fishy scent the breeze carried did not detract from her delight. "It's marvelous!" she exclaimed, not bothered by the noise and dirt of the area immediately surrounding the depot. "I've never been this close to the ocean before. Do you suppose I'll get a glimpse of it?"

"Gulf," Luke corrected absently, dragging her in his wake as he made his way toward the railcar that held their horses. "It's the Gulf of Mexico, not the ocean. And since the town is on an island just a couple of miles wide, you can almost spit across it. Just hang onto your hat, little darlin'. You'll see the beach soon enough."

The first order of business, after collecting their horses, was to make the rounds of the taverns and gambling establishments in search of Dandy.

"Yeah, he was here a while back," one gambler informed Luke, taking a break from his game. "Haven't seen him for a couple of weeks, though, now that you mention it." Upon further inquiry, there was speculation that Dandy might have gone south, toward Corpus Christi or Brownsville.

Immediately, Luke secured booking aboard the next steamship traversing that route, and was frustrated to learn that it would not be departing for two days. Still, it was faster than going by horseback, particularly since there was little between here and there where Dandy might be tempted to stop, especially inland. The delay, and the trip by steamer, would also give them and the horses time to rest up and renew their energies after the long weeks of arduous travel.

Luke rented a single room in one of the hotels closest to the beach. After supper they rode their horses along the hard-packed sand, splashing through the foaming surf, getting wet and salty, laughing and having a grand time. At sunset they dismounted, and Charity stood enfolded in Luke's arms as they watched the dying sun paint the Gulf waters and the few puffy clouds with shimmering orange and red, pink, and gold.

The sky darkened as twilight gave way to night. Stars twinkled to life overhead. The moon hung full and heavy on the horizon, lending its soft light to that of the stars, turning the sea into silvered glimmers, sprinkling diamonds over the crests of a thousand waves. The surf sang its ageless, rhythmic song in sweet accord with the beauty of the night.

Peace enveloped Charity, shattered only when Luke whispered into her ear, "Let's take a swim."

She shook her head, offering the first excuse that came to mind. "I don't have a bathing costume."

"You don't need one. You can swim in your undergarments, or better yet, nothin' at all." He gestured about them at the deserted beach. "No one will see except me." As he spoke, he threw off his own clothes and stripped Charity down to her camisole and bloomers.

"But isn't it dangerous?" she countered. "Aren't there sharks in these waters?"

He laughed softly. "I'll protect you from any sharks that might want a nibble of your tasty flesh. I'll tell them that you're mine, and I'm not of a mind to share."

A snort of laughter escaped her, imagining such an exchange. "And I suppose they'll listen and go their way," she suggested dryly, "seeing as how you're something of a shark yourself!"

Giving her no more time to argue, Luke swept her into his arms, carrying her shrieking and wriggling all the way. When he was chest-deep in the swirling water, waves crashing into them, he swung her about in a circle and, without warning, let her drop into the dark brine.

In an instant, she was lost in a black, silent world, completely off balance, unable to tell up from down. She hadn't had a chance to catch her breath as she fell, and now it was too late! Thrashing, kicking, a silent scream welled up inside her, a scream she didn't dare let loose, one that would not be heard if she did. Stark terror engulfed her, robbing her of all reason, filling her with panic such as she hadn't known since that awful night when Johnny had died.

And now she was about to die, too! She knew it as surely as she knew her own name, her own face in a mirror. Her chest was on fire, her lungs begging for air, her eyes wide open and staring at nothing but murky darkness. Her leg brushed against something hard, and in fear she jerked away from it. For a brief moment, her toes brushed the sandy sea bottom, but the waves buffeted her about before she could gain solid purchase, pulling and pushing at her as if she were no more than a rag doll. A blackness even darker than that in which she floundered swirled inward from the edges of her vision. On a silent, final plea for help, she gave in to the demand of her aching lungs, her next breath sucking seawater into her nose and mouth.

Above and just a few feet away, Luke scanned the surface of the water with worried eyes. When he'd first tossed her playfully into the waves, he'd expected to see her bobbing back up, laughing—or even railing at him for dunking her. But, to his shock and bewilderment, she hadn't come up. Or if she had, she was deliberately keeping silent, perhaps to teach him a well-deserved lesson. Now, the seconds were fast lengthening, and he was becoming frantic. Had the tricky current caught her and dragged her farther out?

Something brushed against his leg and was gone in a heartbeat, before he could grab hold of it. Again he tried to see beyond the churning waves, cursing them and the darkness, and himself for being so stupid.

Once more, something caressed his leg, something as fine and gossamer as cobwebs—or hair! Lunging beneath the surface, he grabbed wildly, wrapping his fingers in the long strands, feeling them strain to slip from his grasp with the pull of the tide.

"No!" his mind screamed, as if the sea were a living thing. "I won't let you have her!"

Inch by precious inch, he hauled her nearer, until his hands found her face, her limp arms swaying with the waves. Then he had her firmly caught and was dragging her unconscious body onto the shore.

Saltwater streamed from his hair, stinging his eyes, merging with his hot tears. Clutching her tightly in his arms, he rocked to and fro, his head low over hers. "Please! Please, God!" he prayed. "Don't take her from me now!" His arms tightened their hold, squeezing her rib cage like bands of iron.

She gave one tiny, gurgling cough. And another. Then she was convulsing and choking, spewing water over both of them as if she would never stop. Suddenly Luke was all action. Tumbling her across one arm, he thumped her on the back time and again, ignoring her weak struggles. "C'mon, sweetheart! That's it! Get it all up and out. Breathe, honey! Breathe!"

At length, the spasms ceased, and she lay panting in his embrace, shaking like an aspen in a storm. When finally she could speak, she squawked furiously, "You bl . . . blithering idiot! I can't s . . . swim!"

Now that the crisis had passed, he yelled back, relief and anger mingling within him. "Why the hell didn't you say so, you twit? No, you yammer on about bathin' costumes and sharks and such, but you don't say one damned word about not bein' able to swim! I could shake you till your teeth rattle!"

"Th . . . they alread . . . dy are!" She gulped, shock fast setting in.

"Well, shit!" That was the mildest of the curses he used as he gathered her and their clothes from the sand, somehow managed to mount his horse without letting loose of her, and headed at a gallop for their hotel. "Stupid, silly female! After all the streams we've crossed, all the times you've stood hip-deep in river water and laundered our clothes, now is a fine time and one hell of a way to let me know that you can't swim! But I'll damn well guarantee you one thing, darlin'! You're gonna learn. I'm never gonna go through what I just did again. And neither are you!''

He was still ranting at her as he marched through the lobby of their hotel, naked as a jaybird, garnering startled stares of disbelief all along the way. He took the stairs two at a time with her still in his arms, both her camisole and drawers all but transparent, her hair hanging in wet strands about her, resembling nothing so much as a sodden Lady Godiva.

24

Tʀᴜᴇ to his word, and despite all her pro-
testations, Luke taught Charity to swim the very next
day. It took three stops at shops dealing in women's
apparel before they found a bathing costume for her.
Casting a critical eye at the thing, which was fashioned with enough cloth to drown almost anyone,
Luke finally agreed, for lack of a better idea. She had
to be clothed decently, after all, if he were to instruct
her on an open beach in broad daylight. They'd already caused quite enough scandal trooping through
the hotel the night before.

It amounted to one of the most frustrating days
Charity had ever experienced. She swallowed
enough water to float a ship, her costume dragging
her beneath the waves time and again. Saltwater
burned her eyes and throat, coating her skin and
hair. Sand worked its way beneath her costume, irritating her skin with each movement. She lost count
of the number of times she scraped her knees and
stubbed her toes. And each time she dared to com-
plain, each time she whined and pleaded to stop,
Luke just glared daggers at her and told her, "Swim,
damn it! You're not gettin' out of the water until
you do!"

"My fingers and toes will turn into prunes and stay that way for the rest of my life," she cried through purple lips.

"At least you'll have a life, without fear of drownin' in the nearest mud puddle," he countered unsympathetically.

She called him everything from a beast and a brute to an arrogant jackass, all to no avail. He stood firm, and by the end of the day she was finally floating and paddling about in a manner that met with his approval. "A fish you'll never be," he told her bluntly, "and you're plenty shy of bein' graceful, but maybe now I won't have to hold my breath and pray whenever we cross a river."

As if to make up for the tyrant he'd been, he wined and dined her at an elegant restaurant that night. Afterward, they strolled the moonlit beach, hand in hand. Wisely, he refrained from suggesting a swim.

He did, however, have amorous ambitions of making love to her there, to which she retorted smartly, "I've had quite enough sand up my britches for one day, Luke Sterling! You can either take me off to our room and that nice, soft mattress, or forget the whole thing!"

Off to their room they went, where he spent the night loving her.

"What are you going to do when this is all over?" she asked him during a lull in their lovemaking.

He answered thoughtfully. "I planned on buyin' some land, maybe in Montana or Wyoming, and tryin' my hand at ranchin'. But only after I've found Dandy, and the rest of the men you're lookin' for. What are you gonna do, darlin'?"

"I don't know. I do think I'll sell the farm, though, and move someplace where there are lots of trees and maybe some hills to look at. I don't really want to go back to Pennsylvania, but my brother and sister are there, and I don't know anyone anywhere else.''

''There are hills and trees in Montana,'' he suggested quietly. ''Wyoming, too. Lots of green grazing land and plenty of water. You could go with me.'' He waited anxiously for her answer.

''I could,'' she agreed softly. ''But I'll have to think on it a while, if that's all right with you.'' To herself she wondered if he were suggesting marriage, or merely a convenient, less permanent arrangement between them.

With all that was yet unresolved in her life and her mind, and not ready to consider either arrangement, Charity was relieved when Luke let the subject drop without further comment. At this point, the only thing she knew without doubt was that she had fallen deeply, wildly in love with Luke, a love that made her serene relationship with Johnny seem tepid in comparison.

The following morning found them aboard a steamer heading southwest along the Texas coastline. The ship hadn't even cleared the harbor when Charity promptly deposited her breakfast over the side. Not much of a sailor himself, Luke was all sympathy, though he thought it a little early in the voyage to become seasick. If she turned green before they'd even hit the open water, what would she do later? Luckily, it would take only two days to reach Corpus Christi, two more if they had to continue on to Brownsville, so there was little fear of her starving en route. Hopefully, it would be smooth sailing, free of storms or rough seas all the way.

Toward noon Charity recovered sufficiently to sit quietly on deck and enjoy the view. She slept most of the afternoon, then tossed restlessly throughout the night, robbing Luke of his own rest. The next day was a repetition of the first. Whenever they docked to take on goods, Luke would go ashore, check for word of Dandy, and hurry back before the steamer left port again. Thoroughly miserable, Charity remained aboard and waited for him, with instructions to gather their belongings and disembark only if he had not returned by the time the ship was ready to go on.

Dandy was not to be found in any of the smaller ports, or in Corpus Christi, much to Charity's dismay. As the trip dragged on, she was fast developing a distinct dislike for the sea, the ship, and all competent sailors, including Luke, who hadn't shown the slightest discomfort after the first few hours of their voyage. When the lighthouse at Port Isabel, near the mouth of the Rio Grande, came into view, she could have shouted for joy, if only she'd had the energy to do so.

Brownsville was a replica of El Paso, only smaller and dirtier, if that were possible. It was just as rowdy, every bit as disreputable. It was also devoid of Dandy, though he'd been gambling in one of the saloons just the night before.

"It ain't no wonder he lit out o' here," another of the card players told them. "He and Charlie were spittin' fire at each other all through the game, and you could see ole Dandy was just itchin' for a fight. Then, when Charlie misdealt twice runnin', Dandy accused him of cheatin'."

"*Was* he cheating?" Charity asked.

The man shook his head and let loose with a rueful chuckle. "Charlie wasn't smart enough to cheat. His only mistake was playin' with Dandy to start with—that and bein' so danged clumsy. That's what got him killed.

"Dandy whipped out that little derringer of his, aimed it right at Charlie's head, and pulled the trigger without so much as a 'by your leave' to anyone. B'fore that, you couldn't have told me a gun that small could splatter a man's brains that far. Beggin' your pardon, ma'am, but hellfire! That damned bitty pistol looked like some kid's toy."

"And Dandy? I ain't never seen a man so indifferent about killin'. Why, he sat there as cool as you please, with this queer, sorta twisted smile on his face. Then he just picked up his winnin's and walked out like nothin' had even happened. It wasn't till he heard that Major Willford over at Fort Brown was a good friend of Charlie's and wouldn't take too kindly to the news that Dandy got a mite ruffled. Guess he figured the U.S. Army was more'n he wanted to tangle with."

"Any idea which direction he took?" Luke asked.

"Word has it he hightailed it right across the border to Matamoros."

Luke nodded. "That figures. Neither the army or the law can touch him there."

A short while later, Charity got her first look at Mexico, and she could only hope that Matamoros was not representative of the rest of the country, for it gave new meaning to the word squalor. Crowding the warehouses that lined the docks was a rabbit warren of crude hovels, some little more than a collection of sticks and mud thrown together for shelter.

Gradually, the rutted road widened and became lined with a haphazard string of saloons and stores that made up Matamoros's main street. They were approaching the single dilapidated hotel when Dandy suddenly sauntered from its doors, heading for a saloon across the street. Before Charity had time to collect her wits, Luke was off his horse, tossing her the reins, and motioning for her to get herself and their mounts out of harm's way. She watched, speechless, as Luke strode forward and yelled, "Dandy!"

The gambler stopped, stiffened, and swiveled

about to face his challenger. "Well, if it ain't the gunslinger himself. I heard you'd recovered and were lookin' for me high and low."

"That why you've been runnin' like some yellow-livered dog?" Luke answered coolly. "I've got a score to settle with you, you back-shootin' son of a bitch. Here and now."

His gaze flickered to the gun belt Dandy sported. "I see you're totin' more than your derringer down here in Mexico. That should even the odds some for you, unless you're too much of a coward to go up against me in a fair fight. In which case, I could haul your scrawny ass back across the border and turn you over to a certain army major who wants a piece of your hide. Or to a lady I know who'd like the honor of puttin' a hole through that black heart of yours."

Dandy blinked, his face blank. "What woman? You talkin' about that good-for-nothin' whore, Paula? Sure, I roughed her up a bit, but no more than she deserved."

"I said *lady*, Dandy. Ever heard of the Widow Witch? She's on a mission of revenge against the six outlaws who attacked her and her husband outside Dodge City last fall. She's already killed Jeb and Cutter, and right now she's watchin' us, just waitin' to see if she'll get her chance at you."

Dandy's gaze skittered nervously past Luke and lit on Charity, who was now standing in the shadow of a nearby doorway, alert and ready. Recognition flitted briefly over his face. Then he focused on Luke again, his features bland once more. "That pint-size runt? Who you tryin' to bullshit, Sterling? B'sides, she enjoyed all that lovin' attention from me and the boys. Don't let her tell you any different."

"She already has, and I'd believe her over any-thing you have to say. My only regret is that I can't kill you twice—once for her, and once for me. But dead is dead, I reckon. They'll be measurin' you for a pine box before the hour's out, and Charity will be sure to decorate it with a bouquet of stinkweed, just like she did for Jeb and Cutter.''

"I'll see you in hell, first, Sterling," Dandy ground out, though he looked considerably less confident now.

Luke smiled. "All in good time, Dandy, but there's only one of us gonna shake hands with the devil today, and I'm bettin' it's you."

The two men stood eyeing each other, each braced for action, each with his hand hovering over the butt of his weapon, while Charity held her breath in anxious anticipation. She watched Luke's hand flash downward, then up again in a smooth arc. In that same instant, she saw a small boy, no more than three years old, dart into the street directly in front of Dandy.

"No!" The cry tore from her throat, echoing that of the youngster's frantic mother.

How Luke managed to keep from killing the lad, he didn't know. His finger was already squeezing the trigger, his Colt aimed precisely at Dandy's heart, when the gambler scooped the child up and held him before him as a shield. Surprise alone seemed to jerk the end of Luke's barrel upward fractionally, enough so that the bullet missed man and boy by scant inches.

Dandy's own shot went harmlessly wild, but now he stood with the barrel of his gun pressed tightly to the boy's dark head. "Go ahead and shoot, Sterling." Laughing wickedly, Dandy backed toward an alleyway, the child squirming in his arms and screaming for his mama.

The mother, wild with fright for her son, was screeching and clawing in an effort to free herself from the arms of another woman, who was desperately trying to hold her back. Luke and Charity stood frozen, afraid to move for fear Dandy would make good his threat to shoot the boy.

The moment Dandy disappeared into the alley, they were running after him. Drawn by the child's cries, they chased him through a labyrinth of rat-infested back streets, past startled peasants and tilted shacks. Their pursuit led them ever closer to the river, until they nearly stumbled over the wailing child. He was sitting amid a pile of rancid garbage at the corner of a shanty, frightened but otherwise unharmed. Unburdened now, Dandy was nowhere in sight.

"Where to?" Charity huffed, grabbing at a stitch in her side.

"There!" Luke pointed to an old warehouse several yards away, butted up to a crumbling pier. The big door was slamming shut as he spoke, and Luke was already loping toward it.

Torn between wanting to follow Luke and aid the child, Charity almost laughed with relief when the mother charged up the alley like an enraged lioness. With the child in safe hands, Charity scampered after Luke.

Guns drawn, they edged carefully into the warehouse. Immediately, two shots sent them lunging for cover behind a stack of burlap-wrapped bales.

"You okay?" Luke whispered.

Charity nodded, stifling a sudden urge to sneeze. Dry white tufts poked out of the jute-covered bales in front of her. "What is this stuff?" she asked.

"Cotton, stored for shipping to the mills." Luke shifted, edging around the side of a slatted crate for a better look at the interior of the huge warehouse. Even in daylight, and with gaps between age-warped boards, lanterns were lit at irregular intervals for the workers who stockpiled and loaded the cotton onto outgoing ships. For a moment, the deserted look of the place confused him, until he realized that it was siesta hour. The workers were all gone, enjoying their noon break for lunch and a nap during the hottest part of the day.

The cavernous building was about half-full of cotton, the bales crated and stacked as high as a man's head, side by side in long rows. And somewhere in this sea of fluff and burlap, Dandy lurked.

"Stay here," Luke murmured. "Watch the door. And your back," he added for good measure. "Don't wander, or we're liable to be shootin' at each other instead of Dandy."

Carefully, quietly, Luke crept to the end of the row. He darted to the next, barely ducked Dandy's next shot, and worked his way slowly toward the opposite end of the warehouse.

Meanwhile, Charity clambered atop the stack before her, raising a small cloud of dust as she went. For something that looked so soft and puffy, the cotton was amazingly dirty. Bits of hull caught at her clothes; the rough jute scraped against her hands. As she eased herself upward and flattened herself over the topmost bale, the ponderous heap wobbled precariously.

From here she could see most of the warehouse, all but the very end which lay in shadow. She could also see Dandy, perched aloft his own hill of cotton like a vulture searching for carrion. Steadying herself, she drew a bead on him, but just as she fired, a sneeze caught her unawares, throwing off her aim. Cursing, she burrowed into the bale as a bullet whizzed past her ear. For long, breathless moments, she hugged the bale and prayed. When she dared raise her head again, Dandy was gone.

Now she could see neither man, though she heard soft scuffling noises that told her both were on the move, each looking for the other. Shots rang out somewhere near the center of the building. She caught a fleeting glimpse of Luke, then one of Dandy, but too fast to get a shot off.

Then she saw Luke's head appear cautiously above a load of bales, as he hauled himself up to kneel on the swaying stack. He saw her and made a questioning motion, as if asking where she thought Dandy might be. Charity shook her head. As one, they scanned the area, ears straining for the slightest sound.

Abruptly, like a child's jack-in-a-box, Dandy popped over the edge of a crate near the opposite wall, his gun raised. With lightning speed, before Dandy could get off his shot, Luke fired. As Dandy shifted to one side, the bullet crashed into the wall behind him, shattering the lantern hanging just above his head.

One moment Dandy was dodging Luke's shot. The next he was covered with flaming lamp oil, surrounded by blazing cotton, engulfed in fire. Screaming. Writhing in agony. Clawing at his clothes. His hair a living torch. His mustache singed instantly from his lip.

Charity could only stare in numb shock, her eyes wide with horror. This couldn't be happening! Before her disbelieving gaze, Dandy's flesh was melting from his face, like some grotesque wax mask, his features distorting more hideously with each passing second. Suddenly the burning bales collapsed beneath him, toppling him and burying him beneath tons of flaming cotton.

Caught up in the terror, Charity could not move, couldn't even look away from the ghastly nightmare taking place before her as screams ripped from her throat. It wasn't until she began to cough, her eyes stinging from the smoke, that she realized the new danger she and Luke now faced. Frantically, she looked about her, but couldn't see beyond the billowing smoke. "Luke! Luke!"

The warehouse was an inferno, the thirsty wood and sun-baked cotton igniting like parchment. Fire flared all about her, sparks flying everywhere, scorching the very air she breathed. "Oh, God, Luke! Where are you?"

Then she felt his hands pulling at her, tugging her down from her smoldering tower. "Charity!" His arms closed tightly around her, catching her briefly to him.

Then he was pushing her onto her knees, yanking her kerchief over her mouth and nose, prying her pistol from her fear-numbed fingers. "Crawl!" he commanded hoarsely, shoving her forward.

It was an eternity in hell. Glowing embers of cotton and jute floated about them and coated the floor, burning their skin and clothes. Fire reached out with flaming fingers to catch at them, blind them, strangle them, deafen them to all but its furious roar. Choking, gasping, they struggled on. Twice, Luke pulled her aside within a heartbeat of being crushed by tumbling, blazing bales. Once, he slapped frenziedly at her back and hair. She scarcely felt the pain.

She couldn't breathe. Her body was becoming so heavy. A darkness that had nothing to do with the swirling smoke enveloped her. She could feel herself growing limp, sinking to the floor. It was the last she knew.

When she collapsed before him, Luke crawled to her side, his every labored breath a monumental effort. With trembling arms, he caught at her waist and hauled her unconscious body with him as he forced himself to continue on. A few more feet. A couple more. Where was the door? It should be there! It had to be there!

Just as he felt himself spinning into oblivion, he felt something pull at his shoulders. A waft of fresh, sweet air drifted over him and filled his aching lungs. On a final, gasping breath, he gave in to the beckoning mists.

Hands were thumping against his back, sending him into racking spasms. People were shouting in Spanish, rushing around, trying to put out the roaring fire. There was noise, confusion.

Ever so slowly his mind began to clear, to function again. When he caught his breath at last, Luke struggled to his knees. "Charity!" he rasped, searching for her through smoke-bleared eyes.

She was huddled within arm's reach, retching and crying and coughing all at once. Her hair was singed and sticking out in all directions, her face and clothes filthy and reeking of smoke—and she was the most glorious sight he'd ever beheld!

He raised his arms to her, and she threw herself into them, shaking and sobbing. "Oh, Luke! I thought we were going to die! I really thought it was the end for us!" she wailed, her voice made even huskier by the smoke.

"I did, too," he admitted gruffly.

Gradually her shaking eased, and still she clung to him. "Did you see him, Luke? Did you see what the fire did to Dandy?" she asked weakly, her hot tears bathing his neck. "It was so awful!"

"I saw." His arms tightened in an attempt to comfort her.

"As long as I live, I'll never forget that gruesome sight. Why, Luke?" She sighed, shuddering. "Why did it have to happen that way? So . . . so appallingly?"

"I don't know, darlin'. Maybe it was meant to be, for reasons we'll never know. Do you remember your peyote vision?"

She shivered against him. "It's all coming true, isn't it?" she whispered. "Just like in the dream. Dandy with his face disfigured; Cutter with his throat slashed; Jeb, with a bullet through his brain, even though I was aiming for his chest.''

''Yes.'' Luke took her trembling chin in his fingers and raised her tear-streaked face toward his. ''Could be we're not in control of what's goin' on as much as we think we are. Maybe—just maybe, now, mind you—there's a higher power directin' our actions, seekin' its own justice through us. Fate, or something. I suppose stranger things have happened.''

''Could it be?'' she wondered, her mind boggling at the thought.

He shook his dark head, as bewildered as she was. ''If you've got a better explanation for everything turnin' out exactly like your vision predicted it would, I'm more than willin' to listen.''

''Where will it all end?''

''With the last of the men you're after, I reckon.''

25

WITH Dandy dead, they headed toward Laredo, the last place along the border where they had yet to search for the remaining outlaws. It took them a week and a half of steady riding.

With each passing day Charity felt more miserable, and Luke became more worried about her. Amazingly, none of their injuries from the fire had been serious, just singed hair, raspy throats, and a few minor burns and blisters easily treated with ointment. But something was ailing Charity, making her stomach queasy, her spirits lag, and her temper flair at the drop of a hat. Had the heat and smoke affected her more than they'd first thought?

When Luke expressed his concern and repeatedly asked how she was feeling, she all but bit his head off. "I feel like I got caught in a stampede," she snarled irritably. "I feel like day-old mush and look even worse. Now are you satisfied?"

"Forget I asked," he retorted hastily, jamming his hat lower across his forehead as if to block out the sight of her.

"No, I will not forget it! This is all your fault. You had to suggest taking that steamer to Brownsville. My stomach's been upset ever since."

He sighed, knowing he wasn't going to win this exchange, but willing to indulge her need to argue nonetheless. "Charity, it's been almost two weeks since we got off the ship. Seasickness doesn't last this long—for anyone."

"Then I must have gotten sick in Galveston. You're the one who almost drowned me, then insisted that I learn to swim and wouldn't let me quit even when my lips turned blue. Heaven only knows what was in all that stinking water I swallowed."

"You're bound and determined to place the blame on me, aren't you?" he declared, her prickly attitude spawning his own in direct proportion. "All right, then. I've got broad shoulders. I'll accept full responsibility. But in doin' so, I have the right to make some decisions, and if you're so all-fired sick, then I think you ought to strongly consider givin' up the chase and goin' home where Doc Nelson can tend to you properly. We've found three of the men. Let that be enough for you."

Her chin jutted out stubbornly. "No. I promised myself that I would hunt down every last one of them, and that is exactly what I'm going to do. Besides, if your latest theory is correct, we couldn't quit now if we wanted to, which I don't."

"Even if it kills you?"

"Yes. And the way I've been feeling lately, that's a distinct possibility!"

To herself, Charity admitted that her malady was, in all probability, not Luke's fault at all. More than likely, it was all an aftereffect of the fire, or her nagging conscience beginning to eat at her. Still, if she didn't know better, she'd swear she was with child, for the symptoms were precisely the same as when she'd first carried Johnny's baby. The morning nausea, the fatigue, right down to a noticeable tenderness in her breasts, all made worse by the rough gait of her mare day after day.

But Doc Nelson had plainly said she'd never conceive again after the rape. It would take a miracle, and after some of the dreadful things she'd done in the past couple of months, how could she ever expect God to bless her so benevolently? Truth be known, this illness was probably just a small part of the punishment He had in store for her for her crimes, for daring to take vengeance into her own hands.

Laredo turned up neither hide nor hair of Bronc, and no word of his possible whereabouts. By now, however, Luke was becoming truly troubled over Charity's continued illness. In addition to everything else, he could tell that she was losing weight. Her face was becoming thin and drawn, the dark circles beneath her eyes more in evidence with each passing day. He had to get her to a doctor, and since the nearest thing to a sawbones in Laredo was the local undertaker, San Antonio was their best and nearest alternative.

When he told her where they were headed next, Charity was immediately suspicious. "But we've already been there."

"For all of two hours while passin' through in search of Dandy," Luke reminded her. "This time, we'll be scoutin' around for word of the others. Besides, darlin', it's a fascinatin' city, and all you saw of it last time was the inside of a hotel room."

He dangled the lure before her and she went for it like a fish after a fat worm. "Then can we stay for a while? At least a couple of days?"

"If we don't hear anything of immediate value, yes."

"Good." A genuine smile lit her face for the first time in days. "We'd better choose a different hotel this time. They might still be mopping up after us at the last one."

They had scarcely entered the city when Luke began to pester her to see a doctor. "Luke! Can we at least get checked into a hotel and wash away some of the grime first? Honestly! You can be such a tyrant at times."

By the time she'd finished her bath, the only thing of interest to her was the bed. It was big and soft, and the clean sheets smelled like heaven. Though she promised herself she would just lie down for a few minutes to rest her eyes before supper, the morning sun was shining brightly through the open draperies when next she woke.

Luke was standing by the window, smoking a cheroot and watching the street below. At her first stirrings, he turned to her, his eyebrow rising in question. "You finally wakin' up, sweetheart? How do you feel?"

She thought about this a moment, waiting for the usual nausea to assail her, but this morning, for some reason, it was blessedly absent. "Fine," she answered truthfully. "Rested. Hungry."

"Tell me what you want, and I'll go down and bring it up to you. Meanwhile, there's a pot of fresh coffee and a cup on the stand by the bed."

"Do you think I might have some tea instead?" she asked, surprising both him and herself. As a rule, she detested tea, but suddenly it sounded very good, and a lot easier on the stomach than coffee.

After a light breakfast, she and Luke took a leisurely walk around town. They ended their stroll in front of a doctor's office. Charity correctly suspected that Luke had planned it this way, first getting her all relaxed and unguarded, then springing it on her at the last moment.

"C'mon, Charity," he told her, grasping her firmly by the arm and marching her inside. "You've had me worryin' my fool head off for a good month now, and it's gonna stop."

She left the office with a bottle of elixir to restore

her flagging energy and a recommendation to try mint for her touchy stomach and frayed nerves. Relieved that the doctor could find nothing more serious, Luke was in high spirits. It showed in the jaunty swagger of his walk and the saucy dimple winking at her from his cheek.

"Now will you stop fretting?" she grumbled, having sampled the medicine and discovered it tasted like wet chicken feathers. "Land's sakes, but you're the biggest pest! And I swear if you don't stop grinning at me like that, I'm going to hold you at gunpoint and make you drink the entire bottle of this horrid concoction! That'll wipe that high-handed smile from your face in a hurry."

Charity could have stayed in San Antonio indefinitely, and Luke was tempted to agree. He hadn't seen her so content in a long time, and it was a joy just to watch her discover new and exciting delights. There were picturesque parks and plazas, where young and old gathered to pass the time, and the *mercado*, where the vendors hawked their merchandise from stalls piled high with tempting fruits and vegetables, woven baskets, colorful blankets and shawls, and almost anything else imaginable.

Spying a pretty Mexican skirt and blouse that had caught her eye, Luke could not resist buying them for her, his reward a sparkling smile and a lingering kiss that promised more to come.

Then there were the shops and open-air restaurants along the shaded walk that ran beside the river. All of it—the people, the appealing mixture of customs and cultures, the varied foods, the calm clean atmosphere of the town, everything from siestas to street dances, pleased her immensely. And what pleased her, pleased him.

She even enticed him into dancing with her, though he'd always considered himself about as graceful as a one-legged horse on a dance floor. Her tonic seemed to be working wonders as they joined the others in a lively Mexican folk dance, then a country square dance, even a rousing German polka, though they fumbled through some of the footwork. A bright glitter lit her eyes, and a charming flush stained her cheeks as she whirled breathlessly about, her unbound hair swirling around her like a golden shawl. Her gay laughter sounded as sweet and clear as a freedom bell, and Luke congratulated himself on his wise decision to take this brief break from their travels.

When it came time to leave, they were both reluctant.

"This has been so lovely." Charity sighed lazily, taking a deep breath of the soft evening air. It was their last night in San Antonio, and they were seated on the small veranda outside their hotel room, enjoying the sights and sounds of the city. Below their balcony, a strolling guitarist serenaded them with a haunting love song. "I wish it didn't have to end."

"It doesn't darlin'. Not that we can lie around havin' endless fun forever, mind you, but we could go on from here. Think about it, Charity. Since we stopped chasin' after those desperados, you've become much more relaxed and cheerful. You're feelin' better, and the color is back in your cheeks. Honey, I think it's time to go home. I don't think you can stand much more of the guilt you've been heapin' on yourself."

"And let the last three go free?"

"If that's what it takes to keep you healthy and happy, yes. We can go to Montana, put the past behind us, and start fresh, you and me."

His hand sought hers, his eyes searching her face in the dim light. "I love you, Charity. In my whole life, I've never said that to anyone else, but I'm sayin' it to you now, and I mean it with all my heart. I want to marry you, to make a life with you, have a family with you, and grow old with you at my side."

At his mention of a family, she stiffened. With a breaking heart, as much as she'd come to love this wonderful man, she knew she had to decline his proposal. "I can't marry you, Luke," she told him regretfully, biting back a sob.

He dropped her hand, practically throwing it from his. She heard the sneer in his voice, watched his features harden, as he asked sardonically, "What's the matter, darlin'? Isn't a gunslinger good enough for you after all? Even a retired gunslinger? I'm good enough to do your dirty work for you, even good enough to sleep with, but not good enough to tie yourself to for the rest of your life?"

"It's not that, Luke. It's not that at all!" she exclaimed.

"Then what is it? The fact that I'm the bastard son of a whore?"

"No! Oh, dear God, no! Don't ever think that!"

"What else can it be, Charity? I thought you cared for me, at least a little, but I guess I was wrong. Honey, you sure missed your callin'. With the act you put on, you should have been on stage somewhere."

"I do care. More than you'll ever know."

"Then why won't you marry me? Give me an answer I can understand, woman. One I can live with."

"I can't have children!" she blurted out on a sob, tears coursing down her face as she recalled that terrible day when she'd heard Doc Nelson render his verdict. "You want a family. You deserve one more than anyone else I know. And I just can't give you one. I love you, Luke, with all my heart and soul, and I'd gladly give you anything within my power, but I can't give you that. You need a whole wife, not a cripple like me, not someone with her insides torn up so badly that there's no hope of ever conceiving another child.''

''Hogwash!'' he retorted sharply.

''It's not hogwash! It's the plain and awful truth.'' She gulped. ''Ask Doc Nelson, if you don't believe me. Ask Sue. They're the ones who tended me after the rape.''

''It's not your word I'm doubtin', sweetheart,'' he said, pulling her close to him. ''Or theirs, either. It's your foolish notion that I need some other woman, when all I want is you. Darlin', do you think not bein' able to have children makes any difference in the way I feel about you?''

''It certainly would to a lot of other men,'' she argued.

''I'm not like other men.''

''But you've already said you want children.''

''I said I wanted a family, Charity,'' he corrected softly. ''You would be my family. All I'd ever need.''

''No. You're wrong, Luke. Chances are, if I married you, you'd be content for a time. Then you'd start thinking about what you were missing by not having children, a son of your own. In time, you'd come to resent me, maybe even hate me for not being able to give them to you. I couldn't stand that, don't you see? And if you strayed in your affections, if you gave some other woman your children, I'd die. After once having your love, losing it would kill me just as surely as a bullet through my heart.''

''I wouldn't do that, Charity. I wouldn't do it to you, or to me, and certainly not to any child. Not after growing up as a bastard myself.''

Her hands came up to frame his face, her eyes straining to see his features in the gloom. ''No. I'm sorry. Call me a coward, or whatever else you want, but I just can't chance it, Luke. I love you too much.''

''If you truly love me, you'll marry me.''

"I can't. I'll love you forever and beyond, but I can't marry you. Please try to understand."

"I'll try, if you promise to consider what I've said." Cutting off further debate, he pulled her to him, and spent what was left of the night trying to convince her, without words, of his abiding love and need for her.

The next morning, Charity's health in mind, Luke suggested they take the stage as far as Fort Worth. "It'll be faster than riding the horses, and even if we tie them to the back, they'll have a rest from our weight," he explained, concealing his real reasons from her. Let her think his concerns were for their mounts, since she seemed to take offense whenever he questioned her about her recent ailments. Still, he was hoping the easier travel aboard the stage would continue her recovery.

This proved a miscalculation on his part. The constant sway of the carriage brought a swift return of her nausea, and by the time they'd reached Waco, they were both eager to abandon the stage.

Charity staunchly refused to see another doctor, though Luke claimed the one in San Antonio was surely a quack not to have cured her. "It was just the motion of the coach," she assured him, already feeling much better. "I'm beginning to think that anything that moves, be it ships, horses, or stage, will lay me low. Land's sakes, I'm half-afraid to sit in a rocking chair," she joked lamely.

On the third morning, at Charity's insistence, they retrieved their horses from the livery. "We might as well go on. This dillydallying is silly. I can't spend the rest of my life in one spot, particularly not here."

They were leading their saddled mounts from the stable when shots rang out. Luke's Stetson flew from his head; a sharp buzz, like that of an angry hornet, flew past Charity's ear. "Crouch down behind your horse!'' Luke shouted at her, his narrowed gaze scanning the fast-emptying street. "Use it as cover!"

As more lead pelted all around them, they managed to regain the relative safety of the livery, pulling the heavy doors shut behind them and barring them. "Close those rear doors and secure them. Fast!'' he hollered back to the frightened livery man, who was standing as if frozen in one of the stalls. Creeping to a window, he peered out cautiously, earning a spray of gunfire for his efforts.

"Who is it, Luke? Can you tell?'' Charity whispered from close behind him.

Before he could answer, a voice called out, "Hey, Sterling! You goin' soft? You gonna hide in there behind your woman's skirts? Or are you gonna come out and face us like the man you used to be?''

Luke replied with a blast from his Colt, a cool smile of satisfaction curving his lips as a yelp of pain floated back. "Gus Newsome and his band of merry men,'' he informed her with a rueful grin. "Old enemies of mine. This is all part and parcel of a gunslinger's life, havin' the past rear its ugly head now and again, I'm sorry to say. As for this bunch, I helped put them in jail about four years ago, when they tried to rob the stage I was ridin' shotgun on at the time. Seems they hold a grudge,'' he added, his brow rising in an expression of nonsensical innocence.

He nodded toward their horses. "Get the rifles and our extra ammunition, while I keep them pinned down.'' When she returned, he told her, "I want you to take your weapons and climb into the loft. You might get a better view of things from there, and you can tell me if any of them tries to sneak around the side or the back. Stay low and keep your head down. And remember—I love you.'' With a smart pat to her backside, he sent her on her way.

From the doors high in the front wall of the loft,

Charity looked down. Hurriedly tallying heads, she scurried back to the edge of the loft, leaned over, and called down softly. "I count four of them, unless there are more at the back."

Crawling back to her vantage point, she raised her rifle to her shoulder and swiftly put one of the assailants out of action. The rebound landed her in the prickly hay, a bullet whizzing over her head. "Three!" she accounted for Luke's benefit.

She wriggled closer to the window once more. Splinters of wood flew everywhere as one of the men below tried to blow her head from her shoulders, making her duck hastily back again. His efforts earned him a bullet through the heart, as Luke took offense. "Two!" he said.

There was one left, by her count, and as she heard glass breaking in one of the windows below, she rose from her crouch, intent on warning Luke. The shot from behind her took her unawares, bringing a gasp echoing through the near-empty loft. Pain lanced from shoulder to fingertips, her entire arm on fire as she fell to her knees. Walls and stacks of bales wavered before her, shimmering and weaving as she tried desperately to dispel the sudden dizziness, not daring to look at the sticky blood flowing from the wound her free hand now clutched.

Luke's Colt barked out close beneath her, and his voice followed anxiously. "Charity?"

It took all her effort to answer him, but she now knew that there had to be one more enemy still lurking in wait. "I'm okay," she managed, biting back a groan. "Luke, there's one more out there."

With that, darkness overwhelmed her, and she sank slowly into the beckoning void.

Swimming up from the fog that enveloped her, Charity murmured, "But I don't want to learn how to swim, Luke."

A chuckle rumbled above her, and she opened her eyes to stare up into a strange face. At first assuming this was the last man who'd been trying to kill them, Charity began to fight. She managed a weak swing with her fist, missing the man's chin by a mile. Immediately, shards of pain shot through her other arm, and she collapsed onto her back with a strangled shriek.

Luke bounded into the room, his eyes wide with worry, even as the stranger said, "Now, ma'am, you've got to lie still while I finish binding this arm."

"Go easy, Doc," Luke warned darkly.

To Charity's amazement, the older man rounded on him. "Now look here, you young pup! I'm not about to hurt this woman any more than is necessary, but you can just hie your tail back out there into the waiting room and stick yourself to one of those chairs, if you know what's good for you!"

Luke blinked in surprise, then turned to do as the doctor ordered. "Just take care with her," he demanded on his way out, throwing one last concerned look her way. "She was feelin' poorly before she took that bullet in the arm."

"So! What's this about you not feeling well, young lady?" the doctor asked as he bound her throbbing arm with yards of gauze.

Her teeth ground together against the pain, she hissed, "It's nothing. Really. Just an upset stomach and feeling tired all the time. The doctor in San Antonio gave me a tonic."

As his hand accidentally brushed against her breast as he wound the cloth around her upper arm, she winced involuntarily. His bushy brow rose, much in the manner of Luke's. "Your arm or your breast?" he questioned bluntly, making her blush.

For a moment she thought about lying to him, but as his bright gaze held hers, she conceded softly, "My breast."

"Been dizzy at all?"

Charity worked up a weak smile. "Not until that bullet met up with my arm. Guess I'm just a coward when it comes to pain."

"This stomach upset," he continued. "When does it bother you most, and how long does it last?"

"Look, Doc, I know what you're getting at, and I have to tell you, you couldn't be more wrong." She frowned up at him through welling tears. "I can't have any more children."

"Then you have one already? Or more than one?"

"No. I lost a child last year, before it could be born." The fingers of Charity's good hand sought the little ribbon pinned inside her pocket, an unconscious gesture for comfort.

"I'm sorry. But are you sure you can't be pregnant? Your symptoms are fairly classic."

"My doctor was certain of it," Charity maintained.

"No disrespect to him, but members of our elite profession have been known to be mistaken on occasion."

"I was beaten and raped," she confessed, mortified at having to confide this information to a virtual stranger, but knowing no other way to convince him. "Doc Nelson said there was a lot of scarring."

"Would you allow me to examine you?"

"No!" Her sharp cry brought Luke running again, a warning frown on his face.

The elderly doctor pointed a finger toward the door. "Out!" he snapped. "Now! And this time stay there!"

The look on Luke's face as he tromped from the room brought a reluctant smile from Charity. "I'm sorry. He's so protective of me."

"So he should be, if he's the father of this child I suspect you're carrying."

"There is no child. And I resent your trying to

build false hopes. It hurts enough to know that I can never bear Luke's child.''

''That remains to be seen. Now, I promise to be as gentle as can be, and bring you as little discomfort and embarrassment as possible, but I really think, for your own peace of mind, and that of your husband, that we should determine the source of your ailments. And that means eliminating all possible doubts as to whether or not you are with child. Then, if that proves negative, we'll investigate further.''

With great trepidation, and without correcting his assumption that Luke was her husband, Charity gave reluctant consent. With gritted teeth, valiantly battling the familiar fear that raised its ugly head the moment the doctor lifted her skirts, as well as acute humiliation at having her modesty flung aside in the name of medicine, she endured the examination. The doctor proceeded as if all of his female patients were prone to such violent flinching at his merest touch.

At last, when Charity thought she could not bear it one minute longer, he gave his smiling pronouncement. ''Well, little Mama, I'd say you'll be rocking that cradle sometime in the early spring. The end of March or first of April would be my guess.''

''It can't be,'' she murmured, staring back at him, hope flaring and dying, then flaring again as he nodded. ''How could it be?''

He shook his head, as if in wonder himself, and said, ''The body has a miraculous way of healing itself sometimes, often by means we don't understand and when we least expect it. It's one of the things that makes medicine such a challenge, and so rewarding.''

''You're sure? There's no chance that you're mistaken?'' she asked, almost fearful that his answer would not be the one her heart longed to hear, needing to have it confirmed yet again to her waiting ears.

"I wouldn't tell you if I wasn't absolutely certain. Now, do you want to break the happy news to your nervous husband, or shall I?"

The last thing Charity wanted at this point was to have the good doctor blurt out such news, or to discover that she and Luke were not married. She needed some time to think, to come to terms with this startling discovery. And as much as she might long to share it with Luke, she also needed to savor it, to hold it close to her heart and truly come to believe it herself.

"No. I want to tell him myself. Please."

26

BUT she didn't tell him. Not then. Not
that night when he was making love to her, taking
great care not to hurt her injured left arm. Not the
next day or the day after that. Her arm was healed
well enough for her to ride without much discomfort, and still she had not told him about their baby.

She was almost afraid to tell him, for fear it would
somehow not be true and both of them would be
devastated. Or that something would happen, as it
had before. She kept remembering that she and
Johnny had just learned of their impending parent-
hood when disaster had struck. As irrational as it
was, she didn't want to chance something similar
happening this time around. To her convoluted way
of thinking, it seemed that the longer she waited to
say anything, the longer she could hold fate at bay.

Then, too, she knew without doubt that the moment she told Luke, he would demand that they get
married. Not that she had any objections to marrying him, especially now that she could offer him at
least one child as well as herself. Luke would have
his family after all, if everything worked out. And
her love for him bordered on desperation.

But she also knew that Luke would want her to

give up her quest for vengeance. He'd already mentioned it more than once. And she was not quite ready to do that, because if she truly was pregnant, she didn't want this child to enter a world with Weasel, Whitey, and Bronc still running amok in it. Even with all the other evils and pitfalls of life that might befall her anyway, she couldn't put aside this pressing need to follow through with her plan to eliminate these murderers—or if she didn't, to bury her lingering fear that they might one day suddenly reappear to once more destroy her happiness.

If Luke wondered why Charity fell silent at odd moments, why she seemed preoccupied, he told himself she was still recovering from being shot. It was natural that she might dwell on it for a while, having brushed so close to death again. Or perhaps her previous ailments were still bothering her, though she seemed much improved. Only rarely did her stomach trouble her as before, unless she was taking pains to hide it from him so he wouldn't fuss over her quite so much. Or maybe she was concentrating on where best to find the remaining three outlaws they sought and how to trap them.

But how to account for that funny little smile that crept over her face from time to time? As they rode along, he would catch her humming to herself, as happy as a lark. Or she'd have this peculiar look, sort of an angelic glow, her eyes all a-sparkle, like she had some grand secret that the rest of the world didn't know.

It irked him that she might be hiding something from him, that she wouldn't share her thoughts with him, but he was too stubborn to come right out and confront her. If and when she wanted to tell him what was on her mind, she would. Until then he would hold his tongue and not ask—and stew himself into a slow simmer all the while.

When they reached Fort Worth, they had a decision to make. Either they could continue on, heading straight north along the Chisholm trail into Oklahoma and eastern Kansas, territory they hadn't yet covered; or they could veer westward toward Wichita Falls and follow the Western Trail north to Dodge City, returning the way they had come. Time played an important factor, since it was already mid-September. The cattle drives were dwindling now. Winter would be coming soon, and they had little time to conclude their search before they would have to give it up until spring.

Of course, only Charity knew that their time on the trail was limited by more than the weather and the cattle drives. Soon her waistline would begin to expand noticeably, and the game would be up. Luke would know. She couldn't ride like this much longer at any rate, unless she wanted to chance losing this second child. And that was the one thing she would move heaven and earth to prevent.

She'd also found herself wondering lately how Mano was doing with the farm. The wheat should be harvested by now, or close to it. It had been exactly a year since she and Johnny had concluded the last harvest and gone into town in such high spirits. It had been a year since his death, her rape, the loss of their baby.

At times it seemed like yesterday to her, most particularly since she'd learned of her pregnancy. Her thoughts naturally seemed to revert to that first time she'd been with child. But when she thought of Luke, of how much he'd come to mean to her, of how much they had shared and had yet to share together, the attack seemed centuries ago, in another lifetime.

That old proverb about time healing all wounds was true after all, it seemed. If only she could find her remaining attackers and deal with them successfully, without jeopardizing a future that looked so bright and was almost within her grasp, she would be truly content.

Once again, the choice was taken from them, as if by destiny's guiding hand. Bronc had left Fort Worth scant hours ahead of them, heading for Wichita Falls. Not even taking time to replenish supplies, they set out after him.

They caught up with him two days out of Fort Worth, on the main trail that cut through the open cattle range, miles from even the nearest ranch house.

He looked like a typical cowhand, from his sweat-stained Stetson to the spurs that gave Charity cold shivers just to look at them, recalling the intense pain they had rendered. His boots were worn, his denim pants faded from numerous washings, his neckerchief more functional than decorative. It was his saddle that set him apart, though Charity would still have recognized his face in any place and at any time, so clearly had she committed it to memory. The saddle was the one from her peyote dreams, black leather trimmed heavily in a unique design of Spanish silver.

When they rode up alongside him, he doffed his hat and smiled widely, appearing no more dangerous than a schoolboy. "Howdy, folks! Where y'all headed?" Though he looked Charity square in the face, he didn't seem to recognize her.

Deciding to play along and see where things led, Luke answered, "Wichita Falls. My wife has relatives there."

Charity couldn't have said a word if her life had depended upon it. She was having enough trouble trying to keep her eyes from straying toward those awful, many-pointed spurs.

"Nice place," Bronc said. "I'm headin' that way myself. Thought I'd have to ride all the way by my lonesome, but I'd sure welcome your company, 'specially if your little missus can cook better'n I can. It's a wonder I ain't poisoned myself by now.''

He gave a short laugh at his own humor and slid a sly glance over Charity's still-trim figure. The shiver grew, slithering along her backbone, and it was all she could do not to let it show. She wanted to scream at him, to spit in his handsome young face, to tear him down from his horse and stomp him into the ground until he was nothing but small, unrecognizable pieces!

''Charity's a right fair cook,'' Luke conceded, watching the man's face closely for any signs that he recalled her or her name.

Bronc's features remained unaffected. ''Pretty name for a pretty lady,'' was all he said.

Unexpectedly, a jackrabbit sprang from a cluster of brush and darted across the trail, startling the horses. While Luke and Charity calmed their mounts with soft pats, soothing words, and a firm grip on the reins, Bronc shouted and cursed like a madam. With vicious intent, he yanked the bit hard against his horse's tender mouth and dug the barbs of his spurs angrily into the rearing animal's flanks, drawing blood.

''Damn you!'' he ranted. ''You'll either learn who's boss, or I'll plant a bullet in that big, stupid head of yours, just like I done to that dumb peddler a month back! You hear me?''

In the next instant, Bronc was all smiles, as if he'd never been upset in the slightest, as if his reaction hadn't been in any way irrational or excessive. ''Sure is a nice day for travelin', ain't it?'' he commented pleasantly.

Charity stared back, pale and shaken by the unwarranted cruelty she'd just witnessed. And what was that offhand remark about some peddler he'd killed? Luke frowned in growing concern.

They rode in silence for a distance, while Luke

sorted various plans through his mind, trying to decide their best course of action, especially given Bronc's peculiar behavior. Suddenly, for no apparent reason, Bronc drew his horse to a halt. Charity and Luke did likewise, not trusting the man at their backs. As Bronc pulled his rifle from his scabbard, Luke went for his Colt. But Bronc wasn't paying any heed. He was staring off in the distance, aiming at something neither of the other two could see.

Firing off a couple of rounds, he yelled, "Gotcha, you dirty son of a bitch! That'll teach ya to go stealin' my cattle, you filthy Injun!" He slammed the rifle back into its sheath, muttering all the while, "Gotta teach those red savages their place is on the reservation, that's all."

Seconds afterwards, Bronc was whistling a merry tune, riding along as if he didn't have a care in the world!

Charity and Luke shared a look of wary disbelief. There had been no Indian, or anyone else, out there; and as far as they knew, Bronc didn't own a steer to his name. It was also as eerie as hell the way he could switch moods as fast and easily as a chameleon changed colors. By all indications, the man was a raving lunatic, more dangerous by far than any of the others.

"Fancy saddle you've got there," Luke offered conversationally, when a few minutes had passed. "Where'd you get it?"

"Thanks. I took to it the minute I saw it. Bought it from some Mexican down El Paso way."

Stole it, more likely, Charity thought, swallowing the bile rising in her throat. Probably after he killed the owner.

"That right? Wouldn't want to sell it, would you?"

"Nope. This saddle is my pride and joy. Most fellas want to be buried with their boots on. Me? I want to be buried with my saddle.''

Luke's voice went suddenly cold and deadly, like a rattlesnake shaking its coiled tail. ''I sure hate to disappoint you, Bronc, but it ain't gonna happen that way.''

Bronc's head came up in surprise, his eyes growing instantly wary. ''How'd you know my name? Have we met somewhere before?''

''We haven't. But you had a meetin' of sorts with Charity about a year back. Just outside of Dodge City. You and five of your friends. 'Course, she wasn't very pleased with your idea of an introduction, or your brand of fun. Sound familiar to you yet?''

As Luke spoke, Bronc's gaze swung toward Charity. He stared at her hard, recognition finally dawning.

When it did, he whipped his horse into a gallop, digging those star-shaped spurs into its flanks. ''H'yah!'' he yelled, urging the animal to more speed.

Not about to let their prey escape so easily, Luke and Charity gave chase. For several minutes they stayed close behind, tagging him as relentlessly as his shadow. Then, suddenly, as if it had been shot, Bronc's horse went down.

Only Luke's quick reflexes saved them from the same fate, as he grabbed for Charity's reins while still handling his own. With a rough jerk that sent her horse's head twisting sideways until its nose almost met her boot, and his own mount rearing up in alarm, Luke brought them to a skidding, sliding halt. They stopped just shy of the wicked snarl of rusted barbed wire in which Bronc and his mount lay tangled.

The poor horse was thrashing about, trying to work its way loose, several of the barbs already imbedded deeply in its hide. Bronc was caught with it, his right leg still in the stirrup and tightly wedged beneath the heavy, bucking animal. Each time the beast moved, Bronc screamed anew with agony, his own skin torn and bleeding; his leg, if not broken, at least painfully crushed.

Still astride his stallion, Luke looked down on him with disdain. This was the man who had laughed as he'd ripped Charity's thighs to shreds with his spurs, leaving deeply furrowed scars on her tender flesh, and Luke spared no pity for him now. "You know, until this very minute I couldn't decide a punishment this side of hell that would be horrible enough for you."

The horse's tormented shrieks were earning Charity's full sympathies and fast wearing on her nerves, though she couldn't dredge up much compassion for Bronc at the moment. To her mind, he had been the worst of them all, the most deliberately evil and taunting, the one who had taken the most unholy glee from her rape and given her the most pain. For the rest of her life, every time she bathed or dressed, whenever she looked at her legs, she would be reminded of his demented cruelty.

"Wh . . . what do you have in mind, Luke?" she asked, still caught in the clutches of her tormented memories and trembling violently.

"I suggest we cut the horse loose. Then I think we ought to wrap old Bronc here up nice and tight in his prickly nest and leave him to the buzzards. Of course, it's up to you, darlin'. He's yours to do with as you please. But I think it's a queer twist of fate, after what he did to you, that he's all bound up in what amounts to about a hundred spurs, don't you? It's almost as if destiny has stepped in again to take the nasty business of killin' him off our hands. And I can't think of a more just death for him than this slow torture."

"We'd just leave him here?" she questioned dubiously, weighing Luke's suggestion. "What if someone comes along and sets him free?" Right now that was the worst thing she could imagine, and the last she would want to chance.

"Honey, I doubt that would happen in a million years. It's miles to the nearest ranch, let alone a town of any size. The roundups are done, and we've ridden pretty far off the main trail. He could scream his head off and no one would hear him. Hell, they probably won't even find his bones until next spring, unless the vultures lead them to his rottin' body."

To Bronc's horror, she agreed. "All right, but you take care of it. Please, Luke, because I don't think I can bear to be near him, let alone touch him. I know it's silly, but as much as I want him dead, I'm afraid—afraid his insane wickedness will somehow transfer itself to me if I get too close. I'll just go collect some weeds, and you come find me when it's done."

She left Luke staring after her with a baffled, worried look creasing his brow.

Martha Whiting was delighted to have them staying at her hotel once again. If she was surprised when Luke requested only a single room for the two of them, she held her own counsel. Rather, she exclaimed in dismay over Charity's wound, which was still bandaged and supported by a sling, and fussed over the younger woman like a mother hen.

"Why, just look at you! Thin as a rail. I don't know what ya'll have been doin' since you passed through here last, but whatever it is, it sure hasn't put any meat on your bones." She ran a critical eye over Luke and added brusquely, "Yours, neither." With that, she hustled off to her kitchen, intent on preparing them a meal they would not soon forget.

Later that night, well-fed on stuffed grouse and

all the trimmings, bathed and tucked between fresh sheets that smelled like sunshine, snuggled tenderly against Luke's warm, naked body, Charity tried to convince herself that she was blessedly content.

It was a lie. While her body was clean and sated from Luke's earlier lovemaking, her mind was in a jumble, her emotions in such a tangle that she wanted to scream just to relieve some of the tension. Her conscience was making a blasted nuisance of itself, on more count than one.

Beside her, Luke gave a soft snore, and she found herself wanting to throttle him, for nothing more than being able to sleep while she lay wide awake. "Hellfire and damnation!" she muttered, shifting irritably into a more comfortable position.

"What is it?" Luke mumbled sleepily. "Your arm botherin' you?"

No, she answered to herself. My conscience is. We're going to have a baby, and I'm dithering around like an idiot, not knowing when or how to tell you. On top of that, I'm trying to justify killing all those men, and I'm wondering why God has seen fit to reward me with this wondrous new life inside me, despite my numerous sins, and what He might do if I continue my search for the last two. That's enough to keep anyone awake!

Aloud, she whispered, "It's all right. I just can't sleep."

"Mmmnn." He nuzzled his nose in her neck and breathed in deeply. "You smell nice."

A wry smile curved her lips. "Amazing what a little soap can do for a person, isn't it?"

"Not the soap. You." His lips nibbled lazily at the lobe of her ear, sending shivers to her toes and making her scalp tingle. His fingers traced patterns on her bare thigh, inching gradually upward toward the juncture of her legs. "Soft. So soft and warm."

He was warm, too, but far from soft. He was hard

and throbbing and ready for her. But he wanted her to be ready for him, too. So hot and wet and ready that she ached with it. He wanted to hear those breathless little moans she always made when she was on the brink of rapture, to feel her hands pulling at him, her nails raking his back as she urged him into her.

His fingers parted the petal-soft folds, seeking that nubbin of flesh that set her wild. They touched and teased and petted, while she writhed in sweet torment, her body arching up in quest of his. Her gasp was thick and throaty as his fingers slipped into her with long, deep strokes.

"Luke! Oh, Luke! Please!" *Help me forget, for just a little while!* With words and hands she urged him up and over her, her tongue mating with his, her teeth gnawing hungrily at his lips as he entered her. Her wondrous sigh was a siren's song in his ear.

What started out slow and easy ended in a frenzy, the two of them racing headlong toward passion's promised land, frantically clawing their way up its steep banks, teetering dizzily at the topmost precipice for endless aching heartbeats, then tumbling head over heels over the edge in spinning, spiraling splendor.

Charity lay panting beneath him, his dark, damp head cradled on her tender breasts, her teeth clamped over her lip to keep her tongue from spilling out the secret she so desperately longed to tell him. The wonder was that she hadn't blurted it out in the midst of passion.

Her heart ached with the need to tell him about the baby, but she had to be certain first. She couldn't build his hopes only to dash them again, all on the word of some kindly, crusty old doctor. In a few more weeks, she promised herself drowsily, tears stinging her eyes. *When we're home again, when I* know for certain it's not just some mistake of nature or my body playing nasty tricks, I'll tell him.

"Marry me, darlin'," he murmured, kissing the shadowed valley between her breasts, lapping at a drop of salty moisture there. "Forget the rest. Just marry me and let's go off together someplace where no one's ever heard of either of us."

He'd hit on the crux of her problems. Could she do that now, with two of Johnny's killers still uncaught? Could she bury the past successfully, so deeply that it would never rise up to haunt her? If providence was kind, she would have a new child to replace the one she'd lost—a new love. It seemed a miracle, but did she dare place her trust in it yet? She wanted to. With all her heart, she wanted to.

"We'll see," she told him.

"I love you."

"I love you, Luke. More than I can say. Just give me a little more time. Please."

Not knowing what else to do, and conceding to himself that this was slightly more encouraging than the last reply she'd offered, Luke silently and reluctantly agreed. At least, this time, she hadn't given him an outright no. He'd be patient a while longer. He'd try to give her the time she needed to decide in his favor.

Time ran out the next morning. For once, Luke slept late. Charity was up a good hour before him, and by the time he came down to breakfast, she'd already eaten and was hanging their freshly laundered clothes on Martha Whiting's back line to dry.

Martha served him his breakfast at her kitchen table, where they could both keep an eye on Charity through the open windows while he ate and Martha kneaded bread dough.

"You can tell me it ain't none of my business, but are you gonna marry that little gal and give your babe a proper name?'' Martha asked out of the blue. "It is your child she's carryin', ain't it?''

Luke almost bit his fingers off, his teeth coming down hard on them as he attempted to take a bite of toast and missed. "Wh . . . what did you say?''

"No need to repeat it, and no need for you to play dumb, neither. You heard me plain as day.''

"Mrs. Whiting, ma'am, there is no baby. You're mistaken.''

"Sure,'' she scoffed with a snort of disbelief. "And George Washington is sleepin' upstairs in my bed right this minute!''

"Hope he's comfortable,'' Luke teased with a broad grin, then sobered. "Charity can't have children, though she'd probably have my head if she knew I'd told you that. She's a might touchy about it, you understand.''

Martha frowned thoughtfully. "Now, who's tryin' to pull the wool over whose eyes here?'' she mused. "Either you're lyin' or she is, or both of you are as blind as bats and dumber than dirt! That gal's got a bun in the oven, or I'm not wrist-deep in flour dough. She turned green the minute she walked into the kitchen this mornin' and smelled that bacon fryin'. Out the door she flew, gaggin' like a duck stranglin' on a bug.''

Luke shook his head, half in denial and half in amusement over Martha's colorful speech. "Sorry to disappoint you, ma'am, but Charity's been doin' that for some time now. The doc in San Antonio gave her some medicine for her stomach, and all we can figure is that it has somethin' to do with travelin', 'cause whenever we stop for a while it seems to ease up.''

Martha stared him straight in the eye. "So, how long has it been since she had her last monthly flow?'' As blood rose upward from Luke's neck, she chuckled. "Now, don't try to tell me you wouldn't have noticed havin' your nightly fun interrupted for a spell—a lusty young buck like you. And don't bother to deny that the two of you are doin' more than sharin' a bed for sleepin' purposes alone. I didn't just fall off the turnip wagon. B'sides, the walls in this place are as thin as paper, and there's not much goes on that I don't hear." Her grin broadened. "And you two were carryin' on fit to shake the rafters down last night."

"I'm not gonna deny it," he said, amazed to find a rare blush creeping up his neck. "And I'd marry Charity in a minute, if she'd agree. I've asked her several times now, and she's finally said she'll think about it."

"Well, she'd best think fast, then. 'Cause she's gonna be rockin' a cradle come next spring or so. I've seen enough of it to know, though Mr. Whiting and I have never been blessed with any children of our own. Has she complained about her breasts bein' tender? Has she been cranky to live with? More tired than normal? Faints easy?"

Luke's eyes widened more with each of the symptoms Martha listed. "But she told me she couldn't have children," he murmured more to himself than her. "I know how much it hurts her that she can't, and I'd stake my life that she's tellin' the truth."

"As much as she knows of it," Martha conceded. "Now, I'm not sayin' she'd deliberately deceive you. She doesn't seem the sort. Maybe she doesn't have any idea she's carryin' your babe."

Luke nodded. "But the doctors? Why wouldn't they know?"

"Contrary to what most of 'em seem to want to think and make the rest of us believe, doctors aren't gods. They make mistakes, just like the ordinary folk—and sometimes they make some real dandies. Why, I knew one who pronounced a man dead, and the old geezer sat right up, spit out the chicken bone he'd been chokin' on, and called the doctor a liar and a quack! Darndest thing I ever did see!''

"I don't know," Luke said, the furrow in his brow growing deeper. The more he thought about it, the more Martha made sense, but how in blue blazes was he supposed to be sure? Or better yet, convince Charity of the possibility? "I just don't know."

"I do," Martha stated firmly. "Now, if I were you, I'd go have me a nice long talk with that young woman and get things straightened out in a hurry. I'd also rustle up the preacher and . . ." She broke off, staring out the window with a calculating gaze. "There she goes again. Hangin' onto the clothesline for dear life and lookin' like she's either gonna faint or heave her stockin's up past her tonsils."

Luke took one quick look through the window and bounded out the back door. "Charity!"

Her knees buckled before he could reach her. He caught her just as the clothesline snapped, sending wet laundry tumbling down around both of their heads.

27

"**Y**ou did what?" Charity shrieked in outrage. She attempted to leap from the bed, but the sudden movement sent her head spinning again, and she collapsed back upon her pillows to glare up at Luke. "How could you? How dare you! I trusted you! And what do you do but bring a doctor in to examine me, while I lie in a dead faint! What gives you the right to do such a thing, without my knowledge or consent?"

"The fact that you're carryin' my child inside you gives me plenty of right," he told her. "And right now I'd say you're actin' suspiciously unsurprised about it all. How long have you known, Charity? Why were you hidin' it from me? And how the hell did it happen to begin with, when you were so all-fired convinced it couldn't?"

He was confused and hurt, ready to be convinced that Charity, the one woman he'd thought he could trust, was just like all the rest. His wariness showed in his face as he awaited some kind of explanation, hardly daring to hope he could believe whatever she told him.

"Oh, Luke!" she wailed in dismay, her own anger dissolving before his disillusionment. "I wasn't

369

sure. Honestly. First, Andy Nelson said I could never conceive, and the doctor in San Antonio didn't think too much of it. Then, suddenly, the one in Waco told me to expect a child in early spring. I didn't know who to believe!''

"I know the feelin'," he assured her, his arms folded sternly over his chest as he stared down at her.

"I wanted to believe it, but I just didn't want to get my hopes up, or yours, until I was absolutely certain."

"And when might that have been? After the baby was born?''

"I know you're angry with me, but try to see it from my point of view, Luke. Please. Just try to put yourself in my shoes for a moment and imagine what it's been like for me. I was scared. Scared to believe, and scared not to, hoping beyond hope that my ailments were an indication that I was carrying your child, especially after seeing that doctor in Waco. Scared to tell you . . .''

"Why in tarnation would you be scared to tell me somethin' you knew would make me love you all the more?'' he cut in with a furious frown.

"Because I didn't want anything to go wrong. Oh, Luke, you don't understand. How could you? Johnny and I had just learned about our own baby the very day of the attack. Maybe I was being silly, or crazy, but I just didn't want it to happen again. I felt that if I told you, then I'd be tempting fate to bring some disaster crashing down around us. I wanted to keep this child safe for as long as I could. I don't want to lose your baby, Luke, the way I did Johnny's.'' Scalding tears streaked her face as she looked up at him, her liquid eyes begging him to understand and forgive her.

She reached out to grab his arm, claiming his hand and clutching it between her own. "Please, Luke!

Please believe me! Please understand how hard it was for me to sort it all out in my mind. In my heart. I don't think I really, truly believed it myself until now. It seemed like such an impossible hope—a miracle that could be snatched away at any moment. I wanted to tell you. I wanted to share it with you. I just was so frightened that something bad would happen if I did."

Dragging his free hand over his face, he closed his eyes and took a deep breath. "Damn it all, Charity! Even if you didn't believe it, you suspected it. You should have told me. You let me walk around like a blind man, worryin' and wonderin' what the hell was wrong with you. Afraid it might be somethin' serious."

"It was serious. To me, it was deadly serious."

"It could have been. We went right on chasin' after Bronc, ridin' hard and puttin' your life and that of my child in danger. But I didn't know that, did I?" he accused righteously. "Because you were too blasted superstitious and stubborn to tell me."

"Luke . . ."

"No more, Charity. No more. We're gettin' married today, if I have to hogtie you and hold you at gunpoint to make you say the words. Then we're goin' straight home."

"But . . ."

"No 'but' about it. Since you aren't capable of makin' a decent decision these days, I'm makin' 'em for you. And as for Whitey and Weasel, forget it. We've caught four of the men we set out after, and that's gonna have to be enough to suit you. Your safety, and that of our child, are gonna have to come first from now on."

"Fine." Her pouting lips spit the words at him, though there was a suspicious twinkle lurking in her sky-blue eyes.

For just a minute he looked stunned, as if she'd shocked him with her sudden compliance.

"Fine?" he echoed. "That's it? Just like that?"

"You want me to disagree?" she asked, arching one fine brow. "Well, think again, Luke Sterling. I love you. I love our baby. I want it to have your name. More than anything in this world, I want to be your wife and bear your child.

"I've already been giving serious thought to giving up the chase, for the sake of our baby's health and my own. After all, we tracked the worst of them down, and if Whitey and Weasel ever do turn up in our lives again, I guess we'll just have to deal with them then. I'll simply have to learn, somehow, not to be so afraid, to trust that between us we can protect ourselves and our child, that together we can handle any problem life brings our way."

"I'll keep you safe, Charity. Both of you," he promised.

"You were right about a lot of things, Luke," she went on. "About it being time to stop the search, and about all this violence and bloodshed amounting to more than I'd bargained for, but I was just too mule-headed to admit it until now. I honestly want to be done with it."

"Can you be done with it?" he asked softly, knowing how hard it must be for her to see the final two go unpunished. "Can you put it behind you, with no regrets?'Cause if you can't, I'll take you back to the farm and go after those two myself."

"I know you would, but I won't ask it of you. I love you too much to risk losing you over the likes of them. If we're going to start a new life together, then let's wash our hands of the whole stinking mess. We'll sell the farm and go to Montana and raise chickens and cattle and horses."

"And children," he added reverently.

"There may be only this one," she warned,

knowing that this child was a special miracle, perhaps never to be repeated.

"I don't care. It'll be ours. Yours and mine." He swallowed hard on the lump in his throat. Lowering himself to the edge of the bed, he gathered her into his arms. "I love you, little darlin'. I always will, no matter what."

"No matter what," she repeated joyously, her heart brimming over with love.

"With this ring, I thee wed," Luke repeated solemnly, producing, to Charity's immense surprise, the most beautiful ring she'd ever imagined. It was a lovely violet-blue stone, intricately cut and standing high and bold in a silver-filigree band.

Her mouth worked in soundless question, earning two warm, calloused fingers across her lips, silencing her curiosity as the preacher continued with the ceremony.

Luke winked down at her, not at all the nervous bridegroom, while Charity felt as if her insides were being dragged across the ribs of a washboard. Yet she'd never felt as proud as she did now, standing next to him, her trembling hand tucked securely in his. Nor had she ever felt so cherished, so beautiful inside and out that she quivered with it.

Looking down at her, Luke thought he'd never seen her quite this lovely, with a radiance that seemed to glow from her soul. Her borrowed dress fit her to perfection, as he'd suspected it might since it belonged to Mrs. Whiting, the very same lady who'd previously loaned her the saloon girl costume.

This gown, however, was much more modest, better befitting a bride, yet not as virginal as most. Disdaining to wear white, Martha had chosen pale blue satin trimmed in ivory lace that rose across the bodice to a high, banded neckline and dipped to delicate points in full-length sleeves. A matching embroidered shawl, as sheer as cobwebs, adorned Charity's golden hair, left long and loose at Luke's request.

As for his own attire, Luke had not fared quite as well. While Martha had pressed his one decent pair of dark trousers and starched new life back into his only white dress shirt and collar, he could not find a coat to match on such short notice. He'd had to content himself with a fancy vest and string tie, hastily purchased and yanked off the back of a gambler passing through town. All things considered, Luke felt fortunate to be decently dressed at all, and he would have been stunned to learn that Charity thought him the most handsome man she'd ever beheld.

With Mr. and Mrs. Whiting standing as their witnesses, Luke and Charity exchanged the vows that would bind them to each other for a lifetime, pledging themselves to each other for as long as they both should live.

As Luke claimed his first kiss from his wife, and her lips answered his softly and sweetly in sacred promise, his heart swelled to bursting. "Well, Mrs. Sterling?" he murmured long minutes later, and much to the Whitings' delight. "How does it feel to be kissed all legal and proper for a change?"

She smiled up at him, her eyes gleaming with love and mischief. "I'll have to collect a few more to make a proper comparison, Mr. Sterling. And let me warn you now, legal and proper had better not mean any less wicked, or you are in a heap of trouble, mister!"

Wonder of wonders, Martha had somehow managed to bake a cake to complement a marvelous wedding supper, all in honor of this grand and glorious occasion. The other hotel guests shared in the celebration, offering hearty toasts of congratulations long after the newlyweds had stolen off to bed.

"I still can't believe it," Charity murmured, lifting her lips from Luke's as they stood, alone at last, in their room.

"Which?" he asked, planting a kiss on the point of her chin, then slowly working his way up her jaw. "That you're gonna have our baby, or that we're married?"

"Both."

Her fingers made a foray into the crisp dark hair at his temples, her wedding band catching the lamplight and sending it back in sparks of red and purple. "Luke, where did you find such a magnificent ring? When you slipped it on my finger, I thought I'd die of shock."

"Glad you like it. I've been carryin' it around since San Antonio, just waitin' for you to accept my proposal. Actually, I've had the stone for longer than that, but I had the jeweler there cut it down and place it in the band."

"Cut it down?" She could only imagine the original size, since it dominated her finger as it was now, flashing with violet fire.

"Yeah." He grinned down at her. "It was the size of a goose egg before, and I thought that might weigh your hand down a bit too much."

"Heavens! I should hope so! But where on earth did you get it? When? How?"

"From the cave, darlin'. It got stuck in the top of my boot somewhere along the line, and I thought it would make a nice keepsake. Now, mind you, it isn't worth near as much as diamonds or emeralds. The jeweler called it amethyst."

"It's exquisite, and worth more to me than anything else you might have chosen," she told him sweetly. "There are cherished memories bound to this, and now I won't ever forget them. But it was your find, and you should have a memento of your own," she added regretfully.

His laughter rang free as he pulled away from her and reached into his pocket to draw out a small pouch. "I do, sweet thing, though I'm not sure yet what to do with it. Maybe you can give me some ideas."

Opening the drawstring, he poured a mound of violet jewels into her palm, until they overflowed and spilled onto the floor. "Oh, my stars!" she gasped, as he continued to laugh at her amazement.

"Think that'll buy a few head of cattle for our Montana homestead?" he crowed. "Like I said, it's a far sight from makin' us rich, but it will give us a darned nice start, don't you agree?"

"If it doesn't, I'm not Mrs. Luke Sterling."

"Oh, you're Mrs. Sterling all right. Make no mistake about it. And you're gonna be Mrs. Sterling for a long, long time."

There was no comparing this wedding night with her first. Between bride and groom, there was no hesitation, no awkward fumbling embraces in the dark. No embarrassment and no holding back. There was just sweet, primitive passion building steadily between them like magnificently orchestrated music.

His hands played over her as a master musician might stroke the strings of a harp. Her body sang a lilting refrain in response, her own slim hands trilling delicately across his flesh as Pan might have fingered his flute-pipe. He led; she followed. She lured; he met her halfway there, their hearts and bodies perfectly attuned.

The melody ebbed and flowed around them, at times with aching poignancy, then soaring to pinnacles of passion. Their frantic heartbeats set the rhythm of pounding drums, their glad cries echoing the crash of cymbals and resounding trumpets, their whispered sighs those of violins played softly. The music built to a wild crescendo, sweeping them along in a wondrous blending of pure, rapturous tones carried on night breezes. And when the last, shimmering note trembled softly into silence, they held its sweet memory still in their hearts.

They were headed home at long last, with promises to write to Martha Whiting and her husband with news of the birth of their child and their new location once they'd settled in Montana. Of course it would be the following spring before they could move to Montana, after the baby was born and Charity had recovered sufficiently to travel. Besides, there would soon be snow in the mountains, with little time to sell the farm and buy new land before winter set in with its icy grip.

They rode north along the Western trail, through the flat plains of Oklahoma and Kansas. All along the trail, the tall prairie grass was flattened now, trampled by countless hoofs. By spring, it would have renewed itself once more into a waving sea of green.

"Won't everyone be shocked to learn about the baby," Charity mused as they rode. "I can hardly wait to see the looks on their faces, especially Sue and Andy."

"They'll probably be more surprised to find you married to a gunslinger like me," Luke grumbled, knowing the news of their wedding would meet with many a frown.

"Yeah." She sighed dreamily, deliberately misinterpreting his words. "Imagine poor, pitiful Charity Prindle wedded and bedded by the most handsome man in the territory. Why, it'll set tongues wagging from here to St. Louis. No doubt, I'll be the envy of everyone who hears, and it will stir new hope in the hearts of spinsters for miles around."

"Poor pitiful Charity my arse!" he retorted with a snort. "How I ever thought you plain, I'll never know, though I have to admit you were a scrawny little mud hen when we first crossed paths. You've improved a might since then. Matter of fact, you're the prettiest thing since sunrise.''

She returned his grin. "Thank you, kind sir. And you can take most of the credit for my remarkable transformation, particularly when this scrawny mud hen is waddling around like a bloated buffalo in a few months. Remember that, when the time comes.''

They were into Kansas, almost home, riding out the last dying rays of the setting sun before stopping to make camp. Suddenly, ahead of them on the dimming trail, shots sounded. Screams rang out. Long, terrified screams that ripped through the still air.

Just that quickly, Charity was taken back to that horrible night one year ago, when her own screams had rent the darkness. It had been an autumn evening such as this, a place so similar that ghostly fingers danced up her backbone. The blood fled her face. "Oh, God! No! Not again!''

"Stay here, Charity,'' she heard Luke say. Then, in imitation of Johnny's words, he told her. "Get back off the trail.''

"No!'' Terrified eyes turned to his, and for a moment she saw Johnny's face looking back at her, before she finally focused on Luke's beloved features.

"Do as I tell you,'' Luke commanded sharply. "Keep your gun ready and wait for me where I know you're safe.''

Before she could reply, he spurred his horse into a gallop, racing down the trail toward the fracas. She watched him go, fighting back old fears, battling to get a firm grip on her unraveling emotions. Within heartbeats, completely disregarding his orders, she was barreling down the trail behind him.

Around a bend, she came to an abrupt halt. The sight that met her eyes was so reminiscent of her own awful memories that it was like looking backward in time through a mirror. A wagon lay tipped on its side. A man lay half in, half out of it. A woman struggled between two captors, the bodice of her dress hanging in tatters at her waist, her frantic screams falling on the deaf ears of her laughing attackers.

What with the rowdy laughter and the woman's ear-piercing shrieks, they failed to hear Luke's approach, had no idea that anyone was near until Luke's Colt barked out its warning. His first bullet caught the bigger man in the shoulder. The second buried itself in the skinny thigh of the other assailant. Both released their prize with howls of pain, scrambling to draw their weapons and find cover. The woman, frozen with fear, stood as they'd left her, her eyes glazed with shock, still screeching.

As Charity watched, the men split up, one rolling to one side, the other hobbling toward a small pile of rocks in the opposite direction. The bigger man gained cover behind the wagon even as his partner returned Luke's fire. His attention dangerously divided, Luke stood his ground, a perfect target.

Charity's heart was in her throat, her pulse pounding madly as she took in Luke's vulnerable position. Reacting completely on reflex, the lessons now so ingrained that they came without thought, Charity drew her gun and fired, catching the larger outlaw off guard just as he was leveling his weapon toward Luke. The pistol spun from his hand, the impact sending him careening sideways. As he lost his balance, his hat fell from his head, revealing a startling streak of pure white in an otherwise dark head of hair. Whitey!

Shock jolted through her, sizzling along her veins like a bolt of hot lightning. Somewhere in her reeling consciousness, as she kept her Colt trained on her target, she was aware of Luke swiftly dealing with the second attacker—the smaller one with the ferret features. Weasel.

One stolen glance at Charity told Luke he was the only one capable of taking further action. Fortunately, the outlaws did not seem to sense this. Quickly, competently, he gathered guns, searched the two men for hidden weapons, and bound them tightly back-to-back with rope. All the while, Charity sat stiffly, stonily in her saddle—and the other woman continued to scream.

28

ONCE Charity's mind began to function properly again, after the initial shock had passed, she tried to comfort the frantic woman. When she had calmed enough to give them her name, they learned that she was Anna McGee. She and her husband, Will, had been heading south toward Texas, to seek work on one of the cattle ranches. Will would be traveling no more. He was dead. Anna, at thirty-two years of age, wanted nothing more than to join him in blessed oblivion.

"If only you had come along just a few minutes earlier," Anna wailed, making Charity and Luke feel even more miserable. "Oh, what am I to do without my Will?"

Throughout the long night, which held precious little sleep for any of them, Anna wept and clutched Will's lifeless body to her. Luke righted the wagon and threw the spilled items back into it. He tended to their horses, built a fire, and kept careful guard over their prisoners.

Though no one was hungry, Charity cooked an evening meal, refusing to offer any of it to the two men who lay tied and groaning just a few feet away. Nor did she tend to their wounds. Luke didn't sug-

381

gest it; and noting the hate-filled looks Charity tossed their way, he made no attempt to do so himself. Their wounds were not life-threatening, though they would probably lose a good deal of blood. And if they bled to death before getting medical attention, or if infection and fever set in, who would really care?

Not poor Anna. And certainly not Charity. Luke didn't have to ask why. One look at her, and he'd known that they had found John Prindle's final two murderers, the last of the six men who'd raped her. Coming upon them this way had brought it all fresh to Charity's mind again, almost making her relive it anew, and she was furious, not only for herself but also for Anna.

"Do you want me to drag them out a ways and kill them?" Luke asked her solemnly.

To his surprise, she shook her head. "No. The gunshots would only panic Anna more."

"I wouldn't have to shoot them, darlin'," he told her.

Again she declined. "I've had enough of killing to last me a lifetime," she admitted softly. "I want no more blood on my hands, Luke. No more on my soul. I have our child to think of now, and what all this violence might do to the tiny life inside me. If it's all the same to you, I'd rather take these two with us into Dodge and turn them over to the sheriff there. Let the judge pass sentence on them. Let the law hang them. My vow for revenge will still be fulfilled if they die by hands other than yours or mine."

Though he wasn't sure his own thirst for vengeance on her behalf would be slaked by handling matters this way, Luke agreed. As unfamiliar as he was with the ways of breeding women, he'd nevertheless heard the old wives' tales of babies being born marked or maimed if the mother witnessed acts of violence with the child inside her womb. He

wasn't sure he believed such nonsense, but neither
was he about to take the chance with his own off-
spring. If Charity wanted the law to deal with these
last two, so be it.

When the sun at last sent its first warming rays
above the horizon, they broke camp and prepared
to ride for Dodge City, two days away.

"Ma'am?" Luke squatted down next to Anna,
hard put to find her eyes in her tear-swollen face.
"Ma'am, we've got to head out soon. You've got to
decide what you want to do with your husband's
body. It would be better all around if we buried it
here and now, but if you insist, we'll take him back
to Dodge for burial there."

As he'd hoped, Anna left the final decision to him,
feeling too distraught to choose for herself. When
the final shovel of dirt was tamped down on the
grave, Charity offered up an eloquent prayer in behalf of Will McGee's soul, and Luke got his first
glimpse of the pious young woman she must once
have been. With a handful of fall prairie flowers and
a crude cross constructed from a broken piece of
wagon board to mark his final resting place, they left
him there.

Since Anna could do little more than weep, Charity drove the wagon team, her horse and those of
their prisoners tied behind. The two outlaws, gagged
and bound, and unable to ride astride, had been
wedged uncomfortably in the bouncing wagon bed.
Charity was tempted to ride roughshod over every
rock and ridge in their path, just to hear their grunts
of pain. The only thing that prevented her from doing so was the added discomfort it would cause
Anna. Luke brought up the rear, riding shotgun.

Nightfall found them camped at the bend of
Crooked Creek. With an early start and no further
problems, they'd reach Dodge early the following
evening. While Charity took Anna in hand, the be-

reaved woman now in a silent stupor, Luke set up camp. Before bedding down for the night, he led each of their prisoners in turn out into the surrounding darkness to answer nature's call. First Weasel, with his wounded leg, who gave him no trouble at all. Then, Whitey, who suddenly seemed prone toward antagonism.

"How do you like knowin' we had a taste of your wife first, Sterling?" he taunted viciously. "Sweet little piece, ain't she? And tight? Damn if she wasn't the tightest I've ever had!"

"Keep it up, Whitey, and you won't need a gag tomorrow," Luke warned darkly, giving the man a rough shove ahead of him.

"Tell me, Sterling," he went on, ignoring Luke's threat, "is she as hot for you as she was for me? Does she squirm and scream when you stick it to her?"

Luke's fist flew out, catching Whitey square in the mouth. The next blow connected hard with the outlaw's nose, rendering a satisfying crunch as the bone snapped. Blow after blow came fast and furious, until Whitey's face was battered and bloody and Luke's knuckles scraped raw.

Unceremoniously, Luke dragged his prisoner back into camp and dumped him next to Weasel, ignoring Charity's wide-eyed gaze as he lashed the two men together. Only then did he turn to her with the triumphant look of a conquering hero, spoiled but slightly by a sheepish grin.

Holding out his swelling knuckles he said, "Darlin', I could use a little tender lovin' care with these, if you don't mind. Old Whitey there needed a lesson in manners."

"Which you so kindly rendered," she guessed, shaking her head over the damage he'd done to his hands in the process.

He shrugged, much in the manner of a little boy

sent up before the headmaster at school. "It seemed
the proper thing to do at the time. And I have to
admit, it sure as hell felt good."

"I hope you hit him a wallop for me," she said.

He wrapped her securely in his arms and chuckled. "I did. Yours loosened several of his front teeth,
so I don't think he'll be givin' us much sass from
here on out."

Dusk was just falling when they rode into Dodge,
riding slowly along Front Street toward the sheriff's
office. The saloons were just coming to life for the
night, but as people recognized Luke and Charity,
the streets started to fill with curious observers. By the
time they reached the jail, a crowd surrounded
them, waiting to see what was about to happen.

Hearing the commotion, Bat Masterson stepped
from his office, his eyes narrowing into bright slits
as his gaze fell first on Luke, then on Charity and
Anna. "What's goin' on here?"

"We brought you some prisoners, Sheriff," Luke
informed him, dismounting and heading toward the
back of the wagon. He made no attempt toward gentleness as he jerked the bound, wounded men from
the back of the wagon, letting them tumble to the
dusty street before yanking them up again and
shoving them toward the open door of the jail, past
the gawking crowd and Masterson. "You want 'em,
or should we turn 'em over to Marshal Earp?"

"Wyatt's gone. Left town about a month ago, so
I guess I'm stuck with them," Masterson said with
a frown. His own popularity in Dodge had dwindled in the last few months, and if he didn't win
reelection in November, he'd be following his friend
for greener pastures. "Who are they?"

"Do the names Whitey and Weasel ring any bells
with you, Sheriff Masterson?" Charity asked. "Just
in case you've forgotten, let me refresh your mem-

ory. They're two of the men who attacked John and me last year. We've brought them in to be tried for John's murder.''

At her words, a gasp rose from the crowd, followed immediately by a hum of speculation. She was making the sheriff look bad, as if she'd done the job of tracking down her husband's killers since he had failed. In retaliation, he smirked and jeered. ''Only two of them, Charity? Where are the rest? Or am I correct in assumin' that you're the infamous Widow Witch I've been hearin' so much about lately? The one who killed three men by the names of Jeb, Cutter, and Bronc, the last body found just four days ago, all left with the Widow's callin' card of weeds? Kinda puttin' yourself above the law, weren't you?''

''If that's what it takes to get the job done,'' Charity replied evenly, vasty relieved to hear that Bronc had not escaped his barb-wire prison to cause her or anyone else any more harm. Evidently, the lawman hadn't learned of Dandy's demise as yet.

Before Masterson could question her further, Luke brought the sheriff's attention back to the prisoners still to be locked behind bars. ''We caught these two while they were attackin' Mrs. McGee and her husband along the trail south of here. Mr. McGee is buried out on the prairie. We brought her back to town with us.''

He turned to Charity. ''Darlin', why don't you get Mrs. McGee down to Doc Nelson's while I finish up here? I'll meet you there as soon as I'm done.''

She nodded, noting the looks on several interested faces when Luke called her ''darlin'.'' As she took up the reins once more, she stared Masterson square in the eye. ''Sheriff, we've gone to a lot of trouble to catch these men. They've killed my husband and Mrs. McGee's, and God only knows who else. Now, I won't presume to tell you how to run your office, but I want these men brought to trial and hung. If they should somehow mysteriously find their way loose from your jail, I'll personally see you run out of town on a rail. And that's only if I'm feeling at all kindly disposed toward you. I do hope we understand each another.''

Masterson glared back at her, his eyes gleaming malevolently. ''I hear you, Mrs. Prindle, loud and clear. And I assure you they won't be going anywhere until the judge says differently.''

''Sterling,'' Luke corrected curtly, confusing all who listened. He went on to explain, much to everyone's amazement, ''Her name is Sterling now, not Prindle. She's my wife.''

They'd been home for almost a week. In that time a lot had happened. The county judge had held a special court session, and with the sworn testimonies of Luke, Charity, and Anna, the two outlaws they'd hauled into town were sentenced to hang. The scaffolding was already being erected at the end of Front Street, and come Saturday Whitey and Weasel would meet their just end. Charity would not attend their execution. She'd already informed Luke that she wanted only peace and quiet for a time, with nothing to mar her homecoming or her happy plans for their child. Luke and Mano and a vengeful Anna would be there to witness the hanging.

Anna was beginning to accept her husband's death, though merely acknowledging it did nothing to ease her deep sorrow. The act of grieving had only begun for her, and it would be many months before her heart would heal. Seeing her husband's killers pay for their perfidy was just one small step toward that day.

Despite the way they had met, or perhaps because of the similarities involved, Charity and Anna were forming a deep friendship. Childless, with a drunken father and four worthless brothers, Anna had no wish to return home now that Will had died. When Charity offered her a permanent place in her household, suggesting that Anna might want to go with them to Montana, the woman readily accepted.

"But I'll work for my keep," Anna said proudly. "You're gonna need someone to cook and clean and help look after that young'un. And once you get the ranch runnin', and some hands hired, there will be a lot more to do."

Mano was staying at the farm for now, and hadn't yet decided to move on with them. He didn't say, but Charity thought it had to do with not wanting to leave Sue. Perhaps by spring the two of them would resolve whatever problems now stood in their way. Charity hoped so.

Even now, Luke was scouting around for land to buy. Almost every day, or at least every other, he sent telegrams and letters to prospective sellers, and investigated open range land that was coming up for sale in Montana and Wyoming. It helped that he'd already been up that direction in his solitary travels before meeting Charity and was fairly familiar with the land there. As soon as he found the property he wanted, they would purchase it and begin plans for building up a herd.

Early one morning, he kissed Charity good-bye and headed into Dodge, as excited as a child at Christmas. "There's a man I have to see about a bull," he told her, laying his hand over her ever-so-slightly rounded tummy. "I should be back by noon, but if I'm not, don't hold the meal for me. Expectant mothers need their nourishment."

A short time later, Charity saddled her mare and rode out on her own, despite Mano's objections. There was something she'd put off doing for too long, and nothing and no one was going to stop her. "I'll be fine," she assured him. "I can look after myself pretty well now, and I won't be long."

She followed the trail toward Dodge, but her objective was only halfway there. When she came to the place she sought, she reined in her horse and just sat gazing out over the land.

It was mid-October, and there was the slight nip of fall in the air, though the days were still mild and there had been no killing frost as yet. On either side of the wagon track that passed for a road, the prairie stretched out before her. A little distance from the track, in the same general area where the attack had occurred, or as near as Charity could recall, a stray patch of sunflowers waved in the breeze.

Venturing closer, Charity was surprised to note that they were still in full bloom, which was unusual for so late in the season. It was stranger still that they should be growing here, in the middle of the prairie, two dozen or more all by themselves. Yet it seemed right, too, somehow, and it cheered her heart to find them.

Dismounting, she left her horse and walked among them, until she reached the center of the cluster. Shielded on all sides from prying eyes, she knelt in the tall grass and closed her eyes. For a long time she simply sat silently. Then she began to speak, softly, earnestly.

"Faith, my dearest darling little daughter, I've come here, to this place, wanting to feel closer to you, because I need to talk with you just one last time. I'll never forget you or the joy I felt when I first knew that I carried you inside my body. I'll love you always, though I never got the chance to know you, or to be a mother to you the way I wanted to. I wanted to tell you this because . . . well, you see, I'm expecting another baby in a few months, and I didn't want you to feel that it would take your place or make me love you any less.

"This baby will be a part of me, just as you once were, and maybe when I hold it in my arms it will be like having a small part of you there, too. I can only pray that it will be born healthy, that God will allow me this chance to know motherhood in its fullest at last, that between us we can protect this fledgling life and see it born into the world safe and whole.

"I hope you can hear me, precious. I hope you can understand. It's not so much that I'm giving you up, as that I am going on with my life. Come spring, I'll be moving away from here, but wherever I go, I'll carry you with me always in my heart. So it's not really good-bye, after all, you see. Perhaps just farewell."

Tears half-blinding her, she reached into her pocket and withdrew a tiny scrap of pink ribbon. Gently she brought it to her lips, bestowing a kiss upon it. For a moment longer she clutched it to her breast. Then, with trembling fingers, she lay the ribbon upon the ground, anchoring it with a bit of dirt. "Thank you for giving me this token of faith and hope when I needed it most, but love has healed my heart now and made me strong, so I am giving it back to you, my sweetest angel," she murmured tenderly. "God bless you and keep you."

It might have been minutes later, or hours. Charity only knew that she was still kneeling there, her tears dried by the playful breeze that rustled through the sunflower stalks, her aching heart at last knowing a full, swelling peace within itself, when Luke's shadow fell across her path.

"I spotted your horse and figured this was the only place you could be."

She looked up at him and smiled, holding her hand out to him and pulling him down to sit beside her. He spotted the ribbon and knew intuitively what she'd been doing, why she'd been drawn here, and he couldn't find the will to scold her for going

off alone, as he'd first intended to do. Not when the
tracks of her tears still showed on her face.

"I just wanted to tell her I still loved her," Charity
said simply. "I needed to do that. Especially now,
with a new baby on the way."

"I know. It's all right, darlin'." He drew her close,
held her tightly, his own heart aching for hers.

"Yes, Luke. It really is all right, I think, at last. I
feel so much better now, so much more at ease and
at peace with myself. I can go on from here, without
constantly looking back. Without all those old fears
and regrets and anger. I feel whole again. Stronger.
Alive and eager for all the tomorrows we'll spend
together, you and I."

She turned her face up to his, her lips brushing
his like a sigh. "I love you. You're my life, Luke.
You're the air I breathe."

"And you're my sunshine," he returned softly.
"I don't think I ever truly knew what it was to stand
in the light before you came into my life. I was fum-
blin' around in darkness. And suddenly you were
there, leadin' the way, showin' me how to love. It's
the greatest gift anyone's ever given me. Probably
more than I deserve. Certainly more than I ever expected."

"It's only fair," she assured him, "since you've
been my gallant knight, slaying fiery demons at
every turn. Freeing my heart to love again. But
there's one more dragon yet to slay, my darling. One
more menace to lay to rest, if you're willing."

"You know I'd do anything for you."

"Then make love with me. Here. Now. In this
place where my life was darkest, give me joy. Help
me replace the old memories with new ones, shining ones. Let our laughter chase away the ghosts;
gladness wash away the shadows. Please.

"If ever I think of this place again, let it be with
peace and love in my heart and the remembrance of

lying in your arms in the sunshine. Your body, your hands touching me. Your lips over mine and your love surrounding me.''

He could not deny her, any more than he could stop the sun from rising or the wind from blowing. There, in the midst of the flowers, hidden and guarded and blessed by them, he lowered her gently into the grass and followed her down. As his hands dealt with their clothing, hers helping and hindering in her eagerness, his mouth sought each newly bared inch of her sweet, warm flesh.

She smelled like sunshine; tasted like honey. Her skin glowed like rare, blushing pearls fresh from the sea and felt infinitely more smooth to the touch. Everything about her beckoned to him, pulled at him; everything within him answered that sensuous, age-old call of woman to man. As she rained kisses over his yearning body, worshiping it with her lips, her whispery voice was sand on silk, sending exquisite sensual shivers through him. Exciting him, bewitching him, making him drunk on the whiskey-rough sounds she made as she fired his ardor ever higher.

He'd meant to be gentle, had promised himself to give her the tenderness she needed. But nature had other plans, it seemed, as passion spun its silken web tightly about them, entwining them in its tangled maze.

Charity, too, was caught up in it, enraptured, beyond herself and greedy for more. She was a tigress, wild and free, calling to her mate with soft growls and enticing mews. Clutching at him with nipping teeth and claws not quite sheathed, soothing him with little laps of her tongue. Wrapping herself around him with a might born of love and need.

And a fitting mate he was, matching her move for move, strength for strength. Dominating without intimidating, laughing softly when she brazenly stole the lead from him. He was savage and tender, a gentle ravager; a bold conqueror willing to be conquered, knowing the prize was his either way.

Fitting her long, smooth legs over his shoulders, with his mouth he sought the heart, the heat of her. On a sharply indrawn breath, she shuddered. She moaned and made small, pleading sounds deep in her throat. Her fingers wove into his hair, grasping, holding him close for her delight and his. The earth trembled and dropped away from her, and all she knew was him, his sweet mouth tormenting her, bringing her glorious, lustrous fulfillment, and a thousand stars exploding all around them.

When he came over her, molding her lips with his, she tasted herself on his tongue. Desire spiraled through her, hot and strong. Her fingers captured him, guided him toward the beckoning threshold of promised splendor.

"Take me now," she whispered gruffly. "Love me now."

On a low snarl of unleashed desire, he answered with a commanding thrust, claiming her fully, making her his as man has done since the dawn of time. Bold, clean strokes; power tempered only with love, as he poured himself into her, bathed himself in the honey-sweet nectar of her quivering depths.

Together they braved the raging tempest that devoured them, the howling winds that pushed them ever higher, the thunder that rolled and roared and made them part of the savage storm. Lightning split the sky, creating a jagged, dazzling staircase to the heavens, flinging them through rapture's gates into ecstasy's waiting arms.

Sunflowers nodded their golden heads as if applauding. The earth was warm beneath their backs, the air filled with the smell of crushed grass and love, as they basked in the afterglow.

"Thank you," she murmured, bringing her hand up to caress his face, her eyes wide and blue and spilling over with love as she gazed into his beloved face. "Thank you for coming into my life, for rescuing my heart and restoring my faith, and chasing all my ghosts away. But most of all, thank you for loving me."

He laughed softly, his eyes like emeralds in the sunlight. "My pleasure, darlin'. Now and always."